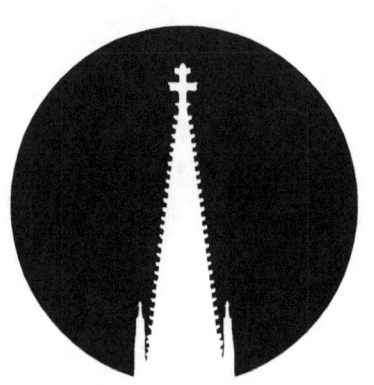

CATHEDRAL
TOWER

Ross Simister

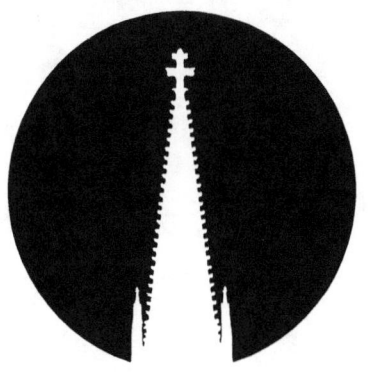

CATHEDRAL
TOWER

City History

Gang City was formed 220 years ago when The Battles between The Vampires and The Christian Vampire Slayers ended with victory going to The Vampires along with their comrades, The Witches. City history states there has only been one war, The War Against The Vampires; this is correct – The Battles were before the city was formed. This victory gained The Vampires power of the city and they ruled along with The Witches after The Vampire leader Niculi and Queen Ziana of The Witches married and ruled together with a reign of terror and darkness. For centuries Europeans have told dark folklore tales about creatures of the night that live off the blood of mortals, or disturbing stories of women conjuring demons and evil spirits; and Eastern Europe is no exception. Wallachia, a modern-day state of Romania but in the 15th Century was its own principality, has been steeped in mystery for many Western Europeans, and in 1480 The Vatican grew disturbed by the tales of evil that were making their way across Europe, and raising an army joined with Britain and France with an aim to march into Wallachia to do God's work. Niculi, hearing an army in the West was planning to slay him, gathered his minions and followers and on February 12th 1480, formed The Vampires. This was the birth of The Battles which would make their way across Europe and eventually be the foundation of 9 Gang City.

Word crossed into Western Europe that Niculi had caught wind of the military plan from the West and the combined forces of Italy, Britain and France formed The Christian Vampire Slayers, or The CVS for short. Niculi was a great warrior and ruled the darkness not only in his native Wallachia but all over Eastern Europe, and it was on the border with Hungary that he met Ziana, a witch whose magic had grown powerful and could not be matched by any other. Niculi and Ziana had met many years previous and by the time The CVS entered Wallachia, The Witches had already been formed with Ziana as their Queen, and together The Vampires and The Witches fought back against their oppressors from the West. The first battle was horrific as The CVS were woefully under-prepared and had underestimated their enemies' power; Niculi, who could break a man's neck with one hand and rip heads off with his teeth, annihilated the oncoming army and The CVS were forced to make a hasty retreat. Unwilling to let the insult of the invasion go, The Vampires and The Witches followed. The Witches obliterated The CVS who had retreated into Hungary and The Vampires made their way into Bohemia (Czech Republic). It was in Bohemia that The CVS regrouped after reinforcements were sent from the West and now knowing what they were facing were a lot better prepared and an epic battle took place. The CVS in their thousands stood on the battlefield ready for their foe to raise from his slumber to face them, and face them he did. With teeth like a snake, the roar of a dragon and the strength of a thousand men, many times Niculi stood against entire armies and won. The battle was immense, many men lost their lives but took a lot of their enemy down with them, the battlefield scattered with corpses and body parts, ash and bonfires from burning witches at the stake. The end of the battle drew near and Niculi peered over and saw his beloved Ziana retreat into a nearby stable, quickly followed by a group of CVS soldiers and a monk who accompanied them for blessings and religious ceremonies. Niculi smashed the door open to see Ziana being tied to a stake ready for burning; with outrage and more ferocity than ever before after seeing his companion in darkness ready to be killed, Niculi launched into attack. The first soldier he came to had his neck and back bent so far back his head was by his feet and then thrown through the stable wall, the next had his throat ripped out with ease, the taste of blood only giving more encouragement to Niculi to spill more. Picking up a sword from his fallen victim, Niculi went to work. Heads, arms, legs, bodies chopped in half as zero mercy was given. The monk was the last man standing, gained leverage in the battle and bought time for more CVS to arrive to help by throwing holy water in Niculi's face, which caused the monster to stagger back, roaring in agony. The monk's crucifix kept Niculi at bay but unknown to them all during the altercation Ziana had been preparing a spell; sat in a circle of blood, the witch queen pulled Niculi into the circle as more CVS soldiers appeared to turn the tide back into their favour. The monk knew what this spell was and demanded the soldiers not to let the witch clap her hands; but diving to stop her, the soldiers' efforts were in vain as Ziana clapped her hands and she and her beloved disappeared in a ball of flame and smoke. That was the closest The CVS would come to victory for 522 years.

Niculi sat up, seeing that they were safe; Ziana had teleported them across the border into Poland. Turning to see his love smiling at him, they embraced passionately at their escape. For the next 30 years Poland was the scene for The Battles, with The Vampires gaining the upper hand and eventually causing The CVS to retreat into the Germanic States where eight decades of fighting brought no peace and no victory, only a stalemate of fallen fighters on both sides; but with The Vampires' ability to bite, infect and turn people, they had no problems recruiting new members, whereas The CVS's reliance on men became obsolete and they began to recruit women and boys to fight for them. This is where The Battles again split into two fights: The Witches moved up into Scandinavia to scatter The CVS who would be obliged to follow them, and The Vampires pushed forward, causing yet another CVS retreat into Austria, Spanish Netherlands and France. A century passed of death, rising from the dead, the undead and many other forms of supernatural, all in the aim of supremacy, until The Vampires were forced to cross The Channel to England. Sensing a holy victory, The Christian Vampire Slayers quickly followed and before long The Battles had stretched the entire Island of Britannia. In 1692 on the North Yorkshire Moors, a new foe was to make their acquaintance, just like centuries past. The CVS, Vampires and Witches brought death and destruction to each other and mid-battle a howl was heard in the near distance. All sides looked at the oncoming attack as The Werewolves entered The Battles, adding a new breed of ultra-violence to the conflict. The rising of the sun brought an end to the battle and Niculi, fresh from slaughtering whatever came near, roared at The CVS.

"What makes you think you can conquer Niculi? For 200 years your kind have tried and failed; what makes you think you are worthy? The rising of the sun is the only reason you still live, you look to the sky and thank the sun you are still alive. Come and conquer Niculi, I challenge you to come and conquer Niculi" were the words he bellowed to the watching CVS as he retreated the sunrise. The Christian Vampire Slayers, eager to not allow another force of darkness add to their ever-growing problems, followed the fleeing werewolves as they scattered across the moor in the devolution of Lycanthorpe, now that the full moon had gone and the sun brought mercy to The CVS. Capturing a werewolf in man form, they held him hostage for questioning about the new threat they faced. He told them The Werewolves were a local people that didn't like or want The Battles taking place on their land and saw it as an outside invasion. Once darkness fell and the moon rose, he was no longer a hostage and could no longer be questioned as he broke free and wreaked havoc through the camp.

Six years had passsed when the fifth gang made its entry, The Cannibals, an elitist upper class English cult that fell victim to a vampire attack; they wanted revenge for the killing of their members and joined The Battles. Almost a century passed and the bloodshed and body count grew and grew and the warfare reached new lows and evils. The Witchcraft Raids are what some people today call a magical biohazard tactic – witches would pose as local women offering help in the fight against evil, nurses, cooks, farm hands anything that would get them into enemy territory unscathed and would then curse and hex the army camp from the inside, in some cases even having sex with the soldiers in order to spread deadly viruses through the ranks. The CVS were hit the worst to a point where they stopped women entering the camp for fear any one of them could be a witch; many soldiers died as a result of these raids.

It was only a matter of time before the fighting made its way to Ireland and in 1776 The Irish were formed, who were conflicted as a strong religious nation to fight against evil for the greater good, but at the same time it was another problem coming to their land from Britain, so in the end they fought against everyone. As did The Chinese who were founded just weeks later in England as for many years Chinese immigrants had made their way west and the first Chinese community in Europe was in Liverpool. The Battles continued and more gangs meant more people which led to more bloodshed, and The Christian Vampire Slayers came no closer to victory; in fact, it was The Vampires and The Witches who edged closer and in 1790 the eighth gang were formed, The Pagans, after a battle around Stonehenge, a site that Pagans hold sacred on land that was Pagan centuries before Christianity, and here The CVS were ordering the local people to join them in their fight. The Pagans did join the fight but as their own gang and not alongside their religious oppressors.

With eight gangs fighting for supremacy, and mortal weakness and tribalism taking its toll, victory finally came in 1802 with The Vampires and The Witches taking their place at the top – 322 years of battles, Niculi and his true love Ziana became the couple supreme. This was met with sheer devastation by the other gangs, but the forces of darkness reigned. Unwilling to accept defeat, the rival gangs did not flee but stayed in the hope of some relief from the nightmare they had experienced, most of them for their whole life. This played into The Vampires' hands as it is always a good idea to have your food source close to you. An agreement was made and on 20th August 1802, 9 Gang City was founded. The day previous, The Vampires realised they would need what they called a guardian of the daylight, meaning they needed somebody to watch over them during daylight hours, so Niculi formed The Messengers, the ninth gang and completing the 9 Gang City collective. It was agreed that The Messengers would serve whichever gang was in power, to which The Messengers agreed as this would make them always at least the second most powerful gang in the city.

Another change that took place was The Christian Vampire Slayers changed their name to The Monks as a tribute to their founders; this came about when Niculi told them that if The Battles were over then they were no longer slayers and that they should look to the future and not the past. The CVS reluctantly agreed.

For 200 years The Vampires and The Witches ruled as tyrants and dictators, taking pleasure in their power, and over two centuries of no law and order paved the way for the other gang members being lambs to the slaughter of vampirism and witchcraft. This kind of leadership only leads to revolutions and some would say why did it take 200 years to revolutionise? The answer is it is easier said than done to defeat such foes. Niculi could crush entire armies alone and Ziana could wipe out hordes with one hex. But along came a saviour, along came Brother Gideon, a gang member for The Monks, who was gaining high praise in the ranks and working his way up. Gideon informed his superiors of his desire to take the city from the evil tyrants that had infected the world for too long; his leaders agreed and gave him permission to hold secret meetings with the other six gangs. The Messengers also joined with them against their controllers and The War Against The Vampires was declared, with all seven other gangs joining forces under the leadership of The Monks to fight back against The Vampires and The Witches. This war was fought with no morals whatsoever, no mercy was given and slaughter was an everyday occurrence. The Vampires call the war The Massacre Of The Vampires because of the tactics used, mainly The Daylight Killings in which rival gang members would enter vampire tombs and slay them as they slept defenceless; some were dragged outside and left to the sunlight. This tactic has drawn much criticism even from the gangs that took part, some going as far as to call it cowardice to slay your victim when it is defenceless, others say it was necessary to take control from an enemy that seemed undefeatable, and in any case the city is better off now than it was. The end came when the seven gangs split into two armies. One fought The Witches and the other attacked The Vampires, bonfires blazed as witches burned, witch after witch was captured and set alight at the stake without mercy; the numbers against them were too many and The Witches were crushed. The Monks burst into a den of witches to see Ziana with two gang members who were dealt with comfortably leaving the queen alone. Ziana hissed at her attackers who surrounded her, throwing chains over her body and arms so she could not fight back and dragging her to a stake and chaining her, leaving no chance of escape. Dowsing her in petrol, Brother Gideon took a flaming torch and stood in front of her. Ziana looked up at him, knowing her end had arrived.

"I cast you to hell" were the immortal words that Gideon spoke as he set the witch queen on fire, bringing an end to her rule of darkness; but before he did, Ziana cast one last spell before screaming as the flames took her. With no time to celebrate, the remaining gang members rushed to assist in the slaying of Niculi. What greeted them was ferocious battle with dead bodies scattered far and wide and as they expected Niculi would be much more difficult to defeat. They attacked him in their droves but he laid waste to their effort with little issue. Gideon stepped forward dowsing Niculi with holy water. The vampire let out a roar of agony as the liquid saviour burnt his face; more and more gang members stepped forward to drench him with more holy water which brought Niculi to his knees until a stray werewolf entered, forcing the other gangs to step back as the wolf pounced onto Niculi, sinking its teeth into his shoulder. Niculi, gripping hold of the wolf, threw the beast. Crashing into the wall, the wolf was quickly back into combat as snarls and roars were exchanged, Niculi crashing a punch into the wolf's, face sending it staggering back; but werewolves are not easily defeated as men and the beast kept on coming. The rival gang members kept their distance, as for mortals to get involved in a fight such as this would be suicide. The werewolf swinging with ferocity, sliced deep into Niculi's body, the vampire retaliating by sinking his fangs into the wolf's face deep and viciously, falling to the floor. Niculi reached for a gun that was on the floor dropped by one of the fallen gang members, and knowing on a night such as this the gun would contain silver bullets – this is because although the other gangs had a pact, werewolves when they are transformed have no control over their actions. Niculi placed the gun to the wolf's head and fired; the corpse dropped lifeless on to him before he threw it in to the air, raising to his feet and letting out a roar of dominance.

The enemy were gripped with fear; they knew it was now or never to defeat the monster their predecessors had failed to slay for centuries and, led by Brother Gideon, they stepped forward. Surrounding Niculi and with copious amounts of holy water they drenched him from all angles, sending the vampire down onto his knees. Gideon stepped forward with a crossbow loaded with a stake, took aim at the monster's chest and pulled the trigger. The crossbow fired the stake directly into Niculi's heart and without wasting another second Gideon drew his sword and swung with all his might, removing the vampire's head and sending the decapitated body of Niculi falling to the ground. All the people present stood in silence, not quite believing what they had just witnessed, 522 years and they had finally achieved what their ancestors couldn't: Niculi was slain.

Brother Gideon, taking his place in history, raised his sword in the air and let out a call of victory. The remaining gang members joined in his celebration as Niculi's corpse was reduced to ash and the reign of terror was over. Quickly taking control of Cathedral Tower, The Monks took the initiative and called an immediate election and made Bother Gideon their leader, knowing that after his heroics they would be voted into power.

Father Gideon won the election by a landslide and became leader of 9 Gang City. New rules and political policies were introduced, and new leaders were in need of election. The Vampires voted in Goran as their new leader, but he did nothing to change the ways of The Vampires and he was replaced by Krul, a young vampire with a more political approach to leadership, knowing that The Vampire's old ways were the reason they were so hated. His new style brought him respect, such as vampires could no longer feed on rival gang members; instead a blood supply was provided for their people. The Witches voted in Rika as their queen – the witch queen is not actually a queen, it is just what The Witches call their leader – but Queen Rika has control now and time will tell how that turns out.

The city is better than it was and the gangs are certainly better than when The Battles were taking place, but that is not to say all is well; in fact, far from it. Father Gideon's respect has hit an all-time low and animosity for The Monks is growing, mostly because of their dictatorial approach, something they complained The Vampires did, but hiding behind religion is their excuse. The future seems bleak for the city as it is now at a point that many gang members think another war is the answer, which would be catastrophic for The Monks as the hatred towards them grows by the day as they are now seen as hypocrites who accused The Vampires of something that they now do and the people of the city have had enough. Once a hero and a legend who took his place forever in the history of 9 Gang City, Father Gideon is now hated beyond repair. If ever there was a time for democracy and political leadership to come to the forefront that time is now, but with a leader unwilling to compromise and a city on the brink, it looks like 9 Gang City will resort to what it does best, violence.

City Details

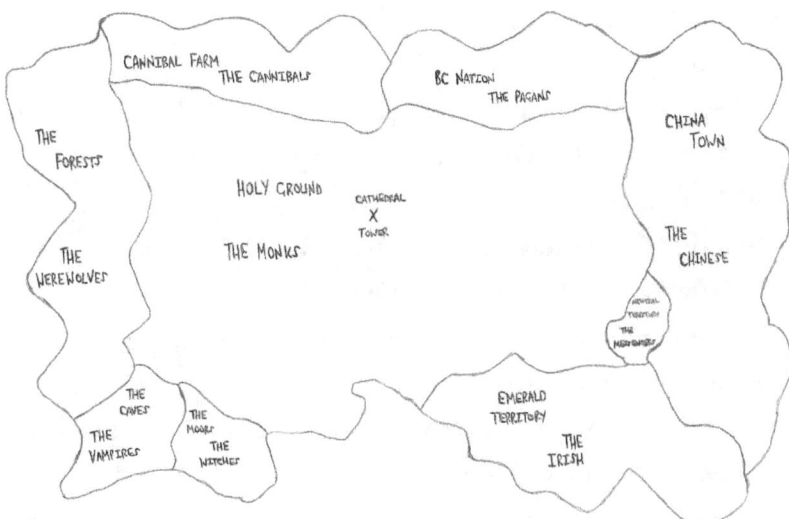

- ❖ **City Name:** 9 Gang City
- ❖ **City Age:** 220 Years
- ❖ **Population:** 1804
- ❖ **Gang Members:** 1804
- ❖ **Non-Gang Members:** 0 (You can't live in 9 Gang City unless you have a gang membership)
- ❖ **Largest Gang:** The Chinese
- ❖ **Smallest Gang:** The Messengers
- ❖ **Largest Territory:** Holy Ground, The Monks
- ❖ **Smallest Territory:** Neutral Territory, The Messengers
- ❖ **The Monks:** 267 (Only 20 are monks, the rest are soldiers)
- ❖ **The Messengers:** 24
- ❖ **The Irish:** 233
- ❖ **The Chinese:** 492
- ❖ **The Cannibals:** 207
- ❖ **The Pagans:** 221

- **The Werewolves:** 176
- **The Witches:** 50
- **The Vampires:** 134
- **Gang In Power:** The Monks, 20 Years
- **Previous Gang In Power:** The Vampires, 200 Years
- **Most Respected Gang:** The Messengers
- **Most Hated Gang:** The Vampires
- **Gang Most Likely To Take Over City:** The Chinese
- **Gang Least Likely To Take Over City:** The Messengers
- **Number Of Wars:** 1, The War Against The Vampires
- **Gang Allegiances In City:** The Vampires and The Witches
- **Territories Most Avoided:** The Moors (Non-Full Moon)
- **The Forests (Full Moon)**
- **City Terminologies:** Father Gideon, Gideon The Great, after his service in The War Against The Vampires.
- **Alice Heart, Alice "Kind" Heart or Alice "Sweet" Heart:** a nickname given to her by Krul because of her good nature and support of The Vampires.
- **The Dog Pound:** The Werewolves' leader's nickname for themselves.
- **Silver Nights:** During a full moon when the other gangs change the bullets in their guns to silver bullets.
- **The Cauldron:** The Witches' gang headquarters, nicknamed by others.
- **The Dark Fairy:** Tunder's nickname.
- **The Countess:** Enigma's nickname.
- **The New Age Vampires:** A new gang name for The Vampires after Krul became leader, Krul rejected the name because he wanted to keep The Vampires as one gang and not two separate gangs; this gained him more respect amongst his members.

- ⌬ **Blood 134:** A term meaning The Vampires' blood supply is running low.
- ⌬ **The Blood Bank:** The Vampires' blood supply.
- ⌬ **Bat Country:** Nickname for The Vampires' territory.
- ⌬ **The Fleas, The Flea Breed, The Parasites:** An insulting term used towards The Vampires by the other gangs, it is considered highly offensive by The Vampires.
- ⌬ **The Massacre Of The Vampires:** The Vampires' name for The War Against The Vampires because of some of the tactics used.
- ⌬ **Past City Atmosphere:** All-out war
- ⌬ **Present City Atmosphere:** Hostile
- ⌬ **Predicted Future City Atmosphere:** War

City Laws

- ⌬ High Council is the highest authority in 9 Gang City.
- ⌬ Sale of territory is allowed.
- ⌬ Gangs are allowed to do business with each other without High Council permission.
- ⌬ Gangs are allowed to have unions with other gangs.
- ⌬ Gangs are allowed to merge but must rename the gang and territory.
- ⌬ Gangs must go through High Council before declaring war.
- ⌬ Punishment for undeclared war is the other gangs join forces and wipe out offending gang and divide their territory.
- ⌬ The Messengers work for whichever gang is in power.
- ⌬ The Messengers are the only gang who can enter any territory without permission.
- ⌬ Attacking a Messenger whilst on High Council duty is punishable by removal of High Council voting power.

- ⚜ Murdering a Messenger whilst on High Council duty is punishable by execution.
- ⚜ No battle can take place in Neutral Territory.
- ⚜ Total City lockdown during full moon.
- ⚜ Werewolves can be shot during full moon if they attack a rival gang member but only as a last resort.
- ⚜ Vampires cannot feed on rival gang members.
- ⚜ No battle can take place with The Vampires during daylight hours.
- ⚜ Execution of Monks, Messengers, Irish, Chinese, Cannibals and Pagans is by firing squad.
- ⚜ Execution of Werewolves is by firing squad with a silver bullet.
- ⚜ Execution of Witches is by burning at stake.
- ⚜ Execution of Vampires is by firing squad with a crossbow stake and removal of head during night hours.

High Council

High Council is the highest authority in 9 Gang City; it is made up of the leaders of each gang and their 2nd and 3rd in command and is where the decisions of the city are made. High Council was formed 200 years after the city's formation and directly after The War Against The Vampires and when The Monks were voted into power. It was the first democracy the city had and finally brought political structure to a place of tyranny and dictatorship. It was the idea of Father Gideon and mainly the work of The Monks but was set up by all gangs. Since the induction of High Council every decision in the city is decided by the vote of the High Council members; each member has the right to vote how they please and cannot and should not vote depending on their leader's command. Each member is free to express their opinion without consequence and no member should feel obliged or forced to go along with anybody, High Council is for the free and democratic, and each member has a legal right to a vote on every policy put to them.

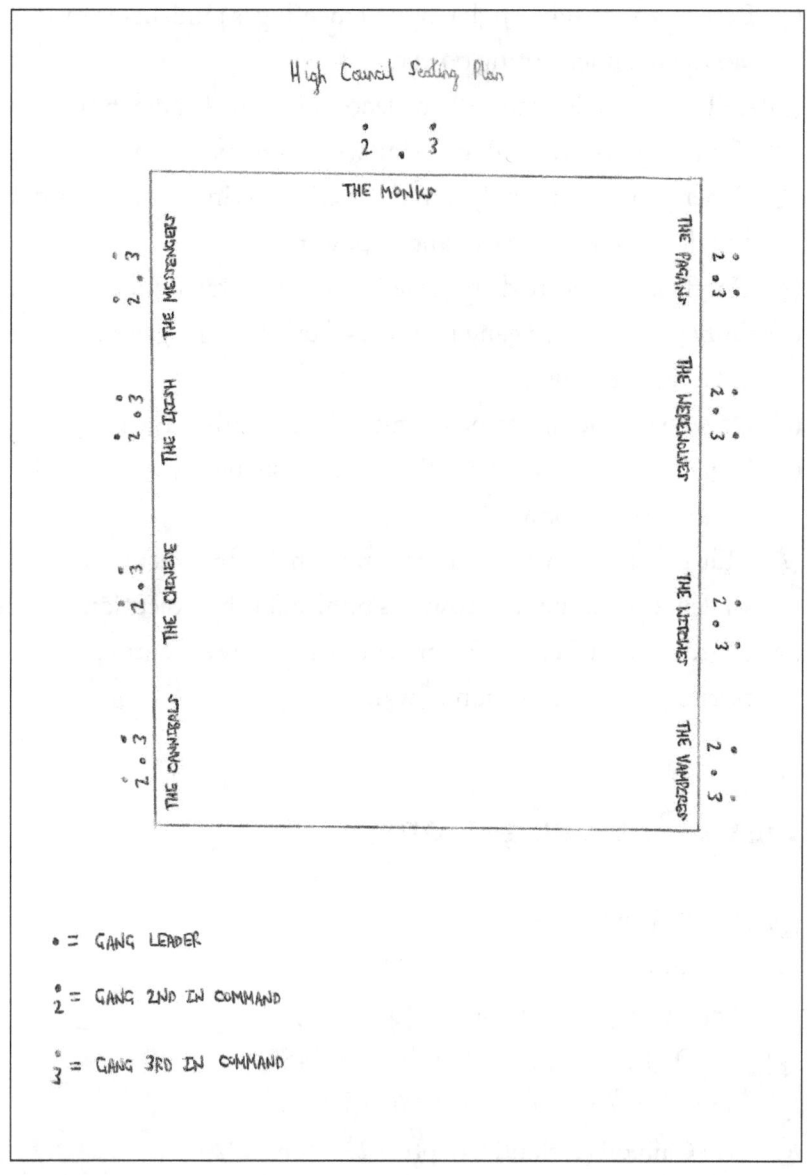

Rules Of High Council

- ◎ High Council meetings can only take place in Cathedral Tower.
- ◎ High Council meetings cannot take place without all 27 members being invited.
- ◎ Refusal to attend a High Council meeting is punishable by loss of High Council voting power.
- ◎ Only The Leader can call an election for The Leadership.
- ◎ Gang in power can call meeting whenever they want.
- ◎ Other gangs must make a request for meeting stating reason, and decision is made by gang in power.
- ◎ Unofficial votes are disregarded and considered undemocratic.
- ◎ Only the top three gang members from each gang are allowed in Cathedral Tower.
- ◎ Other gang members must wait in The Waiting Yard.
- ◎ Violence in The Waiting Yard is punishable by loss of High Council voting power.
- ◎ Murder in The Waiting Yard is punishable by execution.
- ◎ Violence in Cathedral Tower is punishable by execution.
- ◎ Murder in Cathedral Tower is punishable by execution, loss of territory and declaration of war.

Days Of Celebration

- ◎ City Day 20th August 1802
- ◎ Freedom Day 18th March 2002
- ◎ Victory Day 20th October 2002
- ◎ Day Of The Saviours 12th February 1480
- ◎ Messenger Formation 19th August 1802
- ◎ Eriu Caibidil (Ireland Chapter) 22nd June 1776

- ⊘ Dong Tai (Eastern Greatness) 10th July 1776
- ⊘ The Feast 11th May 1698
- ⊘ The Harvest 14th April 1790
- ⊘ Sonnes Of The Mona (Sons Of The Moon) 30th November 1692
- ⊘ Kiralyno Emlekezik (Queen's Remembrance) 18th February 1480
- ⊘ Vampir Ceremoniilor (Vampire Celebration) 12th February 1480

The Gangs

Name: The Monks

Members: 267
Territory: Holy Ground
Founded: 12th February 1480

Information: The Monks were the second gang to be founded and were formed on the same day as The Vampires. Previously known as The Christian Vampire Slayers or The CVS, they are the product of The Vatican who wanted to save Eastern Europe from the dark deeds that were taking place there. A combination of Britain, France and Italy, The CVS were eventually pushed back across Europe into Britain and Ireland where they eventually, along with five other gangs, surrendered to The Vampires and The Witches. After 9 Gang City was founded another two centuries passed before the city declared The War Against The Vampires (the war was also against The Witches), which they won after six months of war. The Monks were voted into power, the first and as of yet only gang to be elected with Father Gideon the heroic legend that slayed Niculi and Ziana as the leader. In recent years The Monks have lost almost all their respect and are hated across the city.

Gang Leader: Father Gideon, The Leader of 9 Gang city who was voted in after The War Against the Vampires and has held the position for 20 years. A Frontline Fighter in the war, he is legendary for slaying both Niculi and Ziana, and was celebrated as a hero, but has now lost almost all the respect people once had for him due to hypocritical behaviour such as refusing to take The Leadership to a vote knowing he would lose, also for hiding behind religion. The Monks are now the second most hated gang in the city and Father Gideon is the main reason for that hatred.

2nd In Command: Brother Francis, a true believer in religion ruling the people, Francis will stop at nothing to keep The Monks in power and is a strong supporter of Father Gideon. A firm believer that if you don't follow his faith then you are less than him. His attitude and treatment of others has him seen as a tyrant and dictator by the rest of the city. Francis does not care what others think of him and believes he is next in line for The Leadership – he is by default, but the city would go to war before they would have Francis as leader.

3rd In Command: Brother Theodore, not as tyrannical as his superiors but enough to believe it is religion first and people second. Brother Theodore thinks peace is best but only on The Monks' terms. Almost used as a lackey by Brother Francis, he is a believer that everybody has their place and that place means sometimes taking orders, not as hated as Gideon or Francis, but still hated enough that he will be a marked man if war should happen, just like his superiors.

Name: The Messengers

Members: 24
Territory: Neutral Territory
Founded: 19th August 1802

Information: The Messengers were founded one day before the city and did not take part in The Battles, they were formed by Niculi to watch over The Vampires during daylight hours. Some people suggested that they should be called The Protectors or The Watchers, but due to their other duties Niculi decided on The Messengers' name. They are the smallest gang with the smallest territory but the second highest political power as they serve whatever gang is in leadership and hold some political clout in the city. Despite the law of serving the leading gang, they turned on The Vampires and joined the other gangs in The War Against The Vampires, an action that doesn't really stand against them as the leader they have now actually supported The Vampires and was against the war. Alice Heart is a highly respected and loved person across the city and almost everybody thinks would be the best leader for 9 Gang City. The Messengers are weak militarily but are in a very strong position politically with Alice in charge.

Gang Leader: Alice Heart, the most respected and well liked person in the city. Alice has been a priceless asset for the city being at peace for 20 years. Her embrace of democracy and diversity have gained her many allies to a point that if The Leadership went to a vote Alice would win. As one of the very few people against The War Against The Vampires, she spoke out openly against The Daylight Killings and she has also strongly supported Vampire Rights as she believes in equality for all. This gained her much respect amongst The Vampires but did not and has not gone down well with The Monks. This is of no consequence to Alice as she is backed up not only by the other gangs but by the law itself – not even Father Gideon or The Monks can remove The Messengers from their position. The Messengers can never fall beneath second most powerful gang in the city which politically is a huge swing in Alice's favour. The Messengers are the least likely to take over the city through war, but are most likely to win The Leadership through politics; this means Alice needs to do all she can to prevent war, a task that seems unlikely given the current climate.

2ⁿᵈ In Command: David Leonard, Leo is an old friend of Alice and a good all-round man who is passionate about his beliefs. A hard worker who spent years promoting democracy he is none too pleased with Father Gideon's obsession with power and has gained respect all over the city. Alice has chosen well having Leo as her deputy as he is loyal to her and their gang as well as being a good politician and a good fighter.

3ʳᵈ In Command: Jessica Heart, the sister of Alice and a passionate believer in fairness to all citizens of 9 Gang City, although she does lack her sister's discipline. It is one of the extremely few criticisms of Alice to make her close friend and sister 2ⁿᵈ and 3ʳᵈ In Command, but in a city like this you need your closest allies to be your most loyal comrades and Jessica loves her sister very much. A supporter of Vampire Rights, she has become popular with The Vampires as well as a growing friendship with The Werewolves leader, which keeps her firmly locked in The Monks' sights.

Name: The Irish

Members: 233
Territory: Emerald Territory
Founded: 22nd June 1776

Information: Founded after The Battles crossed the Irish Sea from England, The Irish saw it as another problem coming from Britain and formed their gang to fight back against the invading battles. Caught between fighting for and against religion, the gang were always caught in two minds and when The Pagans joined The Battles, this added to their torn agenda as The Pagans honour and worship the old Gods. Since the end of The Battles, The Irish and The Pagans have shared a strained relationship but at the same time a mutual respect. They have gained prowess in resect years and with a long-serving, respected leader, The Irish are in a strengthening position.

Gang Leader: Aiden O'Riordan, one of the very few gang leaders that was in power during The War Against The Vampires, Aiden is a strong leader who is well respected by the city and loved by his gang. Political gain is the game now and Aiden is ready for war but has the intelligence to know when and where war should begin. He is a good leader and has raised the stock of his gang; if the city should go to war, The Irish have a chance.

2nd In Command: Cormac Shea, a worthy deputy and always up for a fight; a military minded man, he leaves the politics to Aiden. A strong presence – people certainly know when he is in the room, the rest of the gang do as he says or they will face his wrath. With a short fuse and a low tolerance for the weak-minded, Cormac is a warrior. Anywhere else he would be considered a thug, but in 9 Gang City he is just what a gang needs.

3rd In Command: Siobhan Murphy, a keen supporter of history and celebrator of culture, Siobhan supports the friendship with The Pagans. A beautiful woman with a fiery temper, she is not afraid to speak her mind, not caring whom she offends. She can fight, is not afraid of war and is ready for The Irish to take control, but she needs to control her mouth because she offends too many people.

Name: The Chinese

Members: 492
Territory: China Town
Founded: 10th July 1776

Information: The Chinese are the biggest gang in 9 Gang City and are also the richest and most armed, making them the most likely to take over the city if war should happen. Adding that to a strong leader whose political power is growing, The Chinese are in an extremely strong position to rule the city. Founded in England by Chinese immigrants, they joined The Battles centuries after they started and mere decades before they finished. They believe the reason the other gangs lost The Battles is because they were also fighting against each other and not just against The Vampires and The Witches. This claim is backed up by the other gangs winning The War Against The Vampires when they joined forces, but as far as The Chinese current standing, they will do things their way and things are looking good for them.

Gang Leader: Feng Cai Cheng, Cheng was voted in after the war and is a formidable foe for anybody in 9 Gang City. Tough in battle and politically powerful, Cheng has the biggest gang, he has the richest gang and he has the most weapons. He tries not to let history get in the way of progress, but at the same time respects his people's past, he is a man who should be respected. Cautiously watching The Vampires' progress as they are his biggest threat militarily and although has nothing against The Messengers personally, he knows they are his biggest threat politically, he isn't worried by The Monks as they have mastered their own downfall. Cheng is highly ambitious and keeps himself educated on all the gangs in the city.

The Chinese are in the best position to take over through war, and with the way things are war looks very likely.

2nd In Command: Son Li Yong, after the war Yong stood for gang leadership but was defeated by Cheng. Although disappointed, he offered his full support to Cheng for the good of the gang; this was rewarded by being made 2nd in command, which he accepted with pride. Yong is a proud gang member who believes his people should rule, but honour and discipline are key. Yong is tough, disciplined and passionate, three things his gang will need if they are to reach the top.

3rd In Command: Zhen Yun, a feisty woman who is well trained in hand-to-hand combat and has worked hard to get where she is and is quite forceful in her approach to her gang's progression in power, which has made her enemies. Zhen needs to improve her political skills to be a good all-round gang member because she has a bad temper that sometimes gets her into trouble.

Name: The Cannibals

Members: 207
Territory: Cannibal Farm
Founded: 11th May 1698

Information: Originally The Cannibals were an elitist upper class cult in England; they were the fifth gang to be formed, which happened after a vampire attacked and killed members of the cult; wanting vengeance The Cannibals were founded and joined The Battles. A disliked gang, they are somewhat in limbo between the mortal gangs and the "monster" gangs due to being mortal but taking part in despicable acts. Despite this they continue their ways and dismiss the other gangs' distaste as a lack of understanding for their ways, taking pride in their gang's past and celebrating their elitist bloodline. They are the least likely to be voted into power, which means they will have to rely on war.

Gang Leader: William Henry Davis, a descendant of the most famous cannibal, Archibald Bartholomew Davis, believing it is his birth right to lead the gang he is another that was voted in after The War Against The Vampires. The Cannibals still take part in eating people and have come to be considered disgusting and hated. With little respect William has almost no chance of being voted in, and with their military power weak The Cannibals are the least likely to gain power.

2nd In Command: James Winston Wycombe, just like his leader he is a highly disliked man. James is war hungry and he is corpse hungry, he and the rest of the gang want war, and with the way the city is, war is what they might get, which means fresh meat to feast on. Having an eye on who he would prefer to eat, James is a sick and twisted individual and people should be wary in his presence.

3rd In Command: Clifford Mitchell White is the least powerful member of High Council, which means he is the 27th most powerful person in the city. He does hold power within his gang, but as far as political prowess his chances are slim; the only thing he has in his favour is that he is not as hated as his superiors, but this means very little within High Council.

Name: The Pagans

Members: 221
Territory: BC Nation
Founded: 14th April 1790

Information: The Pagans were formed in 1790 and were the eighth gang to be founded and the last to join The Battles. After much pressure from The CVS to join the fight against evil and the last straw coming after a battle at Stonehenge, The Pagans joined and fought, but much to the fury of The CVS, they joined as their own gang and fought against all. Although they did join the other gangs in The War Against The Vampires, they have often fallen foul of religious tension from The Monks, leading to arguments and sometimes insults back and forth in High Council. The Pagans are in a mid-position for election, and they are growing in power, especially with the city turning more and more against The Monks. It is unlikely they will gain power soon, but with more allies and more guns they might have a chance; that chance grows more and more by the day. They have a faltered friendship with The Irish.

Gang Leader: Arch Druid Brigacos was voted into gang leadership after The War Against The Vampires and a well-chosen leader by his gang; focused on a balance between nature and nurture, military and politics, he is a rising force in the city. With still a way to go before he is a true contender, he works hard to improve his and the gang's chances, but is on the up and up. With growing tension between him and Father Gideon, Brigacos knows other gangs will back him over The Monks, so politics is not his issue; however, if war should happen they have members and guns, but will they have enough to conquer a city that he and his gang believe is theirs through sacred history?

2ⁿᵈ In Command: Druidess Gwendoline, a spiritual person with a love and admiration for nature and culture and a distaste for the destruction humankind have on the Earth. Gwendoline is a good balance between war and politics; this is why Brigacos made her his deputy. On current standing, The Pagans are gaining in terms of politics, but their military power is lacking compared to other gangs; this is being worked on and Gwendoline is right in the middle of it. She is a she-wolf type woman and will not take trouble lightly. Although she loves the natural world, Gwen knows war is human nature.

3ʳᵈ In Command: Druid Bryson, a strong fighter, almost a mystical warrior with a passion for his ancestors' Celtic roots. With a distaste for Christianity due to the demonising of Celtic Gods and Goddesses when Britain was Christianised, Bryson is regularly in conflict with The Monks, especially Brother Francis due to Francis' religious tyranny and belief that The Pagans are beneath The Monks. This gains support from other gangs, but The Monks are becoming tired of The Pagans' troublemaking.

Name: The Werewolves

Members: 176
Territory: The Forests
Founded: 30th November 1692

Information: The Werewolves were the fourth gang to be formed and were founded by English men in North Yorkshire. Taking their names from Old English names for wolf, they embrace their history well; add that to their current political gaining of their leaders and The Werewolves are on the up, which will always cause worry and concern with the mortal gangs. Growing closer to The Vampires and The Witches, the three gangs that are considered monsters see this as an insult and discrimination and are fighting back against this politically. Bringing up the issue in High Council meetings, some support has come their way, mainly from The Messengers as an equal system for all gangs is what will keep the peace, and peace is exactly what the city needs as far as The Messengers are concerned. Uncontrollable during their wolf stage, 9 Gang City goes into full lockdown during a full moon, for the safety of the other gangs. The Forests are the most feared territory during a full moon.

Gang Leader: Cuthwulf, means famous wolf; well suited to being a wolf, he is a proud man and a good leader who has improved his gang's discipline and strengthened their position within High Council. Unhappy with what he and the gang see as a discriminatory attitude from the rest of the city towards themselves and The Vampires and The Witches, Cuthwulf is beginning to think a union between the three gangs may be the answer; whether this materialises remains to be seen, but what is in no doubt is the positive influence Cuthwulf has had on the political rising of his gang. He is fair as a man, but brutal and merciless as a wolf.

2ⁿᵈ In Command: Wulfric – means wolf power – is a very good deputy for Cuthwulf and is passionate about the gang's position within the city and High Council, and is working tirelessly to get them into power. Knowing at the moment they have their best chance The Werewolves have ever had, Wulfric is a good politician and advisor to his leader; there are gangs in better positions to gain control but Wulfric knows sometimes that doesn't matter.

3ʳᵈ In Command: Randall – means shield wolf; a well-disciplined gang member who performs his duties well, Randall is eager for his gang to gain power. Working on his political skills and learning that sometimes politics is sometimes not the answer, he is prepared for war. A good warrior for The Werewolves, he will be an asset if war should happen and going to war during a full moon will always put The Werewolves in the driving seat.

Name: The Witches

Members: 50
Territory: The Moors
Founded: 18th February 1480

Information: The Witches were the third gang to be formed and were founded one week after The Vampires and The Christian Vampire Slayers. They were set up to help The Vampires fight against what they saw as invaders from the west. Originally Hungarian gypsies, The Witches were led by Queen Ziana whose powers were the strongest people had ever known; she was dark, evil and merciless and would work her way to victory for herself, her gang and Niculi by any means necessary. Some people feared her even more than they feared Niculi, as she was twisted in her desire for power and would curse and hex for pleasure, whereas Niculi was brutal but once he had fed he was happy. The city celebrated when Ziana was slain as it rid the world of an evil existence, but despite this she was loved by her gang and even to this day is celebrated as the greatest witch ever. After The War Against The Vampires, The Witches voted in Rika as their Queen and this new leader has somewhat embraced the city's democracy; but the other gangs will never trust a witch; in fact, The Witches are the least trusted gang and their territory is the most avoided during a non-full moon. Queen Rika has a fondness for the gang's history and welcomes the continuation of her gang's affiliation with The Vampires; having said that, The Witches want power back and want to share that power with The Vampires but are willing to go it alone if necessary.

Gang Leader: Queen Rika. Rika has been in power since the end of the war and is a powerful witch who the other gangs are wary of and the city is fearful when The Witches are around. Believing The Witches are the true rulers of the city along with The Vampires, Rika is prepared to rule 9 Gang City by hook or by crook but knows achieving it through democracy will be the better way; this is highly unlikely but Rika is willing to try. Unlike the typical image of a witch, Rika is young looking and beautiful and along with her sisters she has gained some but little ground in changing the city's attitude towards her people; there will always be animosity towards witches.

2nd In Command: Princess Katalin, the younger sister of Rika and a specialist in shapeshifting, which comes in useful for spying missions. Katalin believes her sister is the true ruler of the city and will do all it takes to get her there, the more placid of the witch leaders she is more of a hide in the shadows type rather than out in the open and fight, and there are plenty of shadows to hide in.

3rd In Command: Princess Tunder, the youngest sister of The Witches and a vicious little creature and is hell bent on getting The Witches back where they belong, controlling the city and will stop at nothing to get them there. Tunder is obsessed with Queen Ziana and idolises the fallen queen. The city should count themselves lucky that Rika and Katalin have their sister under control because if war should break out, Tunder will show no mercy. Seeing no progress through democracy, Tunder wants action and has waited long enough for it; now she is sick of waiting and her powers are growing.

Name: The Vampires

Members: 134
Territory: The Caves
Founded: 12th February 1480

Information: The Vampires were the first gang to be formed and they were founded by Niculi to fight against the oncoming threat from Western Europe. Having a long affiliation with The Witches, they fought their way across Europe to Britannia where, after 322 years of battles, The Vampires claimed victory, making Niculi the leader of the newly founded 9 Gang City. Niculi was slain 20th October 2002 and after the formation of High Council, a vampire named Goran was elected as The Vampires' leader. Goran did nothing to change the gang's ways and the animosity towards the gang continued, until a young ambitious vampire joined the ranks. Krul is more politically minded and brought forward a new way of thinking, suggesting that the old vampire ways were the reason their kind were so despised and suggested The Vampires should modernise their way of thinking and their behaviour. This gained Krul positive attention from the other gangs and his fellow gang members saw the impact he was having across the city. Krul defeated Goran in an election and The Vampires have slowly but surely grown in political power; add this to their undead powers and The Vampires seem to be on the rise again, much to the dislike of some of the other gangs, especially The Monks. Despite the positive impact Krul has had, The Vampires will always be hated as people can never seem to let go of the past. Krul has countless times tried to convince the city to leave the past behind them, but that is easier said than done. The Vampires and The Witches still continue the tradition of their friendship, and in this city friends are always priceless support. They have also grown closer to The Werewolves as the three gangs are seen as dark, evil and abhorrent by most of the other gangs' members. The hatred between The Vampires and The Monks continues, and unfortunately almost everybody in 9 Gang City thinks this hatred will always exist; even with a fresh, more vibrant leader, a vampire will always be seen as a monster by most people and they are still the most hated gang in the city. They have a long road back to power, but The Vampires will always be in with a chance and they should never be underestimated.

Gang Leader: Krul (pronounced but not meaning Cruel) was voted in 10 years after being turned and was not around for The War Against The Vampires. For him to become leader in such a short space of time is testament to his political prowess and embrace of the new ways. The Vampires no longer feed at will on whoever they want, they find their blood elsewhere, taking away some but not all of their fear. It was Krul who brought in this new policy which has gained him respect from High Council. Krul has repeatedly argued against The Monks clinging to power and called for an election, which has gained him support from the other gangs but has made him an even stronger enemy of The Monks. This matters not to Krul because the more The Monks refuse a vote for The Leadership, the more Krul will call them out on it; this means his support from the rest of the city will grow. With the strength of ten men and a political gaining in respect, Krul is on the up, and along with his deputy and 3rd the city is becoming nervous about The Vampires' gain. Krul is hated for being a vampire, but he is highly respected for what he has achieved.

2nd In Command: Victuis, the best friend of Krul and himself a young vampire; Victuis has been a priceless asset to Krul and his quest for gang leadership. It was Krul who turned Victuis and as they were best friends as mortals, so they are as the undead. Not as politically strong as Krul, but still well liked and respected, Victuis is a keen celebrator of the vampire's history and embraces his existence to a point he is glad he was turned and thanks Krul for it. The Vampires' leaders are the closest to one another out of all the gangs, which is good for the gang but worrying for the rest of the city. Krul made a wise decision choosing Victuis as his deputy: their loyalty to each other is unmatched.

3rd **In Command:** Enigma, the girlfriend of Krul and the vampire who turned him; 10 years ago she was outside the city borders hunting mortals to feed on when she attacked and bit a man named Michael Krulton – whilst feeding she felt a connection to him and turned him. Enigma is 208 years old and is one of the few surviving vampires from the war and is a hardcore extremist of vampire dominance, and her mind is still set in the old ways. Luckily for the city she listens to Krul and keeps herself controlled, but she is itching for war. Although disappointed when Krul made Victuis 2nd In Command, she understands they have a strong friendship and that strength passes through the gang. Enigma has become good friends with Victuis and they get along very well, much to Krul's delight. Her past as a mortal must have been bad because she doesn't speak about it, not even to Krul, and considering she is over two centuries old very little is known about her, hence her name.

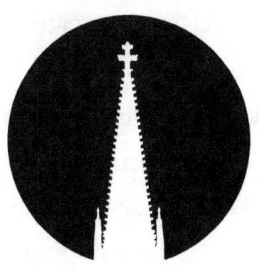

Chapter 1

With all seven documents ready and a duty to uphold, Alice gets into the car where Jessica is already waiting and sets off on their journey around 9 Gang City. In a day and age where technology can have you send a text message or email to multiple people in a matter of seconds, it will seem silly to some people that The Messengers still deliver the notices of High Council meetings in the traditional way by hand delivering them to each gang, but some traditions are upheld. Besides, Alice likes the task as it gets her away from headquarters and gives her a chance to spend some time with her sister. Jessica is always keen to get out and about as she enjoys travelling around the city, and she likes meeting each of the gangs and seeing their political approach and their cultural differences, which gives Jessica knowledge and an insight to how each gang operates. This is a privilege held only by The Messengers as they are the only gang allowed to enter any territory without permission, so in this aspect her gang has the upper hand. On a more serious note, tonight's meeting will be an interesting one; tensions have increased between the gangs of late, which is no surprise whatsoever to the residents of this city, but recently they have grown more and more hostile. There have even been murmurs of war, but these have been whispers in dark corners and shadows, and we all know what lurks in the shadows – the darkness holds beings that are best avoided – but at a High Council meeting they cannot be avoided; however, at least Cathedral Tower is well lit. The first stop isn't far, China Town, and Jessica sits up in her chair as they approach the checkpoint. Each gang should be respected, and out of the mortal gangs The Chinese are the ones to keep an eye on – since the war they have steadily grown in power both militarily and politically, mainly thanks to their leader Cheng Cai Feng or Feng Cai Cheng, depending on what culture is writing it. Cheng is a strong leader, not just physically – he is tough and well trained in battle – but also politically; knowing he is gaining respect across the city, Cheng is happy to push for a vote for The Leadership, but knowing that may never come is keeping his arsenal well stocked and his members well trained. The checkpoints as they are called are the gateways into each territory and are the only way in and out of each gang's turf, officially; any entry into territory over or through the perimeter fences is considered an invasion. Alice slows the car's speed to a crawl as she enters the Chinese checkpoint, seeing the guards already waiting for her; the checkpoint guards are always on high alert as they are the first line of defence. A guard bends down and pops his head into the car through the window, a bit much for Alice's liking but she is a placid lady and lets it go.

"Hello," Alice says in a soft polite voice, leaning back slightly to avoid contact with the guard's head. The guard bows his head in a show of respect which puts the two women at ease. "We have a notice for a High Council meeting" is all Alice needs to says and the guard instantly removes himself and returns to the security hut, pulling his phone out, pressing a button and holding the device to his ear; clearly he has the boss on speed dial. Alice and Jessica hear his voice make a light humming noise, but can't hear what he is saying. Within seconds he hangs up the phone and the barrier opens. Alice looks at the man and thanks him, he bows to return the gesture, and off into China Town the two Messengers go, technically enemy territory but they are not frightened here, they know The Chinese won't cause them harm or trouble in this way, their leader is too disciplined for such cowardly attacks so they are quite safe. Anyhow, Jessica loves driving through China Town with the traditional style buildings and the statues and monuments of leaders and warriors past not to mention the dragons. Whether it be a celebration with people dressed up, or artwork on walls, China Town is a colourful and vibrant place which they wouldn't be able to see if the notices were simply sent through text or email; sometimes technology takes the heart and soul out of things and it's best to get out and about. Although safe from danger, that doesn't stop the odd rival gang member stopping and staring as the car passes, giving a dirty look and a snarl their way. Alice knows this is part and parcel of gang life and has come to accept it; Jessica gets irritated by it and just stares back, safe in the knowledge that the slightest attack, even if a stone is thrown at their car, the gang will have their High Council voting power removed and then the offending member will have Cheng to deal with, which is the last thing they want – so Alice and Jessica cruise past in bliss. As they pull up to the gang headquarters, Yong, the Chinese deputy is waiting for them. Yong Li Son is a proud, disciplined man who takes things very seriously but is well mannered and polite, provided you stay on his right side. He lost the vote for gang leadership to Cheng all those years ago but such is his loyalty to his gang he supported Cheng to the full and was rewarded with the 2nd In Command role. Yong is here as the welcoming committee – not to accept the notice, as the notices are handed to the gang leader except for The Vampires and The Witches, their notices are placed in a secure box for later pick up. The two ladies exit their vehicle and are greeted with an honourable bow from Yong. This is typical of Yong's respect as although The Messengers are in truth an enemy gang, Yong believes in respect and honour so he is happy to bow his head. Alice and Jessica return the bow to respect him and his culture, and Yong bows again. Alice doesn't need to speak; Yong knows why they are there, and spinning on his heels Yong heads towards the headquarters with Alice and Jessica in pursuit, entering the building stood in all its grandeur and up the stairs to the office. Stood outside, Alice and Jessica look into the next room and see Zhen Yun training, majestic in her movement, almost gliding through the air as she floors the four men she is in combat with, and after reaching for a crossbow fires the stake at a mannequin, catching it perfectly in the heart, clutching a sword and launching it sideways decapitating the dummy, clearly practising her vampire slaying. Alice and Jessica have to hand it to her, she is brilliant; but her well known attitude is soon on display when she notices the two rivals watching and storms over to the doors and after giving them a filthy look and not saying hello, slams the door in temper. The two sisters look at each other and smile, Alice shrugging her shoulders when Yong comes back into view and welcomes them into the office. Upon entry Alice smiles as she sees Cheng rise to his feet from behind his desk to greet them, shaking hands followed by a bow; the ladies return the gesture before Alice makes the visit official by handing over the notice.

"And what delights does Father Gideon have for us tonight" Cheng jokes with a smirk.

Alice smiles back but all in the room know she can't divulge. "You will just have to wait and see," she replies, attempting to continue the humour but at the same time making it clear she won't tell him. Alice takes her duty very seriously and even in moments like this when she knows nobody will snitch, she still keeps the information to herself. Mostly because she believes in sticking to the rules, but also because you never know who is listening – an eavesdropper or worse could be lurking; with plenty of hiding places in 9 Gang City and a shadow never far away, Alice is very cautious, so Cheng will have to bide his time for knowledge until the High Council meeting. Cheng nods in acceptance at Alice's professionalism and unwraps the scroll-like notice and reads it, shrugging his shoulders and handing it to Yong to read.

"No doubt The Vampires will have something to say," Yong utters as he reads.

Cheng laughs, knowing he is right, Krul and Father Gideon are always locking horns, keeping the tradition of monk and vampire hatred alive and well. Alice, knowing she and her sister cannot hang around too long as all the other gangs need their notices, bids her farewell and after a bow from all in the room Alice and Jessica return to their duty.

Heading towards Emerald Territory, Jessica turns to Alice with a thoughtful look on her face and a curious look in her eye, Alice knowing she has something on her mind as her sister is always thinking about something, whether it be history, politics or just an opinion on gang matters.

"Do you think Cheng would be a good leader?" Jessica asks looking back out of the window.

"Yes," Alice responds almost instantly. "But not as much as he thinks he would, nobody would; it is easy to be an opposition leader giving fanciful opinions on what is best but the truth is when you are in a position of authority you have an impossible task of trying to keep everybody happy," Alice adds almost in a support of Father Gideon but also first-hand knowledge of what it is like to be a leader.

Jessica knows her sister is yet again just giving a balanced answer which she is so good at and not really supporting Gideon, just offering a fair alternative to the continued complaining about current issues facing the leader of the city. Having said that, Alice knows the current situation with Father Gideon and the rest of the gangs is getting very serious and she fears it will boil over to a point of no return. Jessica is more headstrong and can't help but think a war would clear the city of deadwood; she remembers Aiden O'Riordan, The Irish leader, once saying war is sometimes just an excuse to get rid of people that democracy can't get rid of, or sometimes it's just business. Jessica agreed with his first point.

After delivering the notice to The Irish and Jessica having a shot of Jamieson's with Aiden, Cormac and Siobhan – Alice has water as she is driving – they then enter Holy Ground. Alice and Jessica make their way across The Monks' territory to The Moors. Jessica gets nervous on witch territory; although they don't have to deliver to them directly, the atmosphere is eerie and she feels like she is being watched – this is because she probably is being watched. The car stops at the checkpoint, nothing, not a soul in sight, not one living thing makes their acquaintance. A felon mood lingers and a shiver creeps down Jessica's spine. Alice swipes her entry card and the barrier rises to let them through and into the territory of the most feared gang. It is moments like this that the sisters don't like the traditional ways, but as always Alice stays professional despite her heart pounding. The Cauldron comes into view and Jessica gets the notice ready so they can quickly deliver and get out of there. The Cauldron is what the other gangs call The Witches' Headquarters; Queen Rika and her gang don't call it that themselves, but like the nickname, which is a good thing because it is probably classed as cultural appropriation these days. Alice stops the car and Jessica leaps out, fumbling with the post box; the more she fumbles the worse it gets and the more her heart races. It feels as though something is sneaking up behind her, she jolts round, Alice smiles and calmly helps her; she knows Jessica gets nervous around

The Witches and it is one of the things she needs to work on. Back in the car and on the road the conversation resurrects about gang leaders.

"Do you think anybody would ever vote for a witch?" Jessica asks bluntly. "Except for The Vampires," she adds, knowing the two gangs have a friendship and if a vote ever did happen The Vampires and The Witches would just vote for each other because in 9 Gang City you are not allowed to vote for yourself.

"Yes, why not?" Alice answers, knowing where this is going.

"Because of what they are," Jessica responds, knowing full well Alice knows what she means.

"Why would that make them unfit leaders?" Alice claps back, the conversation rising a notch in tension. "What if people didn't vote for me because of what I am, a woman, what if people didn't vote for Cheng because of what he is, Chinese, these things would be called sexism and racism, so why is it ok to treat a witch like that?" Alice finishes her educating of her sister on equality issues and shows yet again why she is so respected within the city and the best candidate for leadership.

Jessica nods in acceptance of her sister's point and considers herself told and realises yet again these are the things she needs to brush up on if she is to improve politically, not to be stuck in the past like too many of the gang members are from all gangs. These conversations always seem to come up when they are in witch and vampire territory – the city still holds a grudge against the two gangs, especially The Vampires. Entering into The Caves, the land is as empty as The Moors, but the atmosphere has gone and although you wouldn't want to be here at night, The Vampires' turf is very safe during the day. The name of the area is in reference to the caves that sit on top of a hill surrounded by a wood, with one small country lane spiralling upwards to the cave mouth. The Vampires were outcast to this part of the city after the war as a punishment for their past crimes against the people of 9 Gang. Very few say an unfair treatment, most laugh at their current dwelling, but after the progress Krul has made in the last decade the smile has been wiped off their face and replaced with a look of concern. The Vampires will always be a threat due to their supernatural powers. Krul himself has the strength of ten men and those powers grow the more a vampire sails along in time. Alice and Jessica have become good friends with Krul, despite being in different gangs. Krul doesn't let rivalry get in the way of decency if you have earned his respect and Alice and Jessica certainly have. Supporting Vampire Rights and being against the war as well as openly opposing The Daylight Killings, Alice has made a good impression with Krul and his crew, but The Monks' eyes have been firmly locked on the blossoming friendship, and Alice and Krul know she still has to do her duty to The Monks. The Vampires have no choice but to accept this as it was Niculi who originally brought that rule into play. Victuis is Krul's best friend and his deputy, he is a loyal friend, the most loyal in the city and together they achieved what nobody thought was possible, bringing structure and discipline to The Vampires. For hundreds of years it was a free for all with the gang, and Niculi encouraged it, killing for pleasure and feeding at will only added to the hatred for their kind; but in the leadership of Krul they have changed their ways and Victuis has been priceless support to that. Enigma, Krul's girlfriend, on the other hand is not so friendly; one of the few surviving vampires from the war she still has animosity towards the other gangs and is longing for The Vampires to rule again; a vampire supremacist which she calls Vampower, Enigma believes her people are the supreme beings and all others should fall in line. This has made her enemies across the city and she is despised by many, but she is strong, tough and not to be messed with.

Vacating the car, Jessica looks around the area she has only ever seen in the daylight and admires the view of the city. Nearby is a large rock that Krul stands on while he looks out over the distance; on a clear day you can see Cathedral Tower and on a clear night the shining lights of the city's focal point make the place seem glorious and grand, and it would be were it not for the local hatred. Jessica stands on the rock and looks out over the city. Seeing the tower on the horizon, the city seems peaceful – this is probably why Krul enjoys standing here, it gives a moment of fantasy, bringing a welcome break from reality. Alice tells her to hurry up and does not approve of her imposition – perhaps that whiskey has gone to her head. Jumping from the rock and delivering The Vampires' notice, they return to duty. After a trip through The Forests to see The Werewolves, who in their man form were very friendly but best avoided on full moons, Alice had to remind Jessica they had other gangs to meet in a way of trying to pry her sister away from Cuthwulf – for a while now they have been flirting and complimenting each other; it has got to the stage where everybody else is wondering when they are going to get it on, but the two themselves are pretending they are not interested.

The Messenger girls then make their way north to Cannibal Farm, not wanting to linger too long as James Winston Wycombe was present and as usual had his perverted eyes all over Jessica, a vile man who has a taste for women and not just sexually – Jessica heard him admit once that he has a list of people in the city he would most like to eat and ever since has given Jessica more than the once over. It then came to driving east to BC Nation for the final delivery before the trip home. BC Nation is the name The Pagans gave their territory to symbolise their faith and the fact that their people were on this land before Christianity; this did not go down well with The Monks, but they could do nothing about it as the name is not obscene and is factual. Druid Bryson had his usual insults for Brother Francis – the two do not get along. Francis is somewhat of a tyrant when it comes down to pretty much everything but especially religion and politics, and looks down upon The Pagans as religiously inferior. This infuriates Bryson and the two have been at odds for many years. Duty complete and arriving home, Leo is there to greet Alice as he always is; the two have been friends for a long time and he likes to make sure they are ok after spending time with such people as this city has to offer. Now that the gangs know of the High Council meeting and with no more tasks to do until then, The Messengers have some free time to kill, waiting for the sunset.

Chapter 2

T he sun sets, bringing welcome relief to certain citizens and that ominous fear to the rest, the moonlight setting free beings that some call evil but they themselves call a breed apart from a normality that has been brainwashed into people from certain power within society. The lid of his coffin flings open and Krul raises to his feet, turning to his side as his beloved stands freshly raised from her slumber and leans in to kiss her man. As always Victuis enters soon after. The first thing The Vampires' leaders do when they rise is check one another is ok – this is a paranoia from The Daylight Killings. The second thing Victuis does is check the box for any post from High Council. He makes his way to the entrance of the caves and Krul turns back to Enigma for some more kissing. Beginning their patrol around the caves, Krul and Enigma take a head count of the gang again because of being paranoid; Enigma remembers all too well what the other gangs are capable of, and after all of the crew are counted, Krul waits for his deputy to return before he gives his orders as if there is a High Council meeting all plans have to change. Victuis returns with a scroll and Krul shakes his head at the sight as he unwraps it.

"Another comedy show awaits," he jokes as he passes the notice back to Victuis, who in turn reads it, none too pleased at the short notice.

"There is nothing going on that couldn't wait until tomorrow," he snaps at what he thinks are mind games from The Monks.

Krul nods in agreement. "But we still have to attend," he responds to an irritated Victuis who already begins to rally the troops. Krul knows Victuis is right: The Monks are making the meeting at such short notice in the hope that The Vampires don't turn up in time and the meeting can take place without them, which makes Krul want to turn up even more to spite them. Although the meeting isn't until 6 o'clock and the sun sets at 4, giving them two hours to get to Cathedral Tower – which sounds like plenty of time, but when you consider waking, getting the notice, assembling the gang, arming the gang, getting the cars to the pickup location, travelling to the meeting, getting into Cathedral Tower, two hours isn't that long at all, especially when the other gangs have had hours longer to prepare.

With more and more games from Father Gideon, Krul is coming to his final nerve and after doing all he can to change The Vampires' ways, Krul believes he has done all he can to alter his people's behaviour and yet the city still hates his gang because of decades and centuries past, he puts this down to the mortal weakness of victimhood. Krul's phone rings once then hangs up; that is Victuis code to tell him the cars are ready. Turning to Enigma to give her the all clear to leave, the vampire leaders enter a separate car each, in case of an ambush. A gang member opens the door for them and after entering the Jaguar Mark 2 the gang member becomes a bodyguard and sits in the back of the car with each of The Vampires' leaders to add to the chauffeur and a comrade in the passenger seat the gang is ready for Cathedral Tower.

Krul looks out of the window but isn't looking at anything; his mind is wondering what the meeting has to offer. He knows he has made headway within the city, and he understands the other gangs still bear a grudge against his people, so he has to find a way to convince six of the gangs to believe or at least give a chance to see his gang have changed, and with Krul at the top the city will be a better place. The reason he has to convince six gangs is because his own gang are already convinced; that is why they voted him into power. The Monks will possibly never be convinced so they are a potential lost cause as far as The Vampires are concerned, and The Witches have continued to honour the pact between the two gangs so it is down to the other six gangs to be convinced. The Messengers are growing closer to Krul's plan, Alice is an angel trapped in hell, and Jessica can be feisty but is loving and caring deep down, Leo is a good man who will support the greater good. Some would argue that The Messengers pose a greater threat to The Vampires than The Monks and in terms of politics they would be right. Krul doesn't see The Monks as a threat if a vote for The Leadership was called; that is when Alice and Cheng would be the problem, Alice especially, but the likelihood of Father Gideon calling an election, it is more likely the city will go to war, so therefore The Monks remain the threat and The Messengers are not, but that then means The Chinese become a bigger threat because of their numbers and arsenal. These are just a few of the thoughts and complications a gang leader in 9 Gang City has to think about. The Irish are growing in power but not as fast as they would like and if the city goes to war Krul doesn't think they pose much of a threat and people probably would not vote for them politically; the same goes for The Pagans; The Cannibals are no threat in either war or politics. The Werewolves are most dangerous in wolf form and are to be feared during full moons, but the sheer number against them and the guns and silver bullets the other gangs have added to the fact that war would take place mostly during non-full moon and daylight takes away their biggest weapon; this is why Cuthwulf has been working on his politics – he knows even during a full moon his gang are outnumbered and outgunned. The biggest danger to The Vampires is of course war taking place during daylight hours; it may be a rule that this cannot happen, but Krul isn't stupid – he knows that although there are laws of war, people don't stick to laws, punishment for breaking laws of war only happen when war is over and by then it is too late for the fallen.

The car slows for the checkpoint into Holy Ground, Krul sees the guards waiting for them to arrive, crossbows, stakes and holy water at the ready; another has a large crucifix in his hand. The car at the front of the convoy stops first. There is always tension during checkpoint stops, coming face to face with rival gang members is always a tense moment and the guards are clearly on high alert. Krul can hear them talking but not what they are saying, and after a short wait the barrier opens and The Vampires enter The Monks' territory. Driving through turf that used to be vampires', after the war the territory was changed and divided and the entire layout of the city changed – the map of 9 Gang City used to look a lot different: The Vampires had almost all of it, The Witches lived on vampire territory and The Messengers had none at all; the other gangs had scraps of land to live off. People still whine about that but Krul argued that the city back then was closer to unity due to the fact that there were only seven territories back then and The Vampires, The Witches and The Messengers lived together on the same land for 200 years and it was The Monks who segregated them. Other says the gangs have more independence now that they have their own land. Both sides of the argument are true, but in a day and age where people say we should live together as one human race yet there are more countries than ever before, you have to ask yourself is it all just liberal nonsense, and the truth is the human race doesn't want to live as one and segregation is what they really want; 9 Gang City falls into this category.

The cathedral comes into view and the roads are packed with cars, The Waiting Yard isn't big enough for all the vehicles as the gangs like to turn up in numbers so the streets around the cathedral are littered with rides. Slowly turning into the yard, Krul sees The Chinese, The Irish, The Pagans and The Cannibals have already arrived, standing tough and away from each other. Stepping out of the car he scopes the yard and eyes every rival member who in turn stare back but with a slight nervousness that they are trying to hide; people are always on edge when The Vampires are around. Cheng is the first to raise a smile in an attempt to play down the stand-off, but Krul doesn't give and focuses solely on The Chinese leader who can't look away now as it will humiliate him in front of his gang. The yard falls silent as the two rivals glare at one another, neither wanting to back down. Victuis and Enigma stand next to Krul and it becomes a gang standoff, Enigma with her vampire supremacist tattoos on display snarling at Zhen Yun. Zhen hates Enigma intently and has no problem staring back. Victuis and Yong follow suit. The stand-off is only broken when a car pulls into the yard and Cheng breaks focus to see who it is, mortal curiosity hands a small victory to the undead as the Bentley Mark 6 parks up; The Werewolves are here. Pouncing out, Cuthwulf looks over at Krul.

"What was going on there?" the wolf leader shouts over as the rest of The Dog Pound huddle round their leader. Krul looks over with an irritated look still present.

"Just a gang of nobodies who dream of being somebodies," Krul responds, to which Cuthwulf bursts out laughing but The Chinese are not so amused.

Zhen Yun steps forward and to the surprise of no one makes her feelings known.

"A gang of nobodies – what about your has-been crew? How about you say that to us in the morning instead of giving it the big talk in a car park? We will meet you any time any place but you can't do the same, can you?" Zhen rants, her voice getting more irate as the red mist descends.

Enigma will not ever have a rival gang member speak like that about her people and not at least say something back, especially a female rival, as in some cases the women are worse than the men; add to this that these two despise each other and it will always be a matter of time before they respond to each other's comments.

"Listen, you mouthy little bitch, I don't give a fuck what yard we are in or what the rules are or even the consequences if you gob off like that again I will lay you flat out," Enigma snaps back as Zhen Yun walks over to her, but Cheng takes hold of her arm to stop her. "Good choice, put your little mutt on its lead," Enigma adds an insult to her threat, much to the amusement of the rest of the yard who all laugh. The laughter soon dies down as a light mist blankets the area and an eerie atmosphere suddenly lurks over the yard; all of them turn to face the entrance. A car coasts through the mist and parks next to The Vampires, the silver Rolls-Royce Phantom is an apt car for The Witches to drive. Krul opens the door and offers his hand, which is accepted, and Queen Rika steps out. A nervous tension takes over the yard as seems to be the routine when The Witches turn up; the myths of old seem to take control of the mortal gangs and folklore of curses and hexes leave people hesitant to approach or in some cases look at a witch. The Witches, on the other hand, would point to the persecution of their kind across the centuries, The Pendle Witches in Northwest England and The Salem Witch Trials in America, not to mention the original reason 9 Gang City exists and The Battles taking place was all because of hatred and almost a lust for the destruction of their kind from The CVS. Rika as usual looks beautiful with her hair tied back and shoulder-less gown kept up by her bust – or magic, nobody can quite tell. Her sisters Katalin and Tunder arrive by her side, Victuis looking over at Tunder, who in turn stares back with a smile, the only time she ever does, and a look of longing and desire. Rika sees this and encourages focus to which Tunder glares around at the other gangs and that trademark hatred comes back as she scowls at anything that looks her way. Enigma, none too pleased at Krul's gentlemanly approach to Rika, which doesn't go unnoticed by the witch queen who smiles at The Countess, ignoring her envy. Krul is just honouring the friendship between the two gangs. The meet and greet come to an end when Alice makes her appearance through the cathedral door and prepares the gangs for the meeting. Making sure everybody is present – even though she knows they are, because Father Gideon has been watching from the window, which hasn't gone unnoticed by Krul, who looks up at the leader and gives a smirk of satisfaction that he has turned up on time – Father Gideon turns away and readies himself. Alice steps aside for the High Council members to enter, Krul shaking hands with Alice as he walks past her but stops when Alice politely asks Enigma to cover up her tattoos as they may be deemed offensive by the other gangs and indecent in a place that is supposed to be professional. Enigma stops and looks at her but doesn't respond, leaving Alice no choice but to look back at her for a short while, but then turns to Krul with a look of expecting him to make his gang member abide by the rules. Krul turns to his 3rd In Command and pulls rank, signalling her to do as Alice has requested and Enigma looks away with a snotty look and puts on her jacket – the very fact she has her jacket with her just goes to prove she knew this would happen but had her tats on display in defiance of the rules and to infuriate the other gangs. Zhen Yun smiles at Enigma being put in her place as Alice thanks her for covering up and, after a smile towards Krul, The Vampires enter the place they used to rule. Alice nervously greets Queen Rika whilst Cuthwulf and Jessica exchange a flirty hello; the rest act tough as they enter, and the most powerful people in 9 Gang City prepare for political war.

Chapter 3

The High Council members enter Cathedral Tower and are met by Father Gideon already sat in his chair at the head of the table; he does not stand for the other members, something that does not go unnoticed by Krul. Brother Francis and Brother Theodore stand behind Gideon either side, which is the way of these meetings – only the gangs' leaders have a chair and the remaining members stand behind their leader. Victuis and Tunder share another glance in each other's direction and Enigma and Zhen exchange a snarl across the table. The last gang to enter as is custom are The Messengers, and after the leaders are seated, Leo and Jessica serve some refreshment which gives Jessica another chance to flirt with Cuthwulf, which doesn't go unnoticed by Krul who nods his head in approval of the werewolf leader's choice of woman. As for the refreshments, wine, water, tea, or coffee and for The Vampires blood is on offer but not the human kind. Jessica pours Krul a glass who thanks her before sampling the beverage.

"Pigs' blood, not the best but thanks all the same," he jests much to the disgust of The Monks, but Jessica is amused. Once everybody is served and seated Alice begins proceedings.

"Hello everybody and welcome to our meeting," she says getting the formality out of the way. Some members nod politely, most just ignore her nicety. "On the agenda tonight is... Who pays for the repairs to the perimeter fence between China Town and Emerald Territory?" Alice informs the council and stops when she sees Krul hold his hands out and look around. Looking at him, Alice waits for his comment.

"Is this really what High Council was set up for?" he asks with a look of bewilderment at such a trivial issue.

Alice doesn't bat an eyelid and answers in her trademark professional manner.

"Yes, because agreements between gangs is allowed but if they cannot come to an agreement then it becomes the decision of High Council; in this case The Chinese and The Irish have tried to come to an agreement but can't so it is down to us to settle it," Alice states, and after accepting the answer Krul sits back and shuts up. This doesn't go unnoticed by Cuthwulf who turns to Krul and laughs, other members join in and the vampire leader responds by giving Cuthwulf the middle finger.

"Haven't you got a moon to bark at?" Krul jokes and gains back some face but Cuthwulf continues his amusement. Alice smiles before continuing with the criteria.

"Next issue, our leaders..." is all Alice can say before some tuts and derogatory sneers ring out.

This does not go down well with Father Gideon and this time he speaks up.

"Yes, that's right, your leaders, the people your gangs voted into power, democratically elected leader," Gideon states, pointing to himself and barking at the room. Francis smiles with smug pride at his master's outburst until his face drops after Krul retorts.

"Didn't Hitler get elected and then take democracy away?" Krul interrupts, much to the amusement of the other gangs; Gideon and Francis not so.

"I haven't taken away democracy, I simply haven't called an election. This is what the other gangs agreed to and is written into the rules of High Council. You were not around then so take this as an education and let's move on," Gideon rants at Krul, much to the delight of Francis.

The rest of the room turns to Krul for his response, almost like a tennis match from one to the other; this is a typical High Council meeting, almost a chance to vent frustration at each other without consequence.

"I have educated myself very well on the history of our city and before, particularly the fact that this all started because your people persecuted against mine and The Witches because our way of life didn't fit in to yours. Some people would call that fascism," Krul bites back.

Brother Francis butts into the argument. "To rid the world of an evil that had plagued the earth for too long," Francis snaps in temper.

"The world, don't flatter yourself; it was Eastern Europe and you failed miserably," Krul hits back, much to the joy of the room as most laugh out loud which only angers Francis more.

"You can mock all you want – who has the power now?" Francis goads with a smug tone. This irritates Krul but he plays it cool to not give Francis the satisfaction of knowing he has got to him and leans forward in his chair to look Francis square in the eyes.

"But for how long?" Krul asks calmy in subliminal threat, causing a tense silence to grip the room and everybody looks at The Monks for a response which does not come, and after a few awkward seconds Alice steps in to play down the argument and continue with the meeting.

"I think it is best if we stick to the list of issues and listen to each other's point of view," Alice states, looking from Gideon to

Krul to calm the situation. "To cover the first issue, The Irish have made a request that we settle between themselves and The Chinese; what points would you like to raise?" Alice asks, turning to Aiden, leader of The Irish, who turns to Cheng and immediately goes on the offensive.

"It was your gang building too close to the border and your members caused damage to the fence," Aiden vents, pointing his finger aggressively, which doesn't go down well with Cheng.

In this city almost everything must be met with equal or worse treatment because to be seen to back down makes you and your gang look weak. Cheng turns to Aiden.

"What I suggest is you put your hand down and drop the attitude," Cheng responds, sitting forward on his chair, the heat rising. "It was your members who tried to fix the fence and made it worse; it is not our fault you have cowboy workmen," Cheng adds, raising his voice.

"They wouldn't have to fix it if your gang hadn't damaged it," Aiden retorts, sitting further forward on his chair.

Yong motions to move toward Aiden, thinking he is getting up from his chair for confrontation, which causes Cormac to step toward Yong. Zhen then moves forward to Cormac, which in turn Siobhan returns the gesture to Zhen. This is gang life: any slight act of aggression has to be met with aggression; a simple disagreement about a broken fence and two gangs are squaring off, risking revoking of voting power, and if the worst should happen, a dead rival and execution. The other gangs sit and watch as any removal of voting power or death makes these gangs weaker and the rival gang stronger, so the other members almost hope violence happens. As usual it is up to Alice to step in and calm the situation, asking politely for them to consider the fact that aggression makes things worse and coming to a compromise is best, that compromise is why they are here, High Council will decide for them. The two gangs reluctantly agree and cool their tensions.

"Now it is time to vote," Alice says, wanting to solve the issue quickly. "Raise your hand if you think The Chinese should pay for the damage to the fence," she asks and looks across the table for the result.

Everybody raises their hand except The Chinese. Aiden laughs with glee.

"That is what you call a landslide," he gloats as Cheng sits shaking his head whilst The Irish celebrate.

Alice makes a note of the result and swiftly moves on, so their enjoyment doesn't go too far. Father Gideon sits like a king on his throne, allowing his servant to run the meeting, but ready to step in at any time. Brother Francis looks around the room like a strict school prefect whose power has gone to his head and everybody hates, and Brother Theodore stands proud and quiet like a good boy. Krul stares at Father Gideon and thinks how did he manage to convince the city to vote for him, how could people be taken in by such a man? It proves that people are easily swayed by a huge event and Gideon played his cards right and played the city to a tee, knowing the people would be caught in the euphoria of the slaying of Niculi and Ziana, to a point it was well played by Gideon. But the stupidity of the other gangs to agree to some of the laws and rules is mind boggling, to actually agree that The Leader in power is the only person who can call an election instead of having a set time in power is a shameful decision, but some would say it shows the desperation of the people under the leadership of Niculi. Anything would be better but now it has backfired big time on the gangs. After catching Krul's stare, Gideon glares back with a look of hatred and at the same time an arrogant expression in the knowledge he holds the power that Krul wants. Gideon looks away when Alice moves on to the next topic.

"Secondly tonight, The Monks would like to make their day of celebration a city celebration to commemorate their service to the city," Alice informs the room with difficultly as some laughter escapes from some gang members. Gideon takes an irritated breath but allows Alice to finish. "Do we have any thoughts before we vote?" she asks with a sense of dread at what is to come, knowing this would go down like a lead balloon. Alice looks at Father Gideon for his side of the discussion.

"We the saviours of the city and humankind..." Gideon starts, until jeers and looks of disbelief flood the room. Gideon talks louder to drown them out. "The Monks saved this city from a dictator and a tyrant who had all of your gangs begging for salvation and it was we, the descendants of The CVS, who gave you that salvation in the name of almighty God, not The Chinese with their military power, not The Pagans with their conquered Gods and not The Cannibals with their blue blood ancestry; it was we, The Monks, in the name of our forefathers and with the will of God," Gideon fumes as abuse is fired toward him from all directions of the room. The Pagans especially fume at his comments.

"How dare you insult our faith – this was Druid land way before your supposed saviour was born," Brigacos fumes, slamming his fist on the table.

Brother Francis is almost leaning over the table at The Pagan leader. "The son of God is our saviour and we are this city's saviour," Francis shouts in rage.

Druid Bryson as to be expected steps into the argument. "Saviour of what?" Bryson snaps, "Your own desire to rule, which is typical of your faith, peace and goodwill to all men, but command and conquer if people disagree," he adds to a still angry Francis.

"You would all be fodder for evil if it wasn't for us, you should be on your knees thanking us for our help," Francis bellows to the room. Alice attempts to step in to yet again be the mediator, but this time Gideon stops her and allows Francis to vent. "You were all lambs to the slaughter until Father Gideon saved you and this is the thanks we get, The Day Of The Saviours should be a city celebration," Brother Francis finishes his outburst, much to the enjoyment of his superior who turns and nods his head in approval.

The rest of the room remain quiet for a short time until Krul breaks the silence. "It is all well and good ranting and raving about what you think or feel, but the fact is it is up to all of us to decide," the vampire leader states, which encourages Alice to nod in agreement and take the vote.

"All in favour of The Monks' day of celebration becoming a city celebration, raise your hand," Alice asks the room and the most predictable outcome of all time is the result: the only people to raise their hand are The Monks. The entire room smirks and sneers as they look at each other, almost congratulating one another on their victory, much to the disgust of Father Gideon.

"Well done siding with evil and tyranny," Gideon says sarcastically, with a furious Francis shaking his head, staring at everybody in the room. "And you, where is your loyalty? It is your duty to serve the gang in power and here you are voting against us and biting the hand that feeds you," Gideon adds, glaring at a shocked Alice who is taken aback at being called out like this in front of the rest of the council.

"I know my and my gang's duty very well, and that duty is to work for the gang in power, not agree with everything you say and want. If we were to vote for everything you want, that would give your gang an unfair advantage over the other gangs and that is not democracy," Alice responds, her voice slightly raised.

"It is your duty to do as we say and you will do well to remember that," Gideon snaps back with a vile tone, almost dismissing her as rubbish, Leo and Jessica wanting to support their friend and sister against such a disrespectful attitude.

"We know our duty and we know our history, but what you don't realise is this is why people have turned against you," Leo says to Gideon, who is waving his hand at him, almost wafting him away like he is unworthy.

"I will speak to your leader later," Gideon casually but arrogantly states.

"Oh really, will you?" Alice answers, getting angrier.

"Yes, I will, come and see me after the meeting; that is my order," Gideon barks, pointing to the paper in front of Alice, meaning let's get on with the meeting.

Alice composes herself and stands for the next issue.

"Final issue on the list is removal of execution from city law," Alice informs the room as she calms herself. The members' interest is piqued. "This was suggested by myself as I think if we are to move forward as a more civilised city, we should not have the death penalty. What are your thoughts?" she finishes, sitting and facing the people.

"What would be the alternative punishment?" Krul asks, sitting forward and looking at all members. "Building a prison, where? Who is going to pay for it? And does it mean people can commit the same crimes but get a lenient sentence?" As he finishes, some nod in agreement, others remain unmoved.

"Yes, a prison would have to be built and we would all be expected to pay an equal amount," Alice answers. "And I suggest it would be built on Holy Ground by the crossroads to The Caves and The Forests," Alice finishes.

"What if we don't commit an equal amount of crime? Do we still have to pay an equal amount? How is that fair? What facilities will be in place for us vampires and The Werewolves? You would have to keep them locked in a more secure facility, maximum security just because of what they are and that isn't equal," Krul responds.

Alice nods her head, thinking he has a point. "These are things we can decide after we vote on the issue," Alice replies, making a good point in return.

"The thing is, if people don't want to be executed, don't commit a death penalty crime; it is that simple," Cuthwulf adds his thoughts on the subject. "If we escape our turf during a full moon and kill somebody, we accept we will be shot with a silver bullet and killed. Why should other gangs have a softer sentence when they can make a conscious decision and we cannot, yet we get shot for it, it's not an equal argument," he finishes, to which he is pleasantly surprised by the support he receives.

"I agree, let's not have mercy on people who commit heinous crimes," Aiden speaks out.

"Let us vote." Alice stands to make it official. "All in favour of removing the death penalty, raise your hand," she asks and raises her own and looks round to take the count. Leo has raised his raised hand, but Jessica has not; Brother Theodore and all three of The Cannibals have raised their hands – this is not really surprising: Theodore is the most placid of The Monks' leaders and The Cannibals are arguably the most likely to commit death penalty crimes, but to everyone's surprise Princess Katalin has raised her hand. This earns her an angry look from Tunder and even a glance backward from Rika, clearly she has thoughts she has not been sharing with her sisters or she has cast a spell to block mind reading. It is all in vain as a heavy defeat for the raised point means execution is still written in law and an eye for an eye remains.

Alice makes a note of the result and looks back to address the members. "That is the end of the criteria for tonight. Does anybody have anything to add?" she asks out of politeness but a sense of dread as to the result.

Krul raises his hand. "How about a vote for The Leadership?" he jokes to irritate Father Gideon. The rest of the room laugh and jeer at The Monks.

"How many gangs do you think would vote for you?" Gideon responds, annoyed by the jibe.

"One, The Witches and we would vote for them," Krul answers instantly. "But everybody else would vote for The Messengers, making Alice the new leader and I'm ok with that," he claims, adding to the joke, leaving Gideon unable to reply and only a glare of animosity is his response.

Alice yet again is the peacemaker and informs Krul a vote for leadership is not on the agenda and after Krul invites everyone to Vampir Ceremoniilor, the meeting is dismissed. On the way-out Alice is reminded by Father Gideon to see him in his office once her duties are finished. Alice keeps her cool but the frustration is clear on her face.

"Don't let that dictator keep you down, The Messengers were created to not only work for but to protect the gang in power, not be enslaved by them. You tell him that," Krul states as matter of historical fact, which gives Alice the encouragement not to take any nonsense from Gideon. She will do her duty, not as she is told. Krul is content but not happy with the meeting – all his votes ended up on the winning side but how will the city ever get the vote for leadership? The more time goes on the more everybody knows it may not be a vote that the city declares.

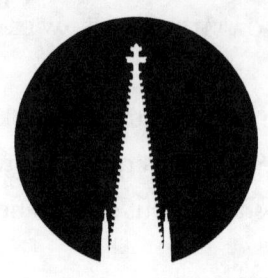

Chapter 4

L eo and Jessica kindly agree to finish the gang's duties, such as making sure The Waiting Yard is clear of any stragglers, and documenting the results of the votes that were taken, although Alice will have to sign off on these later – as leader, everything falls on her head. Making her way to Father Gideon's room like a beckoned schoolgirl, Alice, still angry from his outburst, knocks forcefully, and after a short wait and a deep breath enters and sees Gideon sat behind his desk glaring at her; clearly he is still angry as well. Pointing to the chair opposite, Gideon utters the word "sit" and looks away in disgust. Alice, feeling her anger grow, remains calm on the surface but boils underneath. Gideon's room is quite grand in appearance; a large desk sits opposite the door with a window looking out over The Waiting Yard to the left and a fireplace to the right. The entire ceiling is covered with a painting of Gideon slaying Niculi, and a picture hanging above the fireplace is of Ziana being burned at the stake: Gideon takes pride in his achievements. Alice sits and waits for Gideon to speak first and after glaring back at her he begins.

"Don't you think you should show some loyalty to me and your duty?" Gideon snaps, staring her in the eye almost in an intimidating manner.

"To you, no," Alice retorts, causing Gideon's face to drop almost open-mouthed. Alice is having none of his bullying tactics. "To my duty as leader of The Messengers, yes and that is exactly what I have," she adds, staring back in rebellion at his dictatorial attitude.

"Need I remind you it is written in law that you work for whichever gang is in power," Gideon barks back, disgusted by her attitude.

"Need I remind you that it is the very first law written that High Council is the highest authority in the city and not the leader of the gang in power," Alice hits back, stating legal fact, to which Gideon has no response, as it was he who created and wrote that law. "And as a member of High Council I have every legal right to vote for what I want for whatever reason I want and neither you nor anybody can stop my vote," Alice says, seeing that her upper hand is irritating Gideon.

"Laws can be changed," Gideon responds in a snotty tone, but really just making an idle threat as he doesn't know what else to say, a threat of Alice and the power that her gang has could be taken away.

"Not without a vote from High Council they can't and where would that get you?" Alice asks, her temper rising at his threatening comment. "Having to deal with the gangs directly and how well will that go down? Do you think The Vampires will want to deal with you? Do you think The Pagans will take orders from Francis?" Alice adds, subliminally stating that Gideon needs her as he has ruined his reputation beyond repair.

"Don't let Krul's praise go to your head," Gideon snaps dismissively, thinking Alice is getting above herself. "That parasite believes his own hype far too much; the reality is I am the leader of 9 Gang City, this is my city and you will obey me," Gideon arrogantly says, almost comforted by the fact he can be leader until his death.

"I will obey my duty to my people and nothing that you want, request or demand that goes outside of that duty; and as for this city, 9 Gang belong to the citizens," Alice claps back, emotion getting the better of her. "And as for your disgusting insult about Krul, you didn't say that to his face in the meeting when he schooled you on history," she says in a mocking tone to point out Gideon's cowardice.

"How dare you speak to me like this, I am your leader, I was the one who burned Ziana at the stake, I was the one who drove a stake through Niculi's heart and I am the one who was democratically elected," Gideon bellows with an air of superiority in his voice.

"More like you stood back and waited for the right moment to look like the hero whilst other people did the hard work and took all the risk," Alice retorts, growing sick of his arrogance and dismissing what he thinks are his accomplishments.

"Get out," Gideon shouts at the top of his voice. The volume makes Alice jump in her chair as the truth hurts for the supposed hero. "You are not fit to be in the chamber of a leader, your people will do as I say or face the consequences," he adds, red-faced with rage.

Alice gladly stands to leave and once she reaches the door turns back to her host. "This is why the people have turned against you and this is why if you don't call an election the city will probably go to war," Alice advises.

"We all know why you want an election: dreams of grandeur," Gideon replies with a sneering tone.

Alice shakes her head in disgust and slams the door behind her. Standing outside she has a moment and composes herself as Krul's words echo in her head. Remembering the advice he gave her, she smiles and returns to Neutral Territory, with duties to fulfil, a gang leader's duty never seems to end. It can be stressful sometimes, being a leader, nobody can ever understand until they have been in a position of leadership, the expectation, the selfish demands, the anger at decisions they disagree with and of course the never being able to make everybody happy. Leo and Jessica sometimes fail to appreciate this – Leo looks away disappointed like he has been let down and Jessica gets angry and argumentative sometimes, even bratty when things don't go her way, and what they need to understand is being a deputy and a number 3 gives you power and privilege, but if it goes wrong it is the leader's cross to bear. Alice accepts this as hazards of the job but when the people closest to you become part of the problem, which they inevitably will, being a leader becomes a lonely and treacherous path. Alice begins to wonder if she is a hypocrite because everything she has just been thinking is maybe what Father Gideon thinks of her, but the difference being Alice knows she is right. There was a time Krul told her to never compromise if you know you are right – more wise words from Krul and more thoughts of him running through Alice's mind. It was nice to see him tonight but not so much Enigma – what an obnoxious attitude she has; that connection a vampire has towards the one that turned them must be strong because it is only Krul that sees the beauty, but maybe that is why their bond is so strong. No such luck for Alice having a soulmate in this city, gang leadership is her husband. Leo is a good friend but she doesn't feel that way about him and even if she did it would only complicate things if she took those feelings further. Maybe it is a good thing that she has remained single – leading the gang, serving The Monks and trying to maintain a relationship might be a step too far. Anyway, there are more pressing concerns at hand, Father Gideon is spiralling out of control and Alice doesn't know how much more the city can take. The meeting alone proved the animosity the other gangs have for Gideon and The Monks, and as for Francis, there are some who hate him even more. Twenty years of peace, which for this city is a miracle, and it could be undone by the very people who masterminded that peace; from a hero to a dictator, a saviour to a failure; Alice worries that Father Gideon's leadership will end in the same way that Niculi's did, a casualty of war.

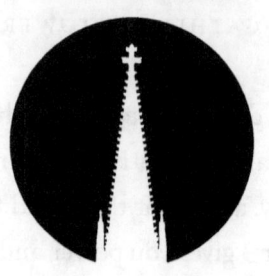

Chapter 5

Wallachia is now part of Romania but centuries ago it was a principality south of Transylvania. Much folklore has come from this part of the world and it is steeped in mystery. In years past, many Western European people believed Eastern Europe to be a place of the superstitious and supernatural, and to a point it is. The human race thrives off superstition and mystery, and it is clear that mystery we think different cultures had was based on our own lack of education on whatever culture it is we find mysterious. Eastern Europe is possibly the most blatant example of this – everybody knows the legends that dwell in the Carpathians, across the Danube and all over the Balkans, and there is truth in some of these legends, which only adds fuel to the fire of folklore. Even before Niculi formed his gang, this land and beyond was ravaged by war and invasion, different tribes, culture clashes, all this has formed the Eastern Europe we know today. For over two millennia, people, both native and invaders, have battled for supremacy from The Roman Empire to the Ottoman Empire and all in between. This part of the world is used to bloodshed and conquest, and Niculi and Ziana were the masters of shedding the blood of invading conquests, taking their fight across the width of Europe, giving their western foes a taste of what it is like to have your land violated. Wallachia, now a Romanian state in which the capital city Bucharest is situated, is a place of much history and unfortunately war. Niculi was no stranger to this even before The Christian Vampire Slayers moved east; as a mortal, which is something very rarely spoken of, Niculi was a warrior for his native land and neighbouring Transylvania. Vampirism made Niculi stronger and even more of a mighty warrior, which only made him more of a threat to his enemies, and the more of a threat you are the more fear and hatred grows within those enemies for you. Somewhat of a self-elected voivode, Niculi commanded in mortal life and reigned supreme in undead life. As a mortal, Niculi fought for and against Stephen III of Moldovia, fighting back against the great ruler's invasion of Wallachia, but 1476 fought with Stephen at Racova. Other than that, and for reasons unknown, Niculi had very little to do with Moldovia, another principality east of Wallachia but its western section is now part of Romania whilst other sections are part of Ukraine and its own country Moldova. Niculi's interests were almost always in Wallachia, Transylvania which was part of Hungary in Niculi's time and Hungary itself; he had a keen interest in the gypsy witches of Hungary, one of whom would later become his wife and queen. As a small boy, Niculi heard stories of the fall of Constantinople, which caused the collapse of the Byzantine Empire by the Ottomans; these 15th Century Turks would be the fathers of the invaders Niculi crossed the Danube and defeated in his later years as a mortal. There is huge mystery around the subject of how Niculi was turned, but conspiracy has it that he was turned by a Transylvanian prince who Niucli had fought with against the Ottomans and this prince was Niculi's mentor in life, granting him undead powers and turning him so Niculi could carry on his defence of the realm; but with undead life come religious persecution and after being turned, Niculi's fight back became against The CVS and not the Hungarians and Ottomans. It is said that the prince had business in London circa 1897 and visited Niculi in 9 Gang City, but city histories say nothing of this and it remains a conspiracy theory that may never be known for certain, which only intrigues people more. The founder of The Vampires never left 9 Gang in the 200 years they reigned, nor did Ziana, but it is said that Niculi was happy when the union between Wallachia and Moldovia was approved and became Rumania, its own country in 1881, after much involvement of many European nations such as Britain, France, Austria, Hungary and Russia. However, Ziana was not so pleased when Transylvania became part of Romania in 1918, something that Niculi and Ziana had argued about, but in the end true love conquers all and they agreed to disagree. Once Niculi and Ziana had gained victory in The Battles and founded 9 Gang City, they never returned to Eastern Europe; their new kingdom was their home now and all the glory that came with it. The couple were never interested in riches – their common goal was power and dominance, and what better power mixed with the most pleasing dominance could they hope for than having their enemies on their knees, their rivals were ripe for drinking and self-righteous enough to be the prime targets of curses for the pleasure and dominance of the witch queen. After centuries of war and invasion across Europe and the hatred of humankind against them, the couple supreme basked in the glory of their victory by adding insult to injury to The Monks, by having built by enslaved rival gang members a "cathedral" and in the tower of this false holy building they had their throne room. That throne room is now the meeting place of High Council, and Cathedral Tower is in truth not actually a cathedral, which is the reason vampires and witches can enter because the ground is not holy.

After The War Against The Vampires, The Monks basked in their own glorious victory by changing the throne room into the meeting place of the democracy they had created, thus making them believe they had been heroic and in the end completed their ancestors' objective to rid the world of Niculi and Ziana. In fact, their ancestors' aim was to rid the world of vampirism and witchcraft, so the objective is still a work in progress that may never be complete, but it is proof of the legacy Niculi and Ziana created if The CVS/The Monks' mindset became almost solely on slaying the couple supreme. Niculi and his bride have left their mark on the minds of the citizens of 9 Gang City to such an extent they will never be forgotten, and their arch enemies can only accept the greatness they achieved and left behind.

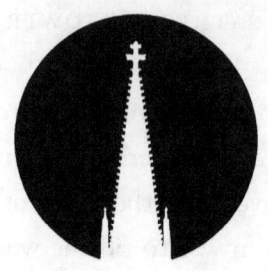

Chapter 6

Having business with The Chinese, The Vampires make their way towards the border with Holy Ground knowing The Monks will have questions to ask and a growing paranoia around why their two biggest threats are meeting in China Town. That paranoia will only grow when they do not get the answers they want, because neither gang are legally obligated to disclose that information. Enigma, with Krul in the back of his car, and Victuis with some henchmen in the car in front, with another two cars tailing behind and one leading the way, The Vampires are going equipped and yet will still be outnumbered, but much to their advantage will not be outpowered – having the strength of ten men, Krul can take on many enemies at once but with The Chinese highly trained and armed to the nines, Krul is taking no chances. Slowing for the border checks, Enigma leans forward to have a better look at what is going on. She hates The Monks with a passion. Krul noticed from the start that she is always tense and on high alert when she is around other gang members, but especially The Monks. The border guards make their way to the second car in which Victuis is sat and a conversation takes place that Krul and Enigma cannot hear but can predict what is being said, until the guards come over to Krul's car, armed with crossbow stakes, holy water and crucifixes. Enigma twitches in her seat, her anger growing. Krul places his hand on hers for comfort and signals to her to calm her temper. Rolling the window down, the vampire leader prepares himself for the inquest.

"Good evening," the head guard says in a tone that is pretending to be polite but you can sense the animosity.

"Good night," Krul responds to be more accurate. "What is the problem?" he adds, getting to the point and nodding his head toward the security gate.

"The problem is you want access to our territory," the guard replies with that tone growing in contempt as he looks in at Enigma, who herself is keeping an eye on the monk gang members who have come to her side of the car and have them surrounded.

"Which means you should be on the phone to your leader to let him know that we are entering your turf and not hanging around my car asking questions," Krul calmly states, knowing the guards are purposely being difficult. One reason is because it is The Vampires they are dealing with, and the second reason, so they can stall The Vampires to give time to their leaders to gather a crew in preparation to either fight or follow them through the territory. Both are understandable and Krul has no problem with it, he is just "playing the game" by giving as good as he gets.

"You mean I should be on the phone to our leader," the guard claps back.

Krul, knowing he is correct but not wanting to concede, takes his turn to gain the upper hand, not wanting to lose face in front of his woman and gang members.

"No, I mean you should be on the phone to the man who, if he thinks at any time he can take me on in a vote, one on one or in gang warfare, should let me know and I will be more than happy to oblige, just like you are obligated to walk away from this car, now, and inform Father Gideon that we are entering your territory and we will go about our business," Krul snaps, becoming irritated, Enigma smiling at her man's alpha male dominance and she would expect no less.

The guard knows Krul is right about allowing them entry – gangs are allowed to do business with each other and if the other gang they are doing business with confirms the meeting, by now The Chinese will have confirmed it with The Monks' leadership, then the guards have to let them through. This is one of the major mistakes The Monks made after the war, taking so much territory and having such a huge turf that they are bordered with every gang means they are the ones who must allow access and have rival members on their patch. No other gangs have to do this, for example where The Caves are situated means The Vampires never have to allow anybody access to their territory, only the invited ones; and the same goes for every other gang. The Monks did this because after The War Against The Vampires they wanted to assert their dominance at the same time as keeping an eye on other gang activity. In the long run it has backfired on them and now they are left with no option but to let rivals travel to other territories if need be. The guard stands with an arrogant smile on his face, but Krul can tell he is just acting tough in front of his crew. They both hear a car door open. Looking to see who it is, Victuis vacates his car with his henchmen and wanders over to support his best friend and leader.

"Is there a problem?" Victuis asks aggressively, staring at the head guard whose men take a step back and arm their crossbows as a warning to the vampire deputy. Victuis is unmoved and continues his standoff with the guard, who by now has grown slightly more nervous now that he is face-to-face with a vampire. After a tense few seconds the guard concedes and walks away to the security hut, calling his men to follow him, each one cautiously walking past Victuis and his members; the barrier opens. Cruising through with nonchalance, Enigma waves and smiles at the guards as she and her gang enter their arch enemy's territory, and after glancing back, she and Krul see two Monk cars follow them. Krul smirks and holds his girlfriend's hand, Enigma leaning in for a kiss as another small victory falls in The Vampires' favour. This is gang life, every tiny one-upmanship is a victory you can claim and leave your enemy reeling with the embarrassment of defeat; to somebody like Enigma these are always moments to saviour. But Krul's mind quickly moves on to the meeting with The Chinese, Cheng will no doubt be ready and although they have agreed to do business with The Vampires, the tension will still be there just like it was in The Waiting Yard; but Krul and Cheng know that was just gang life, a show of defiance to a rival gang and being cocksure in front of your crew, but some of The Chinese gang members will not be happy with rivals being on their patch; however, they will have to do as they are told.

Cathedral Tower comes into view and the focal point of the entire city stands glorious in its appearance, reaching high into the sky and watching over the land. Krul peers out of the window at the place he would like to call home. Enigma joins him in the pleasant viewing of their dream to rule – for now at least it is a fantasy, but a fantasy that is possible to fulfil. Krul suspects Father Gideon will be looking out of the window now, watching his members tail The Vampires to China Town, the paranoia growing and growing, desperate to know what business Krul and Cheng could have – is it a union that could conquer the city, or is it a mere gathering to discuss the avoidance of future conflict? Enigma slides across the back seat and snuggles into her man as they coast past Cathedral Tower, Monk gang members out on guard watch as their enemy through the centuries passes. Fast approaching The Chinese territory, Krul is ready for business, and after a nervous but peaceful transition from Holy Ground to China Town, and a tense but enjoyable ride through the colourful streets, the undead arrive at the headquarters and as predicted Yong is there to greet them. With a battalion of gang members who are heavily armed protecting him and a few on the roof for added safety, another of Krul's predictions is coming true.

The pleasantries take place between an honourable Yong and a respectful Krul and Victuis. Enigma nods her greeting, and after Victuis removes the money from the car The Vampires are taken to Cheng. On the way Krul has a quiet word with Enigma to be a bit more respectful, informing her that what she already knows, that they are on somebody else's turf and are here to do business, not to cause anger and animosity. Enigma agrees with a solemn expression and looks away. Entering Cheng's office, they see the leader sat at his desk but he rises as soon as Krul enters. Zhen Yun is stood behind him and the room is full of gang members looking tough, but Krul knows their hearts are pounding. Zhen Yun and Enigma lock eyes, the hatred in their stare instantaneous. Victuis reminds her of what Krul has just said and Enigma sulks as she is forced to lose the stare out by looking away and the arrogant smile widens on Zhen's face.

"A sample, I think, is in order," Cheng begins the business and signals to bring the merchandise out, a tray of three glasses of blood.

Krul takes the offering and gently swills it around like somebody would with a glass of brandy, lightly sniffing the drink.

"That is fresh," he states with delight and downs the blood in one, feeling a burst of pleasure run through his body and the sheer thrill of the drink leaves him smiling, and he nods his approval to Cheng, who smiles back.

"Freshly drained," Cheng says in response to Krul's comment.

Krul smiles at the news as Victuis and Enigma sample the goods and give their glowing approval. Cheng's supply comes over from China, shipped to him from his connections in the east, traffic victims, kidnap victims, missing people, homeless people, they are all collected, rounded up and shipped to 9 Gang City. They are then drained of their blood, which is then sold to The Vampires who are only too pleased to have fresh human blood for their pleasure and survival. They pay with cash they steal from banks outside of the city – they used to rob blood banks but there wasn't enough for their fill as blood samples are only taken in syringe amounts, whereas Cheng drains the entire body for them: more blood, higher price. Krul signals to Victuis to hand over the money, who places the large bag on the table and opens it. Cheng nods his approval and turns to Yong, who removes the bag from the desk and leaves the room. Zhen, still standing behind Cheng, disgusted by The Vampires' behaviour and need for the blood of another to live, remains silent. Krul glances around the room, looking at the high number of Chinese gang members surrounding them, smiling and looking back at Cheng.

"Have we made you nervous?" he asks with a teasing gesture, nodding his head to the members in the room. Cheng shrugs and shakes his head.

"No chance, just a precaution," Cheng fires back.

Krul laughs slightly but holds his stare. "Do you know how hard it is to hit a vampire in the heart from any distance with a crossbow?" Krul asks, amazed at how deluded a lot of the gang members are in the city – most of them have never done it but still carry them as if they are experts.

Cheng smirks, knowing what he is getting at but does not concede. "Do you think we just carry them to look good?" he answers back in a cocky tone of voice.

Krul is unmoved and sits relaxed in the chair and nods his head. "Yes," he replies in an equally cocky manner.

Cheng takes this as a challenge and looks around at Zhen Yun, who glances at her boss and then stares at Krul. Cheng rises to his feet and offers a demonstration, which The Vampires accept. Making their way to the next room, Krul sees it is a training room with racks of weapons to the side and dummies set up for combats' training. As they are gathering, Yong returns to inform Cheng the money is all there and accounted for. Zhen Yun prepares herself for the demonstration, attaching a crossbow loaded with a wooden stake to her back, two small swords on her hips and a staff that is sharpened at both ends to form a stake on each. Krul thinks that is a good idea from a mortal point of view. She looks impressive but looks don't count in combat. Cheng signals five of his gang members to step forward as would-be assailants and turns to Krul to make sure he is watching.

"This is how we train," Cheng declares proudly and tells Zhen to begin.

She spins the staff around with expert precision as the first man steps toward her, attempting a roundhouse, but gets flattened onto his back with a sweep to the legs from Zhen, who quickly rises with a kick to the face of the second, sending him to the floor with a thud. The next three attack her all at once with Kendo sticks, but Zhen is an expert and blocks every blow with her staff. Whacking one between the legs, he sinks to his knees and is dropped onto his back with a smack to the face with the staff. Turning to the next attacker, she ducks his swing and elbows him in the back whilst at the same time kicking the other to the side of the face. Grasping her staff, she swings with lightning speed, cracking them both around the face, causing them to flake to the ground. Taking her double staked staff, she hurls it through the air at a mannequin, catching it perfectly where a vampire's heart would be. Within a split second she removes the crossbow from her back and fires the stake almost without aiming, but lands it perfectly again in the heart. Pulling both swords, Zhen Yun throws them through the air sideways, at the same time chopping the head off the dummies. Turning to The Vampires, she stands proud of her performance, awaiting their comment. Cheng smiles with pride at her showing, clapping his hands and staring at Krul for a reaction. Krul himself must admit she was impressive and far better than even he thought.

"Very impressive," he states, nodding his approval and staring at Cheng, who is still smiling. "But you seem to be under the impression vampires stand still and let you stake them," he adds, referring to the mannequins.

Cheng's smile fades slightly, knowing he is right. They stand silent for a short while, Zhen Yun turning to look at Cheng, who stares back deep in thought knowing what she wants but wonders whether it is the right thing to do. Zhen makes the decision herself and turns back to The Vampires, pointing at Enigma, laying down a challenge. Krul glances at his girlfriend with a slight smile followed by a shrug of the shoulders as if to say it is your choice. Enigma removes her coat, handing it to Victuis who begins to rile her up even so far as to rub her shoulders like a coach would to a boxer. Enigma then removes her vest so the top of her body is only covered by her bra so she can display her vampire supremacist tattoos for the whole room to see. Zhen snarls with disgust at the gesture, Cheng and Yong remain unmoved. The Countess steps onto the mat and a deep tension blankets the entire room; all present know these two hate each other intently and this could get serious. Krul and Cheng both watch on as bragging right for their gangs is at stake, because whatever the result this will spread across the city like wildfire and the loser will have a crushing defeat to deal with in the way it will weaken their reputation across 9 Gang. The winner will cement their place as a major force throughout the land, driving fear into all other gangs; all this because two women are squaring off – that is gang life.

The two step forward with their defence up, Zhen in a martial arts pose, Enigma like a street fighting boxer. Zhen steps in for a punch but it is dodged with ease by the vampiress who lands her own punch perfectly to the face, instantly drawing blood, which excites her, followed by another in quick succession, sending Zhen crashing to the floor. Krul smiles with glee as Victuis slaps his back and cheers. Cheng stands, unable to help, and Yong twitches at what he has just witnessed. Zhen jumps to her feet in fury, spinning into a roundhouse, to which Enigma simply steps aside and lands another rapid one, two into her opponent's face. The anger grows in Zhen as she lunges into another attack; again the vampire embarrasses her nemesis by avoiding her angry assault with a sidestep, grabbing her with both hands around the back of the head, easily outpowering her, pulling her head down, landing blow after blow with her knees, then clutching her throat and choke slamming her to the floor. Zhen gasps for breath at the beating as Cheng looks to the floor, knowing he shouldn't have allowed this, but human ambition is sometimes their worst enemy. Zhen struggles up, looking at Enigma who, not needing to catch her breath – she hasn't got one – feeling no tiredness or pain, stands awaiting the next move from the woman who believed she could defeat a vampire in hand-to-hand combat. Mortal arrogance stems from pride in your ability and pride is a sin.

Zhen staggers forward not thinking straight and, unable to formulate a plan, lunges cluelessly toward Enigma who almost humiliatingly steps behind Zhen and clutches her in a choke hold, lifting her off her feet. Zhen struggles to breathe and chokes as Enigma has her at her mercy before dropping her to the floor and kneeing her in the face. Enigma stands victorious as Zhen lies on the mat, a humiliated woman. The Vampires cheer and celebrate with Krul standing a proud boyfriend and leader and Victuis holding his arms in the air in celebration. Enigma smiles at the bragging rights she has given her gang, knowing this will spread around the city. Walking away, Enigma turns her back on her defeated foe. Zhen Yun, unable to accept defeat to anyone but especially the creature she hates the most, and on her own turf is too much for her to take and she grabs a stake from the weapons rack and lunges at Enigma. Krul calls out and Cheng orders Zhen to stop, but his demand falls on deaf ears as his 3rd In Command risks all-out war because of her hurt pride. Enigma turns, blocking the cowardly attack, grasping tight hold of Zhen's arm and twisting it round, sinking her fangs into her fingers and ripping two off. Zhen screams in agony and slumps to the floor. Enigma spits the fingers at Zhen and licks the blood from her lips and swallows with a smile. The Chinese gang members draw their weapons and surround The Vampires. The tension is immense – is this it, the war everybody knew would happen but did not think it would be here and now? Krul stands calm but knows this could be the moment and is ready at any point to leap into action; if Cheng orders his troops to fire Krul is going straight for The Chinese leader who himself is stood straight faced with the biggest decision yet of his leadership, his adrenaline pumping.

"Is this how you train?" Krul asks, mocking but also serious. "Attack somebody when their back is turned? I thought you were an honourable man," he adds, knowing it will shame Cheng who knows Krul is right. Cheng signals his members to lower their weapons.

"You are right, Zhen's behaviour has shamed me, please accept my apologies," Cheng states, staring at Krul who, after a pause, nods his head in acceptance. Enigma smiles as she walks to her crew and gets dressed, Victuis holding her coat open for her so she can slip in, followed by a playful shove and a celebratory compliment for The Countess, who laughs, loving the attention.

Krul comes over to offer his congratulations. "That's my girl," he tells her with a passionate kiss and a hug, Enigma proud she has represented her gang and come out on top.

Yong helps Zhen to her feet and collects her fingers in the hope they can be reattached, but when Enigma bites she gets the job done – just ask Krul. Cheng offers to show The Vampires out and has to listen to their enjoyment all the way to their cars. Some vampire gang members lift Enigma up onto their shoulders and carry her out like royalty. Cheng knows tonight's event will set his crew back and it is the fault of his 3rd In Command. A war could have started tonight all because of the indiscipline of somebody he has chosen to represent him and the gang, so that means it must fall on his head; this is the heavy burden of being a leader. Cheng watches as the cars disappear into the distance. The moonlit sky watches over China Town as if goading mortal life in that all that has just happened is because darkness falls every day in 9 Gang City and at this time of year the dark appears for 16 hours a day, bringing life to the supposed dead. The mortal gangs hate the winter months and long for summer, more daylight, fewer monsters and some of those "monsters" have just taken a step forward in reputation.

Chapter 7

Voted into power after the war, Rika, or Queen Rika to give her her proper title, is only the second leader of The Witches. As with most things these days, politics has complicated issues that in the old days would be settled by war, most will say that shows the human race has become more civilised, but to a gang like The Witches being despised simply because of what you are exposes the lie of the human race being more civilised. As far back as 1000 AD when King Stephen I gained the throne in Hungary, becoming the first Christian monarch, changing Hungarian society forever, this brought a fresh persecution to witches at the time. This came a century after The Magyars had invaded and conquered Hungary, a nomadic people who to this day are thought about with conflicting opinions. Some say they were savages bent on rape and robbery; others say they brought a new culture to Europe with their spirituality and dress sense; some say they were the first people in Europe to wear trousers; but this is debated. It sounds similar to the way The Vikings are viewed in Britain and it gets to a point where it may just be how humankind sees outsiders until they get to know them. The Magyar invasion came circa 600 years after The Huns settled in what we now know as Hungary, a horde of fierce and mighty warriors who fought and at times defeated The Romans and Germanic Tribes, the most famous Hun being Attila. With certain types of people having no desire to differentiate between a good witch and a bad witch, they were all judged the same to a point where the only good witch is a burned at the stake witch; this attitude still exists today in some sections of 9 Gang City. England is one of many countries with a history of persecution against witches, even before The Battles crossed The Channel, as far back as King Alfred The Great who banned witchcraft and introduced the death penalty for somebody found guilty of murder by witchcraft. King Cnut even went as far as to cast the same punishment on non-witches who supported witchcraft. It is said by many that the witch trials of 15th, 16th and 17th centuries were based on a number of things: the first, radical Christianity believed witches were in league with The Devil and did his work on Earth; some say The Devil himself joined in, but the persecution of witches cannot be solely down to Christianity because witch hunting was going on centuries before Jesus was born and within cultures who were not or are not Christian. The word witch is taken from the Anglo-Saxon word Wicca many years before they were Christianised; Norse mythology speaks of Valkyries who were women who flew through the sky; in ancient Greece and Rome they believed in witches and punished their bad deeds; in Mesopotamia they feared magic and people who could heal with sorcery so the witches who could do good with their magic were still demonised. Secondly, the blame is credited to misogyny – apparently the witch trials across Europe and North America were down to men within society hating women so much they made up everything about witchcraft so they could kill them – but this theory is quickly destroyed when you consider that men or in this case warlocks were killed during these trials as well as children, both boys and girls, and Jacques De Molay, the last Grand Master of The Knights Templar, was burned at the stake. Thirdly, a fungus is blamed that infected the crops all over Europe and gave people hallucinations to the extent they saw women riding broomsticks and speaking with The Devil in the darkness of the night – this is plausible at first, but when you consider the witch trials went on for circa 300 years is it realistic to suggest that the fungus was around for all that time and made its way to America and was this fungus infecting the crops in ancient Egypt, Rome, Greece, Mesopotamia and Canaan, because all these places have tails of witches and witchcraft? The fourth reason is that it is all true and witches do exist – how else would anyone explain all the legends from all the different cultures throughout time? They can't, not truly explain it, and this is the reason many people are intrigued by these myths, legends and folklore tales of magic, sorcery and covens all these millennia and we still don't know for certain; that leaves the mystery in the tales and people like mystery.

The second highest selling book from 1487 to 1687 was Malleus Maleficarum; translated to The Hammer Of Witches it is a witchfinders bible. In this book you will find how to tell the different types of witch, what part The Devil plays in corrupting the conceiving of mortals, different types of torture for different types of heresy, and how to pass sentence on the different types of witchcraft, and much more. In this book it states that people who believe that anybody who thinks a person can change for good or bad by anything except God's will is worse than a Pagan or heretic, so it is un-Catholic to say these things are done by witches or to have such an opinion. The book also asks whether God himself allows such things to happen because to say witchcraft is the work of The Devil is to believe The Devil is more powerful than God and that is heresy, so therefore is witchcraft allowed by God? It is a fair question because if God created everything then God created the evil, people will question why; perhaps because if there is or was no evil then we would no longer need to pray to God for salvation as our saviour, but if evil exists then we do need to pray to him for help and mercy and maybe this is what God wants? There is a high probability that these attitudes and beliefs will always exist, the hatred will never subside and people will always be controlled by their religious belief, controlled by society and what the fashionable opinion is or their own disgust in what they think is wrong.

Despite all this, Rika knows the best way for her people to regain power will be through politics, but the likelihood of that is very slim. However, with her desire to rule and her devout belief that The Witches and The Vampires are the true rulers of 9 Gang City, Queen Rika will not stop until she is either ruler or burned. With a loyal following from her sisters, Rika is in good company with one aim and one goal, they are a unified trio – only The Vampires are more united, which is a huge advantage to the cause of the gangs who ruled for 200 years together. This only makes the other gangs nervous which in turn causes animosity to grow. This lowers the chance of people voting for a vampire or witch, that then leads to discrimination against the forces of darkness, which then creates hatred towards the mortal gangs. This causes the fear to grow in mortal gangs even more, causing the chance of them voting for a vampire or a witch to disappear altogether. It is a vicious circle of fear and hatred, bringing the conclusion that The Witches and The Vampires will only get into power through war, and it is caused by mortal fear and hatred of what their opinion of evil is. The Witches have become used to this, but the anger never stops, and for hatred and discrimination to be something anybody gets used to tells us how long it has been an ongoing issue.

Princess Katalin, the loyal deputy and second sister of the witch leaders, has no desire to be leader herself, she believes in birth right and rank taking precedence, and is firm in her belief that her elder sister is the true ruler of the city. A sneaky shadow-dwelling sorceress, Katalin is an expert in shapeshifting with a black cat her favourite animal of choice, which only adds to the stereotyping of witches in the city, but also a raven and a rat amongst others. The virgin princess has remained pure as her sole focus in life is to gain her people the leadership of the city and extracurricular activities would only cloud her aim and focus. She is dedicated to her older sister.

Princess Tunder AKA The Dark Fairy is not so accepting of the modern ways. A ferocious temper and a lust for the dark ways have led her to an obsession with Queen Ziana. With a hunger for domination, the youngest of the three witches is a merciless serpentine who is cold and calculated and has a merciless brutality towards her enemies. Tunder is frustrated with The Vampires' more accepting approach to the mortal gangs; this is also a frustration towards her sister for considering the democratic side of modern times. Where was democracy when they travelled across Europe to annihilate their people? Where was fairness and acceptance when they were burning witches at the stake? People say it is all part of history and people should move forward, but it is easy to say that when you have the power.

Rika and Katalin have managed to keep Tunder under control for now, but with growing hatred and her powers gaining by the day, she is a devout to magic and is a ticking time bomb ready to explode. Perhaps a festival will lighten the mood – Vampir Ceremoniilor is fast approaching and the day that celebrates the beginning of all this warfare is a chance for The Vampires and The Witches to commemorate their bond and with Kiralyno Emlekezik a week later, it is a happy time for two of the three original gangs. Krul loves the celebration, it is a chance to forget the troubles of the life they live or in his people's case unlive, and enjoy the moment.

A party for The Vampires to which he has invited everyone but knows some people will not attend, and then at The Witches' dinner a chance to discuss the past, present and future in an agreeable manner. Hopefully Enigma with be more approachable towards their allies; her jealously is beginning to irritate Krul – it is one thing to love somebody but when you begin to show anger and hatred to every woman who so much as looks at your boyfriend then it is safe to say the problem is you. When that problem then starts to affect your people's political cause, then it is time for your leader to step in or get rid. Enigma is not quite there yet, but her behaviour of late towards Queen Rika is not to be tolerated; 542 years of collaboration will not be ruined by one woman's jealousy. It will be interesting to say the least who will attend the party as on the same date Day Of The Saviours takes place, The Monks' celebration. Krul made sure High Council all heard his invitation, he went so far as to invite The Monks, and the look on Gideon's face was amusing. If ever there was a time to score points over The Monks that time is now. Father Gideon will be reeling from the loss of his proposition at the meeting, but did he really think the city would vote for The Monks' day to be a city-wide celebration? If people turn up to The Vampires' day it will rub salt in the leader's wounds. After the meeting with The Chinese and the goods being delivered, the festivities can begin. Krul awaits the anniversary of his predecessor, the vampire who started the gang culture in this city and across Europe, the vampire who founded 9 Gang City, and the vampire who fought back against persecution to heroic affect; it is time to celebrate vampirism.

Chapter 8

The sun disappears beneath the horizon, which is a beautiful sight, lighting up Cathedral Tower, if you were to view it from The Caves, but it is a sight Krul will never see. Despite the season it has been a clear day free from rain and gloom and the UV rays filtered down to light up the city as if God himself was shining down to bring mercy and celebration to The Monks' heroic fight against evil, the undead and dark magic. The most complicated day of the year in 9 Gang City has arrived; the arch enemies of The Battles, the original gangs from whom all other gangs were imitators, were born on this day. Today is the day that tells its own story of present times, because despite it being a celebration of history it also gives an indication of the current political climate of the city. The people who accept Krul's invitation to Vampir Ceremoniilor will be sending out a clear message to Father Gideon and The Monks. Krul knows this and played his cards brilliantly by inviting everybody at High Council with a friendly tone and expression directly after the bitter and crushing blow to The Monks' desire to have Day Of The Saviours made into a city celebration.

As soon as the sun faded, The Caves erupted with cheer and the blood flows, bringing pleasure and satisfaction to a species that, although superior in strength and survival, is thought of as a parasitic existence, and if you consider they need human blood to survive that way of thinking is true despite how insulting it is to The Vampires. Cheng's merchandise is more than satisfactory, as it always is, and the business dealings between the two gangs is proof that, despite being enemies, business can still be done.

Krul finishes making himself look presentable, fixing his tie and tucking it neatly into his waistcoat, adjusting his trousers and brushing down his jacket, and after a quick inspection of his shoes he is ready to be host. Enigma is looking equally impressive in her gothic-style dress with two thin straps over the shoulder, just enough to keep the goods hidden but little enough to have her tattoos on display, with high heel shoes and her deep black hair tied back into a tight ponytail. Victuis, like Krul, is suited with a pocket watch adding a classic style, the chain escaping his pocket and tied to his lower button, his handkerchief folded triangularly and neatly placed into his top pocket and cufflinks completing the look, one with V engraved and the other with C.

Guests begin to arrive and like a good host Krul is there to meet and greet with Enigma on his arm and his trusted deputy ready to lead his guests to the main hall. The Phantoms begin to pull up and as is custom on this event, The Witches are asked to arrive first to honour the friendship and support they have given The Vampires all these centuries. The door creaks open and Queen Rika elegantly steps out, locking eyes on Krul and exchanging a smile, Enigma grasping his arm all the more and pulling herself into him as a show of possession or obsession from one alpha female to another. Rika notices this but pretends she doesn't.

"Welcome, your majesty," Krul greets the witch queen with a bow, taking her hand and kissing it gently.

Rika smiles and gives a curtsy, thanking him for his invitation and glancing at Enigma who glares back. Katalin stands awaiting her turn to thank Krul for his offer as Victuis is busy greeting Tunder. A small but noticeable smile creeps its way across her face, bringing a glimmer of light to The Dark Fairy's usually disturbed look, Victuis holds both her hands, leaning forward and kisses both cheeks, bringing a crimson glow to her pale complexion. This doesn't go unnoticed by all who are present, causing Rika to call her sister to her side. Victuis, feeling awkward, quickly moves on to welcome Katalin, who, between her sisters' special greetings has been neglected.

"My apologies, Princess," Victuis says in a gentlemanly-like manner. "Welcome to our celebration," he adds as Katalin smiles and gives a slight bow of the head in acceptance of the apology. Bringing an end to the niceties, The Werewolves arrive, which brings a sweet satisfaction to Krul that they accepted his invitation, Cuthwulf more and more has been thinking the "Monster Gangs" should stick together.

"The creatures of the night," Krul jests as Cuthwulf vacates his car, and the pack leader himself joins in the joke – "What sweet music we make," he says with a grin to which they all laugh.

Victuis takes the guests inside whilst Krul and his Countess await the other guests. They know at least one more gang is attending but maybe more as the festivities rise a notch, the volume inside growing with every drop of blood consumed. Enigma glances into the distance, seeing the lights of the city glisten and a dream of ruling with her true love begins to bring pleasure to her usually twisted thoughts.

"I can just imagine Gideon fuming while eating his Hotpot, Francis desperately trying to console him and Theodore not knowing what to do until he is told," she says, turning to a laughing Krul.

"If most of the gang leaders turn up tonight, that should be the nail in his coffin," Krul states, turning to look at the approaching car, and after seeing who it is smiles with a mixture of happiness and victory as Alice smiles back through the window. The Messengers are between a rock and a hard place on this date ever since The Monks gained power, having to serve the gang that rules but at the same time it was The Vampires who created The Messengers so do they honour the law or honour history? Tonight Alice has decided her gang honours history – they honour the law the rest of the year. Dressed to impress, the messenger girls very rarely get a chance to dress up, twice a year in fact, and they are two nights in a row: Messenger Formation, which is their gang's day of celebration and City Day which is the only city-wide celebration of the year where all gangs celebrate the one thing they all have in common, 9 Gang City.

"I can only imagine what our great leader said when you told him you were partying with Nosferatu tonight," Krul says as he embraces Alice fondly who returns the gesture, their arms gently but firmly wrapped around each other, and Krul becomes transfixed with her scent – not her perfume, he can get past that, but her human scent. He becomes almost hypnotised as he inhales, her neck mere centimetres from his fangs, and temptation grows within him. It is as if the world has stood still so they can share this moment to a point he opens his mouth just enough to bite, the urge growing as his fangs prepare for the nectar that gives life. Until the thought of doing such a thing to an angel amongst demons like Alice brings him to his senses and he pulls away. Alice smiles nervously as she knows she has just taken a risk, but it shows the trust she has for Krul. Enigma thinks she is too close for comfort and stares at her, Alice plays down the aggression by smiling and saying hello, to which Enigma reluctantly follows suit.

"I didn't tell Father Gideon, although he will know by now," Alice informs Krul with a friendly smile, Krul gazing back with the feeling of a growing loyalty and bond for somebody who has always been kind to him and always stood up for Vampire Rights. Although Alice fought in the war, she was simply a gang member following orders and openly spoke out against The Daylight Killings, which made her enemies amongst the other gangs, even some in her own, but as time went on and the city knew it had to at least try to be more civilised and Alice's way of thinking grew more powerful, this meant Vampire Rights grew more acceptable. Seeing the impact this was having on the city rubbed off on Jessica who herself had leaned more and more towards equality for all, seeing the other gang's attitude as hypocritical. Leo being a fair man and supporter of democracy was already on board, and before The Monks knew it, the second most powerful gang politically were supporting The Vampires. All this was before Krul was a vampire, and after a decade of knowing Alice his fondness for her has grown year by year into a blossoming friendship.

Snapping out of his thoughts, he greets Leo and Jessica with a firm handshake for Leo and a playful greeting with Jessica, almost like a brother and sister would. Entering the party, music booming, drinks flowing and people dancing, Krul is pleased with the night so far, but the night is young and after a few drinks and comradery politics and beliefs start to make their appearance and that's when rivalry comes into play, so although peace is present at the moment, the future awaits. Krul offers The Messenger leaders a drink whilst the rest of their gang mingle, Gin and Tonic with a dash of lemon for the girls, and Leo starts off with a beer with the promise of moving on to the hard stuff later, a classic way of starting a night of alcohol consumption. Alice looks around the room and sees Queen Rika with her sisters stood to the side with a goblet each. Alice assumes it is a witches' brew, her gaze caught by Rika who stares back with a slight smile but a look in her eye that makes so many uncomfortable – or is it a spell of mind control that makes people think that they feel uncomfortable? If so, then it is a powerful trick that could prove extremely problematic for the city and a priceless tool for The Witches. Imagine if an election is called and Rika corrupts the minds of High Council for all to vote for her, who's to say the recent meeting wasn't the result of her mind games? Or perhaps Alice is thinking far too much about it – if Rika's mind control did exist, she would control Father Gideon to call an election and she would already be leader of the city. Alice smiles back with a nod and looks away quickly and notices Jessica and Cuthwulf already exchanging the pleasantries. Krul's phone rings and after answering excuses himself he heads toward the front door to welcome more guests – another gang has accepted his invitation. Alice is interested who it might be; it could be The Pagans to spite The Monks, or The Chinese – she knows they had business recently and Alice also knows that despite his military power and his larger numbers, Cheng sees Krul as his biggest threat, so it could be a tactic of keep your friends close and your enemies closer from Cheng.

Leo shakes hands with Wulfric and Randall, the latter giving Alice a very friendly hello. She assumes it is the vodka talking and upon glancing towards the door, Alice discovers the identity of the new arrival. She was right in one of her predictions and the appearance of such a guest will send shockwaves through Holy Ground and have Father Gideon nervous, without a doubt. Cheng and Krul are in conversation as the room looks over at the two leaders in surprise at the Chinese attendance, Yong nods a hello to Alice who returns the gesture, as Victuis makes his way over to fulfil his duty of respect as deputy. Shaking Cheng's hand followed by a bow from each of them and repeating the process with Yong,

Victuis looks around for Zhen Yun, but Cheng informs him he "left her at home" – in other words, he didn't want her to have a rematch with Enigma or she is still too battered and bruised to socialise. Krul signals for The Messengers and The Werewolves to join them as a tray of shots is provided by a vampire bartender; giving them to his guests, he raises his glass.

"Here's to the slim chance of an election being called and if it does may the best man, woman or beast win," Krul declares and sinks his shot once his toast is complete.

The rest cheer in agreement as Cheng and Alice drink theirs in the knowledge that the two of them plus Krul are the three most likely to win or conquer the city. Alice through politics, Cheng through war, and Krul is the dark horse in both categories. Krul, looking up and seeing The Pagans walking in, rushes to greet them, thanking them for their visit and showing them around. Brigacos informs him that the reason they attended was to piss off Father Gideon and Brother Francis. Bryson tuts and shakes his head when Francis' name is mentioned, the druid needing a drink to tame his tension, and Gwen hugs Alice in a girly manner. As the night goes on, Krul basks in the success of the celebration, his kind hated for so long and yet now it seems the tables are turning – 542 years of hatred and animosity and in a decade Krul seems to be changing people's views and opinions of his people, and The Monks who see themselves as saviours of 9 Gang City have dwindled into oblivion as far as hope and respect go. Krul thinks of Gideon and how much he will be seething when he finds out how many people attended and that he will find out eventually brings a smug smile to Krul's face. That smile turns to laughter when Alice shows him a missed call on her phone from Gideon himself. Krul, Victuis and The Werewolves despite being "monsters" are still males and talk about one of the only two things that men talk about – and 9 Gang City doesn't have a football team.

"How fit does Alice look tonight?" Randall compliments, or at least gives an animalistic honesty about her appearance; the rest nod in agreement, all of them glancing over for a look but not wanting to get caught looking over to have a look. Krul smiles and stares at Cuthwulf who returns the stare.

"She's not The Messenger for you though, is she, wolfman?" he teases, giving him a slap on the back. "Oh no, your nose is in the air for another certain female, that scent wafting over on the wind," Krul finishes as the rest join his laughter and Cuthwulf smiles with confirmation.

"I've been trying to get on Jessica for months, had a thing for her for years, hopefully mating season is approaching," the wolf leader reveals, although everybody already knew this.

"Yes, we know, how slow do you work? I've been banging Enigma since she bit me," Krul continues the teasing, much to the delight of the rest of the lads.

Cuthwulf accepts the banter but tries to deflect onto Victuis. "What about you?" he asks, pointing at the vampire. "What is going on with you and Tunder?"

"Nothing, just being polite," Victuis replies with the fakest comment ever, to which the rest of the group jeer and mock to a level that people look over at them, including Alice, Jessica and the witch sisters, and wonder what they are talking about, but think it is nice they are getting along.

Victuis puts his head down with a smirk as he knows his answer was awful, sinking a shot of blood he prepares a better response. "You know when you feel a connection with someone, it just feels right," he states, Krul nodding his head knowing exactly what he means as he feels that connection with Enigma.

Cuthwulf looks across the room and sees Jessica stood watching people dance and thinks this is a good time. Sinking a shot, he makes his way over, Krul stopping him as he does.

"Absinthe, my friend," he informs Cuthwulf who looks at him confused. "It is an aphrodisiac, visit the green fairy–" Krul suggests, pointing to a bottle on a nearby table and offers to show them how to prepare the drinks.

Cuthwulf thanks him for the help and tells himself that this is the moment, tonight is the night. As he approaches, Jessica's face lights up almost as if she had hoped he would come over, maybe even stood alone to look lonely so he would come and keep her company. He shows her the bottle of Absinthe, she agrees nervously and they sit at a quiet table to prepare the drinks. Krul approaches the couple and stands at their table like a waiter and being a good host gives them a tutorial of how to prepare the infamous beverage.

"This is called the Absinthe Ritual and is the correct way to prepare absinthe," he informs the pair who are watching intently.

Jessica has never had the drink before, but has heard myths surrounding it. What a place and night to see if the myth is true. Krul pours the absinthe into the glasses and then places an absinthe spoon over the top, on this "spoon" he puts a sugar cube which he then pours iced water over.

"Why use water and sugar?" Jessica inquires, interested in the ritual.

"The sugar to sweeten the bitter taste and the water to dilute the very strong alcohol," Krul replies, as he looks up from the glasses to make eye contact. "Don't drink absinthe straight – it is prepared this way for a reason," Krul adds, picking up the glasses and handing them each to his guests who look at one another, Jessica with rebellious excitement and Cuthwulf with an animalistic intent. They drink, Krul smiles and bids his farewell, leaving the two potential love birds to it. With Victuis and Tunder getting friendly, Cuthwulf and Jessica taking a step closer, the bond between The Vampires and The Witches growing in strength, the leader of the most powerful military in the city joining him for a drink and six out of nine gangs accepting his invitation, Krul certainly has made yet more massive strides in his gain of power in the city and his respect grows even more. Alice proving allegiance if she needed to choose is with his people and the "monster" gangs getting closer, all this is on the day The Monks wanted to make a city celebration for their gang but instead the democracy that they so proudly created came back to haunt them and the people of 9 Gang City have sent out a message to a tyrant that still waxes lyrical about slaying a tyrant and will be left to ponder what is his next move. When he slayed Niculi, he thought he had The Vampires in check mate and the city would back him forever; little did he realise much to the embarrassment of wannabe heroes that politics is a fickle game where one day you can be cream of the crop and the next you are stale and unwanted. Instead of evolving with the city and its desires, Father Gideon assumed he would forever be admired and that kind of pride in your achievements is a sin. For such people to be hypocrites within their own religion does nothing to convince others that their faith is the superior force and if God exists and he/she/it very well may exist, could be left ashamed of what he has created hence the reason people question whether God exists because surely his apparent absence is evidence or proof of him abandoning his creation.

Chapter 9

Taking a car and taking his favoured conquest for a ride, Cuthwulf struggles to keep his eyes on the road. Jessica, looking more beautiful than ever with her dress stopping halfway down the thigh showing enough leg to interest a would-be suitor, she has played the game well. Easily achieving the two things she wanted to achieve tonight – have fun and pull the man she has fancied for God knows how long, and here they are, finally alone. It is a short journey to The Forests and after passing through the security check for the first time Jessica feels a freedom she never thought she would feel, on rival land but not on duty, the shackles feel like they have fallen off and she is at liberty to do as she pleases. No Father Gideon and his tyrannical demands, no Alice with her honour and discipline, and no Leo playing the faithful deputy to her sister and then the superior with Jessica. It would be understandable to think these thoughts are a criticism of Alice and Leo, but they are not; her sister is a great leader and wonderful person, and Leo is a trusted friend and gang member that any crew would be happy to have, but there comes a time when anybody and everybody becomes tedious and you need time away from them. This is Jessica's moment. Cuthwulf shares that feeling, he has only just noticed he is always with a gang member – as leader he always has somebody with him, Wulfric, Randall or even just another gang member, henchman, chauffeur, he has become so used to it that he didn't notice it, but now they both feel rebellious – being alone with a rival gang member is very rare, it is allowed but so few people do it that it is still considered shocking, almost scandalous; and the city will gossip, but the two of them are thrilled by the notion.

Stopping outside werewolf headquarters it is a familiar sight for Jessica and yet looks different in the dark.

"You have never seen inside, have you?" Cuthwulf asks, turning to her with a smile although he knows she hasn't. Jessica smiles back with a shake of the head. "It seems it is a night of firsts, first time drinking absinthe, first time in Werewolf HQ, what other first times will we have together?" Cuthwulf asks in a suggestive tone.

"You will have to wait and see," Jessica teases in a flirty manner as they enter the building. Stepping inside, she sees a corridor with multiple doorways. On the walls there are pictures, flags and memorials to The Werewolves past and present, a nice setting filled with pride and honour which is exactly what you would expect from wolves, but not much glitz and glamour which is what you would expect from a gang mostly made up of men and of course in a wolf pack the alpha wolf is more often than not the top male, so of course there is going to be a male influence on how the gang operates. Giving the guided tour, Cuthwulf shows Jessica every room. Most of them are offices and dormitories for the gang members and the theme of celebration in their kind continues throughout, almost in every room their symbol takes pride of place on the wall, door or ceiling, an emblem of a face which is half-man on one side but half-wolf on the other. This emblem/symbol is a modern crest that was introduced after The War Against The Vampires; almost everything changed after the war, the previous symbol was a more traditional style symbol of a wolf and a man on each side of a full moon, but Cuthwulf changed it as he believed in a new crest for a new beginning in his gang's existence, although they still pay homage to the old badge as it makes an appearance in the important places of werewolf turf.

Coming to a door grander in appearance and both symbols engraved, the new crest above with the old below, Cuthwulf allows Jessica to enter before him in a lady's first approach, stepping in she sees it is his office, his desk opposite the door and behind it on the wall a map of North Yorkshire Moors, the place where The Werewolves were founded and joined The Battles. Jessica is slightly surprised by this – she suspected he would have a desk and some symbolic decoration on the wall, but she assumed it would be a grander design of the werewolf symbol; however, she thinks it is a nice touch and tribute to their founders.

Cuthwulf offers her a drink and tells her to make herself comfortable. He has all the hard stuff – Whiskey, Vodka, Brandy – but to her nice surprise he has a bottle of wine which she gleefully accepts as she has had enough hard stuff tonight. Leaning on his desk, she looks around the room once again and takes in a more detailed view of his office, seeing a map of The Forests on one wall and once again the new crest on another. She notices there are no windows in the room – perhaps Cuthwulf is worried about spies and assassins, but Jessica does not ask. There is another closed door at the back of the room that she is yet to see.

"What is in there?" she asks, wanting to make conversation as the silence was growing a little bit awkward.

"My bedroom," Cuthwulf responds with a smirk.

Jessica smiles back at the fact he could have taken her anywhere in his territory, but they end up mere metres from his bed. Cuthwulf returns to her with the drinks, her wine in an elegant glass that is way too feminine to be for a man, which makes her wonder who he has had visiting him.

"And why does a masculine alpha wolf have such lady-like glasses?" Jessica intrudes into his reasoning.

His response is swift and honest, one which takes her by surprise but at the same time flatters her.

"Because I got them for you," he responds, looking to the floor almost embarrassed, "Tonight was the night I was going to invite you here after the party; this was all planned," he adds, sipping his drink and looking for a response.

Jessica's heart skips at the thought of him thinking about her and she thanks him for the gesture. That awkward silence returns gradually and Jessica finds herself looking around the room again, Cuthwulf staring into his glass and swilling round his drink in a slightly annoying manner. Men become weird when they are in the presence of a woman they like, they either get over enthusiastic and make a fool of themselves, thus destroying their chance with a woman, or go quiet, clueless what to say. Cuthwulf's silence tells Jessica what kind he is, so she takes it upon herself to get the conversation going.

"Is it true you can't control yourself when you have turned?" Jessica asks, eager to know how far to trust a man that is a beast.

Cuthwulf looks at her, knowing he needs to tell the truth but not wanting to.

"Yes," he replies in a solemn tone. "You can't trust me when I'm a wolf," he adds, catching her sad expression.

Jessica knows he is flawed but so is everybody – it makes her want to help him, but she can't.

"What does it feel like?" she asks, moving closer to him.

He looks at her for a few seconds before answering. "It feels right," Cuthwulf tells her with a spark in his voice. "It feels natural, like a release inside that being human is holding me prisoner but that full moon is my moment of freedom," he adds, almost going into a daze of joy, beginning to feel desire to change and run wild.

Jessica smiles at his response, glad that he feels that way – she always thought it was a curse that he was unhappy with, she never thought he or his kind would be happy with their "condition".

"You sound like Victuis," Jessica informs him, to which he nods agreeing with her. "He is glad Krul changed him, he likes being a vampire, no more illness, no more waiting for death, no more living just to die," she adds, wondering if it would be easier than being mortal.

"He is right about all of those things, our existence is a release from human imprisonment," Cuthwulf responds, attempting to convince her that The Werewolves' and The Vampires' so-called "evil" or "monster" life is not necessarily the burden mortals think it is.

Moving closer to her, Cuthwulf places his hands on her hips, looking her in the eyes as she looks up at him, putting her hands on his shoulders. He leans in, kissing her gently, responding by kissing him back; the two pull one another closer and passionately kiss. Cuthwulf wraps his arms around her as she sinks into him. Years of desire disappear as finally they embrace each other for filling the fantasy they have not so secretly shared; his hands begin to wander slowly, moving down, taking a soft grip of her arse; their tongues begin to intertwine. Moving deeper into him, Jessica feels his cock already hard rub against her, which makes her wet with anticipation; as the passion grows, the kissing intensifies. Cuthwulf moving down to her neck as Jessica invites this by tilting her head to the side, his hands continue exploring her body. Stopping for breath, they gaze into each other's eyes, Jessica displaying a sweet smile of satisfaction that she finally has her man, Cuthwulf celebrating in his mind but his animal instinct wants more, kissing her again before taking her hand and leading her to his bedroom. Removing his shirt, the passion resumes, Jessica rubbing her hands across his ripped body, her excitement gaining with every stroke; his belt unbuckles and his trousers drop, his cock standing tall and bulging in his underwear. Holding her against the door as she pulls down his last piece of clothing leaving him naked in front of her, her pussy soaking with desire. Almost ripping down her wet knickers, he lifts her against the door gripping her arse as she wraps her legs around him, inserting his dick into her; she moans with pleasure as he breathes deeply at the feel of her warm pussy, thrusting into her. Jessica gasps as she is slammed against the door, the pace picking up and the passion building every time he enters – for years Cuthwulf has waited for this moment, for years Jessica has longed for this passion as he fucks her hard, making sure every inch feels the warmth of her dripping pussy. Feeling his end is near, Cuthwulf tries to hold back to make the moment last as long as it can, but years of neglect mean he is unable to and he climaxes. His legs go weak and his body shudders as he comes, Jessica feeling it inside her as they embrace. The two lovers share a smile and a look of conquest that they have at last put their desire into reality. Cuthwulf, pulling out of her and relaxing on the bed, lights a cigarette in celebration, Jessica removing her dress and joining him naked for a snuggle. Enjoying the moment but wanting to talk, she notices he has gone quiet, the smoke beginning to fog the room. Jessica wonders whether she should ask another question about Cuthwulf's life, or maybe it is too personal and he may not want to share it yet. After a moment's thought she asks what she has always wondered but never found the right moment.

"How did you become a werewolf?" she inquires with a reluctant tone, wanting to know but worried he may find the question intrusive. "I mean who was it that turned you?" she adds, looking at him for his reaction.

Cuthwulf never speaks about this or at least Jessica has never heard him speak about it; Krul and Victuis are very open and quite often mention their turning from time to time, but Cuthwulf does not. He looks back at her, wondering why she seems worried about asking such a thing – it's not as if it's secret, it is just that in this city it is not really a big thing and he doesn't talk about it because he didn't think anyone would care. In a place that has many werewolves, vampires and witches, and these things are out in the open and are part of the everyday, not just the stuff of horror stories, it has taken away the "glamour" of being a monster. Add to this that the story is actually quite basic, which brings up another problem – mortals believe the stories from the other side must be scary and horrific but those tales are very rare; the truth is, Cuthwulf was recruited, just like any mortal gang or military. You cannot just wait for people to come to you and hope they join, you have to go out and convince or tempt them into joining your gang, and Cuthwulf was one of these recruitments.

"I was recruited," he answers, stubbing out his fag end. "We were brought in from the outside and signed up, taken into the maximum-security wing and bitten," he finishes.

She looks at him a bit surprised – Jessica didn't know they did this to gain gang members.

Cuthwulf looks back in the same manner – he thought she knew their recruitment process.

"You just go into a room with a werewolf and let it bite you and that's it, you are a member?" she asks in an almost dismissive tone as if it is a normal thing to do. They both laugh at how it sounds.

"Not really as simple as that, but not far wrong," he responds with a smile. "We are taken into a room with a werewolf in a secure cell and then when he or she changes we have to put our arm through until it bites," Cuthwulf finishes, watching the looks on Jessica's face.

"You just stick your arm in a cage until you are bitten?" she asks with a slightly bewildered look on her face.

"Yes," he confirms with a laugh and a confused thought of why she finds it hard to believe. "What did you think we did? Just wait for someone to wander into the city? When has that ever happened? We have to go out and bring them in," Cuthwulf informs her as she nods in acceptance, thinking he has a point.

Cuthwulf lights another cig and Jessica checks her phone, seeing she has a text from Alice asking her where she is; Jessica does not respond. She loves that her sister cares so much, but tonight she wants the pleasures of being a woman and snuggles back into Cuthwulf, their naked bodies rubbing together, flesh on flesh. Sliding her hand down she teases his manhood to see if he is ready for the second round, and he looks down, smiling, kissing her softly as she rubs him to an erection. Dropping his smoke into the ashtray and rolling over – she has done her work well because he is ready for more. Slipping his finger between her pussy lips and flicking her clit, he returns the favour as she gasps and moans as she starts to get damp, up, down, side to side and round in a circle her juices are flowing, dripping onto the bed. He slides inside her as they kiss, thinking the second time is for her, Cuthwulf wants to give her the pleasure she deserves, a caring woman, a fair woman, a friend and now a lover and at the same time a rival. That rebellious feeling returns and Cuthwulf grabs hold of the headboard and slams her hard, Jessica spreading her legs wider to give him easier entry. Rubbing her hands all over his body – his impressive physique turning her on even more as he leans down, kissing her neck and making his way down to her breasts. Lifting her legs so they are over his shoulders Jessica smiles with ecstasy as she feels his every inch hitting the right spot and after whispering in his ear not to stop, Cuthwulf knows he can't let her down now, ramming into her until she gasps. Her eyes roll and she shudders in orgasmic pleasure; he feels proud. That is what she needed, it has been a long time since Jessica had a man, and after sharing a grateful kiss, Cuthwulf continues until he too has his way followed by lying side by side breathless and a slight sweat on both of them.

Cuthwulf suddenly springs to his feet, pulling a Glock from underneath his pillow, and rushes to the door, putting his ear against it to listen. Jessica, not knowing what is going on but knowing there must be a problem, gets dressed quickly. Cuthwulf signals underneath the bed. Jessica looks and finds a sawn-off shotgun which she grasps ready for whatever lurks outside. Cuthwulf quickly puts his trousers on, ready to investigate. Taking the lead he slowly opens the door, making sure Jessica is safe behind him: nobody. Creeping out as quietly as possible but with purpose to kill whatever intruder has entered his turf without permission, Cuthwulf puts his nose in the air to smell the draught slipping through the bottom of the front door. He drops his guard with a dismissive laugh.

"It's Alice," he tells Jessica, who looks at him surprised – she didn't know the wolf's sense of smell could still be used as a human but apparently so. Cuthwulf swings the door open and as stated Alice stands alone, looking slightly miffed but not surprised, while Jessica stands like a naughty girl who has just been caught. Cuthwulf smiles awkwardly and invites Alice in for a drink and to get warm; a shivering Alice accepts with a polite nod and smile. Standing in the kitchen and waiting for the coffee to be poured, there is an awkward silence before Alice break it with an even more awkward comment.

"No prizes for guessing what you two have been up to," she says, looking at her sister who cringes a bit.

"I was just showing her around," Cuthwulf responds with the worst lie ever, knowing full well Alice won't believe it.

Even Jessica gives him a weird look, thinking is he being serious. Alice looks at him unconvinced as she looks him up and down, topless and his fly is undone. Beginning to laugh, Cuthwulf heads for the bedroom to finish getting dressed.

"For God's sake, remember you are my sister not my mother," Jessica says, irritated by the arrival but understanding why. Alice nods her head in agreement, almost angry with herself. "I know," she replies in an apologetic tone. "I was just worried about you," Alice adds, giving her sister a hug.

"No need to be worried," they hear Cuthwulf's voice say as he re-enters fully dressed. "It's not a full moon," he jokes preparing the cups for their night-time beverage.

"It's not that I don't trust you, it is also if word gets out about you two it will cause more animosity with Father Gideon," Alice states to them both. She is right: the leader will not be happy about his gangs' servants fornicating with an enemy, especially a member of a "monster" gang. Cuthwulf and Jessica already know this and are caught in two minds whether they care, it will cause more issues for Alice and Jessica with The Monks, especially Gideon and Francis, but on the other hand why should they hide their love from that gang of has-been heroes and tyrants?

Chapter 10

T he phone rings that familiar tone and Leo and Jessica look at Alice, who glances back with an air of predictability; they knew this would happen. The ring tone is Father Gideon's and Alice knows he will be demanding to know why she and her gang attended The Vampires' day of celebration and not The Monks'. Alice has just the answer. Answering the phone, she braces herself – she has been beckoned as Father Gideon demands to see her at once with a fiery spark in his voice; this will not go well. Jessica and Leo watch her leave and then look at each other, both wanting to help but knowing they can't; Jessica thinking she has made it worse by associating with rival gang members and Leo thinking it is Jessica's choice who she is with, but it certainly hasn't helped matters.

On the way from Neutral Territory to Holy Ground, Alice begins to wonder if this gang life is worth it, what has any of this rivalry achieved, are any of the gangs right about what they say, do or stand for, or is it all just a pointless exercise with no winner in the end? At the security check, Alice notices the monk guards are a bit off with her, a little less respectful, by now the whole city will know who did and who didn't attend Vampir Ceremoniilor, and many people will be wondering the true extent of The Messengers and The Chinese attendance; but one thing is for certain: Father Gideon will be both furious and nervous. Furious that the gang who are supposed to serve his crew socialised with the eternal enemy, and nervous that the two biggest threats to The Monks' hold on power are now not only doing business together but celebrating as well. Entering Cathedral Tower, Alice sees some monk gang members staring over at her; one even looks her up and down like she is a piece of dirt and then mutters something to his comrades. Alice ignores this and continues on her way to Gideon's office. Down the corridor, Brother Francis and Brother Theodore stand outside, Francis glaring as she comes toward him. Alice knew he would make an appearance, not passing up an opportunity to lecture and criticize anyone and everyone who he believes needs it, religion, politics, social graces, you name it, Francis will lecture you on it.

"Careful, Theodore, we have a traitor in our midst," Francis warns in an odious tone with a disgusted look on his face, starting as Alice gets to the door.

"Excuse me," Alice snaps, insulted but not surprised by his outburst. "Don't you ever speak to me or about me like that," she adds with a venom to her voice.

"That is exactly what you are, a traitor – how could you after all Father Gideon has done for you?" Francis moans, his anger growing.

Alice looks almost open-mouthed. "Done for me?" she questions, not knowing what he is talking about. "What has Father Gideon done for me?" she asks, made curious by his ridiculous comment.

"Kept you in a job, kept you in a position – you are technically the fourth most powerful person in the city and Father Gideon allowed you to keep it and this is how you repay him," Francis bellows, his voice almost turning to a whine as if his emotion is getting the better of him.

Alice lets out a sarcastic laugh, not knowing if he is being serious or just saying the first thing that came to his mind.

"Father Gideon has no choice in my position – it is written in law…" Alice educates until she is cut off by an ever-irate Francis.

"Laws can be changed," he butts in, stepping forward to her. Theodore holds out his hand to stop him, but Francis orders him to back off and he does. Alice, shocked by his behaviour, is forced to step back or have Francis right in her face; the monk deputy seeing this, stepping forward again.

"Not without a vote from High Council they can't, and I advise you to step away from me – who the hell do you think you are?" Alice demands, maintaining eye contact with him so he knows she is not intimidated by his bullying. The conversation is ended by the door opening and Father Gideon standing in the doorway, glaring at all three of them like a headteacher staring at naughty students.

"Francis, Theodore, please continue with your duties; Alice, come in," he orders, to which the two monks respond "yes, sir" and go on their way, and Alice takes a breath and enters Gideon's office. Sitting down at his desk the two prepare for loggerheads and Gideon gets straight to the point.

"Explain to me why you didn't attend Day Of The Saviours yesterday?" he asks, attempting to say it professionally but failing as his anger creeps in at the end.

"Because I attended Vampir Ceremoniilor," Alice responds bluntly.

"Yes, I know," Gideon snaps. "Why?" he adds with a bark.

"Because I was invited by Krul, which meant I was left with a choice to attend The Vampires' celebration or The Monks', and I chose The Vampires' because they were the founders of my gang," Alice replies honestly and positively, which seems to cause the temper in Gideon to grow almost as if he is even more irritated by the fact she is right.

"What about your loyalty to The Monks?" Gideon fires back, twitching in his chair.

"I have none," Alice states with a shrug of the shoulders. "I have a legal duty to The Monks but my loyalty is to The Messengers and last night was a celebration of the history of the gang who formed my gang, which means by celebrating with The Vampires I was in a way celebrating my own gang's birth." Alice adds meaning to every word she says with no feeling of guilt whatsoever.

Gideon stares at her, fuming, with what he sees as a rebellious attitude from somebody who is supposed to be his servant; he puts this down to Krul being a bad influence on her. "No need for me to guess who has brainwashed this attitude into you," Gideon sneers with an obnoxious look on his face.

"What is that supposed to mean?" Alice claps back, becoming sick and tired of the leader of the entire city being so disrespectful and one-dimensional.

"This is Krul talking," Father Gideon replies, his tone getting no better. "He has brainwashed you into supporting him and his cause to get his evil existence back into power," he adds with bite; his paranoia is becoming more and more evident.

"I don't see how me stating historical and political fact is Krul brainwashing me…" Alice fights back, keeping a firm grip on the moral and factual high ground of the argument.

"You wouldn't see it if you are underneath him with your legs open," Gideon shouts, standing to his feet, leaning forward on his desk. "Your sister must get it from you," he adds, banging his fist on the desk.

Alice leans back in her chair, her heart pumping, but she knows she cannot give in now. "How dare you? Because Krul and I have a mutual respect does not mean we are sleeping together; and as for my sister, who she associates with is her choice and nobody else's,"

Alice fires back, deciding as she does that this is the last time she will take this treatment from Father Gideon and Brother Francis. No more will she be treated like a lackey or a verbal punching bag for their frustrations because the city has turned against them, a turning that they have brought on themselves with their tyrannical policies, clinging to power by any means necessary; it will happen no more.

"Your sister is a disgusting slut who takes part in bestiality, fraternising with werewolves," Gideon rages, striding around his desk his face seething.

Alice jumps to her feet to retreat. "Don't you dare speak about Jessica that way, you are only like this because you are afraid of Krul," Alice says as she walks backward to the door, Gideon still coming at her. "You are terrified, you are a coward, you are paranoid that Krul will take your leadership, paranoid that Cheng will invade and crush your failing gang, you are scared that The Vampires and The Chinese have had meetings together; your mind must be in overdrive thinking about what they are doing, scared that if you call a vote you will lose miserably," Alice rants, not having anyone talk about her sister like that or treating herself in this manner.

"You are relieved of your duties, your gang no longer has its privileges, and as far as the law goes, I will call a meeting with my members and we will have the law changed; 9 Gang City is to have an overhaul of legality. Say goodbye to The Messengers," Gideon declares, returning to his desk and picking up his phone.

Alice storms out, slamming the door behind her, quickly texting Leo and Jessica to round up the gang members, planning a retreat – she can't take any risks and with Father Gideon's threats and behaviour mixed with the animosity from Brother Francis, the lack of defence from Brother Theodore who had an opportunity to speak up for what was right and didn't, mixed with the overall tension from The Monks' gang members, Alice can no longer trust The Leadership of 9 Gang City. She also texts Krul to let him know what Gideon has threatened to do, knowing he will want to know about this. She also knows he will back her up, which at the moment will be a priceless support. On her way out she is greeted by a seething Francis, still intent on a tirade of abuse, Theodore agreeing with Francis and Monk gang members, sneering and insulting with their superior's blessing. Alice should not have come here alone, but she didn't imagine for a moment it would come to this. She thought Gideon would be angry but, in the end, give his opinion and keep the peace and honour the law; she thought Francis would mouth off about what is right and wrong, but at least have a modicum of respect for her role as Messenger Leader. Alice no longer feels safe, her heart pounding so much she wants to stop and calm herself but she can't, which only makes it worse, needing to take a breath but leaving as fast as she can only makes her worse. She hasn't felt this way since the war, but even then she was surrounded by other members and people fighting for the same cause; now she is completely alone.

Slamming her foot to the floor, the car wheels spin into action. If there was a speed limit in 9 Gang City she would definitely be breaking it. When she reaches the security checks, Monk gang members stand at the border, guns in hand, signalling her to stop, which she reluctantly does.

"Sorry, traitor, you no longer have the right to be on our land," the gang member tells her, leaning into the car and taking the keys. She should have just smashed her way through, but that would have been classed as an attack and the security barriers are reinforced enough that cars cannot smash through.

"Says who?" Alice asks angrily, her adrenaline making her dizzy, her vision becoming blurred as the gang members surround her car.

This is how gang life can turn out, all this over attending a party. "Father Gideon has no right to remove my power and privilege, that is for High council to decide. Father Gideon cannot change the law and your gang can certainly not empower that change without the permission of High Council. You and your leader are risking a war, for what? Because I chose to honour history instead of modern politics?" Alice adds, attempting to endear herself to the gang members' sensible side. It is in vain: he cares not a bit about her side of the story but what his leader has ordered, this is gang life; your leader could be a liar, but you follow that lie; your enemy could be telling the truth, but to hell with truth, your gang comes first. As she finishes, her crew arrive at the border, Leo and Jessica leaping from the car and running to the fence, demanding to know what is going on and demanding Alice be allowed to pass. Alice herself hurries to greet them to tell them to retreat from Neutral Territory – that is her order as gang leader. Informing them she has texted Krul, but knowing they will have to wait for sundown for him to respond, Jessica tells Alice she has told Cuthwulf about the issue and The Werewolves are arming their troops – despite it being daylight and tonight is not a full moon, they can still fight as humans. Alice knows The Chinese and The Pagans will have none of this, The Irish will never shy away from a fight and The Cannibals will fight anybody if necessary, leaving The Witches. Queen Rika will honour the pact between her people and The Vampires, Princess Katalin may even be watching them right now, and if the rumours about Princess Tunder are true, she has been aching for this moment for years; The Monks may be in serious trouble. As soon as he got the message from Jessica, Cuthwulf sprang into action, rounding up his troops; and after not receiving word that everything is ok, The Werewolves are moving toward the border with Holy Ground, knowing if the news is true the other gangs will do the same. Worrying about Jessica, his feelings have complicated things, as he knew they would, but fantasy and desire took over and now with not just a war to worry about but a new love. Thinking The Monks have been tactical in their planning, knowing if war should happen and there not being a full moon for weeks The Werewolves will be men and men are easier to kill than Lycans. On top of that, taking control of The Messengers by daylight with The Vampires unable to help by the time the sun sets they could have removed The Messengers' rights altogether and claimed their territory, making them either political prisoners or banished refugees, 20 years of peace may be about to end.

Alice, surrounded by Monk soldiers at gunpoint and seeing her sister's eyes filling up and her dear friend Leo risking a gun fight by drawing his own weapon, tells her members to retreat from their turf and go to The Forests, knowing Cuthwulf will take them in if Jessica is there. Jessica and Leo refuse at first, but after being ordered to by their leader, and the knowledge that a fight now will mean defeat, they are outnumbered and outgunned by The Monks; however, if they only wait for a few more hours the odds will stack in their favour. It is a retreat but a tactical retreat. Father Gideon, after consulting with his deputy and 3rd, makes the call to the security staff at the border – the order is to take Alice prisoner for treason against The Leadership by breaking the law for not serving the gang in power, and because her gang followed her command, they too have broken the law and their territory is removed; their members will be allowed to leave and claim political asylum on another turf, their leader will face the consequences alone. Alice is placed under arrest and taken to Cathedral Tower. Jessica cries as she watches, and Leo tries to scale the barrier but is stopped by security. Looking into the distance, Alice sees the sun setting and knows within a matter of hours she will either be a free woman, or the city will be at war.

Chapter 11

A s soon as the sun disappears, The Vampires appear, raising from their slumber, and if the tales of old are to be believed they will haunt the night, the nightmare breed who so many fear. If that is the case, then surely mortals haunt the day, an even worse nightmare during the daylight hours who have caused more horror to each other and more damage to the world than any of the so-called evil creatures the legends of folklore speak of. Mortals need those horror stories, those dark tales to convince themselves that they are not the evil ones, but the monsters that only appear at night are the beings to be scared of; they are wrong. Fear is a strange thing, people have a fear of dying although they know they must die, a vampire can give people eternal life but they fear vampires – it doesn't make sense but the human race very rarely does; in fact, it often contradicts itself. The Monks' predecessors The Christian Vampire Slayers were exactly that, vampire slayers, because they believe vampirism is evil, an act of the demonic, an abomination on God's earth, and yet The Messiah they follow said drink this wine it is my blood at The Last Supper; and as for rising from the grave, Jesus did that as well. There are various examples of hypocrisy within Christianity and none of them are Christianity's fault; it is the fault of hypocritical Christians. For example, imagine a woman during the witch trials walked on water or turned water to wine – she would be burned at the stake as a witch; but because the Bible says Jesus did these things, he must be the son of God. Imagine a suspected witch cleansed a leper or made a blind man see, it would be used against her as evidence and she would be judged to be in league with The Devil; but if Jesus does it, what a miracle! It is sad to know that if Jesus did perform these miracles – and he may have done – for them to be belittled because of centuries of hypocrisy and contradiction from his followers only proves that circa two thousand years after his crucifixion, his sacrifice may have been in vain. Time will tell. It was a devastating day for the other gangs when they surrendered to The Vampires and The Witches, some felt they had let down their ancestors, some questioned their religious belief; all felt like failures – they were failures. They had failed to do what they set out to do, they had failed in their conquest to rid the world of "evil" and they had failed to realise that maybe in this world we are all God's creatures and if The Lord created everything then he created the "evil" as well; perhaps that is what led the victors to glory. The Christian Vampire Slayers were hit the hardest; after all, it was they who had started the whole mess by playing the saviours. Having to bow on bended knee whilst Niculi and Ziana sit on their thrones with a smile of gratification on each of their faces was a humiliation for all, but especially The CVS. Those who refused to bow, some were killed in full view of all in The Throne Room as a lesson to others who refuse to abide; most were kept for "farming" as it was called – this is when mortals were kept in cages and drained of blood for feeding, but kept alive to produce more. This was highly criticized by the other gangs until they were reminded it is similar to what people do to animals for meat and dairy products; but humans think things are different when the shoe is on the other foot. Despite his joy and pride in watching his enemies bow and beg, Niculi's favourite hobby was The Hunt – taking some captured mortals to The Forests and letting them loose, he gave them one hour to run and hide before he and his gang gave chase. Those rival gang members have long since rotted beneath the dirt of what is now The Werewolves' territory. This was one of many reasons the six gangs joined forces to fight for liberty and take the city from their leaders, this is where Gideon became a hero and in those days he was. Brother Gideon, as he was known back then, was a brave, bold, intelligent man who insisted on being a Frontline Fighter – as the name suggests these were the soldiers who fought on the frontline in The War Against The Vampires; they were always the first into battle and had to be the bravest of the brave and were selected from the six remaining gangs. Gideon did not have to be one of these fighters, he had enough connection and respect from his superiors that he could have taken a safer role within the war, but Gideon refused this mollycoddling and joined the frontline. People should remember this when they down talk or insult him. It all comes down to perspective on how heroic Gideon was – there is no doubt he was a hero but to what extent? He took up arms and fought in the war when he could have taken a back seat and given orders; this he deserves respect for. Gideon slayed not just Niculi but Ziana as well. For the same man to have done both of those things is a great and heroic as well as historic moment, but he could not have done it alone; in fact, some people criticize his glorification in this part of history. It is true many people were killed in action on the night of those historic slayings, and Gideon has very rarely acknowledged their contribution. Also, when Ziana was slayed, he only stepped forward when she was chained to the stake and it was safe for him to do so; other people did the hard work. However, during the Niculi slaying he did step forward when it seemed the assault was a lost cause. The truth be told, he was not as heroic as he and The Monks make out, but he was more heroic than he gets credit for today. The only real victor in this city is hatred, hatred for what is different than yourself, hatred for what you have been brainwashed into believing is evil, and hatred for what you don't want to exist; and all of these things breed war. Everybody has their own agenda, and it may not be the same agenda as their own gang but they find themselves pressganged into going along with the gang, which may only be the leader's desire. The Cannibals, for example, only formed for vengeance against The Vampires after a vampire attacked and killed a party full of cannibals; it is worth noting that the party was a cannibals' cult meeting and human flesh was on the menu. These people had been kidnapped and killed for the meal, but The Cannibals conveniently forget about that part when they play the blame game against The Vampires. It is true that The Vampires and The Witches have been blamed for most of the wrongdoings across the entire saga, mainly the 200 years they reigned, but as with every event in history there are not two sides to every story, there is only the truth, and the truth may not be what is remembered. History is written by the winner – that is why the current city history portrays Niculi as a horrendous monster, but when he reigned, he was portrayed as a heroic legend by his members for his centuries of fighting back against religious tyranny and a supreme victor for defeating six other gangs. As for Gideon's portrayal, time will tell how it will change; but what is almost certain is that it will change from how it currently stands. If Niculi had not been slain, the history of the city would read differently; if The Vampires and The Witches had lost The Battles, they may been remembered as less infamous. The irony for Father Gideon is if he had not been voted in after the war, history would remember him better and more fondly, so in a twisted way the slaying of Niculi and Ziana have almost worked against him in that his election was rushed through and his ego took over. If the election was done gradually, people might have voted differently and therefore Gideon's reputation would remain intact; but now what remains of a hero is a hollow existence that has forever ruined his legacy.

Chapter 12

Before he had even finished reading the messages, Krul's anger had exploded within but at the same time an excitement at what this night may hold. Giving the order to Victuis to ready the troops, he tells Enigma to take a group of members to scout the border, knowing by now The Monks will have sent reinforcements to back up their security forces. Krul rings Alice's phone on the off-chance she still has it. No answer, as he expected – The Monks will have taken it from her when she was arrested. Secondly, he calls Queen Rika, to request honouring the pact between the two gangs – if war should happen their people will fight side by side once again; the witch queen confirms the pact will be honoured and the conjurers of dark magic rally their members. Krul also asks to meet at the border between their territories. Thirdly, he phones Cuthwulf, asking if Jessica and The Messengers are now political refugees on his turf, Cuthwulf confirms this and informs Krul that both gangs are armed, ready for action and camped on the border. Fourthly, Krul calls Cheng – the east side of the city have borders with Neutral Territory and may have information on any activity they have seen or heard; also this could be the moment The Chinese have been waiting for. Cheng reveals he has spoken to Father Gideon and issued him with a warning to free Alice and restore The Messengers' rights and privileges to the full extent of the law or face invasion. Father Gideon responded by warning Cheng against an illegal war and that Alice had been arrested for breaking the very law he wants restored. Cheng also tells Krul that all the military activity in China Town has The Irish and The Pagans nervous and they too armed their troops. The Cannibals will have no choice but to fight if war should break out. Finally, Krul phones Father Gideon, who clearly has been expecting the call from the way he answered, an almost planned to perfection delay in picking up the phone – it rang four times. If someone is desperate for your call, they are waiting by the phone, maybe even have it in their hand and answer immediately after one ring. If someone is not expecting a call they maybe are not by the phone or are considering ignoring it, so it rings maybe eight to ten times; but if someone is expecting your call and they don't want to speak to you but know they have to, they delay answering to prepare for the conversation or to make it look like they are not waiting for your call, so they allow it to ring four or five times even though the phone is next to them and they are watching it, waiting for you to ring. Krul is on to him and smiles.

"Father Gideon," Krul says in a fake politeness to break the ice. "It seems we have a problem that only you can rectify," Krul adds, listening to Gideon's breathing pattern down the phone. The leader is nervous, which is a good sign – it means there is a chance to negotiate Alice's release without bloodshed.

"We have a very big problem," Gideon responds, trying to calm his heartbeat, knowing within minutes a full-scale attack could begin and yet at the same time wanting his authority respected. Vampires can pick up on things that mortals can't, and to Krul, Gideon's heartbeat is echoing down the phone. "The Messengers broke the law last night on the order of their leader. I have shown mercy on the rest of them because they were just following that order, but Alice knows the law just as much as you or I, so her illegal activity cannot go unpunished," Gideon finishes, trying to hide his breathlessness.

"What law was been broken?" Krul inquires, already knowing but wanting it confirmed.

"The eighth law," Father Gideon answers without hesitation, as if answering instantly makes the charge more legitimate.

"The Messengers work for whichever gang is in power," Krul claps back, quoting the law word for word. Gideon murmurs the confirmation but doesn't actually say it. "The law is work for, not serve or do as they are told; it is a role of duties and requests to do with the running of the city, not to be your gang's lackeys," he adds, becoming irritated, knowing full well this is because Alice attended Vampir Ceremoniilor and not Day Of The Saviours.

Gideon thinks for a while before continuing. Krul knows Gideon doesn't want war – if he did he would have barked a load of tough talk down the phone and hung up.

"They were required to work last night to prepare our celebration; they were not available to work – the law was broken," the leader retorts, almost clinging to a reason to keep Alice prisoner.

Krul laughs at his ridiculous comment and decides on his next move. "I am going to call you back in two hours. If Alice is not released, I will be the first to attack your gang," Krul declares and hangs up before Gideon can respond.

Victuis returns, telling Krul the gang is ready for battle and Enigma calls to confirm there are extra monks on the border. Time is ticking and Krul gives the order for Victuis to take the troops and meet Enigma and the others and march on the border but not to attack. Krul heads to The Moors to discuss tactics with Rika. Arriving to an invisible presence hanging in the air, an atmospheric haunting grips the darkness and the view of The Moors sees a hollow and soulless place. Krul turns way from the fence to look into the distance, but quickly darts his eyes back to see Queen Rika standing before him. A look of conquest tells Krul she is ready.

"It was on a dark night on a border that Niculi and Ziana met," Krul charms the witch queen, who takes the bait and smiles with delight.

"A historic couple bonded by love," Rika responds, her gaze never leaving Krul's, who nods his respect to the legends of their gang's past.

"A historic couple taken from our people by religious fascists who right now threaten the city our gangs built," Krul says with a solemn but angry tone.

"So the histories tell it," Rika replies cryptically. Krul's expression changes from anger to confusion, not knowing what she means. "Taken from us for a time but not forever, the city history states that before Gideon burned Ziana at the stake, she cast one last spell. The other gangs thought this was just legend and Gideon assumed when she burned that would kill the spell's power. It didn't," Rika reveals with pride at her predecessor's genius.

"Can a spell live on after the witch has died? I thought that was only curses," Krul inquires, growing interested in what Ziana has conjured.

"If the spell is complete then only magic can counteract it, the spell was completed and only we can counteract it, the spell will come true," Queen Rika informs him as his mind runs wild with anticipation of what the spell is and when it will happen.

"What is the spell?" Krul asks forcefully, almost desperate to know.

Rika smiles at his eagerness and moves closer to the fence.

"Queen Ziana and Niculi will return," Rika reveals with fire in her eyes and she grows slightly in height. "The witch queen and the vampire leader will rule together again," she adds with a desire for power and bond in her heart.

Krul steadies himself after this revelation. If this is true it changes everything, suddenly instead of Krul fighting to gain power he may just be clearing the way for Niculi's return. Queen Rika seems certain of what the spell was and yet at the same time she was not there, the only people present were Ziana and The Monks, Gideon and his men could not understand what she said because legend has it she cast the spell in Hungarian.

"How can you be certain?" Krul asks, digging for more information. "Ziana was the only live witch there," he adds, at which Rika smiles at his factual knowledge but slightly annoyed by his lack of understanding in magic, though this is to be expected.

"We have ways," Rika responds with a snide look in her eye. "A witch gains power with every moment of magic, a witch can specialise in a certain type of magic or she can spread her learning and knowledge across the spectrum of magic," she adds, Krul becoming intrigued by the different magic styles a witch can have – there was once a time he thought a witch was a witch, but he was wrong. There are good witches, bad witches, good spells, bad spells, there are even different good witches and different bad witches; the list is long, so long that only a witch truly knows how long.

"When will the return happen?" Krul's curiosity is taking over.

"That was never told, the Goddess Of Witches will return when the time is right," Rika replies, her excitement growing every time she speaks of Ziana.

Krul looks her in the eye for a moment; her stare back is intense and the vampire leader is sceptical of the revelation. Anyhow, with Alice locked up and the city on the brink of war, Krul needs to get the meeting back to its original purpose and looks back at the witch queen after looking into the distance at the border with Holy

Ground, which is visible on the horizon.

"War may be upon us," Krul states, bringing the conversation back.

Rika smiles, unfazed by the situation they find themselves in. "You want me to send Princess Katalin to Cathedral Tower to spy on The Monks?" the queen replies, confident she knows Krul's plan, who looks at her with surprise – but with a witch you should never be surprised by what they can do or know.

Krul nods, confirming the plan and thanks Rika for her help as a black cat appears by her feet, Rika looking down at the shadow-like feline before it runs towards the border. Krul watches Katalin as she disappears into the darkness to do what she does best and upon looking back at Rika he is distracted by something behind her, a pair of eyes looking at him as Princess Tunder appears.

"Szia, Princess," Krul politely says as Tunder comes into full view.

"Hello, Krul," Tunder menacingly replies.

Krul, not knowing what to say, turns the conversation onto their common ground.

"Victuis has taken our members to the border in case we go to war," he tells Tunder in case she was wondering.

Tunder looks into the distance at the border as if looking for Victuis. "There will be no war tonight," she responds to Krul's surprise.

"Is that a spell, a prediction or future sight?" the vampire responds, his eagerness for knowledge giving away his desperation to gain power.

Rika steps in to reassure him. "If my sister says there will not be a war tonight, there will be no war tonight," the queen states in full knowledge and trust of her sister's powers.

Krul has ended up with more questions than answers and has come to the realisation that it may be a lot more complicated than just going to war and taking power – there are other forces at play.

"It may be lot more complicated than just going to war and taking power, there are other forces at play," Rika tells him his thoughts. Krul begins to wonder what else his mind has given away. "Clear your mind of complicating thoughts, I can help you with that," she adds with a look of desire and control.

Krul informs her he must get back to his gang and prepare for possible battle, despite what Princess Tunder has said, who has disappeared amidst all the talk of thoughts and complications. An hour has passed by the time he gets back to his troops and Krul informs Victuis and Enigma of the plan and that Princess Katalin is on a spying mission and all they can do now is play the waiting game; and as he does, Krul goes over in his mind what Queen Rika said to him and – can it be true? – a return from the dead of Niculi and Ziana, a victorious conquest of 9 Gang City reinstating the legendary figures of vampirism and dark magic, or is it all a mirage of the mind? Has Rika misinterpreted the spell, has history created a myth that generations to come will talk about? Krul is glad of the knowledge but he didn't need it right now as it is distracting him from what could be the biggest moment of his vampiric life, even more so than when he was elected leader. Imagine the impact a return would have, imagine the devastation it would bring to the other gangs, it would demoralise them potentially beyond repair, thinking all these years they have destroyed and rid the city of their evil foes only to have to face the realisation that they had to face them again would bring some of the rival gang members to their knees, again.

Krul gets a text message from Brigacos informing him The Pagans and The Irish have moved their troops to their borders with Holy Ground, meaning The Monks are now almost fully surrounded – only The Cannibals are yet to move or announce a move to their border; perhaps they are biding their time. Krul wouldn't put it past Davis to wait until war has started and spring his attack after the gangs have decimated each other, giving them a better chance of outright victory. It is a good plan from The Cannibals because as things stand it is probably their best way of gaining power. Krul will keep an eye on that situation because the other gangs have either forgotten or been dismissive of The Cannibals by not inquiring as to their plan of war, or almost taken it for granted that they will attack just because everyone else has.

After texting Aiden for confirmation of The Irish advancement and receiving it almost instantly, Krul moves his mind onto Katalin's mission and what she has found out – by now she will have made it to Cathedral Tower and seen how The Monks are forming and listened in to what they are planning. She will also have spoken to Alice to ask her how she is and to inform her on how much the city is supporting her. Krul knows The Monks would not have mistreated her, but she will be locked up in a room. These rooms will be familiar to Alice as they were the sleeping quarters of The Messengers during Niculi and Ziana's reign – they are not damp, dark prison cells, but to be locked up against your will is bad enough. Krul predicts The Monks' tactic will be to have most of their troops on the defensive and protect Cathedral Tower; they don't really have a choice – if they were to scatter across Holy Ground they will be horrendously outnumbered, better to stay with safety in numbers although they will still be outnumbered; but the more they stick together, the stronger the defence. Time is running out and the vampire leader glances over to his friend and true love with a feeling of nervousness beginning to fester and the thought of whether he should order Enigma to stay with him so he can protect her, or send her out with a battalion to attack from a different angle – after all, she is much more experienced in war than he is and can certainly look after herself. The pressure of being a leader is relentless and your duty is never finished until you are dead or kicked to the kerb, but you can be remembered forever. Krul's time to make history may be minutes away.

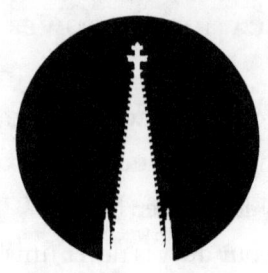

Chapter 13

Alice sits on the bed in a room she recognises. It her was her room before the war when she served Niculi and Ziana, and it says a lot about the current regime because, despite their "evil", they never locked her up as a prisoner like she has been by Father Gideon. The Leader thought it would be rubbing salt in the wounds by putting Alice in her old room and giving her a taste of what defying her master is like, and if she had've been more loyal to her duties, she would be free with her people on their land. In fact, the imprisonment has had the opposite effect – it has proven beyond doubt that in some ways Gideon is worse than Niculi, 9 Gang City has become more divided since The Monks gained power, and the time has come for Alice – if she gets her freedom – to request a High Council meeting and put to the vote The Messengers being released from their service to the leading gang and have their own free will.

Alice hears a light flutter outside her window, the stained glass is difficult to see through and has bars on the outside, but the way the light is shining she can make out the shadow of a bird on the window ledge. A fog seeps into the room but Alice remains unmoved, not frightened and yet a slight nervousness of being alone with her visitor. The fog gradually takes the form of a woman and Alice's visitor comes into full view.

"Hello, Katalin," Alice says calmly, but her heart quickens.

Katalin smiles, hearing the thud of Alice's heartbeat, and sits next to her on the bed and stares at her.

"Good evening, Alice," Katalin replies in a well-spoken and soft voice. "You have a lot of friends in this city and they are all at their respective borders," she adds a subliminal twist, which Alice picks up on and looks at the witch cautiously.

"Thank you for your visit, but be careful – there are assassins in Cathedral Tower," Alice politely warns, but the comment is itself subliminal. Katalin smiles at the retort and moves closer to her host. Alice feels the tensions rise.

"I am the spy for my people; if it were an assassin being sent, my sister would have massacred the place by now, a banquet for wolves and crows," Katalin reassures her, but at the same time hinting at her desires and tastes. Alice tries to remain calm by remembering that Katalin has probably been sent by Rika on the request of Krul. Now that darkness has fallen, she knows it is only a matter of time before Gideon is forced into a decision. Katalin stands and faces Alice, causing her to look up at the witch, who stares down with a glow in her eye. Turning to the corner of the room, Katalin removes something for her possession but Alice cannot see what it is until she sees the witch draw a circle of blood on the floor before turning back to face her.

"My sister taught me a spell; it is a brilliant trick and a historic one too," Katalin informs Alice, who is still sat on the bed, glancing at the circle of blood before looking back at Katalin, who has stepped into the circle and motions Alice to join her. Cautious but willing, nervous but intrigued, she joins the witch, the circle so small they are face to face, almost making contact. Alice's heart pounds, Katalin's face lights up.

"During The Battles, the closest The CVS came to slaying the fallen Queen and King was in Bohemia centuries ago and they would have succeeded had it not been for this spell," Katalin explains as she wraps her arms around Alice, holding her position for a short time and then clapping her hands. Going up in a cloud of flame and smoke, Alice feels a dream-like sensation, almost as if she is travelling quickly in slow motion, a dream that feels real and yet she knows it isn't. She feels so light it is as if she is weightless, almost as if the life has evaporated from her body and she is in spirit form, floating through a gravity-less realm between life and non-life but not death. Alice feels a soft force against her lips as a firm but dilatate grip encircles her body, a light headedness takes control, and her vison becomes blurred. Alice awakens bolt upright looking around the creepy and decrepit house and catches the glare of the three witch sisters stood staring at her; the feeling of discomfort is instant. At the back of the room she sees more witches gathering, some climbing out of the walls. The Cauldron is packed with the queen and her hive. Alice stands quickly and on the defensive, looking around at her hosts. Rika becomes slightly irritated, Katalin almost rolls her eyes at how predictably she has reacted and Tunder likes the smell of fear oozing from her.

"Why are your kind always so frightened in the presence of my people?" Rika asks with a concerning voice but a hint of anger at the constant discrimination against witches.

"Folklore runs deep," Alice responds, attempting to explain her reaction to her surroundings, but at the same time understanding that her behaviour may be offensive.

"There are not two sides to every story, there is only the truth and the truth is your kind have persecuted mine a lot more than the other way around," Rika fires back. Alice nods her head in acceptance. "Is this your gratitude to us after we have just freed you from your captors, your religious, political, social and legal superiors, who you helped get them to where they are and that was how they treat you simply because you honoured history and celebrated the gang who founded your own? We too played a part in your formation so perhaps a little respect is in order," the queen barks, her voice turning almost to a growl as she rants. It's enough to put Alice in her place but also raises the fear factor – she has no hope of escaping, she is at The Witches' mercy. Alice needs to play the diplomat and play down the tension; quickly thinking, she comes to the person they have in common.

"Where is Krul?" Alice asks, looking around at the room as if looking for him, but really she is checking how many witches surround her. "Does he know I am here?" she adds, suspecting he doesn't but hopes he does.

"He is at the border, ready to attack if you are not released," Rika replies, knowing Alice is hoping Krul is on his way. "We will let him know you are free," she adds.

The look of relief becomes evident on Alice's face, knowing the current situation falls perfectly into her hands but the reason The Witches have brought her to their headquarters cannot just be a helping hand. Why bring her here without telling Krul?

"Then why bring me here and not to the border? Why the secret escape?" Alice inquires.

"Because I want you to do something for me," Rika answers immediately, almost as if she has been aching to tell her. "When an election is called, I want you to vote for The Witches," she adds, causing confusion with Alice who looks at her shocked.

"An election?" Alice replies as a question. "What election? Has Father Gideon called a vote for leadership?" Alice adds, unaware of such an announcement.

Rika smiles and gives a slight shrug of the shoulders.

"Not yet, but it is only a matter of time, you were his only leverage and now nothing is in the way to attack The Monks," the witch queen tells her, believing her plan is already in motion to gain power.

"I can convince the other gangs not to go to war," Alice states, confident of her diplomacy skills – there is no need to go to war; her escape will embarrass The Monks enough.

Queen Rika shakes her head at the lack of forward thinking from Alice; the good girl approach all the time is growing irritating for Rika and her sisters.

"Always the girl guide, the school prefect, the law-abiding citizen who never puts a foot wrong – doesn't your life ever get boring?" Queen Rika asks in an obnoxious tone.

"Keeping the peace is never boring," Alice snaps back, taking offence at the comment. "You remember the war – do you want those burning at the stake to happen again? They will if war happens," she adds, warning Rika to be careful what she wishes for.

"Guilty conscience?" Rika responds as a question, meaning Alice was on the side of the people who burned witches during the war.

Alive stands unresponsive to the comment, thinking it was a snide remark that doesn't need answering, but The Witches take her silence as a confirmation of guilt. Tunder twitches with fury at the lack of response or apology and steps forward, Queen Rika holding out her hand motioning her to stop. Alice, staring at The Dark Fairy, sees her cold, merciless eyes glaring at her, the look of animosity enough to make Alice look away with a haunting chill running down her spine. Her options are non-existent, and Alice ponders what Rika has said and finds it almost impossible to believe her vote will make any difference whatsoever as The Vampires will be the only other gang to do so. But with Rika's request taking a vote away from The Vampires, if a vote did happen Alice would vote for Krul; what does this mean for the friendship between The Witches and The Vampires?

"If I did vote for you that would mean Krul loses a vote. What about your union and friendship?" Alice inquires, attempting to make Rika feel disloyal in her request, but the witch stares blankly at her, carefree of the consequence.

"The union will be honoured, Krul will be made deputy and rule with me," Queen Rika responds in a dismissive manner as Alice should worry about her own issues. "I know you have desires of your own about Krul, but do you really think he would choose you over a chance to rule with me and have our people join together again like the times of old and restore this city to its former glory?" she mocks with a snotty tone at what she believes is Alice's fantasy.

"I think you overestimate your desirability; Krul and Enigma have a vampire bond that cannot be broken, not even by magic," Alices answers abruptly, causing a fury to grow in the witch queen before composing herself.

"Estimates and desirability are whatever magic make them, a mortal woman with limited desirability and a clueless dismissal of magic wouldn't realise that, your gang are a limited people with limited use in a city of limitless prosperity, which is clearly the most powerful city in the world and tag-alongs like you should consider themselves honoured and privileged to be along for the ride," Queen Rika fires back with venom and insult, still fired up from Alice's comment. With one final question to ask and proud of herself for at least putting up an argument in such intimidating circumstances, Alice looks at the queen who glares back, irritated by her attitude.

"What if I refuse?" she asks.

"You won't," Rika responds with an evil smile. "You either agree of your own will or you agree by our power – your choice," she says, warning of her taking no refusal.

Alice takes a moment to think before nodding her head in agreement. "Yes, I will vote for you," she replies, frightened of what the future holds.

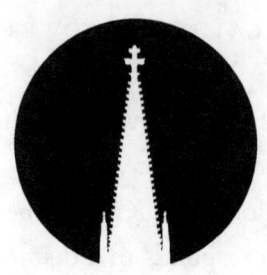

Chapter 14

Krul feels the soft but forceful impact against his leg and immediately recognises the feeling. Looking down, he sees Katalin purring as she turns to rub against him again. Looking into the distance, the black cat stares as if telling Krul to look – he does and can't believe his eyes: Alice walking across his turf from the direction of The Moors. Not knowing quite what is going on, but delighted to see her, he rushes to greet her with a passionate hug. She embraces him back, knowing it was since his involvement that action has been taken and she is free. Pulling away from the embrace, Krul sees the three witches stood behind Alice and thanks them for their assistance, not only in freeing Alice but turning the tide completely in their favour because now The Monks can be given an ultimatum and the outlook of the city begins to brighten for the citizens. Now with seven gangs combined and waiting for a decision from Father Gideon that can no longer be made, the combined forces hold all the cards.

Krul's excitement grows as he makes the call to Gideon, who surely by now knows he is a prisoner short and his leverage has gone. The phone answers instantly; with a fearful tone and a breaking of his voice, Gideon knows his time is up.

"Father Gideon," Krul barks in a demanding manner and a tone of victory, the perfect victory where your enemy knows they are defeated and you have not had to cause any bloodshed. "As I am sure you are aware your prisoner is no longer your illegal captive but is a free citizen of this city. We are mere seconds away from attacking, but we are willing to show mercy," Krul adds, hearing Gideon's heart thunder and his breathlessness giving away his fear.

"I am willing to negotiate" is the reply from a decimated Gideon, his confidence shot and his pride and motivation destroyed; once a mighty warrior but now a dictator brought crashing down in shame by his very own hand. He should never have had Alice arrested, he should never have taken The Messengers' territory and privileges, he should have just accepted it was Alice's choice what celebration to attend, and most of all he should have stepped down long ago. Now he is scared of what the future holds.

"You have two choices," Krul offers, but really it is a demand and a threat. "You either call an election or have your gang wiped out," Krul adds.

The tension grows and all around wait for his answer. Gideon hesitates as if agonising over the decision. Krul falls silent, Victuis looks confident, and Enigma's excitement is evident for all to see as the witch sisters remain calm until a decision is given and Alice is nervous of what the result of either may bring.

"What guarantees will you give me?" Gideon asks.

"If we go to war, I guarantee at the very least we will be renamed 8 Gang City," Krul threatens, echoing his previous threat of monk annihilation. "If you call a vote your fate will be decided by High Council," he adds, not revealing his intent for the soon-to-be-fallen leader, which only strikes more fear into Gideon.

The hero of the past and the present dictator knows his time has come and he must make the best decision for his gang; no matter what happens to him he doesn't want his gang to fall, but it could be too late. Father Gideon takes a deep breath.

"I will call an election," he utters in a heartbroken voice.

Krul's smile beams across his face, giving away to the people around him what choice Gideon has made; they celebrate. The cheers roar across vampire territory so much that The Werewolves and The Messengers can hear in The Forests coming from the distance, so much so that Cuthwulf phones Krul and after hearing the engaged tone phones Victuis. The vampire deputy gives the lowdown and the fresh development from Cathedral Tower and informs him to tell Jessica and The Messengers that Alice is free. Tears build in Jessica's eyes and she wants to hug her sister to celebrate her freedom. Krul tells Gideon to reinstate Alice to her position and her gang to their territory instantly, and demands the vote be held tomorrow night, to which The Leader reluctantly agrees.

Father Gideon sits alone at his desk, alone in the room and alone in life. He casts his mind back to his heroic days, when he was brave in battle; now he feels a coward in leadership. The glory days when people called him Gideon The Great, now only the bootlickers call him that to suck up to him. It has been a long road to failure for Gideon.

The Vampires and The Witches escort Alice back to Neutral Territory. Cuthwulf and his crew bring the rest of her gang across Holy Ground, making sure they beep their horns and cheer louder every time they see a monk gang member, who are stood humiliated and defeated without a shot fired only seems to rub salt into their wounds even more. Giving up without a fight, surrendering without at least a show of pride in their gang and belief only goes to show the monk gang members that perhaps the opinion from the city about Father Gideon is true and their thoughts begin to turn on their leader.

Stopping outside Cathedral Tower, The Vampires gather to celebrate and humiliate, the witch sisters join them in the joy of their bitter rivals' downfall; The Werewolves and The Messengers arrive, Jessica jumping from the car and embracing her sister; Leo hugs both. The gates to The Waiting Yard are chained shut, some gang members try to force them open but stop to shout abuse at Father Gideon when they see him standing in the window of his office, Francis and Theodore nowhere to be seen. Gideon disappears from view and Krul's phone rings instantly; it is Gideon requesting they leave the area now that an agreement has been made – let us wait until tomorrow to discuss proceedings. After speaking with Alice they agree to Gideon's request and take the gangs to Neutral Territory. A party erupts, Alice inviting The Vampires in and also inviting Cheng, Brigacos, Aiden and their gangs, which makes the festivities even bigger than the previous night, Aiden informing Krul the only reason he and his crew had not attended Vampir Ceremoniilor was because of his strong Catholic beliefs and seeing vampirism as an act of indecency against humankind on God's earth. Krul responding by telling him he sounds like Father Gideon and to not take the place of The Monks, Aiden telling Krul he has nothing against him personally, just his way of life. Krul tells Aiden to ease up on the drink as he is beginning to sound insulting. Aiden stops talking.

Krul walks away and mingles with the party goers, has a friendly dance with Jessica, followed by a passionate dance with Enigma, all the time noticing that Queen Rika has been making her way around the present High Council members and is in conversation a lot more than usual. Wondering what her game is, he asks her to dance. The queen is very beautiful; it seems as though she becomes younger and more beautiful as time goes on. With his hands firmly but respectfully gripping her waist and her hands around the back of his neck, at times gently stroking the back of his hair, they glide and sway around the dance floor, their eyes never leaving each other's gaze. Enigma is furious but Victuis tells her to calm down – they are just discussing politics,

"You seem to be getting along better than usual with our rivals," Krul says, but what he really means is what are you up to?

Rika laughs at his failure to disguise his true meaning – does he not remember she has already told him his thoughts? Her smile lighting up her face to a point people would be forgiven if they forgot she is a witch, it is a smile of angelic-like beauty, a smile that makes people take a second look in shock, they have never seen her like this before; is it the thought of a vote, a new leader and a brighter future for 9 Gang City or is it just the effect Krul has on women? She pulls him closer, gently caressing the back of his head, losing herself in his stare. He returns the gesture by holding her in a more passionate embrace, her eyes becoming kaleidoscopic, drawing Krul in even more. The room has stopped to watch their performance as the two allies of darkness rise from the ground and hover as they glide, lost in the moment, lost in a realm of fantasy within reality.

"I am recruiting votes for our rise back to the top," Rika informs him as they touch down gently back to the floor.

"Our rise to the top?" Krul asks with an inquisitive look.

"The witch queen and vampire leader will rule together again," Rika repeats the spell cast by Ziana before her demise. "Your mind is occupied by trivial issues like freeing servants and equality for unequal beings; let me give you an insight of our glory," the queen adds.

Krul suddenly pictures in his mind sitting proud and honourable on a grand throne with a crown of glory placed neatly on his head, holding his queen's hand across their thrones in the throne room where Niculi and Ziana once sat. The entire room kneeling to pay homage to their leaders and celebrating the true leaders' rise back to their true position as rulers of the city their predecessors had built after the most glorious victory this world has ever seen; that queen is Rika. Snapping out of the image he wouldn't think himself he sees the belief on her face and begins to wonder how Rika can be so certain the spell is true, and if it is, where does that leave Enigma – if Krul did become leader he would want to rule with his current love and even the thought of being with another woman makes him feel disloyal.

"If I rule, it will be Enigma I rule with," Krul informs the witch queen, who pauses for a moment as if composing herself before giving a fake smile.

"Your loyalty is admirable, but destiny awaits," she replies, pulling him into her again to continue their dance, Enigma seeing enough has to be held back by Victuis.

"Get your own man," she shouts over, seething, the room falling deathly silent as a bigger event than the vote for leadership could unfold, a falling out between The Vampires and The Witches would be catastrophic for them, great for everyone else and the biggest shock this city has ever seen. "Sat in your dingy shithole with your spell book and your hocus pocus and you can't even conjure up someone to fuck you. Stay away from him, bitch," Enigma adds, blowing her lid; this, the final straw, and still trying to get over to Rika with Victuis holding her back as she erupts. Her anger so intense that Katalin and Tunder are over to back up their sister. Krul rushes over to calm things down, grabbing his girlfriend and ordering her to stop. The atmosphere is toxic and the rest of the gangs are shocked and clueless what to do or think. Alice, as they are in her territory, attempts to play mediator but she knows she can do nothing in this circumstance but still tries and is thanked by Krul for her help and diplomacy; but Enigma turns on her as well. "You can fuck yourself as well, you fake bitch, always the good girl, always saying and doing the right thing, but always with your eyes on Krul, it is time all of you sluts in 9 Gang were put in your place. I am the number one woman in this city, I am the alpha female and any bitch who thinks otherwise, step forward and prove me wrong. Fuck Rika with her magic, fuck Alice with her obsession with leadership, and fuck The Chinese with their military," Enigma rants to the entire room, the aggression and insult so bad that Victuis pushes her forcefully towards the door and tells her to get out, with Krul left to apologise for the outburst to Alice, Cheng and his deepest apology is given to Queen Rika and her sisters.

Rika points to Enigma as she looks at Krul.

"Over five centuries of affiliation, union and bond, and you are going to throw it away for that?" the witch queen asks with a look of bewilderment.

Krul responds by apologising again and walks away with a feeling of shame and anger that this could jeopardise everything, Enigma still ranting as she is ushered to the door by Victuis. Krul glaring at his raving 3rd In Command, having to walk past some of the rival gang members and feeling the embarrassment build. As he passes The Irish, Aiden laughs and gives his opinion.

"There goes the election, Krul," he sneers at the vampire leader's potential defeat before the vote has even started. "You should keep that animal in a cage," Aiden adds insult to political injury.

In his current mood and added to the comment Aiden made earlier, Krul snaps, turning to the Irish leader and flooring him with a punch. For a split second everybody freezes, shocked at what he has done. This is the death of The Vampires' hope for leadership and Krul's quest for ruling 9 Gang City; people can't quite believe he has done it, Alice and Jessica almost open mouthed as Cormac steps forward to attack Krul, Siobhan lunging at him in retaliation.

Victuis and Enigma charge over, followed by their crew as Krul drops Cormac with a punch as Siobhan crashes a glass across Krul's face, a brawl begins. After seeing Siobhan attack Krul, Enigma goes to work, charging her down and laying a horrendous beating, blow after blow to the Irish woman's face and body before opening her mouth to bite. Victuis seeing this stops her, pulling her back after he finishes laying into Cormac and dropping a few rivals. Aiden up off the floor and knowing his gang are outpowered but not taking the attack lightly, breaks a chair, taking the leg from it to use as a stake, an old trick from the war – use anything as a weapon against your enemy and if it is made of wood then it can be used as a wooden stake. Siobhan lies unconscious and beaten bloody on the ground, her face covered in crimson, Cormac struggles up to fight on as many of his gang are laid out, and Aiden goes for Krul. Aiming the stake at Krul's heart and about to strike, he is thrown across the room crashing into the wall, an unseen force bringing an end to the fight as the fighting gang members are all floored by a wave ripping itself across the ground. Only Victuis remains standing. Everybody looks around to see Princess Tunder standing glorious in her display of power, making sure all present know she is not going to squabble or brawl, she will destroy and conquer. Alice is obliged to speak up but struggles to find the right words in the immediate aftermath of a city-changing event.

"Somebody needs to see to Siobhan." She thinks is the first concern, maintain life. Jessica crouches down to the blood-filled face and battered body of The Irish 3rd In Command, Cormac helping her attend to his crew member, Aiden slumped motionless against the wall. "I suggest you all return to your territories," Alice adds, her voice still shaken from the event as The Pagans attend to Aiden who is coming around but very groggy.

"He will be fine," a voice floats across the room from Tunder; all around still standoffish after her performance, but in the back of their mind wondering if the city should go to war how would they defeat such power if she can flatten an entire room with going near a soul? The gangs exit, the celebration turned sour, all cautiously and with both eyes firmly locked on each other, the mood toxic and out of all of them Krul's mind is the most conflicted as to what consequences he will face and the chances of a victorious election have dramatically faded because of his snapped temper caused by the obsession of his most loved person.

Chapter 15

Outside The Messenger Headquarters, Krul approaches Enigma to give her a dressing down but The Countess wants nothing to do with his telling off, still fuming from his recent behaviour, the constant flirting with other women, the obsession with power; the only time he talks to her these days is to give an order.

"I don't care what you have to say," she rages as Krul approaches her, the tears streaming down her face.

Krul continues towards her, his face like thunder. "I know you don't care," he snaps, having none of her attitude. "You only care about your own obsession, twisted by jealousy. Do you realise you have ruined everything, ten years of hard work down the drain because of your possessive behaviour?" Krul shouts at her.

"My obsession – what about yours? The only thing you care about is power," Enigma shouts back as they get in each other's face, Victuis attempting to calm them but failing as the rest of the gang pretend not to look and listen.

"It is not the only thing I care about but if that is what you think you can step down from your position and leave whenever you want," Krul fires back, not wanting to give in. "I've had enough of your attitude, go," he shouts, pointing into the distance for her to leave.

Running to a car, she takes the keys from a gang member and wheel spins off, racing down the road as Victuis tries to stop her and turning to Krul with a look of disappointment that the night has ended like this and their chance of power has ended, Krul stares back, somehow feeling a failure in how things have turned out, watching the car disappear into the distance as he ponders the repercussions. This will be considered a breaking of the law – no battle can take place on Neutral Territory and Krul knows he has no excuse or way out; in fact, if anybody else did it he would be the first one to speak out against it. JHe has no hope of getting away with this, but the result is far from clear. One thing is for certain: The Monks will have a field day with this and it will soften whatever defeat they are likely to have at the vote, but as they are still in charge they will either have Krul arrested, ban The Vampires from voting, or take away their High Council powers – all of these things are possible, even all three outcomes could happen. What he has done is a serious offence; the way Alice looked at him told the story of how much trouble he is in. All this on top of what The Irish will do; there is a chance they will ask for a vote with High Council to go to war with The Vampires, Aiden will not want to let Krul get away with his attack, and both Aiden and Cormac will want revenge for Enigma's beating to Siobhan. There is a chance High Council will vote to allow the war and also some gangs may go as far as to join with Aiden and his crew to assist in their vengeance. The Monks will certainly make such an offer, The Pagans might join them, and there is a chance The Chinese would do the same to take away their main military threat which at the moment is The Vampires – and not forgetting The Cannibals: they could join to gain some respect and leverage from some sections of the city, so straight away that means most of the city will be at war with Krul and his members. The Messengers may be dragged into this possible future war because of having to work for the gang in power, so as much as Alice wouldn't want to, she might have to because if The Monks promise to join The Irish in war and the other gangs see this, it could very well gain The Monks some votes; so one heat-of-the-moment punch from Krul because of a snide comment and his anger at his girlfriend's behaviour has cost his gang dearly and now given The Monks some breathing space.

Krul's problems don't end there. After such a damaging act, his own gang may turn against him and rebel against his leadership, causing him to call a vote for gang leader. This is a possibility but not a certainty; the rest of the gang know that if a war should happen then it would more than likely be better to have Krul in charge through such a war, but if not, then a vote would have to be taken and the likelihood is that Victuis would win, maybe even Enigma as there are still some old school vampires in their ranks who would vote for her if she stood. There is another possibility as well: there is a chance Enigma could break away from the gang altogether and form her own; there was talk when Krul became leader about separating into two different gangs, but Krul himself stopped it because he knew a unified gang is a stronger gang; however, there were certainly vampires who wanted to break away. Enigma is well loved by certain sections of the crew and there is no doubt some would join her and they would be the hardcore crew members, the warmongers and extremists who would be what Krul needs to back him if war should be declared.

All this is racing through Krul's mind as he gets into his car, not saying a word to his deputy who knows his best friend's time may be up, and is it best if Victuis stands for leadership of the gang or is that rubbing salt into his wounds? There are big decisions to make and one of them is arming the troops and preparing for war.

Enigma wipes away the tears that are still rolling down, leaving a mascara trail down both cheeks that she cannot see in the rear view because vampires don't have a reflection and with nobody with her to wipe them away she will have to leave them to run. What is she to do? Is this the end of her love for her leader? The way he spoke to her as if it is her fault, is she just supposed to watch him flirt with every woman in the city? How can he not know he has caused this and all for what, some votes? She has noticed his growing obsession of late – he is always talking about the city and how he can gain the upper hand over this gang or how he can outsmart that gang. He spent more time with Rika tonight and more with Alice last night, all for a step closer to dominance. Enigma, still in Neutral Territory but close to the border with Holy Ground, looks in her mirrors and sees nothing, no rivals and no vampire cars following her home; they must have stayed a while longer to resolve some issues. Driving on and with her mind running wild, she is suddenly hit by another car coming out of a pathway into a wood. The car sideswipes hers and she spins into a 360 before looking to her side out of the window as the glass is smashed and her face burns, leaving her in agony and for a few seconds unable to react. This gives the attacker enough time to open the door and dowse her with another batch of holy water, melting her face and the side of her head. The Countess is helpless and defenceless. Dragged out of the car and thrown to the floor, Enigma looks up at her assassin and sees a figure stood over her, dressed in all black and a hood over their head covering their face. The killer produces a crossbow, aiming at her chest, and Enigma, too weak to fight back, thinks of Krul. She regrets what she has done and her love for him has always been true. The assassin pulls the trigger, the crossbow firing the stake from point blank range plunging into her heart. Enigma gasps as it penetrates; fading away, she pictures her beloved in her mind's eye – he looked very handsome at the celebration last night, she loves him in that suit and remembering the night she bit him it was love at first sight. The way he looked up at her terrified and dying but at the same time his eyes hoping she would help him even though it was her killing him made her feel a sorrow that a vampire like Enigma had never in all her centuries felt like that about a mortal or victim – or vampire for that matter. The bond between them was instant even before he was a vampire, it was true love for certain, and a vampire bond can never be broken. The killer removes a sword from their waist and strikes hard at Enigma's neck, removing her head before standing over their successful hit. Enigma reduces to ash and The Countess is slain.

After arriving back at The Caves, Victuis notices that the car Enigma took is not back yet so informs Krul of her absence. Krul looks concerned but says nothing – she should be back by now. The fact that Enigma left before them and is not back yet suggests she has chosen not to come back, and Krul thinks she must still be angry from the falling out; but the fact they left right after her but didn't see her on the way home worries Krul that she took a detour to Monk, Irish or Chinese territory for a showdown; however, considering neither of those gangs have phoned Krul to tell him suggests otherwise. Neutral Territory is bordered with Holy Ground, China Town and Emerald Territory, so it would be easy for her to travel to the borders with those turfs and with the mood she was in and with everything that has gone on lately, added to her hatred for certain gangs, it is possible she would do such a thing. Krul calls her phone: no answer. The worry grows; he has three choices. Go looking for her, which means The Monks will know she is missing and be on high alert, knowing what she is like and capable of. Another option is to wait to see if she comes back, but how long does he wait? The third choice is to call Alice and ask if she will send a patrol out to search for her. He calls Alice. She answers with a nervous tone of voice. Krul assumes she doesn't really want to speak to him after his behaviour, but after informing her Enigma may be missing, her nerves change to anxiety. Alice agrees to send a search party out.

Leo volunteers to take some members and patrol the territory as The Messengers don't know what to think, Alice tells him to search all the borders in case Enigma is scoping out the enemy. Leo investigates the area as he and his crew drive down a road next to a wood. Seeing lights in the distance, he peers out for a better look and upon seeing the Jaguar Mark 2 with its headlights still beaming, the door wide open, Leo's heart sinks, ordering his men to hurry. Leaping out, The Messengers rush to the car, looking all around as they do, into the woods, down the road and into the car itself. The car engine is still running and as Leo reaches in to switch off the engine, he looks down to the road beneath and sees the pile of ash in the shape of a body. His heart sinks, He stares at the remains of Enigma blowing away on the breeze, his members huddle round as all present look at each other knowing war is on the way. The nervousness becomes fear and the next move is crucial. Leo orders them not to tell anybody until Alice gives the all-clear whilst on the phone calling his leader. Upon answering, Alice doesn't seem herself and after being given the news she begins to panic. Ordering Jessica to rally the troops, Alice heads out to the assassination scene, head in her hands, dreading telling Krul and hoping Leo has got it wrong. Arriving to her deputy and members with faces of fear and a sickening feeling in their stomachs, Alice looks down at what remains of Enigma on the floor. Looking at Leo who says nothing, she makes the dreaded call to Krul. The vampire leader answers instantly, asking what they have found if anything and a distant Alice struggles to compose herself, which angers Krul slightly and asks her to just tell him.

"We have found Enigma… she's…" Alice stutters and takes a deep breath. "She's dead, she has been slain," she adds, knowing there is no right way to say it.

Krul sinks into his chair, the emotion hits him like a stake to the heart, the tears begin to build in his eyes and from his reaction Victuis knows what has become of her without being told. He consoles his friend, hugging him as Krul cries on his shoulder, the pain too much to keep inside. Alice gives him her condolences but at the moment they mean nothing. She also offers to help in any way she can, asking to come and see the scene for himself. Alice agrees instantly. Jessica texts Alice to tell her the gang is armed and prepared, but for now it is just precaution, ordering Jessica not to tell anyone – this needs to be kept top secret until the time is right, but even then it may be with a declaration of war.

After confirming with Alice that Krul has a meeting arranged with her, The Monks allow access back onto Holy Ground, but after they have already allowed passage tonight they grow suspicious of something going on – nevertheless, after all that has happened with Alice's arrest they say nothing and keep a close eye on The Vampires' journey until The Messengers turf. On the journey Krul stares out of the window, not saying a word but with Victuis along for the ride he is not alone, unlike Enigma when she died. Racing through his mind, Krul thinks of his true love all alone in her time of need and suffering in her last moments, all because Krul chose to argue with her instead of calm and mediate, he let his anger get the better of him and look at the trouble it has caused, the ultimate loss.

Coming to the road heading towards the murder scene, Krul takes in how lonely it is and that the killer has chosen carefully where to commit the murder – this was a planned assassination and planned to perfection. With Alice and Leo coming into view, their car slows as Krul and his best friend and deputy begin their investigation. Seeing the side road into the wood and the smashed glass on the floor, vacating the car, Alice is the first to greet them with a hug for Krul, a warm and passionate embrace tells him she is sorry for his loss and she will be there for him if need be. After seeing what remains of Enigma, a mound of ash on the road, some of which has blown away, Krul's eye begin to fill up again. Victuis looks around for any evidence and notices the skid marks on the road telling him that Enigma stopped suddenly, the tyre marks starting just after the side road into the wood and continuing until just after. The glass on the floor and the smashed window are evidence of how Enigma was disabled and upon investigating the interior, Victuis' assumption is confirmed that holy water was used; she must have suffered greatly. Attempting to keep this from Krul to save his pain, his attempts fail as his leader is behind waiting to examine the car himself, after already noticing the tyre marks on the road. Alice asks to speak with Krul before he leaves, attempting to make it sound comforting, but Krul sees right through it. She wants to know his intentions to decide if she should prepare for war.

"There is no need for us to talk," Krul tells her in not so much a dismissive manner but enough to get the point across that her attempt at conversation isn't working. "What you really want to know is what I am going to do. Are you expecting me to believe you haven't already rallied your troops on the suspicion of war? Don't insult my intelligence. As soon as Leo told you the news you would have armed you members," Krul adds as the look on Alice's face is proof that his response is accurate.

"I am just asking what your intentions are," Alice asks, heart pounding and anxiety growing at the answer she knows is coming but dreads hearing.

Krul turns to her as he gets back into his car. "Prepare for war," he replies with a tone of hatred for all in the city and a look of conquest in his eye. Vengeance has become the aim and leadership is already a distant memory in his mind.

Chapter 16

After he heard the news, Father Gideon launched into action – the slaying of Enigma, or in the interest of equality the murder of Enigma, will have the biggest repercussions around 9 Gang City since the war. Knowing the city is on the brink, The Monks have a lifeline in keeping their power, but knowing Krul and his gang will suspect foul play from The Monks, Gideon has put his gang on high alert, sending extra troops to the border with The Caves. Brother Francis and Brother Theodore are frantic in their pursuit of the truth behind the assassination, because although they hated Enigma and are glad she is dead, they have a law to uphold and as they are still in power it may help their cause if they achieve justice. Summoning Alice for information and obligated to attend, The Messengers' leader is exhausted but arrives at Cathedral Tower. Her passage was much more peaceful this time and she saw some of the monk gang members who disrespected her during her arrest – they had their heads down this time and didn't say boo to a goose. Alice hasn't slept for at least 36 hours and even then it was only a couple of hours; she is drained, tired, moody, in need of a hot bath and as for her hair and make-up, they have seen better days.

Just off the phone with Aiden, the news about Siobhan isn't good and from the sound of it she won't be the same again, giving The

Irish even more reason to want revenge – and perhaps they already have it, but murder isn't the diplomatic answer. As far as Krul is concerned, Alice hopes he does not resort to war, but knowing how much he loved Enigma she isn't holding her breath for peace. She feels for Krul – last night was the first time she has ever seen him cry and his response to her embrace was emotional. She cares for him a great deal but now Alice must focus on assisting The Monks in the identification and capture of the assassin. It is safe to say Enigma will not be missed by most of the city, but that is no excuse for murder, and in this city the killer would know exactly what the consequences would be for carrying out such a hit – most probably war, but at the very least execution. Alice has racked her brain trying to put together a list of suspects and in the end she came up with the entire city! Alice knows to some people she will be on the list of suspects – not only Enigma, but also Father Gideon and Queen Rika have all accused her of having desires for Krul, this has raised suspicion in other citizens of the city to a point Alice has noticed some looking at her differently when Krul is around. Krul is a good person and a great friend, handsome too, but do people really think Alice would stoop to such a level and risk everything for a possible boyfriend? Yes, people do think such a thing and Alice will be on many people's list of suspects.

Leo and Jessica offered and were eager to accompany Alice to this meeting after what happened last time, but Alice convinced them Father Gideon wouldn't dare to repeat his behaviour, especially with all that is going on and a murderer needing catching. Walking through the hallway of the cathedral, Alice notices some sheepish monks glancing over and when she looks back they nod their respect and put their head down. Alice holds her head up high and is lot more confident than yesterday – what a difference a day makes. Approaching Gideon's office and as usual Francis and

Theodore are sniffing around, but when they see Alice walking towards them they pretend to be busy and walk away. Alice smiles to herself and stares as they leave. Glancing back, Francis sees her gloating smiles and a look of fury spreads across his face, but he says nothing and hurries away. Theodore, who doesn't look around, is in quick pursuit following like a dog. Upon entry, Father Gideon stands to greet his guest and his demeanour is polar opposite to how he usually is – gone is the high and mighty attitude, gone is the demanding tyrant, and in his place an almost brown-nosing slimeball who knows his best chance of keeping power is to get Alice onside and solve the murder. As he offers her some refreshment for the first time in 20 years, Alice knows his game yet plays it cool, returning the politeness and playing the act in return with the thoughts in her mind that if she does win the election, if the election happens, she will be remembering the two decades of tyranny and not the one occasion of arse kissing and an offer of tea. Her smile beams from ear to ear, which does not go unnoticed by Gideon but he says nothing. Suddenly a feeling of guilt comes over Alice, all this gloating and feeling of satisfaction and she is here to discuss a murder and avoid war, but that is what power can do to people, even Alice – she has noticed her self-pride go up a notch since last night and wonders if she is mistaking pride and confidence for arrogance. Father Gideon's face turns to concern now that the falsities are over and after pausing for a few seconds he looks at Alice intently.

"What has Krul said to you about his intentions?" Gideon asks, fearful of the answer but wanting and needing to know.

"He last words to me last night were prepare for war," Alice replies.

Gideon sighs and takes a deep breath, fiddling with his phone. Alice doesn't know whether he is assembling more troops or texting Krul for a meeting to discuss matters – he doesn't tell her, which puts her on edge slightly because if Gideon is sending more troops to the border it means he is accepting war is going to happen without trying to negotiate peace with Krul. Although extremely unlikely Krul will agree not to start a war, Gideon and Alice have a duty to the city to at least attempt to hold peace talks; this is why Alice questioned Krul last night, despite feeling her timing was terrible she has to carry out her duty no matter what, and Father Gideon should be doing the same thing. One reason he may not do this is if The Vampires start a war without a High Council vote, then this breaks the law and the legal punishment for that is all other gangs join forces and wipe out the offending gang and divide their territory. If Gideon wants to wipe out vampirism from 9 Gang City, then allowing Krul to attack is one way to do it.

"Who are your suspects in the Enigma assassination?" Gideon asks.

"There are many suspects, but the prime suspects are Zhen Yun, Aiden O'Riordan and Cormac Shea," Alice declares, not wanting to put the blame on these people but they are the most likely to have committed the murder.

"I understand The Vampires and The Irish had a fight on Neutral Territory last night," Gideon says with a false tone of concern, but the excitement in his voice gives him away. "Do you see what happens when you rebel against my command?" he adds, not letting go of the fact that this happened when they were celebrating getting one over on The Monks.

Alice gives him a look of disdain that he threw that comment in, but lets it go.

"They did, Aiden made some offensive comment and Krul lost his temper," Alice replies, knowing where this is going but obliged to tell the truth. "Siobhan is in a bad way. I phoned Aiden this morning and she has a broken nose, a broken jaw, a fractured cheekbone and two broken ribs, and needed ten stiches on her face wounds. She will be scarred for life," Alice adds, feeling sorry for Siobhan.

Father Gideon shakes his head in disgust.

"Who gave her a beating like that?" he asks, assuming the answer but having to ask.

"Enigma," Alice replies.

Gideon now understands why The Irish are on the list of prime suspects, and following the fight Enigma had with Zhen Yun, this adds her to the list also. For Zhen, this would have been the perfect time to commit such an act fresh from The Vampires fight with The Irish, who would have been reeling from the defeat and yet at the same time Zhen would know she will be prime suspect after her own beating and the fact that the entire city knows she hates Enigma with a passion. Father Gideon ponders his best move. This has become a game of chess and the leader has numerous options – he can allow Krul to attack, which means by law the rest of the gangs will have to turn against him; but what laws are adhered to during war? Another move could be placing Krul under arrest for the attack on Aiden and the other gangs would have no choice but to accept because, unlike Alice's arrest, this one would be valid; however, this could anger The Vampires even more and cause a war anyway. A third option would be to suggest a pact with The Irish and fight side by side against The Vampires until they are defeated – with strong Catholic beliefs in both gangs they have that in common, so it is possible, but where would that leave the friendship between The Irish and The Pagans? A fourth choice would be remove The Vampires' voting rights at High Council – that way Krul cannot ask for a vote to declare war and also he and his crew can't vote in the upcoming election. None of this would stop a war happening, so it is an option but not the best. Final choice could be joining with The Chinese, similar to option three, but the alternative would be a pact with Cheng and his gang, who know The Vampires are their biggest threat and would consider any idea that damaged their main contender. All these thoughts rush around Gideon's mind and is on top of an imminent election plus a murder case to solve. The Leader has work to do before his probable exit in the vote. Alice knows her position has become more difficult than Gideon's – being the favourite to win the election it looks as though that won't happen and with the weakest gang militarily The Messengers have gone from probable leaders to maybe being forced to fight on the frontline for The Monks. Having to work for the gang in power is valid in war as well as peace time, and The Monks will most probably send them to fight on the frontline. This is not the worst place to be for The Messengers – it would be worse if they broke the law and went it alone, then they would be alone against the city and would be decimated in no time. They could ask for an allegiance with another gang, but that is not guaranteed, so fighting on the frontline of a war is the best option Alice and her crew could have. This is the periless position they are in, which is why Alice must do all she can to avoid war.

"What is the stance of The Werewolves?" Gideon asks, thinking they may join with The Messengers if war should happen.

"I haven't asked and Jessica has been carrying out her duties," Alice answers with a sigh.

Gideon assumes that because of Jessica and Cuthwulf's relationship that they tell each other everything – that would be very romantic if they did but extremely foolish; after all, they are still technically enemies and as werewolf leader Cuthwulf would not divulge his gang's true plans at a moment like this and neither would Jessica the other way; and besides, Father Gideon was only yesterday hurling disgusting insults at Alice about her sister, yet now he is hoping to have werewolf help if war should happen and using Jessica's help to get it.

"Cuthwulf, I assume, is preparing for war," Alice adds, with her mind going back to Gideon's text message. He hasn't had a reply, which could mean he texted Krul and will have to wait until sunset for his answer.

Gideon ends the meeting with a request that Alice speaks to all gang leaders to ask their intentions and preparations for the situation. Alice agrees with a smile and was going to do it anyway and wants to start with The Chinese. She didn't tell Father Gideon, but Cheng has had his army on high alert since they found out about Enigma's death. Alice has had her members patrolling the border and The Chinese have been on manoeuvres. Gideon has most of his gang on The Vampires' border and very few on the east side, presumably because they don't think the gangs to their east will attack, or they have The Messengers to fight on that side for them.

Walking through a building she may be ruler of by tonight, Alice looks around the corridors at the decorations on the wall, filled with either monk gang emblems and art, or religious Christian text or paintings. Father Gideon certainly did his best to make the cathedral as religious as possible. Stopping at a picture of Jesus on the cross, Alice looks and admires. Wondering what Jesus would make of all this, would it be sadness that the human race has not or cannot change? Is it anger that many of us know what the problems are in life and do nothing about them? Perhaps he is angry with himself and his Father for giving humanity another religion to argue and fight over. When you think of the history of hatred and rivalry between Protestants and Catholics, the way Irish Catholics were treated by their British rulers and vice versa in France the way the Catholics treated the Protestants, you have to wonder if people of the same religion can have that much hatred for one another and if Christians are treating Christians that way, what hope is there that different faiths can live in peace? Hope is all well and good, but in a lot of cases it is a pointless emotion and some people are deluded enough to think if they hope passionately enough their dreams will come true. These people need to ask themselves if their dream is possible, and for those who dream of world peace perhaps the problem with that dream is you have be asleep to have it.

Texting Krul to ask to speak to him before he takes any action, and then another text to Cheng telling him she is on her way, it seems as though her work is never done. It will be interesting speaking with Cheng – he will be ready and willing to go to war, but knowing many people may see his gang as the biggest threat with his vast numbers and greater arsenal, it is possible some gangs will join together to defeat The Chinese, which will leave Cheng anxious. The more powerful you are, the more hatred you receive.

Arriving at the security check, Alice sees a battalion of Chinese camped along the perimeter fence fully armed, a sniper on top of the security hut and assuming they are the same at every other border, Cheng has shown his hand. Knowing The Monks will have most of their troops on the border with vampire turf, The Chinese have flooded the border with Holy Ground in an attempt to take Cathedral Tower if war should erupt. The Messengers will not be able to fight them off, and The Pagans and The Irish will have to contend with a smaller number but still well trained and armed Chinese gang members. Alice thinks it is a tactic that could very well work and yet is a bit predictable. The Monks could retreat from The Caves border and allow The Vampires right through their turf to fight The Chinese head on. The Monks could retreat onto Neutral Territory or could join with The Cannibals and seek asylum on Cannibal Farm, and allow the other gangs to inflict heavy casualties on each other and then launch their attack, which is the tactic The Cannibals seem to be going for because nobody has heard from them. Alice decides to speak to them later.

Passing through a security check that had more than the usual security guards with more than the usual weapons on show, Alice drives a little quicker than she usually would, her nerves getting the better of her. The streets of China Town are almost deserted, just a few gang members carrying out some lackey duties – clearly these are the weaker members or are being punished, but the rest will be armed and ready. Cheng has certainly built the place up since his election victory and given his territory a stylish look, and yet honoured history, which is hugely important to Chinese people and in ancient times had historians and scholars record the events of the great dynasties of China. Unlike 9 Gang City, these records were not biased towards their ruler, but were accurate descriptions of events. In fact, the Chinese emperor had no legal authority to read the texts until the Tang Dynasty, which began circa 618 AD. Considering Chinese records began circa 1600 BC, that is 2218 years of unbiased and truthful recording of historical events in China's ancient past; it is doubtful any other nation can boast this. Imagine the different version of history 9 Gang City would have if this was the case here, no storytelling from a religiously heroic point of view from The Monks and no darkness reigns supreme from Niculi, just a truthful series of events that portray the city, its creators and citizens in an honest and accurate way, that hatred for one another is the downfall of us all and although we know it we continue to hate and that only makes the people of this city worse. One thing the ancient Chinese have in common with The Monks is that the people of ancient China had a great love and respect for Heaven; the difference is they did not believe it to be a place that should be worshipped, their belief was it gave guidance to the mortal world and their Emperor was, for want of a better word, the middleman between the people and Heaven. Cheng is a great respecter of history, not only for his ancient culture in China, but also the history of his birth nation and most of all 9 Gang City. This is not only his personal belief but also a cultural tradition also. The ancient Chinese believed, as do other cultures, their ancestors were the foundation of the people's identity and it was their duty to respect their memory by recording history accurately, but also to decipher the meaning of ancient songs and poems to give as accurate an account as they could of their ancestors even before the invention of writing. One of the main reasons The Chinese under Cheng's rule have become so powerful is their embrace and mixture of English-born and Chinese-born gang members, mixing the west with the east, combining western and eastern powers, almost a best of both worlds attitude from the gang; and Cheng was and is at the forefront of that collaboration.

Approaching Chinese HQ, Alice is greeted by a garrison stood to attention outside but step into action and lock and load when they see Alice's car approach, waiting for command to shoot or wait for attack. They stand down when Yong gives the order. Thinking it is a bit much but understanding the reason, Alice greets Yong with the usual grace and respect. Entering HQ, Alice see gang members lining the corridor to add more protection to their leaders. Knocking and opening the door, Alice is greeted by an attempting-to-look-relaxed Cheng in his chair and Zhen Yun stood behind him almost like a bodyguard; and after they meet and greet, Alice sits to discuss politics and takes a snide glance at Zhen's missing fingers. It is clear to see they couldn't be saved – the middle and ring fingers on her right hand are missing from the knuckle to add injury to the insult that she suffered at the hands of Enigma, but is it motive for murder, in this city – and knowing Zhen, yes, it is.

Cheng smiles in an attempt to play down the tension in the room. This is one of Cheng's weaknesses – he gives himself away when he is nervous by either smiling or laughing in an act of playing down the atmosphere; he did it in The Waiting Yard with Krul. Yong and Zhen don't do this; they stay straight-faced and do not give away their thoughts and emotions, perhaps because they are Chinese-born and their childhoods were spent in China, whereas Cheng was born in England to Chinese parents. Cheng has that western irritation of displaying emotion. There were slight murmurs of Cheng only being elected because he was westernised, but people put this down to bitterness from the Chinese traditionalists. Cheng has proven his worth as leader because his crew are the most powerful they have ever been.

"What is the word from Krul?" Cheng asks, making it clear where his thoughts lie. "How is he coping?" he adds, attempting to not sound as though it is all about war and not Enigma's murder, but Alice see right through it.

"He has a loved one to mourn," Alice replies, purposely referring to the murder before discussing war. "As for his plan of action, I don't know what his true intention are, but I am sure you can guess what he said he is going to do, or else why the heavy defence of your HQ?" Alice asks, knowing those gang members were not because of her arrival.

Zhen fidgets at the comment and Alice looks at her with a mind full of suspicion. Zhen Yun stares back, not liking another gang member and certainly not liking another woman coming on to her turf and having an attitude.

"How I defend my territory is nothing to do with you. I simply asked how Krul is coping with his loss," Cheng responds, trying to be polite but making it clear he will have no lip from Alice.

"He is coping as badly as somebody copes when their soulmate has been murdered in cold blood by a coward who didn't have the courage to fight her face-to-face, so they ambushed her and slayed her in a way that would cause her agony and suffering," Alice rants. Zhen fidgets again, much to Alice's annoyance and glares at her. "Have you got something to say?" she snaps to the surprise of the three Chinese leaders.

An awkward silence lingers over the room as Zhen wants to punch Alice for her attitude, but knowing if she does she will be breaking the law, and the last thing her gang need is an arrest and removal of High Council powers. Cheng holds out his hand in the manner of telling Alice to calm down.

"I assume you are stressed at the current situation, but I cannot and will not have you coming on to our turf and speaking to us like that," Cheng tells her, calmly at first but towards the end spiralling slightly into anger.

Alice concedes, knowing he is right. "I'm sorry, after everything that has happened I'm not myself," she responds, looking the three leaders in the eye as she says it.

Cheng nods and accepts the apology, knowing the last few days have been eventful to say the least. Attempting to move the meeting on, Alice asks what Cheng's intentions are – everybody will be anxious to know what The Chinese will do, but at the same time Cheng knows he will have to bide his time to see what the other gangs do. China Town is bordered with Holy Ground, Neutral Territory, Emerald Territory and BC Nation; this means despite their superior numbers and arsenal, The Chinese could very well be outnumbered if The Irish and The Pagans unify, and with The Messengers already working for The Monks, Cheng and his crew could be completely surrounded. It is best for The Chinese to wait and see if Krul attacks The Monks from the westside therefore taking The Monks' attention away from Cheng and his crew and freeing up the east side of Holy Ground for an attack. Alice knows this, but for the sake of political unity she must ask and report back his answer to Father Gideon. Cheng knowing this is the case has a choice whether to tell the truth and score points with The Monks and The Messengers, therefore getting them onside, or lie to either catch them off guard or spring a surprise attack. Alice also knows this is what Cheng will be thinking, but doesn't know which one he will choose. Cheng, knowing Alice will be suspicious but not knowing the truth from a lie, knows that the ball is in his court but that can change with one bad decision; this is just a taste of gang politics and it gets to a point that people become blinded by second guessing their rivals to the extent it causes themselves to make a wrong choice in their own tactics.

"I am going to sit right here and wait to see what The Vampires do," Cheng answers openly and looking Alice in the eye.

Alice believes him and it is the best decision as far as The Chinese are concerned.

"What is being done about finding Enigma's killer?" Cheng inquires, either because he wants justice to be served or he is digging for information on how close the people in power are to the culprit.

"We are still in the shock of the aftermath, but we have a list of suspects and a list of prime suspects," Alice answers, not wanting to look at Zhen who is right at the top of prime suspects. Cheng glances at his 3rd In Command and back to Alice.

"Are we on the list of suspects? And is Zhen on the prime suspect list?" Cheng inquires to Alice's surprise and in front of Zhen who knows she is but remains unmoved; she doesn't care that Enigma is dead and thinks the city is better off without her, she was a liability to peace and yet here the city is on the brink of war over her death – oh the irony, Zhen thinks.

"At the moment everybody is on the list of suspects," Alice reveals honestly and Cheng nods understanding in such a case and considering the victim who had many enemies, the list of would-be assassins will be long. "But yes, following the fight Zhen had with Enigma it does put her on the list of prime suspects," she states, returning the honesty and glancing at Zhen who stares back and only speaks when Cheng allows her. This is commonplace in 9 Gang City when gang leaders are discussing politics or military issues, the deputies and gang members in the room keep quiet until asked for their opinion – they are welcome to speak freely if it is an open conversation, but when it is official only the leaders speak; it saves everybody speaking out of turn and over one another.

"I was in my car on my way back to China Town when Enigma was slain," Zhen states, meaning she has an alibi, her chauffer.

Alice nods at the statement but throws a spanner in the works. "Meaning your only alibi is a low ranking gang member that will lie for you. If you were in a car that gives you means and ability to get to the hit sight, we already know you have motive and how do you know when she was killed? Are you just assuming she was murdered when you were in your car going back home? The time of her murder is unknown, we just know it was some time between one o'clock and three o'clock because they are the times that she left my headquarters to when she was found. Considering it only takes 10 minutes to get to China Town from Neutral Territory, that gives you more than enough time to commit the murder." Alice states her case against Zhen, who along with Cheng and Yong stay silent thinking about the case against her.

"That is all fair enough and it sounds like Zhen is top of your list, but none of it is hard evidence and I'm sure you will be conducting more of an investigation before making any legal judgements," Cheng responds with a hidden message of 'make sure you prove your case against Zhen before you repeat your statement to the wrong people around the city, mainly Krul'. This kind of comment only raises suspicion in Alice and does not intimidate her, rising to her feet to leave she smiles.

"I will be carrying out an investigation and yes, Zhen Yun is at the top of my list," she claps back boldly and offers to see herself out, and leaves without looking back but feeling their eyes burning into her back. Sitting in her car, Alice checks her phone, a text from Aiden asking what is being done about Krul attacking him, a text from Gwendoline asking for any news on the war front, and a text from Jessica telling her that a trace of an Emblic plant has been found on the car seat of Enigma's car on the patches of holy water that was used to disable her – Emblic is used in Traditional Chinese Medicine to purify the blood. Alice takes a deep breath as a step closer is taken in the pursuit of the killer, and after looking back at Chinese HQ she sees Yong stood in the doorway staring intently as she drives away; looking in her rear view at the car following, her heart begins to beat faster, wondering why Cheng has sent a car after her; he has never done this before. With plenty of ambush sights between here and home, and even more members to commit such an attack, Alice begins to wonder if she will suffer the same fate as Enigma.

Chapter 17

After receiving Alice's reply telling him Krul's arrest is on hold until the outcome of Enigma's murder is decided, Aiden fumes at what he sees as special treatment for a friend of Alice's, despite the fact Alice doesn't make the decisions; Aiden also thinks this is a bargaining tactic from The Monks in exchange for votes at the election. Showing a furious Cormac the message, they rant how they are sick and tired of the politics of this city always being about The Monks and The Vampires with The Witches and The Messengers tagging along, it is time for a fresh approach and certainly time for the other gangs to be taken more seriously. Not just making up the numbers in how history focuses mostly on Niculi and Ziana's rule, Gideon's slaying of them, The CVS, Wallachia, Hungary, vampirism and witchcraft, with minuscule mention of the part the other gangs played in The Battles and the formation of 9 Gang. They have made their decision, The Irish want to form a union with The Pagans and with the Celtic cousins showing a fractured honour to each other all these years, Aiden thinks he has a chance of convincing them. Brigacos and Bryson have a hatred for The Monks, especially Bryson for Brother Francis, so Aiden will prey on that as a bargaining tool, plus a union will mean they will be able to cover The Chinese from the north and south, meaning The Chinese will have to fight at both ends stretching their numbers;

this will even things up dramatically. They will also appeal to their ancestral connection – Celtic Paganism stretches back centuries and arrived in Ireland circa 270 BC and is said to be derived from multiple cultures from mainland Europe, mainly the Gauls, but also as far as the Urnfield culture from Central/Eastern Europe and are thought to have crossed Doggerland to what we now know as Britain – or Albion as the Celts called it, which comes from Albiyo a Gaulish word taken from the Indo European language which said to be the origin of modern day European languages; in this language the word Albo means white, clearly a reference to the White Cliffs of Dover. Eventually crossing to the land we now know as Ireland, there are conflicting statements from multiple sources as to what part the Druids played in Irish society; some say they played no part whatsoever within religion and had no status as priests within Irish Paganism, but is this just Christian denial or demonisation of a faith they want to conquer. This is highly likely as it is well known some of the Celtic Gods and Goddesses were demonised as witches and when Julius Caesar himself said the Gauls worshipped Gods similar to the Roman Gods (in his opinion) and Albion Celts are descended from the Gauls, these Celts crossed to Ireland and Irish mythology has a text called The Book Of The Dun Cow in which a higher force is considered a God and Irish Druids acted as priests for this God, then we must consider that any comment of down talking or making false statements about druids playing no part in Irish religion is perhaps down to Christian demonisation of Paganism. The Pagans of 9 Gang City, however, may not be so accepting of Aiden's offer, with The Irish crew and their leader being strong Catholics Brigacos may not want to associate with a faith that demonised his own. This is why their friendship over the years and decades has been a difficult one – both gangs want to honour their people's past but at the same time religious belief has affected their attitude to each other. This is one topic that The Vampires and The Witches have led by example on, they have not allowed the difference between a vampire and a witch do damage to their union, they have joined for the common cause which is fight back against oppression. This is the tactic Aiden should use in his talks with Brigacos – appeal to his ambitious side of political conquest but at the same time pay homage to the ancestors of their kind. The Pagans can be persuaded but it is not guaranteed. There are stories of St Patrick taking part in what can only be described as a magical contest between himself and an Arch Druid on the Pagan festival Bealltainn, which is a Gaelic festival celebrating the coming of summer. During this celebration a bonfire is lit to honour the Pagan God Beli. At this festival it is said that only the Arch Druid can light a bonfire, but in the distance a blazing fire could be seen coming from Tara, which at that time was the capital of Ireland. Furious, the Arch Druid went to see who was responsible and found St Patrick and his followers chanting around the fire. Taking the saint to the king, the Arch Druid challenged Patrick to prove his powers of faith to decide which is the greater. The Arch Druid cast a spell that caused snow to fall upon the waving of his wand, Patrick is said to have made the sign of the cross and the snow disappeared, the angry druid then cast another spell that brought a thick fog around them, St Patrick said a prayer and the fog lifted and faded. The contest was settled when the druid and St Benin, a companion of Patrick's, swapped possessions, the druid carried a Christian mantle and St Benin wore the Arch Druid's cloak, and both entered a tent each; these tents were set on fire to see who and what would survive. St Benin survived but the Arch Druid's cloak he was wearing burned and in the other tent the Arch Druid died and was reduced to ash. The only surviving thing in the tent was the Christian mantle, thus proving Christianity to be the stronger faith. We have to consider three things in this story: the first, is the story true; second, the hypocrisy of Christianity that a pagan conjuring snow and fog and is considered an unholy faith otherwise why would St Patrick be in Ireland to Christianise the Pagans? Add this to St Patrick himself being able to destroy the spell with the sign of the cross and lift the fog with prayer. Are we not going to think what a prayer is in this context, a spell perhaps, what is a prayer that lifts fog if not a spell, the druid said words and waved his wand and the fog appeared, St Patrick said words with his hands together, eyes closed and the fog disappeared – what is the difference? The difference is history is told by the winner and Christianity defeated and conquered Paganism in many parts of the world, but especially Europe, and most notably Britain and Ireland in this case. These are the reasons Brigacos may refuse Aiden's request and this is why the friendship between The Irish and The Pagans has been a difficult one; shared history, different faith. Aiden accepts part of this as a legitimate reason – his people know all too well about being conquered from The Tudors to William of Orange, Ireland has had a turbulent relationship with Britain, especially the English. Although their dealings with the Scots overtime has not been one of friendship, it is their treatment at the hands of the English that has plagued Irish history. The Tudors, for example, wanted to change the Irish elites into a more noble English type which would bring them under an English controlled law; this ended badly as a number of rebellions ended up destroying some of the elite in Ireland. Another is the persecution of Irish Catholics by English Protestants after The Battle of the Boyne, which would lead, believe it or not, to religious tension between Protestant English and Protestant Scots, which started on a plantation in Ulster, so now the Irish people who were proud Catholics had English and Scottish Protestants at each other's throats on Irish soil.

Aiden O'Riordan makes the call to Arch Druid Brigacos who answers like he is eager to speak with the Irish leader. At this stage of the game it would be counterproductive to stand alone. After the pleasantries have been exchanged, and enquiring about Siobhan's condition, the two leaders get down to business.

"It would be foolish to allow The Chinese such dominance on this side of the city," Aiden thinks out loud but really it is in the hope that Brigacos agrees with him.

"I agree," the Arch Druid confirms with a voice of cautious optimism – cautious because any union will cause anger in China Town putting The Pagans firmly in The Chinese sights, but optimism due to the fact The Irish and The Pagans will be stronger together. "The Chinese will be focusing on The Monks and nervous at what The Vampires will be doing; if we unionise after they attack The Monks, perhaps even help them destroy The Monks and then announce our joining and attack The Chinese..." Brigacos reveals his plan.

Aiden smiles at the suggestion and thinks it is the way forward.

"I think The Vampires may even help us in that fight, especially after Enigma's murder," Aiden responds.

Brigacos pauses for a second before replying, "Is that your way of telling me you had nothing to do with the assassination?"

"Whoever it was, the murder has put a hold on Krul's arrest," Aiden replies in an angry tone. Brigacos notices that his response has not answered the question. "It is tactics from The Monks to take The Vampires out of the vote, or favouritism from Alice because she has a thing for Krul," the Irish leader adds, venting his frustration about the lack of immediate justice.

"Alice doesn't make those decisions and if she does have feelings for Krul it would turn Gideon against her," Brigacos responds in a slight support of Alice but more putting the blame onto Father Gideon. "It's all Gideon, in an attempt to save his position," he adds, making it clear his hatred for The Leader.

Aiden thinks this is a lot of blame for one person in a city full of suspects and culprits, almost as if Brigacos wants Gideon to be blamed for things he hasn't done – does he hate him that much or is he taking the attention away from himself?

"You think Gideon himself committed the Enigma killing?" Aiden asks, sceptical. Father Gideon may have ordered the hit but to carry it out himself is extremely unlikely.

"I do, at that time of night he is always alone and never disturbed, he could easily have slipped out. It's Gideon: he has a lot of experience slaying vampires – who else could carry it out in such a professional manner?" Brigacos states, confident in his theory.

Aiden thinks it plausible but still can't believe Gideon would do it himself and gives his theory. "Alice," he answers point blank. Brigacos doesn't respond, just takes a deep breath and waits for Aiden to finish. "Alice knows Neutral territory better than anyone, Alice could have got there in time and Alice is the one most likely to win the vote and wants Krul to rule with her," he finishes.

The Arch Druid casts his doubt on the suspicion of Alice and, after some final words of compassion for Siobhan and union support, the call is ended with Aiden feeling good about his gang's chances if war should arise and Brigacos content with the future joining of the gangs. It puts them in a much stronger position and heaps more pressure on The Monks should they have to fight The Chinese, The Irish and The Pagans on the east side of the city with only The Messengers for support, all this on top of having to fight The Vampires, The Witches and The Werewolves to the west. The Monks will not be able to handle such an attack and may even be better off sacrificing one of the flanks of their territory, which would be the west, they have more of a chance on the east side despite The Chinese numbers and arsenal. This is all music to Brigacos' ears as he pictures the downfall of Father Gideon and dreams of Paganism being the faith that rules.

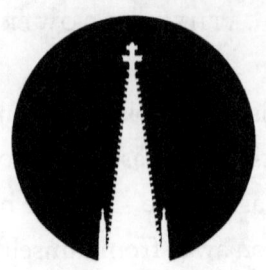

Chapter 18

Living a life without worldly goods and the pleasures women bring seems a lonely life to most, but to a monk it is the life they were destined to live, and honouring God is their only priority. Father Gideon believes his life was pre-planned by the almighty and everything he does is the will of The Lord to either educate humankind or defeat evil for the greater good. There are some who follow this belief – Brothers Francis and Theodore, for example, but many more think it is arrogance to the point it is a sin. Gideon is certainly not lustful – monks are celibate; he is not gluttonous, quite the opposite; neither is he sloth-like; but the rest of the sins could be argued play a part in The Leader's life. Envy – Gideon was certainly envious of Niculi and his power; it was quite obvious from the start that Gideon wanted some sort of power, whether that was gang privileges, gang leadership or city leadership this was apparent during his rise to the top; but it turned out he wanted and achieved all three, which takes us into greed. What is clear for 9 Gang City to see is that Gideon wants everything for himself, the power, the decision making, he wants his fingers in every pie almost to a point he regrets creating High Council, but at that time he needed the idea to get the other gangs on The Monks' side to fight against The Vampires. Wrath has undoubtedly played a role in Gideon's life, almost twisted in mind for revenge against

Niculi and Ziana for the defeat they handed to his descendants during The Battles, revenge for the way the citizens of the city were treated during their reign of terror and darkness, and revenge for God on all vampires and witches for living a life of horror and evil. Father Gideon's biggest sin is pride – so proud of his achievements he has them painted on the walls of Cathedral Tower, so proud it has made him angry at the democracy he created, and so arrogant in his self-righteousness he has come to be hypocritical against his own faith for the sake of power, but so blinded by his beliefs that he has not and cannot see it.

Brother Francis, Gideon's brown nose but a tyrant to the rest of his gang, likes to fantasize that if the worst should happen to his superior that he is in line to the throne; he is, in 9 Gang City, if The Leader dies or steps down The Leadership goes to the 2nd In Command of the gang in power because in this city you vote for the gang in power not the individual you want as leader – the leader of the gang who wins the vote takes The Leadership. This has received some criticism from sections, but they have not gathered much support, the main criticism being a gang could be voted in with a certain leader and then that leader steps down to make way for another; this is possible but the likelihood of it happening is almost non-existent. Brother Theodore, who by default would be a preferable leader from the other gangs' point of view, is a believer in hierarchy; accepting his place firmly below Gideon and Francis, he is a good servant to his superiors but offers nothing to the rest of the city. When people question Gideon's faith, the type of people who quote the Bible to point out what they see as foolish or hypocrisies in an almost mocking of religion kind of way, he gets agitated and over defensive. Gideon sees this as an act of defiance against God and believes all humankind should follow the law of The Lord. The fact remains it has never been proven or disproven if there is a

God or not, so both sides of the coin should remain open minded. The Monks of 9 Gang fail in this way of thinking because they are closed to the possibility that God may not exist and class this as blasphemy and if they had their way would have you locked up for it. From The Monks' point of view, Father Gideon is a great leader who has achieved great things, hence his nickname Gideon The Great, and from a certain point he has been inspirational in the fact that he did achieve what he and his gang, along with the other gangs, tried and failed to do in 522 years. Is this not the will of God inspiring him to inspire others and fight for freedom and truth, if not then what is it? Gideon has his Bible in hand and reads the passage most relevant to 9 Gang City, Matthew 12:25: "Every kingdom divided against itself is laid waste, and no city or house divided against itself will stand". What more can be said about a place such as this? The divide has always existed, man killing beast, beast killing man, man killing man and woman, how can a city so divided expect to stand? Gideon begins to wonder if the scripture of 9 Gang is already written, as if it was all planned by God to show the world everything is at his mercy and nobody is perfect because God made imperfection, and if his followers are not perfect how can they criticise the naysayers. Sodom and Gomorrah, two cities in the Old Testament, destroyed by God who himself said, "Because the outcry against Sodom and Gomorrah is great and their sin is very grave, I will go down to see whether they have done altogether according to the outcry that has come to me and if not I will know." Genesis 18:20 and 18:21. Has God himself stood in 9 Gang City and made his judgement? If so, all hope is lost. Will the borders be broken down and the city destroyed like Joshua did to Jericho, the city? "With its king and mighty men of valour" are how God described the rulers of Jericho, Joshua 6:2 – is this to be the fate of 9 Gang City? Revelation 18:2: "Fallen, Fallen is Babylon the great, she has become a dwelling place for demons." Revelation 18:10: "Alas, Alas you great city, you mighty city, Babylon, for in a single hour your judgement has come." Gideon's own holy book reads like a devastating prophecy of downfall, but if it is God's will Gideon must accept and if the worst should happen the only question is should Gideon ask The Lord why he has forsaken him.

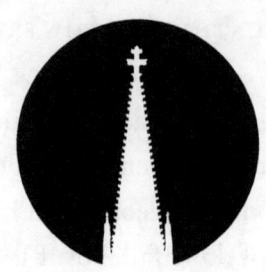

Chapter 19

Another day has passed, a few hours of daylight giving the other gangs that few hours' advantage over The Vampires to prepare for whatever is to come. For the first time Krul rises from his coffin without Enigma by his side; looking at the empty space next to him he pictures his fallen love in his mind. The happy memories come flooding back, her smile that only he saw – everybody else thought of her as an angry, intimidating, aggressive supremacist but Krul knew that deep down a lot of that side of her was a twisted side effect of her past. Enigma never spoke about her life pre-vampire, and Krul never knew how she was turned or who turned her, all he knows is she fought in the war and was around when Niculi and Ziana ruled. Krul asked her a couple of times about her past, but she would change the subject to a point he stopped asking and just accepted she didn't want to share that information. By now the other gangs will know. Krul informed The Witches last night upon his return and Krul knows Alice will have to tell The Monks, after that the information would have been a free for all, Jessica would have told Cuthwulf, The Monks would have told everyone who didn't know and to a point Krul doesn't blame them – a crime like this should be reported to the entire city, a killer is on the loose and the more people who know, the more people can gather information to catch the assassin. Someone in this city is the killer; that means Krul knows the person responsible but doesn't know who it is. That person could be laughing right now at their hit, mocking and insulting his Countess and proud of their action, or at least that is what is racing around Krul's mind.

Victuis enters to fulfil his first duty of the night, the ever-present best friend and deputy and the most loyal of all in 9 Gang City. Wanting to get to the point but not wanting to be intrusive, Victuis hovers around making it obvious he wants to say something. Krul turns to him and sees his deputy looking sheepish and asks what is on his mind. Victuis stutters at first but then just comes out with his thoughts.

"We need to discuss our plan of action and who we need to hunt down to avenge Enigma," he states, thinking forward and not back, dwelling on mistakes and memories. Krul nods, knowing he is right and approves of his friend's desire to get revenge on the one who has taken his love.

"Our plan of action is already decided," Krul replies, staring directly into his deputy's eyes, who stares back with a glint of anticipation for what is to come. "We are going to war regardless of who the assassin is," Krul adds, leaving his tomb and making his way to his office, with Victuis close behind. They fall silent as they pass other gang members who either stand to attention or nod their heads with respect or condolence. After entering his office, Krul sits at his desk and pours himself and Victuis a drink left over from the party. Staring at his beverage, Krul remembers a story Enigma told him of a vampire who could tell the blood type of the blood he was drinking; he was slain in The Daylight Killings. Sinking his shot and pouring another, he gets down to business with Victuis, who is awaiting his thoughts.

"Unfortunately, there is a long list of names who could be the killer," Krul begins. Victuis nods in agreement. "The killers could be The Irish in response to the fight we had with them and revenge for the beating Enigma gave Siobhan, but is it possible they got to the hit sight in time?" Krul asks. Although he knows the answer, he wants to know what his deputy is thinking.

"Yes, it is unlikely but yes they could have got there," Victuis responds instantly.

"It could have been The Chinese – Zhen Yun will still be bitter about losing the fight and her fingers, and could have chosen that moment to do it to frame The Irish," Krul states his second suspect. Victuis has already been thinking this and agrees it would be perfect timing for vengeance from The Chinese. "Thirdly, it could be The Monks, not wanting to go to the vote and causing a war instead. This is unlikely because if they wanted war, Father Gideon would not have agreed to the vote and allowed war to be declared, but I would never put it past The Monks to do such a thing," Krul adds, sinking his second shot.

"It could be The Monks," Victuis responds, sitting forward on his chair. "The reason they would do it is to raise suspicion against other gangs, therefore making our side weaker, giving them a better chance," he adds.

Krul thinks this is a good point and hadn't thought of that himself – if that is their plan it has worked because Krul is suspecting everyone.

"Another suspect is The Messengers," Krul states, looking down for a second and then back up to Victuis who is looking with surprise at his leader's comment.

"Are you serious?" Victuis asks, shocked by his suspicion. Krul nods with confirmation.

"Queen Rika told me Alice has plans to rule 9 Gang with me as her deputy amongst other things, Enigma would only have gotten in the way of that," Krul reveals to a still surprised Victuis, who finds it difficult to believe Alice would go to such a level, but truth be told it makes her the perfect suspect. Nobody would believe it would be her and who else knows Neutral Territory better than her? Nobody; so out of every gang member in the city, she is the one who could get to the hit sight in time for the assassination.

"Which means Leo and Jessica are suspects as well," Victuis adds to the list. "Leo because he would do anything for Alice, and Jessica for two reasons: one, to help Alice in the theory you have just said, and two, if she and Cuthwulf want to start a war to take the leadership," he adds, drinking his shot of blood and Krul pours him another.

"Which means Cuthwulf becomes a suspect as well as Wulfric and Randall," Krul states, pouring the drinks. "The only people we haven't accused is The Cannibals, but I have no doubt they would do it because their best chance of taking power is through war or if The Monks persuaded them to do the hit for them and promised them power and privilege if The Monks keep The Leadership," Krul finishes his list of suspects.

Victuis pauses with a hesitant manner that tells Krul he is thinking something that he does not want to say but it is on his mind. This irritates Krul a little and he snaps at his deputy to speak his mind.

"If everybody is a suspect then that means The Witches are suspected," Victuis answers in a remorseful tone almost as if he is being a traitor to the union between their gangs just by thinking it. "But also me and you, we were with each other when the hit happened but that doesn't mean we are not involved, we could have had somebody do the hit for us," Victuis finishes his thoughts out loud to an almost emotionless Krul who does not get upset or lose his temper at such a comment, only looks straight faced at his best friend knowing he is right. Krul doesn't know for certain that Victuis is innocent and vice versa; not for a second do either think the other is guilty, but the quest for power can make people do despicable things. When Krul said everybody is a suspect he really did mean everybody including the person closest to him and until Victuis is proven innocent, Krul will just have to hope his innocence is proven. Krul and Victuis trust each other but at the moment they are still suspects, the reason they both could have committed such a crime is to put an end to Enigma damaging the gang's chances of being voted in, her constant aggression, the intimidation, the hatred for anything and everything that is not vampire was having a negative effect on their gang's prospects. The other gangs have a respect for Krul and Victuis but hated Enigma, leading to the probability that Enigma being in a position of power across the city would put people off voting for The Vampires; this is problematic for Krul and his gang.

It is a problem The Vampires need not worry about any longer, but it takes their problem to another level – one murder means many killings in war and that is what Krul wants, but as with any attack there is a time and a place to do it. Knowing Cuthwulf has had ideas of a three-way union between what are known as the monster gangs, and with war approaching, Krul decides to give his crew the best possible chance and that would be to make allegiance with a gang that can inflict huge damage to rival gangs. Krul knows when he will attack but is not letting the other gangs know when; he knows this will leave them anxious, and rivals with anxiety may be forced to jump before they are pushed, therefore placing the blame on them for the outbreak of war.

Krul is going to invade Holy Ground in two nights' time, when the moon in full and beaming down on 9 Gang City, when Cuthwulf and his pack are Lycan, when the creatures of nightmares come out to play. The Vampires will have blood fresh from the vein and ripe for drinking, The Witches will have the freedom of the city to inflict all kinds of darkness upon their enemies; it will be a night of horror.

Responding to Alice's text message by informing her he has already given the answer to her question and instead of trying to prevent war she and her people should be preparing for war. Cuthwulf will be between a rock and a hard place –, if they were to unionise with Krul and Rika, attacking The Monks will mean they are against The Messengers, therefore Cuthwulf and Jessica are enemies of war. Such is life in 9 Gang City and they knew complications would occur. Unless Alice decides to turn on The Monks, which is likely because Alice and her crew would rather align with The Vampires, which would take them back to their original gang affiliation with The Vampires and The Witches, things have become complicated, and nobody truly knows which gang will do what and at the moment it is all second guessing and hope. Hope that certain gangs will do what unintentionally helps your gang – for example if The Irish, The Pagans, The Monks and The Messengers join together and attack The Chinese, it will help every gang in the city, but if those gangs mentioned join with The Chinese and attack the monster gangs, it will give the mortal gangs a better chance of defeating supernatural forces who have an advantage over mortals. It gets to a point where politics and military tactics cross over and pollute each other to a level nobody truly knows what to do and waits for someone else to make the first move. That obligation is on Krul because of what happened to Enigma, but in that case the first move has already been made by the assassin, which means the first move falls back onto Krul unless the killer is identified and captured. This brings Alice into the picture, she needs to find out who the assassin is before war breaks out because that means High Council can hold the vote for The Leadership. If she cannot catch the killer and war breaks out, her chances fade dramatically. The countdown to war started as soon as Enigma was attacked and time is ticking for 9 Gang City. As troops assemble on borders and affiliations are planned, one thing is guaranteed: there will be blood.

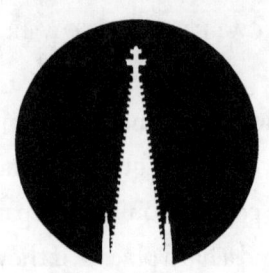

Chapter 20

After Father Gideon informs Brother Francis and Brother Theodore about his decision, Francis' smile stretched from ear to ear and Theodore nodded with delight at their gang staying in power, for now. Dismissing them so he can call Alice and order her to spread the news around the city, knowing this will raise tensions even more, Gideon sees no other option and in this case he is correct. The rules of High Council are clear and all gangs have agreed to the rules, meaning unfortunately for Alice democracy has to wait and Gideon still rules. Only yesterday it seemed as though The Messenger leader would become The Leader and she would be a servant no longer, but in the current climate there is no way the vote can happen and if it did the rules of High Council would be broken.

Gideon sits eagerly as the phone rings, waiting to tell her the news, knowing full well the fury it will cause to seven of the gangs. The Vampires cannot be any more on the brink, but this may push the other gangs over the edge. Alice looks at her phone and assumes Gideon is calling to organise the High Council meeting, although thinks he has left it a bit late. After the pretence of greeting each other respectfully, The Leader gets down to business.

"I am afraid we will have to cancel tonight's vote," Gideon informs her, which causes her jaw to almost hit the floor.

Stuttering for words, Alice manages to utter just one word. "Why?" she demands, suddenly the shock being replaced with anger.

Gideon's excitement raises a notch after hearing the tone of her voice. "Because we can't hold the meeting after Enigma's death," Gideon replies making himself sound heartfelt until revealing his true game playing. "The rules of High Council clearly state a High Council meeting cannot be held without all 27 members and The Vampires have not announced their replacement for Enigma as their 3rd In Command, so as it stands High Council only has 26 members." He smiles to himself.

Alice opens her mouth to speak but just exhales with disappointment at the fact he is right. Father Gideon plays his cards perfectly and Gideon the Great is back in the game, a laughing-stock in recent days, a despised has-been for years, but a simple playing of the rules keeps his position in his grasp and nobody can do anything about it, yet. Giving her an order to inform the leaders of the gangs, Alice agrees with a feeling of will this ever end and there is a chance it might not, hanging up the phone without saying goodbye.

Alice sits in quiet contemplation deciding what her tactics are going to be when war breaks out, because this announcement is the nail in the coffin for her desire for peace; she now knows war is the only way to solve the problem 9 Gang has. After telling Leo and Jessica the news, Leo hits the roof whilst Jessica gives Alice a look of sorrow that her sister may not be leader of the city, followed by an expression of anxiety, knowing the clock is ticking towards conflict. Cheng responds as if he knew there would be some sort of tactic from Gideon – did anybody really think he was just going to hand over power? After informing Alice that Siobhan is gaining strength by the minute but her wounds are still looking bad, Aiden exploded at the news of the vote being cancelled, and Alice could hear Cormac bellowing in the background about how there is now only one option. Brigacos vented his frustration by telling Alice he is moving more troops to the border with Holy Ground and William Henry Davis is finally contacted and tells Alice she is not the first person to ask him his plans – Krul has already contacted him with a proposition that he cannot divulge to Alice, which only frustrates her, mostly that Krul has been sneaking around without telling her. Davis also informed her that he is glad war is going to happen as the city has become far too discriminative towards The Cannibals and their lifestyle. To a certain point he is right, the other gangs treat The Cannibals with disgust, and Davis and his people are somewhat in a no man's land between the mortal gangs and the monster gangs. With no hope of victory within democracy, war is the only way The Cannibals could gain power, and in this city, power is the aim. Alice keeps her composure and politely tells Davis she has other calls to make. Cuthwulf tells her it doesn't matter now anyway, and after being asked his meaning he simply replied the first blood he spills won't be as a man. Queen Rika was seething, the phone lost its signal and suddenly came back with a ranting Rika spiralling off into a disturbed demonic voice about how this is a conspiracy against darkness and death and destruction will fall upon 9 Gang City. This reminds Alice about Queen Rika's comments after Katalin saved Alice from Cathedral Tower, the confidence she prophesised with added to the absolute belief that somehow she was going to gain power leaves Alice confused about how Rika could have gotten it so wrong – clearly her powers are not as strong as people thought or they have waned, but from her reaction to the news the witch queen is furious.

That leaves one call to make: Krul; and she will be demanding some answers. Upon ignoring her first call seeing no need to answer, Krul grows frustrated as his phone rings again, thinking Alice is starting to get high maintenance and even a bit needy – he would never have thought this before but since Enigma's death a piece of him is missing. Having Victuis on the list of suspects, The Witches also being on that list, not wanting to speak to Alice, not caring about Cuthwulf and Jessica's relationship and pitting them against each other in war, Krul doesn't feel anything but hatred for the city and his hatred is the only thing keeping him from being hollow.

"Alice," Krul barks as he answers, taking her by surprise. "You are getting desperate, I've told you what my intentions are. If you want my advice you will break away from The Monks, abandon Neutral Territory and come and join us," Krul adds with a bite in his voice.

"Father Gideon has cancelled the vote due to Enigma's passing, because all members cannot attend," Alice informs him.

Krul stays silent for a moment, knowing Gideon would find a way to keep power, and in a twisted way he is a genius the way he has kept that power for two decades. The original plan to overthrow Niculi and Ziana, the idea of High Council, become monk leader, the rise to leadership of the city – it is all down to how Gideon can think, plan, implement, and manipulate, meaning yet again he has found a way to conquer, which only adds fuel to the fire of war.

"It was too late anyway," Krul replies in a solemn voice, knowing it is partly down to him not announcing a new 3rd In Command, but did people really expect him to replace his love straight away? "Did you really believe it was going to happen? Did you honestly think he was going to let you take his place?" Krul asks with an anger racing around his head but attempting to remain calm so as to not let Alice know he is losing his control.

Alice can't help but be disappointed in his reaction; she hoped he would be more supportive, she longed for more passion in his defence of her, but already in the past few days it is as if he is a different person. She begins to regain her compassion – over the past day or two she has become obsessed with all that is going on and her humanity was replaced with a heartless crusade of investigating everybody's whereabouts and intentions, to solve a murder and prevent war, but now she returns to herself and tells him if he ever needs her she will always be there for him, always.

Chapter 21

uthwulf kisses Jessica as they enjoy their last moment together before tonight's moon. The second full moon of the year is the snow moon named after the weather in the northern hemisphere, but also known as the hunger moon by Native American tribes due to the lack of food either through difficulty to grow crops or the lack of animals to hunt. Other cultures call it the storm moon, but one thing is for certain: The Werewolves will be at one with nature and their release from human imprisonment will make them pure for the hours of darkness. With The Vampires and The Witches ready to strike, the west side of the city will be drenched in blood; no matter how many gang members The Monks have to defend their border, they will not have enough to keep out their rivals. With the law being broken, The Monks have not gone into lockdown this full moon; clearly the law is different if Gideon breaks it.

Gazing at her newfound love, Jessica worries at what is to come with Krul being evasive of his intentions and Father Gideon cancelling the vote, all on top of a killer on the loose and the military action to the east leaves Jessica stressed and anxious. Cuthwulf senses this and sinks into her neck, gently kissing and caressing her. She enjoys the loving embrace and slides down on to his couch, wrapping her legs around him; they share the moment. Knowing time is getting on, Cuthwulf tells her it is time to leave. Dusk approaches and after that, love won't save her from the beast. She smiles a nervous smile and leaves after a passionate kiss, the most passionate they have shared, and her feelings have gone from not caring about what a wolfman does in wolf form to being strangely worried for his safety. Straying onto enemy turf will get him shot, but unknown to Jessica that is exactly what Cuthwulf has planned. After one last loving gaze they part ways, Jessica with hope of a future together and Cuthwulf with a hope that they see each other again.

Darkness falls and Krul stands on his rock, staring into the distance at Cathedral Tower with thoughts rushing through his mind of who will take the throne of the city when the war that is about to start ends, who will survive, who will die and what will remain of each gang. The future history of this city will be a long road to create and not everyone is going to make it. Krul spares a thought for Alice – he has been abrupt with her of late but under the circumstances that is understandable, and he hopes they meet again when peace resumes. With his troops assembled just off The Monks' border, they know their signal to attack, with Victuis leading them into battle – the vampire deputy has longed for this moment. Krul suddenly looks toward The Forests as a howl rings out and the moon brings 9 Gang City into a new war. Leaping from his rock, Krul heads toward Holy Ground. Victuis leads his troops into battle, the waiting, the planning, the anticipation is over and a fresh start awaits until after the bloodshed. Monk gang members rise to arms when they see The Vampires approaching and scaling the security barrier. Leaping onto a rival, Victuis draws first blood, sinking his teeth into the neck of a monk, tasting the fresh blood pumping into his mouth, he can feel the pulse of his victim as he drinks before ripping the throat out to guarantee death. Standing in search of his next victim, he sees corpses already littering the area with some of his comrades fallen and reduced to ash. A panicking monk gang member calls through to Cathedral Tower that an invasion has taken place, just in time to let his superiors know before Victuis ends the call in furious fashion, removing the rival's throat and face. A blood lust has come over Victuis and all he wants is more, frenzied and berserk he goes on the hunt for another. At the security check with The Moors, a monk member sits in the hut with his heart pounding, adrenaline racing and a paranoia at every noise he hears. He is right to be. Princess Tunder is stood in the corner just as the light goes out, bringing darkness to the room. The monk, not knowing what to do and wondering where his back-up has gone, his knife is removed from his waist and plunged into his neck. Tunder turns him around to watch him die – she enjoys seeing the life disappear from people's eyes as they drift helplessly into death. Stepping out, The Dark Fairy goes to war.

On the border with The Forests, gunfire rings out as soon as The Monks see wolves running towards their borders, silver bullets bring down Lycans and return them to man-form but being outnumbered and panic causing aim to falter, The Werewolves penetrate their defence with ease and a bloodbath ensues. Cuthwulf at the forefront leading his pack, the alpha male proves his dominance as he lays waste the monk border force.

Krul phones William Henry Davis to inform him the war has started, which springs The Cannibals into action. This is their moment. With guns loaded and cars at the ready, The Cannibals smash and shoot their way through the perimeter fence, bringing them crashing down and shooting their way into monk turf. Krul then texts Cheng to goad him into attacking The Monks from the east.

Entering Holy Ground, Krul views the scattered remains of his enemy and joins his deputy and crew. They advance towards Cathedral Tower, knowing The Monks will send another squadron out to cut them off, but knowing they are totally surrounded on the western front will either heavily defend Cathedral Tower or retreat into Neutral Territory. Knowing Father Gideon, Krul thinks his obsession will be his downfall. Gideon won't want to leave the cathedral and allow it to fall into another gang's hands, so his own possessive ownership will make it easier for rivals to get to him.

Gideon orders his troops to assemble a defence around Cathedral Tower and orders a number of members to go out and stem the flow of rivals across the territory. This is a death penalty for the unlucky gang members that are selected – there isn't a hope they will stop all four gangs from reaching the cathedral, so it is a matter of when the gangs get to the cathedral and not if. Phoning Alice, he orders her to come to protect Cathedral Tower, and her already armed gang travel to Holy Ground, a nervousness filling their body and a return to the bad old days for Alice as memories of The War Against The Vampires come flooding back. Leo checking his gun is ready although he knows it is, this is simply a reassurance for himself as he heads into battle. Jessica sits worried about what is to come and let down that Cuthwulf didn't tell her about the plan to attack – only hours ago they made love, possibly for the last time and he didn't tell her his intentions. Cuthwulf has shown where his true loyalty lies and it is with his wolf pack just like any alpha wolf should be, loyal to the gang and although he does love Jessica, she is not his she-wolf, she is a rival and his honour to his people has remained his number one priority.

The Messengers' orders are to protect the pinnacle of the city, Cathedral Tower, the symbol of 9 Gang, the object of every member's desire. They are to be stationed in The Waiting Yard to add greater protection to Father Gideon and will be helped by some monk gang members. In the east, Cheng advances his army forward with ease as his superior firepower crushes The Monks' protection on the east side, and after Aiden's spies see this, The Irish, without

Siobhan, join the fight, which means it is only a matter of time before The Pagans attack after Aiden phones Brigacos to inform him war is upon them.

The Monks now being attacked from all sides and corners of the city learn the hard way as to why it is a bad idea to be landlocked by rivals; the force against them is too strong and with only The Messengers for back-up the countdown to their destruction has begun. It would be easy to blame Gideon's cancellation of the vote, but truth be told Krul knows it bore no meaning to his decision, he was always going to invade and was just waiting for a full moon to take advantage of The Werewolves' extra force in wolf form – the lunar cycle had more to do with his timing than Gideon's decision. The Vampires advance across monk territory, thirsty for more blood as they hear howls and gunfire in the near distance. It seems as though The Werewolves and The Cannibals have crossed paths, just as Krul planned it. He knew if he didn't reach out to the disillusioned cannibals, that Gideon may make them an offer they couldn't refuse, so Krul got there first with a tempting offer of war and possible supremacy preying on their victimised side about how they are oppressed by the city for their way of life. How the mortal gangs think they are monsters and how the monster gangs say they are mortal, leaving The Cannibals with nowhere to turn and feeling outcast from society. This is where mental manipulation comes in – Krul made offers of joining forces to fight back against oppression as he and his crew know how it feels and to a certain extent they did join together in destroying The Monks on the west side, but little did Krul tell them and much to The Cannibals' lack of forethought they have been cut off by The Werewolves, so now the war has already split into another gang battle.

Clifford Mitchell White hears growls all around him. Spinning in all directions he realises he is surrounded by werewolves and isolated from his gang, firing his gun in all directions in a panic, hoping a silver bullet hits a target until Wulfric pounces from the bushes, ripping the cannibal to pieces who stands no chance against the wolfman. Leaving the corpse in shreds, Wulfric heads off back into the night.

Alice and her crew arrive at The Waiting Yard and are greeted by panicked monk members with Gideon, Francis and Theodore nowhere to be seen. Alice takes control as she has experience in battle situations and strategically positions what little she has around as much area as she can realistically defend. Knowing that most of their immediate attack will come from the west, but they only have to hold out until sunrise, and The Vampires will have to retreat and The Werewolves will be much easier to fight against, although still very difficult. This leaves The Cannibals. Alice sends snipers up onto the roof to pick them off as they advance, and for The Witches, Alice prepares the stakes for burning and assembles gang members with flame throwers in a circle covering each other's back as she is all too aware one witch can teleport. Over on the east of the cathedral, she takes over the defence against the east side gangs with a barricade of fire power, positioning cars as the first line of defence with the petrol tanks facing the cathedral so they can be snipered and explode when The Chinese approach. The Irish and The Pagans will meet the same resistance. Rushing inside to speak to Gideon, Alice is furious with the leader and demands he stand with his troops.

"Gideon the Great," she sneers as he kneels to pray, Francis also in prayer and Theodore almost cowering in the corner. "Oh how the mighty have fallen," Alice mocks and exits the chapel room and heads back to her people. Taking the stairs to the roof to be with the snipers, Alice lies in wait with her scope out investigating the distance for the oncoming attack, with Leo on the east flank and Jessica on the ground ready for The Witches. Alice grips her walkie talkie and gives a team talk to the troops.

"Snipers, keep a look out for werewolves and cannibals, although most of The Cannibals will be decimated by now because they will have been cut off by The Werewolves, but some may have got through. Jessica, you stay alert for any witches, and Leo, don't just look for The Chinese, remember The Irish and The Pagans will be coming as well," Alice plans before looking back through her scope – no movement, no sound; the squad Gideon sent out will have reached the invasion by now.

Tunder stands in the road as a car hurtles down the road, the monk gang members sent out to intercept the oncoming attack see the witch stood awaiting their arrival and as they aim their guns to shoot, The Dark Fairy raises her hands as the car hurtles towards her. Waving her hands down, the car flips into the air, rising over her and smashes to the floor onto its roof. Tunder marches on to her destination as another monk carload makes its way toward her, lambs to the slaughter as Tunder teleports into the back seat of the car, startling all inside. Before they can react, she pulls a gun from the waist of a monk gang member, blasting him in the chest and shooting the passenger seat member through the back of the head, the bullet passing straight through and shattering the window. Turning to shoot the monk next to her, she lets rip the rest of the clip, leaving him lifeless, eyes open. The driver slams on the brakes in an attempt to send The Dark Fairy through the windscreen, but she does not move, not even a flinch. The monk sits in a panic, breathing deeply, his heart pounding and adrenaline making him dizzy and his fear makes him want to throw up. Not wanting to turn around, he slowly glances in his rear-view and sees Tunder staring at him from the back seat, her demonic eyes pierce his soul and he hears her voice in his head. Pulling his gun, he places it under his chin and pulls the trigger, blowing the top of his head to bits. Tunder sits and enjoys the moment before collecting trophies from her victims –

eyes, teeth, blood, things that can be used in spells. Vacating the car, she takes a step closer to Cathedral Tower. Grinding to a halt, the monk members form a barrier as extra defence against Krul and his gang, with stakes, crosses and holy water at the ready. Undeterred, The Vampire rush the barrier, breaking through the defence with ease and laying waste to what little resistance they managed to achieve, Krul and Victuis having their fill of enemy blood and onwards they march. Princess Tunder arrives at a house halfway towards Cathedral Tower. It is an arsenal used to stash weapons for a moment exactly like this; Father Gideon had it built after the last war so the security forces at the borders could fall back and re-arm. Tunder enters the house as she hears voices approaching. Hiding in a dark corner she sees two monk soldiers enter with some more waiting outside. The lights go out. Fumbling for a torch, one man searches the room for ammunition; the other keeps watch for anything lurking in the dark. Tunder crawls up the wall, her body facing them to keep watch, on to the ceiling slowly and surely, like a spider she peers down at them as their comrades outside tell them to hurry. Hearing a creak above, the soldiers shine the torch up to the ceiling, see a demon-faced Tunder drop on to them with a hiss, savaging their throats like an animal, blood spirting from their necks, they bleed their last as back-up from outside arrives. Seeing the bodies lifeless in a pool of blood, one suddenly rises up and hovers in the air, his head twisting around, breaking his neck and facing the opposite way, the remaining soldiers begin to fire blind into the darkness. The gunfire ends, bringing an eerie silence to the house. The gun smoke lingers, fogging the room, making it difficult for the soldiers to see if they have hit their target, but searching for a body they find nothing. Turning to escape, Tunder appears, latching on to a fleeing gang member like a ravenous beast sinking her teeth into him, the remaining soldier flees in terror, after the mutilated corpse falls to the floor. The Dark Fairy gives chase. Running into a nearby wood, the soldier looks back to see the witch chasing him, her eyes evil and never looking away. He runs faster, his heart feels like it is about to burst. Again glancing back, he sees she is still in pursuit – until he can run no longer and falls to his knees exhausted and gasping for breath. He looks up at the bushes in front of him as Tunder steps out. The fear is too much for the soldier whose eyes fill up and he weeps at the sight of his predator. Tunder slides his knife from its holster, the man too frozen stiff with fear to stop her, slowly slicing his throat. He chokes and struggles as she watches his passing, allowing the blood from his wound to soak on her hand; Tunder wipes it over her face in ritual so his life becomes part of hers. He drops to the floor motionless.

Heading towards the cathedral, Tunder looks into the distance. Her powers give her the ability to see all. A smile creeps its way across her face, but a smile that is not a twisted evil grin or even a smile of sick gratification, it is a smile of longing and love as she sees Victuis is still alive and fighting well for the cause. Her distant vision comes back to her surroundings and that demonic face returns; she has more hunting to do.

Back east, The Chinese plough through Holy Ground with ease, The Monks haven't even sent out a squadron to stop them and the eastern gangs make light work of the trip to Cathedral Tower; the only respite The Monks get is that The Irish and The Pagans have stopped a mile or so out, allowing The Chinese to continue on their path of destruction. Cheng wants to flex his military muscle and Aiden and Brigacos let him do just that; it makes it easier for them. Like a wave tossing ships out of the way, Cheng's army can't be stopped. Spying through his scope, Leo sees the first sign of invasion. Cheng stops his troops a little way out from the cathedral and through his binoculars smiles at the defence in front of him.

He thinks to himself that Alice must have organised this because it is well planned and from the mind of somebody who has fought in a war before but will fall eventually.

Leo readies his snipers and informs Alice of The Chinese presence. Joining her deputy on the east flank, she sees Cheng's army camped and after scoping around and seeing no Irish or Pagan presence, she knows they have stood back for Cheng to do the dirty work. Locked and loaded, both gangs pause for the other to fire, but neither does, becoming a standoff, but after a tense few moments Cheng make the first move, ordering his rocket launchers to fire like archers toward a castle. The walls of the cathedral explode on impact. The shock from Alice and Leo freezes them for a moment, but Alice quickly gives the order to sniper the rocket, launching gang members before they can reload. Gideon hears the explosions and sinks even deeper onto his knees, Francis rushes to a window to view the carnage and Theodore runs for his life.

Cheng orders his members to launch another round of rockets, but as they step forward they are all downed by monk and messenger snipers. Cheng orders more members to take their place. This time, he orders his soldiers to let fly a hail of bullets as cover for the rocket launchers, some Chinese gang members are picked off, but the rockets get through, obliterating the side of the cathedral. Alice and Leo know it is only a matter of time before the wall comes down. If they stay they will be sitting ducks, so they change tactics. Gathering all available gang members, including Father Gideon and Brother Francis, they leave the cathedral and break into two groups and spread out to go on the attack from either side of Cheng's army. The shootout is immense, with monks and messengers falling to their death.

Alice, along with Gideon and Francis, head northeast toward BC Nation, and Jessica and Leo take a team southeast toward

Emerald Territory. Alice calls Gwendoline, asking her to back her up, knowing The Pagans will be camped, biding their time. Gwen speaks with Brigacos and Bryson. If they attack The Chinese from both ends with The Irish coming from the south, they can have Cheng hemmed in where he will either have to retreat back to China Town or move west to the cathedral. By then the monster gangs will have arrived, now that they have wiped out the resistance that was sent their way. The Pagans agree and convince The Irish to attack: Alice's plan has worked.

As The Chinese unleash more firepower toward each flank, Cheng hears added gunfire coming from the north and south of his position. Knowing this is The Irish and The Pagans attacking, he fumes and orders Yong and Zhen to split into two groups and return fire toward each side whilst Cheng himself moves toward Cathedral Tower to take control of the symbol of the city. Approaching the cathedral, he hears howling coming from the near west and orders his crew to stay alert; the adrenaline pumps in each of them, the monster gangs will not be so easily defeated. Knowing The Vampires and The Witches will be here soon, maybe even here now, watching, Cheng enters Cathedral Tower, taking the showpiece with ease just like everybody knew he would – but keeping it will be much more difficult.

Brother Theodore, hiding in the cellar of the cathedral, knows he has nowhere to run – how would he survive out there? – slumped in a corner he is all alone, or so he thought. Theodore hears a noise coming from a dark corner. Trying to focus on the position the noise is coming from, he cannot make out what it is, he strains his ears in an attempt to identify the noise; the sound is like a cat purring. Suddenly realising who and what it is, the monk attempts to run towards the door, but a force field stops him in his tracks. He is paralysed, the only part of his body that works are his eyes so he can see the horror unfold in front of him. Princess Katalin forms into half-woman half-cat, with claws like knives on her fingers, her humanoid feline face stares at him menacingly before she plunges her claws into him. Ripping up as the blood streams from the wounds as Theodore gasps his last breath and slumps to the floor, the witch princess stands victorious still in the realm between woman and animal, she now has a taste for death and wants more. The Irish and The Pagans make little progress in their attack on The Chinese, Yong and Zhen have their squads well drilled and well defended, but the east side is now in the grip of a deadly battle, leaving the western gangs a clear passage to Cathedral Tower, where Cheng awaits their attack. Hearing gunfire from the north-western corner of the cathedral and roars of fury, Cheng knows The Werewolves have broken through his defences and sends back-up, to cut off their advance, or at least stall them, whilst Cheng secures Cathedral Tower.

The Vampires now covering the west flank of the city pick off some straggling cannibals. Krul orders his members to surround the cathedral and kill anything that isn't vampire or witch who approaches or leaves. Looking up at Cathedral Tower, he sees Chinese gang members on the roof ready to defend their newly gained prize to the death – and they will have to. The Vampires remain stationed outside, allowing The Werewolves to wreak havoc through Cheng's crew and hearing how much gunfire is coming from the east, Krul knows The Irish and The Pagans must have surrounded The Chinese. Meaning they will either push them toward the cathedral, then his crew will pick them off, or make them retreat back to China Town, or The Chinese destroy both of them; either way it is of little consequence to Krul. At the moment whatever destruction they bring upon each other is nothing but good news to the other gangs, and bringing destruction upon each other is what the human race does best.

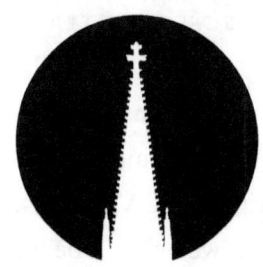

Chapter 22

The Chinese soldiers barricade themselves into a room within the cathedral after The Werewolves ripped through their defence in the corridor, with body parts scattered across the floor and blood spurts up the wall; Cuthwulf and his crew have served the cause well. Cheng orders his gang's flag to be raised from the top of Cathedral Tower and flown with pride so the entire city can see he has taken the flagship building of 9 Gang. Peering down from the roof, he sees The Vampires have surrounded the area and Krul looking up at him.

"What are you waiting for?" Cheng hollers down, arms outstretched as if fronting him for a fight. "Come and take it from me," Cheng adds, holding up a crossbow stake. Krul stares up unmoved, thinking Cheng has moved too soon, his desperation to take the tower has separated his crew into three sections; instead of biding his time and sticking together, now his gang are fighting on three fronts.

"Your hollow achievement means nothing, only a fool would separate his army into three groups and still be surrounded," Krul mocks Cheng's tactics, but the Chinese leader shakes his head, knowing it is all talk.

"Only a limited gang with limited power would have to run and hide as soon as the sun rises," Cheng returns the mocking with an obnoxious tone. "Just a few more hours and you and those ankle biters will be at my mercy. I might even put one on a lead and keep it as a pet." Cheng laughs as the insults fly.

Krul knows he is right. The Vampires will have to bed down for the day and The Werewolves will be human again soon, which swings the advantage into Cheng's favour. An explosion draws everybody's attention to the northeast near BC Nation as The Pagans are pushed back closer to their border by Yong and his squad. Alice ducks for cover as a Pagan gang member falls at her feet, choking his last after being hit in the throat by a Chinese bullet. It is a sight you don't want to watch but can't look away. He stares at her, breathless and motionless; it is said that when men die, they think about their mother and so she was with you at birth she is with you at least in mind at death. Turning and seeing the anxiety on Gwen's face as her gang are beginning to scatter as The Chinese move forward picking off The Pagans one by one before another explosion sends some more of them into pieces and to a gruesome death, Alice realises the collaboration wasn't a good idea after all.

In the southeast, The Irish are putting up a better fight, but Zhen is gaining the upper hand, spreading her crew across the border with Emerald Territory, meaning Aiden and his gang will either have to retreat or come at them head on, and with The Chinese firepower that isn't a good idea. The plan is not turning out how it was imagined as quadrupling up on Cheng's gang up until now has failed. The Monks, The Messengers, The Irish and The Pagans have been dealt a hammer blow and their gangs are in tatters. Cuthwulf rips through another Chinese gang member, leaving him in pieces, and approaching the barricaded door gunfire comes from small hole just big enough to fit the end of a gun through but fails to take down the alpha wolf, rushing the door and smashing into it, the barricade is obliterated and the Chinese gang members who were so sure their defence was sound are flung across the room. Wulfric and Randall, along with their crew, enter the room and lay waste to whatever moves that is not Lycan. The floor, walls and ceiling are turned red and body parts are scattered across the room. The Werewolves make their way in whichever direction they please. Cheng turns his attention to The Werewolves' advancement through Cathedral Tower, leaving The Vampires a chance to enter the cathedral from multiple sides, Krul entering through The Waiting Yard and Victuis around the main entrance. The Vampires march on to claim back the building their founder built as Krul steps over Chinese body parts and dead werewolves, up the stairs and into the old throne room where High Council meetings take place, now the scene of a war. Hearing fighting on the upper level, Krul orders his troops to stay alert and, if need be, take a gun from the dead gang members and shoot The Werewolves – easier to shoot them than fight them; his crew arm themselves.

Tunder approaches a cathedral deep in conflict and yet no resistance to her approach; knowing her sisters are here, the magical force strengthens and The Witches ease their way towards their queen's throne where she once sat with Niculi by her side. Yong successfully pushes The Pagans back onto BC Nation and Brigacos and his gang have suffered major losses, Gideon for the first time in 20 years feels the horror of war, realising he has had it too easy in his two decades in leadership, and Francis in panic mode fires blind and runs. Yong leads his squad over the border with little issue and a wave of conquest enters pagan turf. Seeing Francis flee like a coward, Druid Bryson turns his attention to the monk deputy chasing him down with some conflicted belief that this is all his fault, when really it is his own hatred being given an excuse to inflict pain, injury and death on a man Bryson sees as a symbol of everything wrong with Christianity and 9 Gang City. The tyrannical control the demonised Gods. Bryson tackles Francis to the ground, laying a beating to the monk who attempts to fight back, but exhaustion and lack of skill and training give him little chance. Pulling his knife, Bryson stabs Francis repeatedly until his arm grows too tired to stab any more. Francis lies lifeless as Bryson stares down at Francis staring back. Hearing someone behind him, Bryson spins around, seeing Alice staring back but saying nothing, just a look of shock and disgust. Druid Bryson has crossed the line between killing somebody in war and murdering another human being.

"This is war, Alice," Bryson utters, standing to his feet and turning to her after wiping the blood off his knife on Francis' clothing and placing it back in its holder.

"That was not war," Alice snaps back with venom in her voice at his audacity to try and excuse what he has done. "That was murder, cold blooded murder," she adds, her tone growing in disgust and anger.

"Splitting hairs, aren't you? How many people have you killed?" Bryson continues with his self-defence.

Alice shakes her head at his comment. "There is a difference between killing and murdering," Alice replies, but their argument is cut short by gunfire, and Bryson ducks for cover as Yong is closing in. They both return fire and retreat deeper into BC Nation. Yong stands over Francis' dead body before watching Bryson and Alice run away, leaving Yong thinking it is not the first time a member of this city has been murdered, and Alice was very keen to put the blame on Zhen Yun for the Enigma murder.

Approaching the rooftop, Krul and The Vampires hear the battle between The Chinese and The Werewolves, Cheng's crew holding firm in their defence and using strategic sharpshooting to down the wolf attack. Without warning, The Werewolves are flung in any direction the force field takes them. Looking behind them, Krul and Victuis see Tunder standing in her typical menacing pose, a look of almost irritation on her face that rival gangs think they have a right to be in Cathedral Tower and a disgust at the mere thought of bowing to anybody. The Vampires storm the barricade to the rooftop, as Cheng urgently calls Yong and Zhen for back-up, not knowing how much longer he can hold out. Readying his flamethrowers and holy water, The Chinese leader frantically searches for a possible escape route from the rooftop – there isn't one unless they jump. Yong tells his leader he is about to destroy The Pagans and claim their territory as their own, but Cheng orders him to bring his squad to the cathedral. Zhen Yun instantly turns her squad around and makes way toward her leader, bringing a sigh of relief from The Irish. Aiden and Cormac regroup and count their losses. Brigacos slumps to the floor as Gwen sees to the soldiers. Bryson still has his mind on Francis' dead body staring at him – he notices Alice looking at him and considers his next move: if he and Alice should survive the war, he could be charged with a war crime. Dowsing any vampires that come near them with holy water, The Chinese continue their defence of Cathedral Tower, but their efforts are waning and Cheng begins to panic. After seeing one of his members thrown from the rooftop by Tunder's magic, he clutches a flamethrower and covers as much of the area he can, forcing The Dark Fairy into retreat. Cheng feels a sharp pain in his back; the pain grows as his body becomes colder, the sharpness intensifies as he looks down and sees five sharp claws exiting his body. Dropping his weapon, he looks up and sees the despair on his gang members' faces with Krul and Victuis staring at him, Krul with a look of 'this is a defining moment in the history of the city' and Victuis with an expression of another rival gone is a step closer to victory. To Cheng it is as if the world has gone into slow motion, back-up won't get here in time, and time is something he no longer has. All the firepower and military might has come to nothing as far as Cheng is concerned. Sometimes clandestine warfare is the greater option – you can have all the guns you can carry, but if you can hide in the darkness and move in the shadows without a soul knowing you are there, then the option to strike without the risk of your victim being able to strike back leaves you in a position to conquer with only the bloodshed and life lost of those whom you need to be rid of. Should Cheng have kept his gang together, should he have stayed with Yong and Zhen to fight off The Pagans and The Irish? The temptation of taking the tower was too much and human desire has once again been its downfall. Looking behind him he sees a cat staring back at him, the eyes marble like but with a human twist, Princess Katalin lifts him off his feet her claws dripping with blood as Cheng is throw against the wall and slumping to the floor. Krul and Victuis with the rest of their gang decimate the rest of the remaining Chinese gang members who have had the fight taken out of them after seeing their leader fall, but before any victory can be claimed The Werewolves burst onto the rooftop, Victuis spraying them with bullets, taking them down, before Cuthwulf enters the fray, swinging at Krul, slicing his chest. Krul lifts him off his feet and he crashes to the ground. Wulfric charges at the vampire leader to support his pack member until Victuis intercepts his attack and a brawl starts between Nosferatu and Lycan. Ferocious and brutal, the nightmare creatures go toe-to-toe; Krul and Cuthwulf tear shreds off each other and Victuis takes on Wulfric and Randall, Krul sinking his teeth into Cuthwulf's neck before the wolfman sends the vampire leader across the rooftop with an uppercut. Taking on two werewolves is a task Victuis handles well, dropping Randall and laying blow after blow into Wulfric, whilst Tunder lays waste to the werewolf gang members with a gun full of silver bullets she has taken from a dead Chinese gang member. Wolf after wolf is dropped to its death and returning to men scattered across the roof of Cathedral Tower. Yong and Zhen Yun meet at the edge of the cathedral and assemble their troops; and with no time to waste enter locked and loaded, exhausted from battle but knowing they need to continue for a while longer at least until the sun rises. Making haste up the stairs like a swat team with every angle covered and watching each other's back, they enter the meeting room to see Queen Rika sat in the chair that once housed Father Gideon but now the witch queen takes centre stage. Yong, knowing the power Rika possesses, orders his troops to retreat as he covers their escape. Rika stands to her feet, eyes locked on the new Chinese leader. Yong stands transfixed on the witch queen as she approaches. In his mind he sees himself as leader of his gang. This is true now that Cheng is dead. He sees himself leader of 9 Gang City. This could be true if the war ends with Chinese victory. Yong then has a vision of Zhen Yun assassinating Enigma followed by a future sight of Zhen killing Yong for her own political gain, her own desire to rule, her obsession with being Empress of The Chinese and have all before her bow and kneel at her feet. Zhen Yun sits on a golden throne, dressed in beautiful traditional Chinese clothing after western values have been crushed, the east rules supreme and her conquest complete.

"Every mind's desire is a toy for me to play with," Queen Rika mocks as Yong stands defenceless, still transfixed on the visions in his mind. Rika breaks her concentration when she sees Zhen Yun approach her with courage and no fear, intent on saving her gang member. Firing flame to burn the witch, Zhen unleashes the full barrel as Rika cackles as she mystifies into a thick fog and escapes to the rooftop and out over the city. Krul watches as she disappears southwest towards The Moors. Turning to see flame and smoke coming up from the old throne room, he also notices the eastern distance begin to lighten and The Vampires' fight is up and a retreat is necessary to prolong their fight in the future.

Cuthwulf drops to the floor and with the morning light bringing release to his man form, he lies naked on the floor. Wulfric and Randall along with their crew scatter the rooftop, wolf become men and one nature becomes another. Clutching a crossbow stake, Cuthwulf is taking no chances with The Vampires; although he wanted a union between the monster gangs, one was never agreed to, meaning they are enemies. The wolf pack retreat with no fight from Krul; he has his own escape to make. The fire has covered most of the meeting room and The Werewolves jump through the flames to their escape, some of them falling to their death as they exit the cathedral from Chinese gunfire who have stationed themselves outside like a firing squad, Cuthwulf claiming a firearm from the floor and returning fire.

The Vampires, needing to slumber, escape the rising sun by going deep into the depth of Cathedral Tower, a place only vampire and witch can go. Niculi and Ziana needed somewhere to be safe during the day, and Krul and Victuis are no exception. Tunder leads the way, exchanging the odd glance towards Victuis who returns the gesture. Entering the secret room that Ziana created underneath the tower, The Vampires now have a place to rest and regain strength to continue fighting another night, knowing their friends within darkness, The Witches, will protect them.

Using dead Chinese bodies for cover, The Werewolves blast their way to freedom, causing Yong and his gang to dive for cover as the flamethrower canisters explode after being hit by silver bullets intended for wolfmen. As Cuthwulf and his crew disappear into the distance, The Chinese themselves know they need to rest and although the thought of slaying The Vampires in their sleep is tempting, knowing they are protected by The Witches, Yong calls Cheng in an attempt to contact his leader, fearing the worst but hoping for the best: no answer. Yong camps the troops on the edge of the cathedral with a feeling of dread that his leader has fallen. With no answer from Cheng, Yong takes command.

Chapter 23

Alice calls Jessica, praying she answers, and after a tense wait, she hears the soothing sound of her sister's voice. Hearing Leo in the background, Alice breathes a sigh of relief that they have survived. Informing Alice of the situation in the southeast, Jessica tells her that The Irish have lost heavy numbers; Aiden and Cormac are still alive but devastated and demoralised at their beating; Siobhan is still recovering and weak but wanting to fight; and their own crew members have fared well and only a small number of monk members remain. Alice returns the gesture by informing Jessica and Leo that The Pagans have suffered even more and would have been conquered had it not been for The Chinese returning to Cathedral Tower. Father Gideon is still alive, but Brother Francis is dead; she does not tell them how he died. Wanting to join up with each other, but fearing a Chinese ambush, the sisters know it is better for them to remain where they are. Alice informs Jessica to rest and stay safe, two things that seem impossible in these times but are also necessary. Alice tells her sister she loves her and hangs up, her eyes filling up with a tear rolling down her cheek. Gwen hugs her for comfort, knowing she cannot say anything as words at a time like this are just noises coming out of someone's mouth.

Watching Krul sleep, Queen Rika stands over him as he lies helpless and at her mercy. The Vampires' reliance on The Witches over the centuries has been extreme, none more so than Ziana watching over her beloved Niculi, a task she saw as her duty as a loyal wife and companion, and she instilled it into her people that it was their job to do such a thing. Noticing Tunder standing close to Victuis' coffin, Rika watches her sister and sees the longing on her face – only Victuis brings this out in her. The queen approaches Tunder unable to read her thoughts and wanting to know her intentions.

"Why have you blocked your thoughts?" Rika asks her sister, who doesn't look back, she barely acknowledges that her queen is there, delaying her answer until she wants to give it.

"Why are you trying to read them?" Tunder replies nonchalantly, which irritates her leader.

"Because I am leader of our people and I need, want and demand to know what each and every one of our members is thinking so I can…" Rika's rant is interrupted by her sister's defiant attitude and an air of disrespect.

"Control everybody, control every witch to worship you, gain The Leadership by mind controlling every thought in everyone's mind," Tunder tells Rika her own plan to conquer who doesn't like the attitude her sister is giving her but also grows nervous when Tunder behaves this way. The Dark Fairy has grown rapidly in her powers to such an extent even Rika and Katalin are surprised by her progress in recent years, but defiantly the last few months, Tunder is obsessed with Queen Ziana and has studied all kinds of different types of magic. Magic does not come in one style or standard, it comes in many forms and is so ancient it is doubtful any witch knows every spell ever created, but there are old spells and newly created spells and these sometimes cross over to create a more powerful hybrid of both the old and new. Tunder's teleportation ability is an example of such a hybrid; in the old times witches used to fly on broomsticks to their destination, now Tunder can teleport to where she wants to go instead of flying – a more modern and in a way more scientific approach to the power of doing what non-witches can't. Queen Ziana is the greatest witch of all time because she was the most powerful, her ability to do things no other witch could do made people believe she was of a higher force, to a point no other witch knew some of the spells she could produce; and when you are the only one who can do something it not only gives you a position of authority, it makes people admire and fear you, depending on the way of thinking of each individual person. Ziana was born a witch; a warlock father and a witch mother, she was destined to dwell in magic but how far that dwelling would go was not expected, but to her, magical advancement is only common sense for any witch that wants to reign supreme and conquer the sceptics and naysayers and most of all the religious tyrants who tell witches they are the whores of Satan and should burned at the stake for heresy.

In her younger years, Ziana used to wander the country roads of Hungary telling fortunes for just enough money to eat. As she grew older, she would venture into nearby towns and eventually cities, so as her courage and custom grew so did her magic. Like an evolution of sorcery, the gypsy girl would advance in strength and power. Some spells are impossible to conjure for weak witches, it is not just about magical power, it is also having the physical strength to handle the power that you need to cast a spell; and the woman who would later be queen of the witches and founder of The Witches gang, to some she is Goddess of Witches, developed that strength parallel to the evolving of sorcery. Ziana heard a song once many years ago from an English gypsy girl which she remembered with great fondness as it reminded Ziana of herself:

A gypsy I was born,
A gypsy I'll remain,
Telling young maids their fortune,
Myself I will maintain.

Gypsy life is a culture and a tradition, and as with most things that mainstream society does not quite understand, they find strange and some even develop a hatred for whatever they don't understand because what people don't understand causes them fear, and humankind hates what makes it fearful. Yet again this brings us back to the one problem in this world, the human race. Not all gypsies are witches and not all witches are gypsies, but in Ziana's case the two are as one. Mythology is rich in stories of witchcraft, the undead, people becoming wolves, animals becoming human, almost a crossover of worlds with one world, and a witch like Ziana is at the forefront of that crossover. Another song she remembered, is an old Scottish rhyme which relates to Ziana even more so than the other song:

Of fairies, witches, gypsies,
My nourrice sang to me,
Of gypsies, witches, fairies,
I'll sing again to thee.

Hearing songs that almost sound as if they were writing about her or for her, only gave a greater belief to the queen that it was her destiny to rule and grow in power, but with power comes enemies and there was no shortage of those when The CVS travelled east with their righteous ideology and dreams of saving what they assumed wanted to be saved. Ziana is an idol of witch kind and Princess Tunder idolises the witch she wants to be. Idolising to a point Tunder has developed a visionary spell that can be cast into her own mind and give her a knowledge of what Queen Ziana did, thought and felt at precise moments in history. Princess Tunder knows exactly how history occurred and it is not what the city histories tell, hence the hatred for mortal kind and animosity towards people who have discriminated against the black arts and wiccan spirituality in the name of a theory of how we came to exist and how that existence wants us to live when in fact we don't know for certain how we came to be and maybe the gypsy magic of which Ziana lived by is the greater force. It is all down to belief and until belief is proven to be wrong by fact, perhaps humanity should stop its prejudgement and consider the alternative… but the chances of that are extremely small.

Ziana's magic started with the gypsy arts but extended into Celtic pagan magic once she settled in Britain and 9 Gang City was founded, therefore within her own power creating a hybrid of gypsy magic and druid celt magic, giving her an advantage over everybody in 9 Gang City and over any witch or warlock she came across. Tunder has continued with this witch philosophy of evolving magic to empower the witch to a point she has grown knowledgeable of the pagan belief in reincarnation, a power that Ziana herself was interested in. To cast a spell of self-reincarnation would be to achieve self-necromancy, meaning when or if you die you can come back as anyone and anything, but it is you in soul and existence. Unknown to The Pagans, Princess Tunder has been studying their culture just as Ziana did. The magic arts of the Druids are split into four sections: Necromancy, Prophecy, Divination and Second Sight. Add this to reincarnation and you have the ability to raise the dead as another being plus having the ability to read the past to gain knowledge of how that person died, so the same mistakes can be avoided, prophesies on when and where this reincarnation will occur and the second sight into the spirit world to make contact with that person. Mix all these powers with future sight and you already know how events will turn out. This could make you invincible. These are all magical powers Tunder has been studying and if she achieves what she wants to achieve, there is no hope for 9 Gang City. In Celtic Druidism speaking to and raising the dead is called Taghairm and translates into English as "An echo", meaning a reply from the spirit world, and these lands Albion and Hibernia have connections to the spirit world, or so myth would have us told. As far back as Moses when he was in Egypt he told people that a fairy princess had told him the way the land should be conquered and this fairy princess was a stone and this stone is in myth said to have been taken from Scone, 9th century capital of modern day Scotland, to Westminster by King Edward as he believed the stone was the fairy princess, Princess Scota and this stone was originally in Ireland but taken to Scotland. Stories of fairy princesses, Moses, conquering land, future sight, prophecy, Druids, pagans, gypsies, it all fits together perfectly for Tunder and her desire to fulfil her destiny grows along with her magical powers.

Queen Rika, annoyed with her sister's attitude, changes the subject to another matter she wants to know about and has been evident in recent months, but has always had a suspicion of affection.

"What is your relationship with Victuis?" Rika asks in a demanding tone.

Tunder glances at the vampire deputy as he rests. "Time will tell," The Dark Fairy responds, dismissing her sister's intrusive question, which only adds to the anger in Rika.

"Then tell me what time has told you," Rika snaps, growing tired of Tunder's defiant attitude.

"I have already told you what is going to happen," Tunder replies, turning to her angrily. "I've already told you about the prophecy," she adds.

"Then if our people are destined to return to power, why have an attitude? Why block your thoughts?" the queen asks.

"Because they are mine and to let you in would be to allow myself to be under your control," Tunder replies, not wanting Rika to know the truth.

"I am your queen and it is my order that you submit yourself to me," Rika barks but instantly changes to a smile when she reads Tunder's mind and sees herself on the throne with Krul as her king, and Katalin and Tunder her loyal sisters and servants. Queen Rika's ego is comforted by the future sight Tunder has given her; The Dark Fairy is quickly becoming a specialist in predictions and prophecies, and Rika has become almost reliant on her two sisters, instead of mastering all magic, she believes reading minds and controlling them is enough to take her to glory. Princess Tunder beds down and rests for the day after one last loving glance at Victuis.

Returning to The Forests to recuperate, The Werewolves approach their HQ when suddenly gunshots ring out from all corners and their members fall like toy soldiers as they are blasted without mercy, Cuthwulf diving for cover and crawling to the safety of HQ. Entering the building he peeps out of the door seeing Cannibals ducked behind the trees and Wulfric and Randall heading toward him. Running for a gun, the wolf leader flinches when a gunshot hits the wall mere millimetres from his face. Seeing William Henry Davis, Cuthwulf dives for The Cannibals' leader, tackling him to the ground. Davis, pulling a silver blade after his gun hurtles across the room, swings at Cuthwulf, who dodges the attack and lays a firm punch into Davis' face, sending him slumping to the floor. Wulfric and Randall rush in and land kick after kick to Davis as he is laid out. Picking the cannibal up, Cuthwulf takes him battered and beaten to the front door to show the rest of The Cannibals their leader is hostage. Seeing Davis, his crew stop their attack, knowing he has failed in his ambush. James Winston Wycombe orders a ceasefire.

"I am keeping him as a prisoner of war," Cuthwulf shouts to James Winston Wycombe, who is crouched behind a tree but can be seen looking out from his cover.

"Give him back to us and we'll leave," Wycombe shouts back. Cuthwulf shakes his head, knowing that will lose him his leverage.

"Retreat, or I will blow his head off," Cuthwulf replies, angry at the assassination attempt on his life.

Wycombe tries to play the diplomat which amuses the werewolf leader.

"That would make you guilty of a war crime," Wycombe shouts, making sure everybody hears and is witness to the threat.

"I find that difficult to take coming from a people that kidnaps, murders and eats other people," Cuthwulf bellows to his unwanted guest. "Also, your scumbag leader just tried to blow my head off in an ambush. Did you spend any time in Neutral Territory a few days ago" Cuthwulf asks referring to the Enigma murder. The Cannibals would have had access to The Messengers' turf, The Monks would have assumed they were invited to celebrate with the other gangs, therefore giving The Cannibals the perfect opportunity to commit the crime.

"Enigma was a liability to The Vampires," Wycombe responds in a heartless tone. "But it wasn't us that killed her. If you ask me, it was The Monks to stop the vote – and look what happened: the vote was stopped," Wycombe adds, piling the blame on Gideon and his crew.

Wulfric and Randall have armed themselves and their gang, and are ready for retaliation. Ushering Davis out of the door, Cuthwulf stands him in full view of The Cannibals, cocks his Glock and pulls the trigger. William Henry Davis drops to the ground lifeless. His gang burst from HQ, guns blazing, The Cannibals shooting back and retreating, with wolves in man form chasing them down. Cuthwulf looks down at Davis' dead body and knows he has just become a war criminal but not caring one bit – it is only what Davis was trying to do to him, in Cuthwulf's mind William Henry Davis got what he deserved.

Yong frantically calls Cheng again with Zhen looking at him worried about their leader, but again receives no answer. Staring at Cathedral Tower, Yong wants to go and look for Cheng but knowing The Witches will be hiding in every dark corner he ponders his chances. Never being a coward, Yong arms himself with a flamethrower and some holy water in case any vampires wake from their slumber. Zhen offering to go with him is refused because if Cheng is dead and Yong should die, the gang needs a leader and that should be Zhen. She reluctantly agrees knowing Yong is right but worrying for his safety. Taking one last look at the cathedral and then back to Zhen, Yong orders his troops to stay where they are and rest before heading into Cathedral Tower. Upon entrance the only sight he is met with is the dead bodies scattered across the corridor, the blood pools on the floor and worst of all the open eyes of dead gang members staring at him – he could have sworn he saw some of them move. Slowly creeping his way up the stairs, the smoke from the extinguished fire pollutes the air. Not knowing how the fire was put out, he continues toward the meeting room, but on hearing a whisper he stops. A gloom begins to lurk over the stairway and it becomes more difficult to see. He hears a cackling laughter and begins darting from one direction to another. Firing some flame just in case and for reassurance, he sees and hits nothing. Climbing the next staircase he hears footsteps below. Darting to the banister to look down, he sees only darkness so fires some more flame to light up the area: nothing. Kicking open the doors to the meeting room, he sees the damage is immense – the High Council table is destroyed and surrounding area is black and charred. Walking slowly and cautiously through the room, he hears more footsteps from the stairway up to the roof. Yong ducks down behind the table where only a few days before High Council were sat discussing matters – how petty a broken fence seems now. Peering out and towards where the footsteps are coming from, he sees Cheng come into view. With a skip of the heart and a gasp of relief, Yong stands to greet his leader who smiles at his deputy and is honoured he came back in to look for him. They bow to one another and then embrace.

"Be careful," Yong whispers cautiously. "There are witches about," he adds, turning to head for the exit, fire at the ready for any shadow dwellers that are hiding.

Cheng nods his head and follows his deputy out of the meeting room. Sticking close to the wall and one another, the two men make their escape from this dingy setting that just recently was a grand set of stairs leading to the symbol of the city, now an almost derelict-looking mess with scorch marks and bloodstains galore, taking it form grandeur to graveyard. Their surrounding has become deafeningly silent, there is no noise whatsoever and it makes Yong nervous, his heart pounding at the sound of nothing, returning to the corpses on the floor. The two Chinese comrades exit into The Waiting Yard, much to the delight of Zhen and the crew. Zhen greets her leader with the cultural bow but her heart beats rapidly with delight and relief. The rest of the gang bow and salute to honour their returned leader. Giving the order to retreat, Cheng prepares to leave much, to the surprise of Yong and Zhen who look bewildered by their superior's plan. Cheng stares emotionless at them and repeats the order, pointing in the direction of Neutral Territory, knowing The Irish and The Pagans will be licking their wounds and will not attack. The Messengers and The Monks are decimated, and even if they do put up a fight they will be crushed, so Neutral Territory is there for the taking.

"But, sir, we should attack The Vampires now whilst they sleep?" Zhen utters confused as to why the gang is retreating.

Cheng shakes his head. "What about The Witches?" he asks questioning her rationale. "They will have put an enchantment on the vampires' resting place. You couldn't get to The Vampires even if you tried, it would be a death trap for us," Cheng adds, knowing Zhen's lust for combat is the downfall of her political prowess; it is not just about fighting and killing, you have to be tactical sometimes, meaning attacking for the sake of it is sometimes the worst thing you can do. Zhen looks at Yong who says nothing and forms his troops for retreat. The Chinese march away from the cathedral and towards Neutral Territory in the hope of some unoccupied turf and maybe even a new addition to their territory. Approaching The Messengers' HQ, Cheng orders a watch around the edge whilst the rest eat and sleep after being up all-night fighting; he will send relief to them later. Yong and Zhen follow him into the building and look around for somewhere to sleep that is not too exposed to an attack. Cheng and Yong find a large room each with some soldiers for protection and bed down for some much-needed sleep, Zhen has a room to herself with her protection outside if she needs them. Zhen's eyes are heavy and her mind slowly fades into dream with the exhaustion of the night's fighting taking its toll and she falls into a deep sleep. But suddenly awaking, eyes locked on the door as she heard a creak outside, standing to investigate she opens the door and sees the horror that awaits – her gang members savaged and killed, body parts scattered and their insides on the outside.

Rushing to the nearest room, which happens to be Yong's, she enters and at first can't quite make out what is happening, until she sees Yong's lifeless eyes staring straight ahead and Cheng crouched down, savaging his throat. Cheng, sensing someone in the room, turns to face Zhen, his teeth coved in blood and throat, and his eyes give away his true identity. Bolting from the room, Zhen runs for her flamethrower, Tunder hot on her heels, crawling out of the door and along the wall. Zhen dives for her weapon, turning and firing without aim. Tunder, seeing the danger, teleports mid-air before the flame reaches her and the room goes up in a blaze. Saving herself by smashing the window and escaping, the remaining Chinese members rushing to her aid, Zhen turns to look at the building for no other reason than to hope Yong is alive, but she knows he isn't. Adding to the heartbreak this also means Cheng is dead, and Zhen Yun falls to her knees and cannot hold back the tears.

After a few hours' rest and desperately needed sleep, Alice asks a gang member for his binoculars to give herself a better view of the smoke pluming from the distance. From the direction she knows it is on her land, meaning somebody has either claimed it or is destroying it. Meeting with Father Gideon and The Pagans, they discuss their next plan of action.

"We have to do something, we can't just wait here for another attack," Brigacos states to the room.

Alice nods in agreement, wanting to investigate what is happening on her land.

"If we join up with The Irish, we can go to their land via Neutral Territory," she suggests and receives mixed responses.

Brigacos and Bryson agree, but Gideon and Gwen think they should hold where they are and defend BC Nation, knowing on their journey south, they could be attacked at any time.

"If the Chinese are between here and The Irish, we will be outnumbered and outgunned," Gideon says, getting the feel for war again, the old days coming back to him.

"I agree," Gwen chips in. "We don't know what is happening from here to Emerald Territory and we have already lost enough lives," she adds, thinking it may be a suicide mission.

Alice shakes her head.

"We can each make our own decision, but I am taking my people south to meet up with Jessica and Leo, and I want to know what is going on back home," Alice tells them in a no-nonsense tone.

Brigacos agrees to the journey and tells Bryson to order the troops to assemble; Gwen urges them to reconsider but the decision is made.

"Did any of you see Francis?" Gideon asks, hoping he is still alive but fearing he is not.

Alice feels uncomfortable and takes a snide look at Bryson, who looks back at her wondering if she will tell Gideon the truth.

"No," Alice replies, feeling awful. "I didn't see him," she says, knowing that at the moment a lie is best for the collective of the mission.

After speaking with Aiden on the phone who told him The Irish welcome their visit and will meet them at Messenger HQ to accompany them back for safety in numbers, Brigacos takes another look at his beloved land, not knowing what will become of it. The journey south begins and who knows what awaits.

Chasing down cannibals, The Werewolves are relentless in their pursuit and take no prisoners – why should they after the dirty ambush The Cannibals committed against them? With every cannibal killed, a feeling of vengeance for their fallen members satisfies Wulfric who only last night butchered Clifford Mitchell White and doesn't know or remember, all he knows now is The Cannibals would do the same to them if the shoe was on the other foot. Almost diving into a car, Wycombe makes his retreat and drives off in any direction to escape. Wulfric calls a stop to the pursuit and watches some cannibal members dart off into the distance. Returning to HQ, Wulfric and Randall see the dumped body of William Henry Davis in the bushes, discarded like a piece of rubbish with little humanity and decency for a man who had none whatsoever for anybody. A man who was elite but in the end was an ambushing coward and even then he failed; a blueblood of ancestry, a descendant of the founder of the gang that he led only now to be left for the wolves, a beaten corpse that has been thrown into the overgrowth with no care or respect.

Entering HQ, Wulfric hears Cuthwulf on the phone. By his tone he assumes he is talking to Jessica – the relief that one another is alive must be immense so he leaves them to it and organises the troops into two groups, one to eat and rest, and the other to keep watch for enemies; they will swap later. Jessica's heart skipped when she heard Cuthwulf's voice, knowing he has survived the night and is safe. After discussing their losses they move on to the pleasantries... Like asking why he didn't tell her about when the war was going to start. Cuthwulf says it was because he didn't want it to get out until the war started – if The Monks found out they would have sent more troops to the border, therefore making it more dangerous for him and his gang. Jessica thinks it is a fair reason, but she would not have told anybody, not even Alice. Cuthwulf's apology and three magic words are enough to forgive him; in a city like this there isn't enough love, so Jessica wants to keep the love she has.

Chapter 24

Approaching home, Alice sends a scout ahead to spy on whatever is waiting for them, if anything, when they get to HQ. Stopping his army, Brigacos phones Aiden to inform them of their position. The Irish leader tells him they will be there shortly but to be careful as he has seen The Chinese in the area. Alice's phone vibrates; it is the scout telling her HQ is on fire and there are dead Chinese members scattered around but no dead members from other gangs. Alice wonders what has happened – did The Werewolves come this far east, have The Vampires occupied the land and are now in slumber in the building, have The Witches claimed the turf as their own? Alice orders her members and informs Gideon and Brigacos to arm their flamethrowers and keep their stakes ready. After word from Aiden that they are approaching Messengers HQ, Alice and Gideon along with their members, split from The Pagans and surround the area, with The Irish covering the other side. The smoke from the blaze gets thicker as the flames engulf the building. Scoping the area, Alice decides to step out and investigate; with her crew and Gideon for back-up she inspects the dead bodies. They have been massacred, some with their throats cut, some disembowelled, decapitated, eyes removed, teeth pulled out – this is witch work. If it were vampires they would be drained of blood and at most throats ripped to confirm death, instead of turning them into a vampire. If The Werewolves had done it, the bodies would be brutalised with no pattern, just animalistic rage defeating an enemy, this is twisted murder but with reason. The reason being to test out new spells, when and where they can, better to try out a new weapon to discover its true power than during a war, trying new magic, collecting ingredients for hexes and curses. Alice knows a witch has been here, clutching her flame thrower for reassurance. Hearing someone approaching, Alice turning quickly sees Jessica. They run to each other and embrace, happy that each other is safe, likewise with Leo. The Messengers are united again and organise what few members they have.

Shaking hands with Aiden, Brigacos talks numbers and tactics with The Irish leader, guessing that if The Chinese took on the monster gangs, they would be surely depleted in numbers by now and should march west to Cathedral Tower whilst there is still sunlight. Knowing that if The Chinese are fewer in numbers and by the scene in front of them they are, The Werewolves will be men during the day and will have retreated back to The Forests to regroup. The Vampires will be in hiding from the sun, The Cannibals will either be wiped out or on their own turf, knowing they cannot match the monster gangs' power. This leaves only The Witches between them and Cathedral Tower. Aiden agrees with his logic but questions his eagerness to take on The Witches, remembering all too well what Tunder did to him in the very building that burns in front of them. The Arch Druid knows it could be now or never; in fact, what other option do they have? Wait until darkness when The Vampires are awake, wait for the next full moon when The Werewolves are Lycan, or stay where they are and wait for the monster gangs to come to them, which they surely will? There is no way The Vampires will leave the east side alone – if or when they conquer the cathedral they will move east to conquer the city. Aiden knows this is true and agrees to march west. Alice and Gideon agree and after collecting supplies from the dead bodies they move toward Holy Ground with the fear that they face creatures unholy.

Back in China Town, Zhen Yun, knowing she has inherited the gang from her fallen and much missed superiors, orders a security force at the border but to retreat to Chinese HQ if an enemy approaches and to inform her of the attack. Sitting in Cheng's chair in his office which is now her chair and her office, Zhen can't hold back the tears and her tough girl image is shattered with the loss of two people she held most dear. Despite the discipline and honour, Yong was a good man who had looked after Zhen when they first arrived in England, he was kind and thoughtful in private, and respectful and professional amongst others. Cheng was the best leader the gang has ever had, he united a people who, although were one gang and one race, they were dived by nationality. China-born Chinese and English-born had a cultural difference which sometimes came between them. Some of the China-born saw themselves as pure and the English-born as westernised mongrels, many were divided by the language barrier, some China-born didn't speak or learn English and the English-born didn't speak any dialect of Chinese. Cheng changed all of that by teaching his gang that it does not matter where you were born or what country you are from, they are as one and should embrace each other as brothers and sisters in arms. He also made it a gang rule that all members must learn to speak English and Chinese, therefore defeating the difficulty of the language barrier with one commonsense rule. It pains Zhen even more that she doesn't know how Cheng died – did he suffer, was he in pain, did they desecrate his body, was he scared? It is all too much to handle, and Zhen's chest begins to tighten, her throat feeling like it is closing up and she cannot breathe. Going into panic mode, Zhen has to calm herself, take her mind out of anguish and breathe slow and steady. Lifting her head to clear the airways, she breathes in slowly for seven seconds through her nose and exhales for eleven seconds from her mouth, this a breathing technique to battle anxiety and panic attacks. Anxiety is caused by your body releasing too much adrenaline from fear or nervousness, this increases the heart rate and therefore your heart pumps faster, meaning the adrenaline is pumped around your body faster, making you more excited, but because you are scared or nervous your mind mistakes this for danger, therefore making you more scared or anxious and it becomes a vicious cycle. You must stop the adrenaline and slow your heartbeat by telling yourself you are safe and breathe slowly but purposefully. This is what Zhen is doing to combat her tense feeling and after a few deep breaths she returns to herself. Knowing that her numbers are depleted and the other gangs will take advantage of this, Zhen Yun must plan very carefully what her next move is and for now it is staying where she is and watching how the other gangs play their hand. There is a danger The Irish and The Pagans will attack again from both sides, but she thinks this is unlikely – to do that would mean giving the monster gangs free run of Cathedral Tower and the whole purpose of war in this city is to gain power, and allowing The Vampires and The Witches unchallenged occupation of the cathedral would be pointless in any quest for glory and domination. Zhen predicts The Irish and The Pagans will join forces and attack the cathedral, especially now that the monster gangs will be fewer in numbers. This gives her gang time to recuperate and plan their next wave of combat.

After such a massacre from Tunder, Zhen wonders how such a force can be stopped, what can kill a witch, a blessed weapon but she would need a blessing from a holy man, and although this city does have them they are few and far between, the enemy and possibly dead. A stronger magic, there is no way she can find that in 9 Gang, burn them, burn them all, light up the city with flame, there is plenty of petrol, alcohol and other flammable substances on top of explosives, the way to defeat them is exactly what The Chinese have, firepower. If what doesn't kill you makes you stronger, then what kills you makes you fearful, and if The Witches fear anything it is God and fire, and if God created everything then he created fire, an infernal wave across the city will bring The Witches to destruction and avenge the brutal deaths her people have suffered.

Zhen springs into action with a new lease of life and purpose, ordering her gang to gather any flammable substance they can find and make petrol bombs and any type of weapon that will explode or cause a fire, an inferno of vengeance and justice. Ordering them to empty the cars, the oil supply, alcohol, aerosols and all that will cause destruction, Zhen herself checks the holy water supply and makes certain the stakes and swords are sharp enough to penetrate a vampire and decapitate them. Before this war is over it will get more brutal.

The combined forces approach the cathedral, cautious but intent on victory and destroying whatever stands against them, stopping and spreading out. Alice views the cathedral through her binoculars and sees a damaged and scarred building but no sign of movement, which causes her to fear what is in there. If it were mortal or werewolf they would have a look out, soldiers on the rooftop and security surrounding the cathedral, but here she sees nothing. This tells her at the very least The Witches have occupied the cathedral with The Vampires deep below out of reach of the sun. No doubt some curse or hex engulfs the building, meaning the task has just become all the more difficult; of course it has, Alice thinks to herself. Aiden and Brigacos discuss their plan of attack without consulting Alice and Gideon, assuming they understand they have joined up with them so do not have authority here. To a point they are correct, but Alice becomes irritated, and Gideon thinks it is arrogant, so already the rift is starting. After eavesdropping on their plan consisting of entering the cathedral slowly back-to-back to cover each other in case of witch teleportation, Alice shakes her head at the suggestion.

"What if a witch appears through teleportation?" she asks angrily. Aiden and Brigacos look at her bewildered that she has snapped and interrupts them. "Just burn them at will with flamethrowers, what if that causes death by friendly fire and we end up shooting in all directions killing each other? The Witches are clever, they will fool you into doing that," Alice adds, as the other gangs members pretend not to listen but they clearly are.

"What is your suggestion?" Aiden asks, acting polite but failing miserably; his irritation seeps through at her interruption and tone.

"If you knew about The Witches you would know it is only Tunder that can teleport, Rika has mind control and Katalin is a shapeshifter; and all three can turn to mist," Alice states, educating whoever is listening on the witchcraft they are about to face. "The rest of their gang only have limited powers and can only hold a spell for so long, a witch's spell is only as strong as the witch itself, and magic can only be as powerful as the witch who conjures it," she tells them, most wondering how she knows this. The gangs listen to her and consider the fact that if Alice is right then the answer to part of the problem they have is right with them: if The Witches possess evil power then surely the alternative is non-evil power; they have monks with them. Father Gideon may be a tyrant in politics, but he is absolute in his religious belief, and his purity of faith is the difference between a mere mortal and an evil witch. Gideon knows his time has come to roll back the years and lead his city to freedom once more; the other gangs clouded by their hatred for him failed to realise the best weapon against evil was with them all along. Aiden, being a Catholic, feels the most embarrassment for putting animosity before shared faith and offers an apology to Father Gideon, which does not go down well with The Pagans. This is why Brigacos had doubts about joining with The Irish, this is the difference between true Celtic Pagans and modern Irish: religion. Celtic Pagans were conquered by Christianity and their Gods demonised in certain ways and modern Irish pay homage to that faith and demonisation in the form of Protestant, Catholic and whatever other denomination of Christianity; how many ways do Christians need to worship the same God? Back when Ireland was Hibernia, the Romans' name for modern-day Ireland and when the Romans wanted to expand their empire, they embraced some Celtic Gods and gave them a new identity so to speak. Between Pagan Gods across Europe there are similarities certainly with the Greek and Roman Gods. Paganism is not split into different groups as an identity, it is split into different sub-sectors of Paganism; Greek Gods, Roman Gods, Norse Gods, Celtic Gods are the most well-known but there are many more. The definition of a Pagan religion is any religion that is not one of the five main faiths which are Christianity, Judaism, Islam, Hinduism and Buddhism; any other religion is considered Pagan. Who knows, maybe in the future one of the main five could become a Pagan religion? Brigacos sighs with disbelief at Aiden's behaviour, Bryson shakes his head with disgust, which Cormac doesn't like and eyeballs the druid. Gwen is dreading what is to come.

"Oh really," Brigacos snaps.

Aiden turns to him, wondering what his problem is. "Apologising to him, what about Celtic origins, brother, what about we are the same at our root, Paddy, this is why I had doubts about unionising with you giving it the big talk about ancestry and brotherhood, but

when it comes down to it you will be on your knees for St Patrick,"
Brigacos rants, getting in Aiden's face so much that his head touches
The Irish leader, who snaps and punches the Arch Druid, who in
return swings back. The Irish and The Pagans get involved in a
gang fight and Alice is left shaking her head at the typical problem
with humanity. How can the human race ever conquer evil when
it is fighting itself? Does The Devil really have to try when we are
destroying ourselves or is that self-destruction The Devil's work?
Either way the human race is its own worst enemy. Father Gideon
rounds up his troops, ordering them not to join in the gang fight;
instead, he asks them to kneel as he says a prayer. Alice closes her
eyes whilst he asks God to protect them from the evil that they are
about to fight against in his name. With Aiden and Brigacos still
fighting, Cormac and Bryson beating the hell out of each other,
Gwen attempts and fails to break up the fight – she likes and honours
the connection between their people and fighting between them is
the last thing she wants. Leo helps Gwen as he separates the two
gang leaders, shouting at them that their behaviour is only helping
their common enemy. After calming themselves and wiping the
blood from their face, Aiden and Brigacos order their crew members
to stop. Looking up to the sky, Alice sees dusk beginning to show
itself and knowing the fight they face is only going to get harder
with the next few hours. Turning to the recovering gang members,
she looks at them with disgust. Aiden, still angry and eager to prove
his gang are the braver and stronger, offers to lead the attack, using
tactics that worked in the last war – small teams covering each
direction, The Irish marching in haste on the cathedral.

Alice warns him the last war was different and this time The
Witches are stronger, their magic has grown and new tricks have
been learned. Alice is right and she has listened to Queen Rika and
Krul over the years and having once worked for Niculi and Ziana.

This is something people for some reason seem to forget, everybody seems to associate Alice with Father Gideon, probably because both of their leaderships have been the same length and Alice has been "servant" to Gideon his entire reign, but she was a gang member for The Messengers when Niculi and Ziana were alive. From that time to now she has noticed an increase in parapsychology and a mixing of the old ways with the new, Ziana was powerful and her magic was very much the old style, cauldron spells, gypsy hexes, but The Witches now have evolved. Aiden doesn't listen and marches on regardless, shouting back to Alice that she talks too much and daylight has almost run out; with this point he is right. Not wanting to lose face, Brigacos follows with his gang, Bryson offering to lead fresh from his fight with Cormac and is always ready for action. Both gangs creep through The Waiting Yard and after a tense wait and a deep breath, they enter Cathedral Tower knowing it will be highly defended, and are met instantly by pitch dark, unnatural darkness with a tense atmosphere. Switching on their torches, they go on a witch hunt. Alice and Gideon take their crews around to the main entrance which will be less defended. Alice enters first, leading her people into an unwanted but necessary danger zone.

Zhen Yun marches her gang back to Cathedral Tower with her mind on nothing but victory and vengeance. After draining their cars of fuel to burn witches, it is a journey on foot but a necessary journey which will not take too long. With a cautious eye watching for Irish and Pagans, and sending scouts ahead to guide the gang on a safer passage, Zhen is surprised how effortless their journey is – she thought at least Aiden and Brigacos would leave an ambush behind, but nothing has attempted to stop their way to the cathedral. This could mean that they have been wiped out or are so obsessed with taking the tower they have thrown all their eggs into one basket; it could be a good idea keeping their gangs together for strength in numbers – perhaps that was Cheng's mistake not keeping his crew together. Being informed by her scouts that the other gangs have entered the cathedral, Zhen ponders her move: should she wait to see if the other gangs make headway into witch burning and vampire slaying, or should she help them destroy the forces of darkness? Zhen decides to camp in view of the cathedral but not let the other gangs know she is there; the waiting game is her next move.

The only noise the Irish and Pagans hear is their own heartbeats thundering in their chest, Aiden suggests he and his crew take the stairs to the tower and Brigacos takes the corridor into the rest of the cathedral. Bryson leads the way with Brigacos bringing up the rear. Gwen amongst the troops edges slowly down the corridor, adrenaline pumping, torches shining everywhere, corners, walls, ceilings, knowing a witch could be anywhere. Aiden leads The Irish up the stairs to the meeting room and after entering it feels like a different place, he even looks at the chair he sits in at High Council meetings – it seems a ghost of the room it once was. After a tense look around, Cormac informs Aiden there is nothing but corpses, his leader nods and signals to the rooftop, dusk has become dark and already mortals hope for dawn, yet no monsters greet them. More bodies more mess, an absolute bloodbath took place here and Aiden recognises some of them as werewolves, the remains of ash that were once vampires, as well as a couple of dead witches chained to stakes and burned, and a whole lot of dead Chinese. Aiden's eyes lock onto a corpse he recognises and, although an enemy he has had run ins with, his heart still sinks a little at the impact the death of such a man will have on the city. Cheng, slumped against a wall, with no question of how he died – his stomach has been stabbed by four sharp blades, his eyes closed meaning either somebody closed them for him or his death was not instantaneous. Crouching down to look at the body, Aiden and Cormac examine the cause of death; the stabs wounds to the stomach are exit wounds meaning he was stabbed in the back and the precision of the stabbing means it was not a werewolf – also a werewolf wouldn't stab with its claws, it would swing and slice, added to the fact that a wolf fights more with its teeth – leaving Aiden with the conclusion that another type of animal killed Cheng. The wounds look like they were made at the same time, meaning it couldn't be a mortal who did it, multiple stabs wounds made by a person in such a tense battle situation would be frenzied and inaccurate, but these wounds were made at the same time by something who was not scared or nervous and an expert in their handling in such weaponry and yet this expert was an animal, leading Aiden to the belief that Princess Katalin killed Cheng. Surviving the last war, Aiden came to know how a fatal wound was inflicted and by what kind of weapon. Seeing such death and horror has become something Aiden is used to, such is the life in this city.

Hearing a noise coming from inside, Aiden and Cormac spring to their feet, their gang members turn instantly, guns pointing. Cormac peers down the stairway, shining his torch to see: nobody, just the smoke-stained walls of the cathedral and stone steps leading down to the meeting room. Cormac looks back at his leader for his orders – they can't stay on the roof and there is only one way in and one way out. Aiden gives the order to return into the building. Cormac is first down the stairs with his crew covering his back, with some of them going down backward to cover behind them. Without warning the chairs that host the leaders of High Council come hurling toward them one by one, an invisible force, poltergeist-like, throws the chairs toward the soldiers, some diving for cover, some frozen stiff and being clattered dropping to the floor, Cormac letting rip with his flamethrower, knowing only a witch could do such a thing. Aiden looks in shock as one of his members is thrown like a doll back up the stairs and over the roof into the distance, panicked gunfire rings out and The Irish soldiers lose their ranks. Hearing the gunfire, The Pagans who have so far been unsuccessful in their hunt for monsters, ponder whether to go and help or continue their search. After a think, Brigacos abandons their plan and decides to help The Irish. But running down the corridor, his crew are met by vampires, cutting them off from both ends, surrounding them. Arch Druid Brigacos fires his crossbow, missing his target, and is pounced upon by a vampire who is about to sink its fangs into his neck when holy water is thrown into its face. Druid Bryson plunges a stake into the vampire's heart and takes off its head without hesitation. Christian-blessed holy water brings saviour to pagans but no crucifixes – they wouldn't work if they had them; you have to believe for those to work. Surrounded by vampires, The Pagans' fight begins to wane until a shriek of fear echoes around the corridor and The Vampires retreat. Turning to see what has caused their fleeing, Father Gideon with cross in hand comes into view, followed by Alice firing a stake with precise aim through a vampire's heart, dropping it to its knees and removing its head. Leo and Jessica soak the fleeing vampires in holy water and their gang members decapitate them; the numbers are evening up. The Irish in their panic scatter from the meeting room, most guns blazing, some just running for their life, the ones that do are slaughtered by Princess Tunder on the stairway, soldier after soldier dropped to their death. Cormac sees this and attempts to cover her in flame, but The Dark Fairy teleports behind him, kicking him down the stairs. The Irish deputy tumbles to the bottom, landing on his dead comrades. Looking up he sees his leader, a devout Catholic with crucifix in hand hold it out at the witch who roars like a beast but with a demonic growl which echoes through the cathedral.

Tunder springs up the wall in retreat, slowly crawling backwards, her face a twisted demon in the midst of holy punishment as Aiden shouts, "Devil's maiden, I send you to hell." The Irish leader bellows as Tunder writhes in agony in the corner of the ceiling. Turning toward Aiden, she vomits a thick black sludge which sprays out over the crucifix and Aiden's face.

Undeterred, the Irishman continues his crusade. "You should have stayed in the shadows, you belong to the darkness," he shouts, holding the cross aloft, aiming as close to the witch as possible.

Tunder, unable to escape, is cornered by the force of the almighty, the one power she has yet to find a way to conquer. Cormac, clutching a flamethrower, bolts up the stairs to his leader and the shrieking witch whose teeth are now taking the form of a snake as if a serpent is behind a woman's face attempting to push its way through. Taking aim, Cormac is about to torch the witch when suddenly he is charged to the ground, crashing into Aiden, which breaks his hold on Tunder. Victuis pounces on to Cormac, sinking his fangs into his neck, with such force the blood squirts out up over his face and on to the floor and wall, making sure Cormac feels every tooth in his mouth as punishment for attempting to hurt Tunder. As the Irish deputy reaches for a stake to slay the vampire and save himself, Victuis staggers in retreat, leaving Cormac on the floor blood still spilling from his neck, Aiden stopping his attack with one cross outstretched and another keeping Tunder in her place.

"Demons of the dark, God repels you," he speaks as Victuis slowly backs away, trying to shield himself from the crucifix with his hands; the pain is clear on his face.

"You think God is with you? Where was God when your people were defeated?" Victuis roars back in fury.

A familiar voice escapes his mouth but Aiden cannot quite make out whose voice.

"God was with us," Aiden fires back, angry at his enemy's doubt. "God led us to victory in the war when your so-called great one was slain," he adds, looking up to Tunder who is forced back even further into the corner by the cross.

Victuis laughs a deep and disturbing laugh that surprises and scares Aiden. "Slain?" Victuis mocks. "There is no such thing." He laughs, which causes Aiden to lose concentration enough for him to not notice who has entered the stairway. Krul fires a stake from a crossbow at Aiden, hitting him in the shoulder and sending him falling to the ground. Struggling to move as the pain is immense, he is nevertheless able to clutch his cross and keep his dark foes at bay.

Tunder falls from the ceiling into Victuis' arms; she is weak from the punishment the crucifix gave her. Victuis flees the stairway of the tower and darts deeper into the cathedral past burned witches and fallen gang members, as The Pagans, side by side with Gideon and Alice, slay some vampires. Aiden nurses his wound, removing the stake before looking behind him at Cormac who lays lifeless on the floor, the wound inflicted by Victuis too deep and brutal for him to survive. Aiden sinks his head into his hand and sheds a tear for his fallen deputy. The battle spills out into The Waiting Yard, Leo and Jessica successfully capturing a witch and chaining her to a stake, Gwen stepping forward to help and torching it to a fiery death. Brigacos and Bryson double up, forcing the undead to become dead, and Father Gideon rolls back the years as he slays another vampire, sending its head rolling across the yard, as Alice covers his back, lighting up an attacking witch with flame. It has been a victorious battle for the combined forces, and The Vampires and The Witches have been dealt a blow to their gang numbers and their quest for glory.

Chapter 25

Z hen Yun watching the fighting that is taking place in The Waiting Yard through her scope is pleasantly surprised by the victory the combined forces have claimed. Checking the west for any advancement from The Werewolves she sees nothing, so Zhen keeps her troops camped. Not knowing if the other gangs would turn on her, she thinks it is better not to intervene and let them continue with their heroics, and up until now they have been heroic. Like Yong going to rescue Cheng, a hero of great magnitude reminds Zhen of the rebellion against The Mongols, a great time in Chinese history when Zhu Yhanzhang, just a peasant at the time but becoming the first Ming Emperor, rose up with his people and fought back against Genghis Khan's grandson, Klablai Khan, eventually taking The Mongol capital of China Ta-Tu, which is known today as Beijing. Zhen Yun likens this to her gang's fightback against the tyranny of both Niculi and Gideon, and now that she is leader of her people perhaps Zhen Yun will be 9 Gang City's Wu Zetian. The first female Empress of China was part of the Zhou Dynasty and the comparisons continue. Zhou was one of the three pre-imperial dynasties lasting circa 800 years and is credited, although barely, with turning China into a more intellectual culture becoming more political; this reminds Zhen of Cheng. Zhen Yun is a proud China woman, and her people are a strong culture, so strong that men in far off lands would give their wives to the Chinese if it made them happy. Malacca, an island under the control of Hsien Lo, modern day Thailand but now a state of Malaysia, was a place Chinese sailors and tradesman enjoyed visiting, not just for the homage that was paid to them or the wealth that could be gained through trade, but the Malaccan women. These women, who were said to be of a higher intellectual standard to their husbands, would offer themselves to Chinese men, seeing them as a higher class of male therefore moving themselves up in society, sometimes having sex with them in front of their husbands, cuckolding as it is called, their husbands not caring as long as the Chinamen were pleased and continued their trade.

Discovering America years before Columbus, and Australia centuries before Cook, history has been changed to suit the west, creating the reason Zhen wants to right that wrong and bring eastern culture to the west. Zhen not only wants to conquer but to change the entire culture of 9 Gang City – for too long have western values reigned supreme, Christian values, monsters from Romania, even as far as dragons being seen as beasts to be slain by warriors and Saints. In Chinese culture dragons are a symbol of good fortune and prosperity, hence the reason Cheng had so many dragon statues erected in China Town. But Zhen Yun must look toward the future now, Cheng and Yong are gone, and it is up to her to lead her gang to victory, she is Empress of her people and could be one great victory away from starting her Dynasty.

Cuthwulf marches his crew across the border with Cannibal Farm, guns loaded and the wolf pack for another 29 days is a brotherhood. The storm moon already waning means the lunar cycle brings a sigh of relief for the mortal gangs, but where last night there was teeth, now there are bullets. Knowing that the rest of the city will be squabbling over the cathedral, Cuthwulf makes his fight about territory; he is a dog after all. With no defence from The Cannibals at the perimeter fence or security barrier, The Werewolves waltz in at will. Quickly approaching Cannibal HQ, Cuthwulf stops his gang within sniper distance and sends Randall around the back and Wulfric through the front, telling his snipers to kill any cannibal that leaves. Wulfric and Randall get into their positions and inform Cuthwulf they are ready through their radios, the wolf leader gives his snipers the all-clear to take out the guards outside the building, and they all fall with ease. Wulfric and Randall make their move, a werewolf gang member smashes through the door and another enters, AR-15 aimed at cannibals and dropping them with one shot each. At the same time Randall has come through the back door with his hit squad and obliterated what awaited him at the back. James Winston Wycombe, hearing the commotion, orders his bodyguards to stay close and protect him. Spying out of the window he sees nothing, so orders a gang member to climb out of the window to check whether it is safe. After seeing that gang member's blood erupt from his head when the sniper bullet hits him, Wycombe knows it is not safe.

Wulfric lays waste to The Cannibals as he meets up with Randall mid-way through the building, they go upstairs together, Wulfric leading and Randall covering his back. Searching every room including what was William Henry Davis' office, they kill what they find but do not find Wycombe, and inform their leader the building is clear. Cuthwulf enters, leaving his snipers in position, impressed with his team's work. He meets up with his deputy and 3rd and examines every room again. Rounding up prisoners as they go – Cuthwulf has a plan for them – he orders Randall and a team to take the prisoners back to The Forests; any of them who resist, refuse or flee, shoot them. Keeping one hostage with him, Cuthwulf and his deputy take the hostage into William Henry Davis' office which has now been inherited by Wycombe, asking the hostage to tell him where Wycombe is. At first he refuses, so Cuthwulf shoots him in the knee cap. Dropping to the floor crippled and whining in pain, the hostage still refuses, so Cuthwulf shoots the other knee cap. Despite becoming permanently disabled the prisoner still refuses to tell Cuthwulf and Wulfric where Wycombe is. Admiring the man's loyalty to his leader, Cuthwulf nevertheless pulls down the man's trousers and underwear, Wulfric holding him down, pulling his knife. The cannibal tries to fight them off but fails. With the threat of losing a man's most prized possession, and feeling the cold steel, the hostage squeals the whereabouts of James Winston Wycombe, nodding his head to the wall. Confused, Cuthwulf checks the wall by knocking on it, and to his surprise a section in the middle is hollow. Quickly pulling all the books out he finally opens the secret passage. Cautious that Wycombe is lurking ready to shoot within the passage, the werewolf leader throws the hostage through the doorway who is instantly shot in the chest falling to his death – Cuthwulf's sixth sense was true. Hearing footsteps running, Cuthwulf and Wulfric give chase. Down some slippery steps into a dingy walkway, firing into the distance as Wycombe escapes, up a ladder and out of a trap door and running into the night. The Cannibals' HQ is built in the old English Manor House style in respect to their ancestors; many of these houses have secret passages from the old days to make escapes just like Wycombe or to hold prisoners, stash contraband or in some cases to hold religious ceremonies. Springing through the trap door, Cuthwulf sees it is a hidden amongst leaves and bushes and looking around it is a few metres away from the house and he sees Wycombe fleeing into the distance. Giving chase, the werewolf leader thinks this is the second time this coward has made his escape, Wulfric backing him up on the chase. Wycombe with his heart racing knows he cannot stop now as he will surely be killed, but being the man he is, a vile person but not stupid, has a car stashed nearby. Looking behind him, he sees the wolfmen closing in. Entering the car, Wycombe fumbles with keys, his enemies getting closer. A gunshot rings out but no contact. The engine stalls followed by another gunshot which shatters the window. Punching the steering wheel, Wycombe shouts at his car as the engine fails to start as another bullet hits the car, causing the cannibal to duck, and after looking out, he sees Cuthwulf and Wulfric aiming their guns, ready to shoot. The engine starts and James Winston Wycombe bolts off into his escape as gunfire shatters the back windscreen and ricochets off the car. Another escape for Wycombe means another irritation for Cuthwulf, but he has a much greater prize. With Davis and White dead and Wycombe fleeing, Cannibal HQ there for the taking and hostages held at Werewolf HQ, Cuthwulf and his crew have just claimed Cannibal Farm as their own and have officially added to their territory.

Victuis lays Tunder down in his coffin; she is weak from the exorcist-like ritual Aiden performed on her. Opening her eyes she sees him gazing at her adoringly, Victuis gently strokes her hair mostly for the contact but also for comfort. Queen Rika almost floats across the room to check on her sister and assess what damage her gang have taken – if Tunder is unable to fight, her crew have lost a powerful weapon, and after the beating they have just taken The Witches need to reconsider their tactics. Looking around Victuis notices Krul has not returned to the secret room and goes to search for him, Tunder grabbing his hand to stop him from leaving. As he turns to the witch princess she gives him that look that only he gets, not the usual evil look she gives everybody else. Rika notices this and doesn't approve but says nothing. The witch queen likes to have complete control over everybody, especially her own gang and a love interest will complicate and compromise her control. Victuis leans in and gently kisses Tunder's lips; she returns the kiss with added passion, it has been so long; they hold the kiss for a few seconds before Rika steps forward to separate them, not liking what she is seeing, but she can't move. A paralysis covers her body like a force field is stopping her from doing anything, even breathing; she begins to panic as the force field tightens around her and she feels crushed, still unable to breathe. Victuis pulls away, Tunder smiles and kisses him one last time and he runs off to find Krul. Queen Rika is suddenly released from the force field and she breaths deeply, catching her breath, feeling the sensation coming back to her body, the panic fading but the slight fear that Tunder can do such a thing to her replaces the panic. Tunder glares at her, almost in a challenging way as if she is daring Rika to test her. Rika won't, she knows Tunder can do things she cannot and The Dark Fairy is too important to The Witches' cause of rising back to the top. The fact that Rika cannot mind control her youngest sister into doing what she wants not only angers the queen, it also scares her, because it means Tunder's magic has become more powerful than Rika's and for the queen to not be the most powerful in her gang is a bad thing – how else do you control your crew? It is all well and good relying on respect, but what if your people don't respect you? Other ways need to be considered and the queen may need other ways to keep her crown.

Aiden struggles out of the cathedral with his good hand clutching his cross, seeing the ashes of slain vampires and burned witches covering The Waiting Yard, impressed by the victory but heartbroken over Cormac. Gwen rushes to help him and sees he has been crying. Knowing Aiden is tough she suspects his tears are not because of the pain of his injury.

"Where's Cormac?" she asks, suspecting but dreading the answer.

Aiden's eyes fill up again. "He's dead," he barks, his voice breaking. "Victuis killed him," he adds, looking back at the cathedral as Alice comes to help, Father Gideon almost incinerating a witch,

Druid Bryson staking vampires, and Leo and Jessica making sure each other is ok as vampires and witches retreat to the safety of the secret room where magic protects them and tonight has been a disaster for Krul and Rika's gangs.

Krul, unhappy with the night's defeat, decides to play a different tactic – the other gangs can fight out in the open all they want, but the loss of life it causes only ruins the gangs' chances of gaining power. Seeing The Chinese camped just out from the cathedral and not hearing from Cuthwulf, Krul makes a tactical retreat, but not one that the other gangs will expect. Knowing it is only a matter of time before they turn on each other, Krul also knows the only reason they have joined forces is to wipe out his crew and The Witches, followed by The Werewolves. If they achieve this, which is highly doubtful but if they do, they will not agree to a combined leader or leadership so will turn on each other; typical human beings, Krul thinks to himself. Krul springs around when he hears somebody approaching from behind; eyes locked on the figure in front of him, he sees Victuis with a concerned expression. Tonight has been horrendous for The Vampires.

"Where are you going?" Victuis asks, wondering why his leader is leaving Holy Ground.

"This isn't war," Krul replies with a tone of anger, mainly at the loss of so many gang members, but also at the sudden turnaround in the mortal gangs' fortunes – only last night they were close to annihilation, now they stand victorious in battle on the edge of the cathedral. "This is tragedy, hit and hope tactics, where is the honour? Where are the heroics?" Krul rants, almost as if he expected more from the city, not just himself but also his enemies, almost as if he had been dreaming of war and being a war hero and going down in folklore like Niculi, but instead he is disheartened by the way things have turned out, even though his gang have Cathedral Tower. Victuis stands silent, looking at his leader and best friend and can't help but feel a little disappointed in his attitude. To Victuis this has always been about the supremacy of the gang, reigning over their foes and vampirism and witchcraft returning to their rightful place in The Throne Room, and not holding political High Council meetings that get the city nowhere. The citizens of 9 Gang have given democracy a chance and it still leads to war; politics gives too many people the opportunity to have their fingers in the pie with their minds twisted for their own agenda.

"The honour is in victory," Victuis replies with a slight tone of anger.

Krul nods in agreement. "Yes," Krul snaps, "victory by any means necessary and sacrificing our people to gain that victory is not honourable, any vampire dead is a victory for our oppressors." He thinks bitterly of his gang members' suffering and the boasting the mortal gangs must be doing right now.

"What is your plan?" Victuis inquires, wondering what the secret escape is all about.

"Time to go into the shadows, time to strike from where they fear: the darkness," Krul answers, before telling Victuis to return to the cathedral before the sun rises. He is handing over control until his return and hopes Tunder is recovering. "I wish you and Tunder all the best, keep her close. I know how it feels to lose the woman you love," Krul tells him growing sad as he thinks about Enigma.

Victuis hugs his friend and watches as he walks into the distance, knowing now that he controls the army the responsibility is on him to regroup the gang and lead from the front to show his enemies vampirism will not be destroyed because of some people's hatred and disgust toward his kind.

Krul heads southeast toward Emerald Territory, his war has become clandestine and playing the mortal gangs at their own game has become his tactic. This will teach them the error of their ways, and with each rival slaughtered The Vampires take a step closer to power.

Chapter 26

T he morning light brings an end to the fighting, at least with the monster gangs, and Father Gideon smiles with pride at the night's work as victory draws to a close. Aiden's shoulder has been seen to and is bandaged in a sling, Brigacos and Bryson are waxing lyrical about their victory, and Leo, Jessica and Gwen are tired but attending to everybody who needs attention for injuries or the stress of seeing a loved one perish. Alice is happy with the win but thinks the rest are overrating it, although she does not tell them this for risk of demoralising the troops; but The Vampires and The Witches are still occupying the cathedral and calling the shots. Having to fight by night has become the mortal gang tactics which only serves The Vampires' purpose and The Chinese still have to be defeated. If the mortal gangs think they can keep this up they are deluded, but Alice lets them have their celebration. This war has become a case of gang warfare where whoever has the stroke of luck, like Aiden being in the right place at the right time to inflict the crucifix on Tunder, like Victuis turning up at the right time to kill Cormac and save Tunder. There is no way the war can be won this way and Alice is worried the rest of them have already become too confident in themselves. Tonight was about evening the numbers and that is what happened, but only with The Vampires and The Witches. Sooner rather than later they will have to march out to either The Forests or China Town and take on Cuthwulf and Cheng. Waiting for the next full moon cannot be an option, and Cuthwulf and his crew need to be conquered before then.

The Werewolves complete the conquering of Cannibal Farm and while the other gangs are squabbling over a cathedral, Cuthwulf has claimed more territory, the cannibal prisoners of war are locked in the cellar of Werewolf HQ and will be kept there for at least another 28 days or so. Moving east, Cuthwulf and most of his crew make haste toward BC Nation after their spies have returned with information that The Pagans have moved all their troops toward the tower to help the combined forces claim the ultimate prize in 9 Gang City. Cuthwulf has a different plan now, that he can make conscious decisions and is not just a wild beast, not for a while yet anyway. Positioning small squads at the borders on his own turf and Cannibal Farm, and demanding his gang's flag is flown on the border with Holy Ground and the newly conquered territories as well as The Cannibals' HQ so anyone approaching will know The Werewolves have conquered land. Leaving Randall behind to run things, Cuthwulf and Wulfric travel east, stopping just before the border with BC Nation. Wulfric, wondering what for, sees Cuthwulf looking south curiously. Taking out a scope he investigates the distance and can make out the top of Cathedral Tower. The Chinese gang flag still wafts in the wind, although after his escape on the first night of war Cuthwulf knows they do not control the tower.

"Take a squad on to BC Nation and claim the land. I want to have a closer look at the cathedral," Cuthwulf tells his deputy, who thinks it is risky – they do not know what is between here and the cathedral and he wants the gang to stick together. Cuthwulf senses this and knows it is a risk, but has given his order and as alpha wolf he expects his order to be carried out. "Take your place in history, our future gang members will read our history books and know it was Wulfric who claimed BC Nation in the name of Lycan," Cuthwulf reassures him, a smile spreads across his deputy's face at the thought of his name in history and he leads his squadron to pastures new.

Cuthwulf takes a battalion south on to Holy Ground, sending spies ahead to scout the area. The scouting mission confirms what Cuthwulf suspected, a free run to Cathedral Tower and the combined forces are camped on the edge, meaning The Vampires and The Witches still control the tower and The Chinese are stationed a way out from the cathedral grounds. It seems to the alpha wolf that all the other gangs are placing their eggs in one basket, such is their obsession with claiming the tower. He understands this as deep down he wants Cathedral Tower for himself; it is the desire of every member of every gang in the city. Like men desire women, women desire money and people desire power, fame, treasure, attention, praise, knowledge, accomplishment, acknowledgement, sympathy, in 9 Gang City all people really desire is the tower. Cathedral Tower is everything in 9 Gang – to control it is symbolic of power, and to rule the city is to have supremacy over all others, and that is what gang life comes down to: power and control over rivals, and Cathedral Tower is the ultimate symbol of that power and control; everybody wants it and Cuthwulf is no different, he is just going a different way about getting it.

Zhen Yun is caught in two minds. Her gang are now fully rested and now would be a perfect time to attack, the combined forces are tired from battle and The Vampires will be resting for the day; but the problem she has is, if her crew deplete the combined forces, she will be helping The Vampires and The Witches, and if she attacks the cathedral now she does not know where The Vampires are and they will be protected anyhow. It is beginning to feel as though war was a bad idea and Zhen thinks back to the times she wanted and encouraged it – it has turned out very different than she imagined. Believing their superior firepower would have The Chinese blast their way to victory and leave the rest of the city in their wake, little did she know The Witches were as powerful as they are; she knew they had magical powers, but she thought it was all just hocus pocus and bubbling cauldrons and could place a hex on somebody every now and then. Zhen didn't realise things like teleportation, moving the ground, anti-gravity, force fields, mental manipulation were things in their arsenal, but she is not alone in that respect. It is almost to a point people think The Witches have been playing second fiddle to The Vampires all these years, when in fact they have been the only priceless asset to The Vampires – Niculi, Krul and Victuis could not have done it without them, and their advancement in magic has shown the city that magical evolution is a fact and as mortals can create new weapons, so can witchcraft. Zhen decides for another day she will sit back and let the other gang waste lives and weapons, and when they are vulnerable attack and claim victory. At this time of year, the sun only brings relief to the mortal gangs for about eight hours before falling into the horizon and nightmares return to stalk humans, reminding them that perhaps they are not the most powerful existence in the world. Kiralyno Emlekezik, Queen's Remembrance, has arrived and no matter what is happening in the city, The Witches' day of celebration will be honoured.

Princess Tunder is on her feet and she would not miss a day like this, embracing her gang members and honouring her sisters, she receives the same from all witches present. The vampire gang members pay their respects to their allies and the atmosphere in the secret room rises a notch. Victuis manages to get Tunder alone and gives her his best wishes before passionately embracing, arms wrapped around her and kissing her affectionately; she returns the gesture. Offering greetings to Queen Rika and Princess Katalin, the latter of whom accepts with thanks but Rika half- heartedly accepts as she glares at Tunder, unhappy with the frolics they have clearly been up to, but after her sister's last protest against her leader's objection to her choice of love, Queen Rika stops short of attempting to stop them. It was 542 years ago today that Queen Ziana founded The Witches to help her true love fight back against The CVS, and every year since the two gangs have celebrated with each other in joy and harmony. On this day tradition reigns supreme and the ceremony takes place with The Witches around a cauldron to honour their fallen Queen, spells and enchantments are performed, one of which Tunder can perform giving her visons into the past to see through the eyes of Ziana so she can honour her in the correct way. This ceremony is not usually performed in front of The Vampires; it is a witch ritual. They are usually invited to a gathering later in the night, but under the current circumstances their friends can watch the ritual. Victuis sits with his gang as The Witches sit in circles around a great bubbling cauldron, it looks majestic in a mythical and fanciful way, the kind that people around the world think is just fairy tale but 9 Gang City knows it is very real. Queen Rika sits on her throne, looking relaxed, but her heart races with excitement at the event; Princess Katalin sits in cat form in front of the cauldron, and Princess Tunder performs the ritual. Collections of ingredients taken from war victims provide the perfect tonic for the performance of witchcraft:

Blood of an enemy (A symbol of victory for witchcraft)

Eyes of rival (To see into the past)

Tongue of a conquered foe (They cannot warn their comrades from the afterlife)

Ears of a corpse (They cannot hear a witch stalking them in death)

The Cauldron bubbles and lights flash, Tunder goes into a trance, her eyes black as the night and her voice becomes a demonic echo from the beyond.

"The time of The Witches has returned, those who desired to burn us to ashes will be slaughtered for their insult, our kind has hidden in the shadows for too long, darkness will reign supreme and enemies will bow before us or fall into despair, the Goddess Of Witches has returned," Tunder bellows from her hypnotic trance.

The witch gang members cheer in ecstasy at the revelation, Rika sits forward on her chair at the news, and Katalin still in cat form looks back at her sister's reaction. Victuis sits unmoved whilst the rest of his gang sit in shock at the news but not knowing whether to believe it or not. Queen Rika attempts to keep her composure, but if what her sister has just revealed is true then where does that leave the prophecy and the thoughts in Tunder's mind that Rika has been reading.

After the ceremony the witch sisters and Victuis sit around a table to dine in celebration, Rika still with her thoughts racing and attempting to read her sister's mind across the table, but Tunder glares as her voice echoes around Rika's head, telling her to stay out of her mind. Victuis stands to toast his hosts and he hopes the union and friendship they share lasts an eternity. Tunder smiles at his kind words before Rika speaks up, bringing the conversation to more recent events.

"Where is Krul?" the queen asks Victuis in a fake polite tone.

Victuis, seeing the anger in her eyes, attempts to play down his leader's absence.

"As we speak Krul is gaining us ground in our bid for power," he replies, knowing by the look on her face she isn't accepting the excuse.

"In what way is he gaining us ground?" Rika instantly responds, barely allowing Victuis to finish.

Victuis pauses but holds his glare at Rika. "There is more than one way to win a war," he tells her with a slight smile. "Meeting head on can be too costly to our numbers and with Gideon and Aiden's faith being a powerful weapon against us, we must rethink our strategy," Victuis declares, finishing his goblet of blood that was taken from a recent victim, a victim that would have happily killed him and not felt an ounce of guilt so are they really a victim or a reality of war? Queen Rika sits dissatisfied with Victuis beat around the bush answers and wants to dig a little deeper, Tunder seeing his goblet is empty fills it for him and shares a loving glance.

"What strategy would he have us take? We have the cathedral and we must defend it," the queen says, wondering why she cannot read his mind. The harder she tries, the more it resists, looking at Tunder who is already staring at her. Tunder's voice once again takes over Rika's mind, demanding the queen stop trying to spy in Tunder and Victuis' thoughts and spend more time leading their people to victory. Realising her power is not as strong as she thought, Queen Rika grows anxious, added to the revelation about Ziana returning, Rika begins to realise that maybe all this time she has not been queen at all, more a guardian until Ziana takes the throne back. Most witches would be honoured at such a position, but Rika's ambition and desires may be her downfall. Krul, approaching The Irish HQ, sees a light on that stands out in the darkness and makes it obvious somebody is home. Siobhan is still recovering from the beating she took and has been unable to fight, no less willing but physically Enigma beat her up badly. Standing outside the window, Krul peers in, stalking his chosen victim; he sees the Irish woman struggling to walk around the room, clearly trying to rehabilitate herself and considering her injuries she is doing well. Her hair red and flowing and her well-toned body make her a pleasure for Krul to view – male vampires prefer feeding on women and vice versa with female vampires, and although he doubts she is a virgin the joy will be all his. Siobhan hears something by the window and spins around, which causes her a lot of pain, but she is certain she saw something move. Picking up her gun and arming herself with a stake, she creeps slowly to the window, switching out the light so as to not give away her position; peeping out, she sees nothing. Knowing he cannot enter without being invited, Krul needs to get his intended victim outside so searches for some fuel to burn her out. Finding some old petrol tanks, he dowses the HQ with as much as he can find and sets it alight. Siobhan peeps out again but still sees nothing and begins to think it was her imagination until she hears a noise coming from another part of the building. Slowly opening the door, she looks out into the hallway and smells smoke. Bursting from the room as quickly as her injuries will allow her, she sees flames engulfing the building with the only escape the front door. As much as she tries to find another way out there isn't one. Her attacker has carried out his plan well and Siobhan has to decide whether to go outside or die in the flames. She walks cautiously out. Making certain she does not get attacked from behind, she turns in circles as she makes her way to a safe distance until she hears someone behind and turns and shoots, catching Krul square in the chest. He shakes his head at his victim.

"You should have known it would be a vampire," he tells her as he listens to her heart pounding. "The mortal gangs would have just snipered you from the trees," Krul adds, mocking Siobhan's decision making, who drops the gun knowing it will serve no purpose and clutches the stake ready to fight.

"Come on, you filthy parasite," Siobhan insults him, not caring if she offends. "Your disgusting kind have infected this city for too long," Siobhan shouts at him, her heart almost breaking free from her chest but her choosing to stand and fight and not run proves her bravery.

"I like it better when they run but I will still enjoy draining you," Krul responds.

Siobhan lunges with the stake at Krul's heart, but her attack is blocked and she is slapped to the ground. Undeterred, Siobhan quickly rises, the pain shooting through her body, but she stands strong, Krul allowing her to come on to him knowing he has the advantage.

"You don't know, do you?" Krul goads her.

"Know what?" Siobhan replies, irritated.

"Cormac is dead," Krul informs her. Siobhan's face drops and emotion takes over. "Victuis ripped his throat out and he bled to death," Krul tells her, making her dive into frenzied attack, her anger uncontrolled. Krul dodges and weaves with ease to avoid the stake and, gripping her throat tightly, lifts her from her feet. Dangling in the air, Siobhan chokes and struggles to breathe, and Krul squeezes harder.

"Victuis should have let Enigma finish you off," Krul says, glaring into her struggling eyes.

Siobhan attempts to speak but can't so Krul loosens his grip to allow her some final words.

"Enigma was a horrible bitch and I hope she suffered," Siobhan chokes, infuriating Krul who sinks his fangs deep into her neck instantly tasting the sweet nectar from her veins. Wrapping his arms around her as she struggles, he sinks his teeth deeper. Her struggle grows weaker but there is still life. A thrill shoots around Krul's body as fresh woman blood is top of every male vampire's list of consumption and his eyes roll back with pleasure as he drinks, still feeling her life inside her but fading. Krul stops, holding her weak body. Her skin pale white from blood loss. Slicing himself with his nails, he forces Siobhan to drink his blood, holding her tightly so she is infected with vampirism. Siobhan shudders as the blood takes effect and Krul holds her tighter to inflict the change. Dropping her to the floor, she is an infected mess as a trickle of Krul's blood dribbles down her chin. Standing victorious over his victim, Krul basks in the glory of one less enemy and another member gained.

Wulfric, deep and unchallenged into BC Nation, surrounds The Pagans' HQ just to be on the safe side, sending in a small hit squad to either capture or kill what they find and secure the area. His crew do their job with ease and no challengers. The werewolf deputy enters and wanders with pride through the newly claimed prize with his leader's words echoing around his head. Wulfric will now be in the history books as the wolf who claimed land for his people. His name has come true and has proven an apt description of his achievement, wolf power is the modern English translation of the old English Wulfric and he has his name alongside his ancestors.

When he calls Cuthwulf to confirm conquest, his leader congratulates him and informs his deputy that he is coming to join him after scoping the cathedral and seeing it is exactly as they predicted. The other gangs have become so obsessed with claiming the tower that they have left their turfs completely free, assuming that all gangs will be attempting to claim the ultimate prize. After checking up with Randall how things are back home, his 3rd In Command confirms all is well, and Cuthwulf heads northeast to join his deputy in the glory of another success and The Werewolves have the north conquered with ease and very little loss, the other gangs clueless to their own land being claimed and Lycan supremacy may become more than just a lunar cycle.

Chapter 27

The combined forces' leaders gather to discuss their next tactic. Although a victory was claimed, the main prize was not, and it will take a victory greater than the previous night to claim Cathedral Tower. An injured and bent-on-revenge Aiden barks and rants his way through his plan which doesn't make much sense and Alice has to inform him fighting with rage only makes it easier for their enemy because the anger clouds your judgement and leads you into mistakes. Aiden knows and accepts this, but Alice's holier than thou attitude is beginning to irritate him. Gideon wants to strike again in the same way as they did last night; Brigacos and Bryson agree; Gwen thinks they should wait and see what The Vampires do next; and Jessica and Leo suggest contacting The Chinese and asking them to join. Alice thinks they are all legitimate ideas, but using the same plan as the previous night is risky, The Witches will be wise to it, sitting and waiting for the enemy to make the first move means they can be picked off at will and it is doubtful The Chinese will join – only two nights ago they and the combined forces were killing each other. Alice looks at Jessica who looks back. Knowing her sister wants to discuss something, Jessica wanders away under the pretence of gang duties. Alice soon follows after.

"Have you heard from Cuthwulf?" Alice asks, considering the possibility of werewolf help.

"Yes," Jessica replies, knowing where this is going. "They were ambushed by The Cannibals outside Werewolf HQ, Davis is dead, Wycombe is cannibal leader now," she adds, seeing Alice's eyebrows rise and a look of concern form across her face.

"Did the werewolf leaders all survive?" Alice asks.

"Yes, they're fine," Jessica replies, her mind wondering what Cuthwulf is doing now.

Alice pauses for a moment looking away and then back to her sister. "Do you know what his plan is for the rest of the war?" she inquires, nibbling away for information, which irritates Jessica.

"No, what is your point?" she bites, wanting Alice to just be clear with her questions.

"Ask him to join with us and take the cathedral," Alice tells her, doubting the combined forces can claim the tower despite last night's victory. Jessica thinks it is worth asking but is not certain he will agree; after all, in the current climate they are enemies and he didn't tell her about starting the war, which made things quite clear where his loyalties lay.

As Jessica makes the call, Alice notices a rat scurrying along the edge of The Waiting Yard against the cathedral wall. The rat stops and looks at her, standing on his back legs. Knowing Princess Katalin sometimes poses as a rat, Alice stops Jessica from divulging too much information on the phone for risk of giving away tactics to their enemy. Alice raises her gun and aims at the rodent, and the rat runs for its life toward the cathedral door, convincing Alice it is indeed Katalin; she fires, the bullet just missing and hitting the cathedral door as the rat disappears into the shadow of the entrance. Looking at Alice, people wonder what she is doing until she informs them they were being spied on, bringing an instant paranoia to the group, looking up to the rooftops, glaring at the windows, the trees, the bushes, searching for witches in disguise.

Jessica waits patiently for Cuthwulf to answer the phone – he usually answers swiftly as if he has been longing to talk to her, but this time the phone rings and rings. Eventually it is answered by a tired sounding Cuthwulf who makes a fair effort to sound pleased to speak to her, but Jessica can tell he is just being polite, which saddens her, knowing some of his feeling for her has waned and whatever relationship they did have may already be beginning to fade. After the pleasantries have been exchanged and an awkward pause, Jessica asks him his position and what he plans to do.

Cuthwulf sighs as if annoyed, surprising Jessica. "Has Alice told you to ask me?" he responds abruptly.

Jessica pauses, knowing he is right and can't deny it, but she is still taken aback by his temper. "I'm just asking what you are planning to do."

"I'm planning to take over the city, hopefully one day with you by my side but at the moment that is fifty-fifty because you are obviously calling to ask me to come and help you claim the cathedral; but when I was there two nights ago you were not helping me, you were off fighting The Chinese, who by the way are camped just off from your position and could have attacked at any point," Cuthwulf snaps, angry at her pretence of being the concerned friend when really he is right – Jessica is calling him for back-up and not because she is worried about him.

Looking up to the possible location of The Chinese, Jessica signals Alice to come over and informs her of what Cuthwulf has told her, and Alice rounds up some troops. Jessica, trying to calm Cuthwulf down, fails and he hangs up. Saddened by his behaviour but with more pressing matters at hand, Jessica cocks her gun and readies herself for action. With the possibility that they are surrounded on both sides, the combined forces must quickly establish their next move. After seeing the massacre sight on Neutral Territory and not seeing or hearing from The Chinese, some people began to believe they had been wiped out, but from what Cuthwulf says they are alive and kicking, waiting for the right moment to conquer.

Alice takes the right flank with Leo and Jessica taking the left, Druid Byson agrees to go with Alice and the rest stay in case of a vampire attack. They slowly but surely spread to attempt to surround The Chinese. Zhen Yun peering through her binoculars is wise to this tactic and sees all that is going on, watching them for a day now the new Chinese leader predicted they might try this and sends scouts out to watch for their approach. Readying a few explosives, she retreats her army slightly to give them a better position to sniper oncoming attackers. It appears the decision has been made for her – only a few hours ago Zhen was considering whether to help them fight against the forces of evil, and here they are sneaking up on her gang instead of approaching head on with a white flag raised, the combined forces have played their hand and it plays right into the hands of The Chinese but even more so The Vampires and The Witches.

The scouts return, informing their Empress that the gangs are closing in. Zhen gives the order for the snipers to fire without mercy – if they wanted some they should have approached in peace and not in a snide manner. Alice ducks behind some bushes just as she hears a whiz past her and one of her gang members falls to the ground with a hole in his face. Ordering her crew to drop and hide, Bryson dives for cover as another messenger gang member is dropped to his death. Radioing Leo they are under attack. her deputy already knows as he has the blood of a member splattered across his face and Jessica is under sniper fire – the bark from the tree she is hiding behind chipping away under the hail of bullets.

Joining her troops at the front, Zhen looks through her scope and sees a cowering enemy quickly realise their plan was a bad one and knowing they cannot make a run for it as they will be prime targets for snipers and have nowhere to go. Phoning Gwen for back-up, the Druidess is thrown to the ground by an explosion as a Chinese rocket is launched at The Waiting Yard, sending body parts of gang members scattering into the air. The Chinese have the combined forces under siege and there is nowhere to run except into the cathedral, but in there is an even more deadly enemy so their options have disappeared. It is now a matter of when they are defeated and not if. Another explosion rings out and parts of the cathedral walls crumble as Gideon searches for a place to run and hide. Alice quickly thinking of a way out as Jessica slumps further down to avoid the snipers' fire. It is a perilous situation they find themselves in.

Zhen Yun, watching through her scope, hears a thud next to her and looks at the gang member who is beside her. Seeing the lifeless body she rolls out of the firing line to a safer position and looks for the perpetrator through her scope, but sees nothing. Another member at the other side of her position is hit in the head by another bullet, forcing Zhen to retreat as another one of her snipers is himself snipered, turning the tide. Ordering her troops to flatten the area with rockets, Zhen wants destruction, but as they attempt to launch their attack the gang members are slaughtered without mercy from a flood of sniper fire.

Jessica, noticing the assault has stopped, stays hidden but wonders what is happening. Alice wants to look around but doesn't just in case, and Bryson is able to peep out from his position, seeing a dead Chinese member and looking around for the person who committed the killing. Gunfire rings out from the west flank as Zhen and her crew come under attack from Randall, and looking at what has saved them, Jessica sees Cuthwulf advancing from the east. Her heart skips at the thought of him coming to the rescue and is told to wake up by Leo, who has risen to his feet and is making his way toward The Chinese with his gun blazing. Seeing Zhen retreat as the gunshots ring out, Cuthwulf phones Wulfric, who is in the process of claiming China Town, to be aware at the border as The Chinese may return. Randall, diving to the floor to take cover and sighting a Chinese member about to launch a rocket at his crew through his scope, drops him with one bullet. Eyeing up Zhen Yun for a kill shot, Randall pulls the trigger just as a Chinese gang member stands to retreat and unintentionally takes the bullet for her, blood splattering over her face; she retreats. Randall mutters the word "bitch" to himself and re-joins his crew.

Jessica jumps to her feet and runs to Cuthwulf, almost diving into his arms and giving him her most passionate kiss yet, wrapping his arms around her so she feels safe and protected; he returns the kiss with equal passion. Alice approaches with thanks and a handshake and asks for an update on current events with his gang. Cuthwulf smiles at her, ever the working woman lifestyle and returns to kissing her sister who is only to keen to oblige. Alice will have to wait.

Siobhan struggles to her feet, wiping her face and seeing blood on her hand, in a panic she rubs her neck and sees more blood yet notices that the pain of her injuries have faded and her sight and hearing seem to have improved. Wandering back to a blazing HQ, she remembers what happened and looks around for Krul but he is nowhere to be seen. Slumping to the floor, Siobhan begins to realise the position she is in and her heart begins to pound. What will become of her? What will her gang members think? Will she be outcast? How will she survive? The fear consumes her and paranoia takes over. All she can think about is Krul and an urge to find him, and yet at the same time Siobhan wants to join up with her people and fight for them in war – this is the crossover, the no-man's land between mortality and vampirism. Caught between wanting to remain human but knowing your change is inevitable, knowing the only thing that can stop the change is to slay Krul before the infection finishes its cycle; after that there is no turning back. Life, or in this case unlife, is going to consume her and the change for some is terrifying. Especially when you have nobody to guide you through it offering advice and understanding, it feels like you are alone and nobody feels as scared as you. Krul felt this when he changed, although Enigma did help in some way, and Victuis had Krul to guide and advise him; but Siobhan is all alone and the panic grips her.

Curled up on the floor in tears, Siobhan watches as The Irish HQ burns and perhaps her infection is the trans period from one gang to another. Already the urge toward Krul is growing, beginning with a thought and evolving into a desire; Siobhan is twisted in two minds whether she should find her crew or seek Krul. Rising to her feet she stumbles in no direction in particular, the infection still taking over her body but not yet full blown. Unless her infector is killed, it is only a matter of time before mortal becomes monster and nothing can reverse the infection.

Under cover for protection, Wulfric watches the distance from as many angles as he and his crew can manage. After Cuthwulf's warning about The Chinese retreat and probability that they will return home, Wulfric and his squad will be an unwelcome sight for them. Claiming China Town was a feather that Cuthwulf wanted in his cap, but true love conquers all and the alpha wolf played the heroics to a tee to save his woman. This means his deputy yet again claims a piece of werewolf and city history, and the wolfmen already have their eyes locked on Emerald Territory and Neutral Territory to complete the surrounding of Holy Ground from the north, east and most of the west, with only The Caves and The Moors left, meaning Holy Ground will be completely surrounded by the monster gangs. The Werewolves have played their hand well and their tactics seem obvious and straight forward, but really it just comes down to knowing your enemy. Cuthwulf knew the other gangs would battle over the tower, so he simply went against the grain and did what others didn't expect. Everybody assumed all gangs would fight for control of the cathedral, so Cuthwulf didn't, and with a loyal wolf pack backing him up the alpha wolf may become alpha leader of 9 Gang City.

Seeing movement through his binoculars, Wulfric quickly changes to his sniper rifle and scopes the distance – another movement, but all he can see is the top of whatever it is, as if it is something creeping and staying hidden, knowing it will not be Cuthwulf or Randall. Cuthwulf is still at the cathedral and Randall is on his way to claim Emerald Territory, meaning it must be an enemy, but he does not want to shoot yet because it is not the right time to give away his position. But whoever or whatever it is is getting closer and Wulfric needs to decide quickly what his decision is; he sends a team out to investigate. Watching their mission through his scope, he sees they have swiftly surrounded the possible invader with guns drawn and approach cautiously. The team leader radios back to his superior.

"It's Siobhan Murphy," he informs Wulfric, who is surprised by the news. "You should have a look at her," the gang member adds, waiting for Wulfric's orders, who, after a quick think, tells his team to take her prisoner and bring her to him.

Seeing the Irish woman for himself, Wulfric sees she is a mess, looking ill and yet at the same time wounds healing rapidly; it is like she is suffering from a virus that is destroying her but making her stronger at the same time. Wulfric knows instantly what has happened – checking her neck he sees the bite marks, lifting her top lips he sees the beginning of fangs piercing through her gums, and the look in her eye is becoming more attentive to her surrounding as if she hears and senses everything.

"Who did this?" Wulfric asks out of curiosity, but Siobhan remains silent. Wulfric doesn't blame whatever vampire bit her because infecting the change is exactly what his gang are going to do to the cannibal prisoners they took and are holding hostage until the next full moon. Wulfric is merely curious as to which vampire has realised that perhaps recruiting instead of killing is a better way of making your enemy weaker at the same time as making your own gang stronger; he suspects Krul. Taking Siobhan to Chinese HQ, which now just like Cannibal Farm and BC Nation flies The Werewolf flag, soon to be followed by Irish and Messenger turf, she struggles but they are half hearted attempts still in the crossover stage. It will be a few more night yet until she is full vampire, but full vampire she will be at this rate.

As Cuthwulf organises his crew to return to Wulfric and continue their conquest, the combined forces' leaders look at him with surprise – they assumed he was here not just to save Jessica but to take the cathedral, when in fact he is just here to save Jessica. Alice in an attempt to stop him and persuade him to join with them is stopped in her tracks.

"Alice," Cuthwulf says politely. "You are a nice person but don't bother trying to convince me to join a lost cause. Do any of you really think you are going to win this battle?" He looks around The Waiting Yard at a group of tired, weary-looking leaders and their even more exhausted-looking gang members. Aiden takes exception to his comment.

"We did just fine last night," the Irish leader boasts.

Cuthwulf looks at him with a wry smile. "But at what cost, your gang numbers are down, you grow more and more tired by the day whilst The Vampires grow stronger, you are fighting on their terms by fighting at night, you want to commit The Daylight Killings but can't because The Witches are protecting them, and tonight you have been fighting and dying with The Chinese and not one vampire or witch has been slain," Cuthwulf truthfully says, and knowing he is right nobody speaks until Alice feels the urge to say something.

"What do you suggest we do? Just leave and let The Vampires and The Witches have the tower?" she asks, knowing it is possibly their only choice.

"Yes," Cuthwulf answers blankly. "You and your people can stay with us, the rest of you can stay and fight all you want," he adds, turning to Jessica to see her reaction, who looks at Alice for her answer.

Alice then looks at everybody else. Leo nods in agreement with Cuthwulf, Gideon thinks a retreat would only spur on their enemy, Aiden wants to stay and fight, as do Brigacos and Bryson, with Gwen torn between the two. Allowing The Vampires to have the tower and retreating would only give them more time to recruit and re-evaluate their tactics and position, but staying would be a bloodbath. Despite last night's victory they have gained no ground and are smaller in numbers, so was it really a victory at all? Alice decides to go with The Werewolves, much to the delight of Jessica and the relief of Leo, but the rest of the combined forces stay to fight.

Cuthwulf leads his crew east to the surprise of The Messengers. Father Gideon notices this but assumes The Werewolves are chasing down The Chinese, the rest are too focused on their own agendas to realise. Riding with her man, Jessica snuggles up to him. She has missed his touch and kisses him, the perfect antidote of war is love and Jessica is in love with the wolfman.

Alice, who is in the passenger seat is wondering why they are heading east, and turning and seeing her sister smooching, she hopes they can unlock their lips enough to remember there is a war ongoing. Cuthwulf looks at Alice with an expression of here we go again knowing she must have some serious question or request, always the bore never the joker he thinks to himself.

"Why are we going east?" Alice inquires before he even asks what she wants. "When you said we can stay with you I assumed you meant The Forests?"

This is met with a roll of the eyes and a shake of the head from Cuthwulf.

"Perhaps assumption is why all the other gangs are fighting over the cathedral and we have almost conquered the city," Cuthwulf replies.

Alice and Jessica look at him with surprise, anticipating him elaborating.

After glancing at both, he reveals what he and his crew have been up to since the full moon faded. "We have already claimed Cannibal Farm, BC Nation and China Town, and the reason Randall left as soon as The Chinese retreated was to claim Emerald Territory," the alpha wolf adds to a shocked Alice and Jessica.

Alice wanting to know his intentions for Neutral Territory and Jessica wondering how something like this could be so easy, but in truth that is exactly what it was, easy.

"What about our turf?" Alice asks, almost knowing the answer but wanting confirmation.

Cuthwulf pauses, feeling awkward to say it but knows they at least deserve to know. "We will be claiming your land as well, that is where we are heading now," he tells them, Jessica pushing away from him in disgust and Alice gives a disappointed sigh. "I'm sorry, ladies, but war is war and a wolf needs to mark his territory," Cuthwulf states, looking at Jessica who doesn't look back and glares out of the window as they approach what used to be their home, now a new conquest of The Werewolves.

"Are we prisoners?" Alice asks as they exit the car at a charred Messengers HQ.

"Diplomatic immunity," Cuthwulf grants them as he investigates the scene, still littered with Chinese gang members relieved of some of their body parts for witch spells. His phone rings. Randall informs him that Irish HQ has been burned to the ground, arson, with empty fuel cans found. Cuthwulf thanks him for the update and orders him to fly the flag and find somewhere to bed down for some rest with a guard on duty. No sooner has he hung up the phone Cuthwulf receives another call, his deputy this time, informing him they have a prisoner of war. Upon asking from what gang, Wulfric hesitates before replying "I don't know", which bemuses the wolf leader until he is told of Siobhan's condition. Once Alice is told she is sad for Siobhan but intrigued as to what vampire escaped the battle and is on the loose. Added to Cormac's death, Aiden will be even more heartbroken.

Raising the wolf flag from a ruined HQ as The Messengers watch and Randall doing the same on Irish turf, The Werewolves have claimed the east side of the city and every mortal gang in 9 Gang City has either had their land conquered or is surrounded by those they call monsters. Another night draws to a close and not one vampire or witch slain, and the euphoria surrounding the victory they claimed begins to fizzle out and feels like a defeat, the combined forces already beginning to look around their ranks and see their numbers fewer. The Messengers have retreated who were the mediation between the gangs, leaving a disunited group of people who only last night were collaborating against the forces of evil, now wondering how they will repeat the heroics, and some wonder if they should cut and run. The mood is hostile and morale has lowered to a point that the combined forces segregate themselves into their gangs and glare at each other across The Waiting Yard. It is almost as if a darker force is toying with them.

Chapter 28

L
ike Atilla with his Huns and The Magyar tribe, The
Witches went from east to west and conquered, and to a
point integrated, with the society they settled in. Defeating
Roman and Germanic tribes, Atilla was a mighty warrior close to
the crossover of time periods between Roman Times and The Dark
Ages, laying waste to whatever and whoever stood in his way. One of
the greatest warriors in history, Atilla ravaged the Roman Empire's
territory as far as Gaul, modern day France, and Constantinople,
and paved the way for the Germanic Tribes to eventually claim
Roman turf. Many historians and scholars argue over the origins
of his name – some say it is Gothic, meaning father, others say it
means wolf, another suggestion is it means universal ruler from
Turkic origin; all these are plausible, but whatever the meaning
Atilla is remembered for the fear he bestowed upon his enemy and
as a mighty tribal leader. The Magyars centuries later travelled
west from Asia settling in Europe, bringing a new culture to The
Carpathians. It all sounds comparable to Ziana and Niculi moving
west, conquering and settling in a new land and leaving a legacy
that will always be remembered. A legacy that Princess Tunder
wants to continue and now that The Witches' day of celebration
is over for another year, it is back to business for The Dark Fairy.
Hearing from Katalin that the combined forces have been fighting

and dying at the hands of The Chinese, and The Messengers have retreated with The Werewolves, Tunder laughs to herself, thinking only mortals could claim a memorable victory and then help their enemy by losing strength in numbers. Queen Rika returns from the rooftop after polluting the minds of their rivals outside, and despite the loss they suffered The Witches are in the driving seat – only a witch could stand victorious after defeat; magic whether it be good or evil is of a greater force than mere mortal combat, and mortals' greatest weakness is their emotions and to affect their emotions you pollute their mind. Prey on something they either hold dear or a bracket they fall into such as race, class system, gender, sexuality, religion, and show them all of the problems they face because of one or each of these things, you then simply brainwash them with these issues at the same time as pointing the finger at those you wish to demonise, whilst mentally manipulating them into believing you or your beliefs and opinions are the solution, and you have successfully created a victim who thinks your enemy is the cause and you are their saviour. Liberal politics has done this with expert precision over decades and decades, and it has produced a western society that is the luckiest, privileged and most free society in history, and yet victim status is at an all-time high, all because that freedom and wealth has been produced by a section of society that are deemed to be the representative of all things wrong in the world, when in fact they are a minority who simply allowed nothing to hold them back from prosperity. Queen Rika has simply changed that way of thinking, keeping the anger and hatred but altering it to be aimed at others around them and not at what dwells in the shadows. While The Witches were celebrating their history, mortals were doing what they do best, turning on each other and killing one another, and these are the people who say witchcraft and vampirism is evil.

When man began to multiply on the face of the land and daughters were born to them, the sons of God saw the daughters of man were attractive. And they took as their wives any they chose. Then the lord said, "My Spirit shall not abide in man for ever, for he is flesh: his days shall be 120 years." The Nephilim were on the earth in those days, and also afterward, when the sons of God came in to the daughters of man and they bore children to them. These were the mighty men who were of old, the men of renown. The Lord saw the wickedness of man was great in the earth, and that every intention of his thoughts of his heart was only evil continually. And the Lord regretted that he had made man on the earth, and it grieved him to his heart. So the Lord said "I will blot out man whom I have created from the face of the land, man and animals and creeping things and birds of the heavens, for I am sorry that I have made them. But Noah found favour in the eyes of the Lord.

Increasing Corruption on Earth, Genesis, Holy Bible, English Standard Version, Anglicized Edition.

When a holy book contains scriptures of the God they worship regretting creating them to a point God then brings destruction upon them, you have to consider many things, four of which are: one, God does not forgive as some Christians say he does; two, the evil in the world is of human existence and not within witchcraft and vampirism; three, if God brings destruction and death, why do we commiserate when somebody dies when maybe we should celebrate their demise as one less corrupt, evil polluter ruining the world; and four, the possibility that God put witchcraft and vampirism on earth to hunt down and punish man for his sins and maybe the draining of blood that kills man and makes vampires stronger is symbolic of God's vengeance on his regretful creation. It is safe to say of all God's creation the rarest is peace, and with hatred being one of the most popular it should make us wonder has it all been made as a test to see if we enter Heaven or burn in Hell when we die, or is this just a story from Holy men to scare us into being good and following God? Or is it because God wants us to hate? Does God want war, murder and rape, is the passage written above just a passage written by a religious brainwasher centuries ago or is it the truth? What is for certain is there are accurate statements in that passage and all these years later the human race is no closer to change. The occult offers the balance of the equilibrium, the balance of good and evil, the Libra effect; we cannot have one without the other; if we did good would not be good, it would be normality, and perhaps this is why God created evil, so we would pray to him to be saved. When The CVS went to Eastern Europe to destroy vampirism and witchcraft, they were attempting to destroy the balance between good and evil. This ended with the formation of 9 Gang City so perhaps this great city is the balance between the two where they both live side by side with Cathedral Tower in the middle as the scales themselves. This would account for Niculi and Ziana's slaying in The War Against The Vampires, the city had become too evil and the scales had tipped to the occult and had to be re-balanced; God saw fit to help the city on its way and gave aid to the other gangs to claim victory and restore the scales to their level of equality. It all fits together, but what the future holds remains to be seen.

Chapter 29

Night falls and Krul stalks, The Chinese fuming from The Werewolf attack and even more irate that those very same werewolves now occupy their land. Krul watches The Chinese watching The Werewolves and the wolfmen watch Zhen's army camped on Holy Ground. This war is quickly becoming a standoff with one gang waiting for the other to move. The combined forces still haven't launched their next attack, The Vampires and The Witches remain in the cathedral, and The Werewolves, happy with their fill of land, are content to sit it out until the next full moon. The Chinese are caught between a rock and a hard place – if they travel north, south or east, Cuthwulf's army will cut them off, if they turn back and head west the combined forces may do the same. Zhen must think and think quickly. Krul watches all this unravel and with The Messengers now with The Werewolves, the vampire leader can now strike the combined forces without mercy once he returns to the cathedral. He had been worried in battle of Alice and Jessica being killed, he bears no ill will toward them for any vampires they slayed, Krul knows this is part of war and the two Messenger women were just doing their duty to their gang. Also, Krul had his fill on some Messenger gang members so the favour was returned.

Krul creeps closer to The Chinese camp like a beast stalking its prey, on high alert. Zhen's troops are anxious and twitchy, with no longer a home to go to and living on enemy land, morale is the lowest it has been and the high and mighty gang they were only a week ago has fast disappeared and is replaced with a worried and paranoid group who may crumble under another attack. Moving nearer, Krul feels the thunder in their chest, hearts racing and adrenaline flooding their body to a point some struggle to compose themselves, the smell of fear from what he sees in front of him has Krul aching for action; he makes his move. A watchman on the outskirts of the camp is pulled into the bushes and struggles as fangs are sunk deep into his neck, Krul cuts himself to inflict infection the same way he did to Siobhan, the recruitment process. Force-drinking his blood into the gang member's mouth, some oozing out and slobbering down the side of his face, Krul leaves the soldier on the floor to be consumed by infection and hunts down his next victim, silent and swift, one after another he repeats the process, taking from one gang and giving to his own. Until he is caught in the act by a rival who without thinking lets rip with his gun. The bullets have zero effect on Krul who stands bulletproof and springs onto the gang member, this time savaging him to death just for the pleasure of killing a rival.

Zhen Yun, hearing the gun shots, leaps into action, rounding her bodyguards and investigating what is happening in her camp. Seeing the bitten members of her gang and trails of blood leading to the woods by where they are stationed, Zhen calls on her soldiers to follow her. A hasty investigation is followed by a cautious pursuit. Zhen leads the way, showing her men she is willing to risk it all for the gang, and her crew members take motivation from this and follow their leader into the unknown. A tension grips the wood and Zhen knows something lurks nearby, waiting, spying, stalking, longing for the right moment to pounce, she feels it in her heart with every thump it beats. Zhen spins around after hearing a noise and sees the bushes moving and a gang member missing. With her crossbow stake aimed, she slowly moves toward the bush, pulse racing and edging ever closer she anticipates a vampire springing into attack. Suddenly something does spring out startling all present, but it is not a vampire but a vampire victim, the missing gang member clutching his neck with blood pumping from the puncture wounds and crimson fluid slipping down from his mouth. Another ambush from behind them as another gang member disappears into the undergrowth; some of the others fire blind into the bushes but are ordered to stop by Zhen as it serves no purpose, but their panic is evident. Another member is dragged into the bushes as the gang are picked off one by one and Zhen is forced to retreat. Krul has his fill of Chinese blood and after tasting Irish he can confirm different races taste different to drink. Zhen will have to kill Krul to save her crew members, or kill them to save them from an undead life, or allow them to become vampire forever. She looks at one of her gang on the floor, clutching his neck; he looks up at his leader for some encouragement or sympathy, anything to stop the panic that is running through him. But the infection that is already taking its grip has only one cure and the likelihood of killing Krul before it takes its full effect is low, and having to control changing gang members and protecting others from their bloodlust is a workload they don't need, especially on top of taking back their land from The Werewolves and fighting for power and claiming the cathedral.

Zhen's heavy heart decides, a decision a leader never wants to make but a conflicted mind must and when your people's prospects come before individuals the ultimate step must be taken. Zhen Yun raises her crossbow and fires the stake point blank though her own gang member's chest, the soldier winces and lets out a welp of pain as his heart is pierced. Slowly and sadly pulling her sword, she removes his head to save him from an eternity of darkness. Bowing her head in respect and apology, she orders her crew to do the same to any infected member. Turning to watch Chinese kill Chinese, Zhen's heart sinks into more agony and Krul has done his work well – his plan comes together perfectly as rivals become comrades and enemies kill their own kind; there is more than one way to win a war and Krul's war is coming together nicely.

The combined forces hatch their plan and Aiden is itching to gain revenge for Cormac's death, gripping his crucifix and a stake as he prepares for battle. Father Gideon suggests they all stick together and attempt to locate the secret room; although it will be difficult they have proven they can claim victory and there is power in faith. Aiden nods, still grasping his cross tightly, dreaming of slaying Victuis, and if that demonic pixie should get in the way she will die as well. Brigacos, not liking Gideon calling the shots, but holding his tongue for now, the Arch Druid knows at a time like this sticking together will give him and his crew a better chance of victory, but he never thought he would be on the same side as Father Gideon. The tyrant Gideon, the fallen hero Gideon, the representative of the religion that demonised Celtic culture Gideon, but Brigacos needs to put those feelings on hold because they are about to enter the lair of creatures that can decimate them in a heartbeat.

Aiden keeps going over and over in his head when Victuis killed Cormac and how close he came to exorcizing Tunder and that voice that came out of Victuis was not the voice of the vampire deputy. Aiden cannot work out what it was, but it had a chilling familiarity. And what he said, what did he mean by there is no such thing as slain? Aiden is snapped out of his thoughts by Gwen who gently taps his shoulder to tell him they are ready to enter the cathedral. Looking at the entrance to Cathedral Tower, Aiden jumps to his feet when he sees Princess Tunder stood in the doorway, a light mist encircles her and she faces her enemy alone with no fear or worry of the consequences. The gang members stand off her worried and paranoid at what she might do, flamethrowers are ready to burn but the hands that hold them are shaky and unsteady. Father Gideon hurries to the front, quickly followed by Aiden, each with their crucifix ready to strike. The Waiting Yard moves underneath them, sending the gang members sprawling to the ground, weapons falling with them. Before they can react, they are elevated and thrown out of The Waiting Yard as The Vampires charge out of the cathedral to attack. The combined forces dither in panic and are set upon by Victuis leading his crew into battle, feasting on rivals and with every bite victory draws closer. Weaponless, the combined forces are lambs to the slaughter and vampires lay waste to a helpless enemy. Father Gideon shouts for a retreat, knowing it is a lost cause; the others turn to run in any direction they can; the distance cannot come soon enough and sunrise feels a lifetime away. The hunt is on and Victuis smiles with gratification as he watches them run in panic, his excitement rises a notch and he gives chase, feeling the rhythm of their thundering hearts is music to his ears and all around his enemy is falling and dying. Berserk vampires overtaken by blood thirst and bent on gang supremacy feast their way through fallen foes, and mortal life falls foul of their own ambition. An ambition to conquer, an ambition to rule, and an ambition to dictate to others what is right and what is wrong based on their own beliefs, those ambitions have become yet another downfall of humankind as the undead send them to death.

Wulfric watches Siobhan through the glass in the door. Each gang has medical facilities on their turf and medically trained gang members. On Chinese turf the medical rooms have glass in a vertical strip so medics can check on the patient without entering the room.

With her strapped to a bed like a lunatic would be in the old days, Wulfric is taking no chances with the soon-to-be-vampire and yet he is still taking a chance – Siobhan has almost healed, her puncture wounds have almost disappeared and soon she will be stronger than any mortal. Although Wulfric is not mortal, she will still be able to fight him comfortably in man form, but during a full moon it won't be so easy. Siobhan hears voices outside like they are right next to her, she can hear a scratching in the wall – a scurrying mouse sounds like a bull in a China shop with Siobhan's new supernatural hearing. Seeing Wulfric through the glass talking to a gang member, Siobhan hears they are talking about how long she has been infected… Approximately 24 hours. How long before the infection takes full hold of her? About five days without blood, or three days with human blood to drink and her infecting vampire's blood to quicken the process. Wulfric knew all this, but he wanted to be certain. This poses a problem because in order to gain more members, The Werewolves have to wait until they have turned and then bite their recruits to inflict their own infection. If vampires can do it between three and five days, then Krul and his crew could have claimed the entire city as their own by then. Siobhan sees Wulfric turn away, lifting his phone to his ear and by the respectful tone of his voice it must be Cuthwulf he is talking to. A guard stands outside the room with his back to the glass. Siobhan's strength is increasing and she tries to force her way out of the straps; they loosen; she forces against the straps again and they loosen more. Stopping and glaring at the guard to see if he has heard what she is doing, she sees he is still facing away so continues her escape attempt. The straps are loose enough for her to slip out of and staring at the window as she does Siobhan is out and standing beside the bed, looking around for anything she can use as a weapon but there is nothing – she will have to break her way out and collect a weapon on the way. Creeping to the glass – the guard is still facing away unaware that the soon-to-be-vampire is standing centimetres away from him with only glass in-between – Siobhan listens for any extra guards in the corridor and from what she can make out they are alone. Smashing through the glass with a force she wouldn't be able to manage if she was full mortal, Siobhan grabs the guard by the throat, who struggles under the attack, reaching through and taking his handgun from its holster she fires multiple shots through his back, although not dead as the bullets are not silver, but it causes enough damage to drop him to the floor. Reaching out, she checks the door for the key which is in the lock, and turning it Siobhan bursts out of the room and runs down the corridor to where she knows the way out is, remembering from being brought in. Hearing werewolf gang members entering, she hides in another room, watching them run past. Siobhan slips out and on to her escape. Entering the main part of Chinese HQ, she hears the gang members following her from the medical unit and more approaching from the front. Edging her way along another corridor, she checks all the rooms, looking for some assistance in her escape. Bursting into a room she sees weapons racked – The Chinese have their arsenal well stocked even after days of war. Grabbing an AK-47, Siobhan ransacks the ammunition, checking their metal – silver – a rush of excitement runs through her body as the tables turn slightly. Locked and loaded, she bids her escape. Taking a couple of grenades and exiting the room, she rolls one down the corridor and takes refuge back in the arsenal, the explosion rings out and the walls and ceiling collapse, blocking the way and any rival coming from that direction. Making her escape with gun leading the way, Siobhan drops the first enemy she sees with a precision shot and another from the opposite side. Knowing The Werewolves are well organised, she will have to have her wits about her, but using the benefits of her new infection, her wits are additional to those she had as a mortal; Siobhan is already using vampirism to her advantage. With two ways to go and enemy troops coming from both sides, Siobhan throws a grenade one way and shoots her way to freedom the other. Another explosion rings out as the building crumbles and during the commotion she has the drop on the squad that is there to kill her. Lacing them with her AK, she keeps the trigger pulled until it is empty, dropping all in her path. Reloading, she springs her escape through the door and out into China Town, when a bullet hits her in the shoulder. Turning, she sees Wulfric with his AR-15 aimed. Siobhan peppers bullets in his direction and the werewolf deputy dives for cover. Before he can shoot again, Siobhan is gone. Running through China Town, which is now a werewolf town but seeing it at the moment it is a ghost town, Siobhan is alone again but at least she is free from captivity and that escape is largely due to the infection she has suffered, but if it has saved her is it really an infection or a saving grace? Wulfric, furious with the night's events, wants a full investigation held before Cuthwulf finds out, an escaped prisoner, dead gang members and in all truth an embarrassment for Wulfric that this has happened on his watch. Only yesterday he was daydreaming about his place in history and the stories that would be told about him, now he is the fodder for Irish and vampire jokes. The wolf who oversaw one woman escape him and his crew and killed his gang members, this is a reality check for Wulfric. A reality that a full takeover will not be so easy, The Werewolves can rave about their achievement all they want, but when other gangs fight back your conquest becomes a lot more difficult. If one rival who has barely changed from mortal to vampire can do this then what can all the full vampires do, especially when they are backed up by The Witches. All of a sudden, the full moon can't come soon enough and the wolfmen have been given a taste of what difficulties they face if they are to rule 9 Gang City.

Chapter 30

Krul, after suitably lowering Chinese numbers and morale, heads east, and after hearing two explosions in the distance he is intrigued to see what is going on. On the border with China Town the Werewolf guards are on high alert and from their body language and facial expressions something has gone badly wrong. Hearing vehicles approach, Krul watches as Cuthwulf and The Messengers arrive at the border and are immediately allowed in by a nervous looking security guard. Krul wants a closer look so scales the fence with ease, his vampiric abilities give him access to enemy land and with borders long and gang numbers down there is no way a border can be totally guarded. Travelling ever closer to Chinese HQ, Krul sees The Werewolf flag wafting in the breeze, a symbolic gesture to not just The Chinese but the entire city that The Dog Pound and their crew have conquered land, but by the sound of what is going on they should have paid more attention to what is happening within instead of showing off their achievements. From what Krul can make out as he spies, a prisoner has escaped and killed ten werewolf gang members in the process. Cuthwulf stands furious and Wulfric stands guilty and ashamed that it happened under his command. Cuthwulf storms into the building, demanding to know the full details of the incident. Krul is happy to see Alice, Leo and Jessica are still alive, but judging by the gang numbers that are with them The Messengers are almost wiped out. After investigating further, Krul sees the destruction the explosions have caused and from his guess he thinks a grenade did the damage, which means The Werewolves have access to The Chinese arsenal but left it unguarded.

Crouching behind a car, Krul cracks the petrol tank so the fuel drizzles out. Before long the fuel has formed a small puddle on the ground and is gradually trickling away from the car. Krul repeats this on the other vehicles present. Lighting the petrol, the cars burst into flames as Krul stands back and watches, werewolf gang members rush over to put out the fires but already the cars are engulfed. Cuthwulf and Wulfric bolt out of the doors to see another setback take shape as one of the cars explodes and flame shoots into the air. Krul hears Cuthwulf shout "Find that bitch" to his crew and they dart off in search of the culprit with stakes, crosses and holy water. Krul wonders whether it must have been Siobhan who escaped and caused havoc and begins to feel a small pride for his new-claimed victim. Leaving a much freer passage into HQ, The Werewolf gang members frantically search for somebody who may or may not be there. Finding the arsenal, Krul rips the steel cage from the window, a feat mere mortals couldn't do but vampire strength has no problem with, the bars are removed as well and entry to the weapons supply gives him even more carnage to inflict. A vampire can bite a werewolf as much as he/she wants, but only silver can kill a werewolf, whether it be a bullet or a blade. Now with access to the precious metal, Krul can really cause destruction. Hearing somebody coming, Krul cocks a gun and hides in the shadows. The door swings open and the light goes on. Krul smiles to himself when he sees it is Alice. Stepping out, she spins around with gun aimed and lowers it immediately on seeing him. They embrace happily, holding the hug to confirm their missing one another, they smile as if long lost friends have been reunited after years apart and yet it has only been a few days.

"Was it you who set fire to the cars?" Alice asks. Krul smirks before confirming. "And Siobhan, was it you that bit her?" she says, looking at him for his reaction.

"Yes," he answers without remorse. "She would happily kill me so I got to her first," Krul adds, noticing Alice's face fall into sadness as if disappointed, but what did she expect? Biting, drinking and turning or killing is what vampires do, why would she think Krul is any different?

"She is somewhere around, it was her who blew up part of the building, she is already on the turn," Alice informs him.

Krul nods at the news and is pleasantly surprised she was able to do such a thing so soon after being bitten – usually people are flaked out for days unable to cope, she must be strong both physically and mentally.

"What is the score with The Werewolves?" Krul inquires.

"They have conquered all of the surrounding mortal territories, Randall is on Emerald Territory now and The Cannibals have almost been wiped out. Davis is dead, Wycombe is alive but on the run, and White is missing," Alice replies, happy to divulge to an enemy but Krul is different – if she is not to be leader she wants it to be Krul.

"How are your people doing?" Krul asks.

Alice shakes her head with sadness. "We are almost wiped out, but Jessica and Leo are still alive," she adds with a beaming smile, a smile so wide Krul's face lights up in reaction. It feels nice to catch up with a friend and both share a silent moment of enjoyment before glancing at one another and sharing another smile.

"Stay close to Jessica and I hope we all get through this," Krul says and hugs her before she can respond and escapes out of the window he came through. Alice stands alone in the room and the more she thinks about her life, the more she is alone. Krul, locked and loaded, makes his way around the grounds, dropping a werewolf gang member to his death and scaling the wall to perch on the ledge that is just above. Peering down, he sees three more members approach and look at the dead body; taking aim he shoots another. The other two look up and one is dropped while the other fires a stake at Krul but misses completely. Krul returns fire and hits his target and makes his way to another spot to kill more.

Hearing gunshots, Cuthwulf wonders why they are shooting guns and not stakes, and rushes to investigate. It is beginning to never rain but pour for the werewolf leader. Taking a gun and a stake, he exits the building, pissed off with the night's events. Seeing his crew members' dead bodies, he ducks down looking all around for his attacker. Jessica storms out wanting to help her man and with gun ready for action she covers his back. The two lovers creep their way over, making sure each other is safe. Cuthwulf looks over the gang members' bodies while Jessica keeps watch. All four killed with a single shot each and with a handgun. Cuthwulf doubts a mortal could be so precise and get the drop on a wolf, especially four wolves, and after seeing a stake has been fired and unable to pick up a scent, he is sure a vampire is definitely at large on the base. He also doubts an unfully turned vampire could do this, and considering Siobhan ran away why would she return? Cuthwulf is convinced a much more experienced vampire is here – Krul or Victuis perhaps. Cuthwulf radios Wulfric to inform him of the situation and his deputy, eager to make amends, loads his crossbow and arms himself with some holy water. Krul, eyeing up his next victim, takes aim and fires, another rival down, another step to supremacy. Hearing more troops approaching, Krul takes the dead soldier's gun and empties every bullet into the oncoming crew. Although the bullets aren't silver it does take them down long enough for him to execute every one of them as they lay on the ground. Telling Jessica to return to base, who at first refuses until Cuthwulf orders some gang members to escort her back and The Messengers to be kept inside, Cuthwulf and Wulfric break up into groups and head toward the gunfire. Taking a flank each they close in on the scene. Taking cover, Cuthwulf peeps out and sees more corpses of his gang members. Knowing he must get up close to slay a vampire but he himself can be shot from a distance, it is a nervous time for Cuthwulf and his gang. Wulfric, wanting to make up for his mistake, slowly heads out to the area they have narrowed down by covering the rest of the base, no movement, no sign, just dead bodies. His crew follow close behind but Cuthwulf hand signals him to fall back as there is no doubt a vampire will already know they are there and has the advantage over them; this is what separates Cuthwulf from Wulfric – the leader has the wisdom as well as the bravery but sometimes his deputy lacks the wisdom. Wulfric can be too prideful, too strong a belief in him and his gang's power, too much intent on his gang's rise to power, sometimes it is the correct choice to sit it out, retreat, hold back or all-out attack and a good leader knows when and where to do each of these things. Cuthwulf knows they are not dealing with a mere mortal here, a vampire is much more difficult to defeat, especially if it is Krul or Victuis, an experienced vampire who has the advantage and could be sitting patiently with his silver bullets aimed at them right now; but Wulfric is eager to put right his embarrassment.

For the first time, Wulfric disobeys an order and the first sign of cracks in the wolf pack appear, said to be the closest to a perfect system in nature but the human virus of hurt pride has broken the purity of a wolf's hierarchy and Cuthwulf sits fuming but at the same time hurt and shocked at his deputy's disrespect. Frantically ordering Wulfric to fall back, once again his deputy refuses with thoughts of heroism and history making, a thought his leader put into his head – maybe history should be written by the future generations. A gunshot rings out and Wulfric feels a thud to his head. He steadies himself but begins to feel cold, he feels a trickling down his face and he begins to panic as blood blurs his vison and he grows weaker. Hearing Cuthwulf shout something but Wulfric can't make out what he has said, but can sense the emotion in his tone, some of his crew run past him toward where the shot came from but more gunfire erupts and they fall to their death. Dropping to his knees, Wulfric can't feel anything, his body has gone numb and his eyes close, breathing ceases and wolf power has become powerless as he falls face down into the dirt. Human pride has destroyed wolf honour and human pride has paid the ultimate price.

Cuthwulf rages at his crew to fall back and orders them to get inside the building and lock all doors and windows, knowing that whatever vampire it is has already been inside so therefore must have been invited in at some point, eliminating the possibility of it being a random gang member, and with Enigma dead that only leaves Krul or Victuis; Siobhan is not yet full vampire so did not need an invite. The werewolf leader is going to sit it out until sunrise, which is only a few hours away. From his emotional state and not seeing Wulfric, Jessica assumes the worst and clutches her man, kissing him for comfort. Attempting to play it tough, Cuthwulf continues his duties but his pain is evident. Jessica can do nothing but give him support as and when he needs it, but The Werewolves have been horrifically exposed as to how vulnerable they are when the moon is not full.

Krul, after seeing the Lycan retreat, cautiously takes a tour of the grounds and knows the plan from Cuthwulf is now to barricade themselves in until the sun saves them, an understandable tactic that they should have used from the start, but such is Cuthwulf's desperation to keep what he has conquered, he saw it as a matter of honour to capture or kill the intruder. Doing a lap of the building, The Werewolves have done well in protecting themselves, this time, with stakes and holy water at every other window and with The Messengers backing them up, Krul decides to head back to the cathedral after doing devasting damage to The Irish, The Chinese and now The Werewolves. Krul said his plan was to go into the shadows and the shadows have proven to be a prosperous war weapon. As he leaves the Chinese HQ grounds heading west, Krul stops in his tracks as a would-be assassin steps out in front and has the drop on him, with crossbow aimed directly at his heart and a bottle of holy water and a crucifix. Krul knows it is either negotiate or be slain. Looking directly into the assailant's eyes, he smiles when he sees who it is and his pride grows at his new friend.

"Good girl," he says with affection. "You have done so well," he adds, gazing at Siobhan who by the look in her eye is caught in two minds to break the infection or give in to her newfound longing. Ever since the bite she has been drawn toward Krul and the vampire bond was instantaneous; the change is already becoming clear on her face, her skin a paler white and her red hair a beautiful crimson glow, her eyes a glistening sapphire blue with her fangs beginning to make their appearance over her mortal teeth.

"If I slay you now the infection is broken?" Siobhan says as a question.

"Yes," Krul answers without hesitation. "But don't miss," he tells her, holding out his arms, inviting her to slay him. She hesitates under the pressure, the decision agonising, which only proves the infection is taking affect. Only last night she was terrified and worried about the reaction from Aiden when he finds out – would he embrace her or disown her – now she is worried about all the weaknesses of remaining mortal and the loss of her new-gained power.

"Why do I feel ill but strong at the same time, like I am aching for something that will make my existence complete?" Siobhan asks, confused.

Krul smiles as memories of his own change come back to him and he gives her a sympathetic and understanding look.

"You're thirsty, I can cure that," he responds, slicing his neck and offering himself to help the change hasten.

Siobhan twitches with anticipation and almost leaps forward at the sight but stops herself, the mortal in her still reluctant, the vampire craves the drink.

"Come to me." Krul waves her forward. Another hesitation is quickly replaced by the crossbow dropping to the floor and a falling into his arms and feasting on his fluid. Her eyes roll with pleasure with every swallow and the bond grows inside as the change strengthens. Krul wraps his arms around her and sinks his fangs into her neck and drinks, she tenses at the initial pain but that quickly turns to a growing enjoyment, Krul now understands why Enigma loved him so much as his affection for Siobhan is growing – this is Krul's first turning of a mortal and the feeling it gives him is beyond mortal understanding.

The combined forces are no longer combined and their fight is up. They have scattered across the landscape and scarpered into the distance. Brigacos stops to catch his breath, spinning in all directions to make certain he is safe, hearing blood-curdling screams in the distance he knows he is not home and dry, propping himself up on a tree he hopes Bryson and Gwendoline escaped. A twig breaks behind him and Brigacos turns around quickly with thoughts of vampires in his mind, seeing Father Gideon, the monk asks if the Arch Druid is ok. Brigacos grunts his response making it clear he doesn't care for his question. Gideon glares at him, irritated by his constant attitude, but lets it go.

"Bryson and Gwendoline escaped," Gideon informs him.

Brigacos looks up with a happiness in his eye.

"I saw them get away," Gideon says, looking around for any hunters.

Brigacos stands after catching his breath and starts to walk back toward the cathedral but Gideon stops him by grabbing his arm.

Turning to the monk, Brigacos snaps. "Get off me, you scumbag," Brigacos shouts, pulling his arm away from Gideon, who stands angry at the outburst but not surprised. Some people will never be able to get over history or forgive for political policies. "It has been bad enough having to fight alongside you, but being stopped from searching for my people isn't going to happen," the Arch Druid barks, almost using it as an excuse to have a go at Gideon.

"Going back is stupid, The Vampires are hunting people without mercy," Gideon says back, attempting to remain calm but his temper is rising.

"Stupid," Brigacos shouts, stepping closer to Gideon to get in his face. "Just because you are happy to leave you crew to die, Gideon The Great who will tuck tail and run when the going gets tough and will claim to have saved the city when in fact others did the dirty work and you took the credit," he insults and goads, knowing Gideon hates it when people question his slaying of Niculi and Ziana.

The goading works as the monk leader heats up. "How would you know? You were not even there, probably worshipping some tree within your conquered religion," Gideon takes the insults a step further and Brigacos snaps, striking Gideon in the face and pouncing on him. Gideon defends himself, taking the druid to the ground, landing on top of him, punching Brigacos in the face multiple times until his attack is stopped by the druid reaching for a fallen tree branch and hitting Gideon in his face. Tasting his own blood, Father Gideon stands toe to toe with Brigacos, and the two religious foes go at one another, the druid swinging the branch but Gideon dodging, another attempt misses its target and Gideon lunges forward, again taking Brigacos down. They both scrap on the ground exchanging blows until Gideon ends up on top and clutching a nearby rock smashes it into the druid's face who instantly goes limp, knocked out or dead Gideon doesn't know, but his rage takes over and he lays blow after blow to Brigacos' head and face, the druid defenceless and lifeless by the time Gideon's arm is too tired to continue the brutal beating. Looking down at the body, Father Gideon now stands, wiping the blood from his face, the soldier of old is now an old man but old habits die hard and Gideon has claimed victory over another enemy.

Bryson, keen to find his leader after the retreat heads in the direction he saw Brigacos run, weary of the vampire hunt, he slowly but surely moves forward looking for his Arch Druid. Seeing blood on a tree branch he inspects the area, from the state he sees that a fight took place here and after a short investigation he see him. The shock shoots through his body and Bryson rushes to his leader. A bloody mess, Brigacos lies with his face smashed in and a sickening killing has taken The Pagans' leader. Bryson sinks to his knees, staring at the state of what somebody has done to him, by the way he has been brutalised this was not a witch or vampire, this is a human killed and it begs the question which beings are more civilised when a human killer is more brutal than witchcraft or vampirism? Scanning the area, he sees a blood trail going off into the distance and with anger inflating his vengeance he runs off in the direction the blood leads.

Father Gideon, with blood not just on his hands but splattered across his face and stained into his clothing, comes across a battle site and it is his own gang members that are the victims. Kneeling to say a prayer for his fallen people, he looks around at the horrors of war and wonders if God has forsaken everything on Earth, if the Old Testament is to be believed then yes, God has forsaken us all. With a heavy heart he checks the corpses for anything he can use, food, water, weapons, he takes as much as he can carry. Closing the eyes of his members, he wishes them joy and happiness in the afterlife. Hearing somebody closing in, he turns to see Druid Bryson, face full of fury, staring at him.

"You murderer," Bryson shouts, full of emotion.

Gideon holds out his hand to deny the allegation. "No, it was self-defence, your leader attacked me first," Gideon correctly states, but Bryson is not going to listen or accept. Instead he picks up a gun and fires off whatever remains in the clip. Gideon dives for cover, firing back, catching Bryson in the shoulder who falls backward from the impact. "This doesn't have to happen, we can still fight against the forces of evil," Gideon pleads to an injured but raging Bryson, who is on his feet and running at Gideon after hearing his gun empty.

"You are the force of evil in this city," the druid shouts, diving at the monk. They struggle with one another but Bryson's younger, fitter, in shape, and strength gets the better of the has-been Gideon and Bryson lays a beating to his enemy. With every blow he thinks of his leader until he feels a sharp pain in his chest left of centre. Father Gideon knows exactly where the heart is from his vampire slaying days and Bryson was too busy looking at the face he was beating and not enough attention to what the hands were doing. Gideon removes the knife and plunges it into Bryson's throat leaving the druid no option but to die. Gasping for breath, a blood curdling choke exits Bryson's mouth that is now filled with his own blood. Falling to the floor, Bryson's blood soaks the ground from the fatal wounds and Father Gideon proves once more that he is not the has-been people think he is, and the battle ground is littered with another victim of war. Just another life lost, just another dead body that if things had have gone differently would have happily added to the death tally themselves. Are victims of war really the victim we make them out to be, or are they just the result of being in a war zone in the first place, putting yourself in a kill or be killed situation; is some of it not their fault and the people they leave behind have to pick up the pieces emotionally? So much hatred causes so much pain and the only true way to cure the world of such hatred is to commit the very thing that causes the pain: murder. An extinction-level event of biblical magnitude to annihilate the human race and rid the planet of its most destructive problem. God showed mercy to Noah and the result of that mercy was the continuation of humanity, the continuation of sin, the continuation of evil, tyranny, rape, murder, theft, genocide, paedophilia and all other manner of mortal wrongs. If God wants to save the world, then maybe a return to Genesis and this time show not one ounce of mercy.

Chapter 31

Victuis glances at the horizon and sees the beginning of orange make its appearance. Knowing his fun is over for one night, he orders his troops back to the cathedral to slumber for however many hours ultraviolet brings saviour to mortals. Collecting some tokens and ingredients for Tunder as a gift, he leaves some of the war dead lifeless, eyeless, tongueless, earless, heartless and even takes the head from a monk as a symbol of the night's victory. The Vampires cheer and roar in celebration so loud that Father Gideon hears it in the distance, still attempting to wash the blood from his hands. The war has swung in The Vampires' favour even more than they think it has, because they are yet to hear of Krul's success in depleting China and Lycan. Entering Cathedral Tower, Tunder is waiting for Victuis who offers her the gifts he collected and she smiles with delight at the thoughtfulness of his gesture. After the gang members have taken refuge in the secret room, The Dark Fairy and Victuis take a stroll up the stairs to The Throne Room, up the stairway that Victuis saved her from Aiden and into the room that democracy polluted Niculi and Ziana's memory. Holding hands as they enter, Victuis gazes in awe at the sight to behold: The Throne Room decked out in all its glory with banners of both gangs on each side of the walkway towards two gothic thrones side by side at the head of the room. Tunder smiles at his reaction, her magic has pleased him as they sit together as King and Queen of 9 Gang City on their thrones, a beautiful fantasy for them, a hideous vison for others. The magical mirage must be cut short though as Victuis begins to feel the burn ever so slightly from the sun's rays creeping in and although short and sweet the fantasy may be a reality before long.

Krul takes Siobhan to Messenger HQ knowing only a small crew of werewolves are guarding the turf and with the sun coming up he needs to hide soon. Siobhan still not fully turned can handle the sunlight, but it is beginning to give her trouble.

"Enjoy the sunrise, it will be one of your last," Krul tells her.

She takes his advice, turning to see the sun peeping over the distance. Krul checks his gun, counting five bullets, Siobhan doing likewise with her AK has enough to slaughter what tries to stop them. Krul takes the front with his accomplice going around the back and with no time to lose as the sun rises. Krul springs out, dropping the two guards on the door, hearing AK fire from the back; his apprentice is coming through the house. Two werewolf gang members kick the door open and Krul goes hand to hand with them both, slamming one to the ground and laying the other out with a punch, the first rising to his feet for a second go until his head splits and his lifeless body slumps to the ground; after Siobhan opens fire now that she has cleared the building, Krul executes the other. The vampire leader quickly finds the darkest room in the cellar and beds down for the day. Siobhan stays up a while longer to enjoy perhaps her last sunrise until the choice she has made completes its takeover.

A few devastating days of war has been damaging for gang numbers and all have felt the effects of battle, all have seen family, friends or comrades fall, and the war looks no nearer to ending so more deaths are likely to happen. Jessica tries to console Cuthwulf after the loss of Wulfric, but the alpha wolf is typically male and pretends he is alright, but Jessica can see in his eyes he is pained inside. Kissing him sympathetically he half-heartedly returns the affection but his motivation isn't in it. He tells her to get some sleep and goes to collect Wulfric's body now the sun is up.

Stepping outside he looks around at the carnage, the damage, the dead members and he feels like he has failed every one of them, Leo offers to help carry the body and Cuthwulf accepts with a semi-smile. Closing his deputy's eyes, they carry Wulfric into the building, laying him on a bench as gang members bow their heads in respect. Cuthwulf allows them all to have a moment for reflection but then asks to be left alone with the body. Looking at the damage the shot did to Wulfric's head, Cuthwulf considers it is not the result of a handgun but an assault rifle. Evidence that taking prisoners of war can backfire and Wulfric's corpse is proof and has shown Cuthwulf that perhaps execution and murder are the only way to ensure dominance of your gang and safety for your members. If Wulfric had had this way of thinking he would still be alive. Cuthwulf still has not told Randall of their loss, his new deputy blissfully unaware of the night's events and his promotion, sat comfortably in Emerald Territory thinking The Werewolves have the upper hand, but instead their crew has suffered devastating losses and a heart-breaking loss.

Zhen Yun, exhausted and drained from the night's events, the eyes of her people looking at her as they were slain already haunting her. Not wanting to have her members infected with that virus called vampirism, she took the ultimate step, believing it was the correct decision, but that doesn't stop the visions repeating in her mind, the crying, the whimpering, the fear and the look of disappointment in her people's eyes when they realised their own leader was going to kill them instead of hunting down the infecting vampire. The likelihood that they could have captured and slain the right vampire is extremely slim, but that doesn't console Zhen. Now to avenge her fallen people, she has become obsessed with vengeance for Cheng and Yong as well as tonight's victims, war victory can wait and it certainly does not have to be achieved now. As far as gang warfare goes, The Chinese are at a standoff and after the defeat of the combined forces, The Cannibals have disappeared and the commotion Zhen heard coming from her gang territory, The Werewolves have also suffered losses, meaning each gang will be licking their wounds and playing the waiting game, meaning the entire war has become a standoff.

Camped on Holy Ground with a view of China Town, The Chinese are refugees. After spying on The Werewolves through her scope, Zhen saw The Messengers aligned with Cuthwulf and his crew on Chinese turf, despite Cuthwulf claiming Messenger land for his own gang. These are the complications of war and in the end even the winner loses something. It gets to a point where the deciding factor in a war is whoever loses the least is the winner, a winner by default, but in the climax of victory all that is forgotten. Lest we forget the fallen, Zhen Yun will not, and she is prepared to die for the cause, a cause that has been drilled into her by gang culture, a cause that she is almost brainwashed by and a cause she has enforced on others, bringing her to the brink on more than one occasion; and yet here she is, the leader of her people. Looking at her hand, the hand from which Enigma removed her fingers, it seems so long ago yet it was only a week or so, how time can change somebody, people, entire lives altered by the events that time allows. Zhen Yun has decided, she is going to return to the cathedral and camp her troops on the outskirts of the grounds but herself only will enter in search of her vengeance, a need that has consumed her and no amount of blood drinkers or magic will stop her from at least trying to get revenge for her dead leaders.

Chapter 32

Krul awakens bolt upright. Looking around he still, for a split-second, longs to see Enigma rising next to him until reality sets in and the loneliness takes over. With no best friend to walk through the door to fulfil his duty, Krul misses Victuis and wants to return to his deputy. Realising Siobhan is not in the room with him, he goes in search of his apprentice. Wandering the building she is nowhere to be seen until he leaves the house and on a chair outside he finds his pupil, lifeless – enjoying her last sunrise was her final act as a mortal and the change is complete. Krul wastes no time with the next stage of the process. Taking her in his arms, he lays her down a short distance from the house, and after returning with a shovel he digs her grave the second to last instalment of the change, 6ft deep. Krul climbs out and respectfully lowers the once Irishwoman into her final resting place. Standing over the grave he has his final look at the mortal body and refills the hole, unable to top the soil with a crucifix, he adds a piece of wood with her name written on as a final show of respect. Krul never thought he would be burying rivals but with this it is different. After his ceremony finishes, Krul heads west, back to the cathedral with no sadness and no tears only anticipation for the next stage, only vampiric nature can achieve that so Krul goes on to his next task. Inspecting the surrounding area of the cathedral, he sees some corpses but very little activity as far as rivals go, and feels a sense of pride in Victuis' achievement; no doubt he had help from Tunder, the two make quite the pair, and Krul is pleased his friend has somebody. He remembers the good times with Enigma and it only breaks his heart even more to think about how it ended, if only he could take it back, the anger he showed her, the fury he felt and memories of her storming off never to be seen again. Krul has to stop and compose himself. He cannot return to his people with tears in his eyes and sorrow on his face, he must return a leader and a war warrior because his accomplishment over the last few nights has been a huge boost to his gang and their prospects.

The Chinese move west to fulfil their leader's plan. Zhen Yun's mind is rampant with thoughts and plans of how she will navigate her way through witch traps, vampire attacks and werewolf fury to get to that gargoyle who calls herself a fairy. Revisiting her memories and seeing Yong's lifeless body and the sight of Cheng doing what he was doing, she is becoming twisted by vengeance and needs to focus on the task that awaits. The Witches will show no mercy and will not tolerate her visit, they will expose any weakness they find, twisted and obsessive anger only leads to mistakes; this is one of the tactics witches use, they use their power to search for weakness, expose weakness and punish weakness. Sometimes fear is the tool they use to expose the fragility of human minds, and mortal fear is one of humankind's biggest weaknesses.

Setting up camp as quietly as possible, Zhen knows Princess Katalin will be spying but that is something Zhen welcomes, she is ready for anything, even death. Alice sits alone in Chinese HQ, in the chair that Cheng used to sit as leader of his gang, now Alice occupies the seat while another gang occupies her land. Knowing there is still more death to come, she tries to concentrate on the positives – Jessica, Leo and herself are still alive and that is something to be grateful for. But such is the negative nature of the human mind her thoughts keep skipping back to all the dead bodies, the blood, the screams, the screams can sometimes be the worst. Spine chill screams from hardened soldiers will haunt her mind forever, screams of agony, fear and the tone of almost begging for the inevitable not to happen when they know they are going to die but don't want to. However, the other side to that is how many would have shown mercy if the positions were switched, before they died how many rivals did they kill without any mercy, how much begging did they ignore on their way to slaughtering an enemy? Alice begins to wonder what the city will be like after this hell is over, will it be a return to dictatorship or will democracy keep its place at the top of the tree? It certainly didn't work this time but that was because of the short sightedness of the other gangs. Caught in the thrill and celebration of victory against Niculi and Ziana, they agreed to anything, so in a way it is partly their fault and not all Father Gideon's, but that mistake will not be repeated. A five-year term for every leader and even then, the chance to strike a vote of no confidence to force an election inside that five years, open borders and a multicultural city where peace reigns over any form of hatred. A secure unit built for The Werewolves, where they can run free but keep the city safe, a blood donation unit so people can give blood in a safe and voluntary manner for the vampires, magic can be used for the greater good and not just evil deeds; this can be encouraged to help all citizens of the city. It is a pleasant fantasy Alice has in her mind, but a fantasy is exactly what it is – the likelihood of people accepting all these policies she would want to bring in is almost non-existent. Hatred and animosity are too far gone and will people really live in peace with others whom they know have killed their loved ones? But because Alice has a nice sounding political policy let's live in harmony. Alice needs to snap out of her dream and get her mind focused on reality; hatred is king and war is its weapon.

Krul swaggers unopposed into The Waiting Yard and is pleased to see slaughtered enemies littered and scattered and from the look of them his people and The Witches have had a field day. A black cat runs toward him and purrs as it rubs against his legs. Crouching to stroke the feline, he thanks Princess Katalin for the welcome. Entering the cathedral, the bodies have been cleared but the bloodstains have been left as symbolic artwork paying homage to their victories, electricity is off and candlelight shows the way to add to the gothic feel of vampirism and witchcraft. Sensing something up in the tower, he takes the now infamous staircase to The Throne Room and sees his friend's face light up as Victuis rushes over to embrace his returned leader. Princess Tunder welcomes him back and a now-woman-form Katalin joins their celebration. The mood alters when a presence enters the room and all turn to see Queen Rika, clearly pleased to see Krul but still fuming he left without so much as a by-your-leave to her and no information on why he was going, to her it was like a desertion. Krul has some making up to do, but he knows exactly how to get round the witch queen, a bow of respect and kiss on both cheeks for affection, followed by a homage to the queen of witches by taking her hand gently and leading her to the thrones that are waiting for her to perch on. Rika can't hide her smile, even with magic such is her delight, and with Krul taking the throne next to her it seems the prophecy has come true and the vision she read in Tunder's mind was accurate: Queen Rika and Krul are ruling 9 Gang City.

After the unofficial ceremony, Krul meets and greets his crew, but a longing grows inside with a feeling of being drawn back outside. Stepping out into the beautiful darkness, the moonshine is a blissful escape from the burning sun, standing in the entrance to Cathedral Tower he waits patiently for what he knows is coming.

Sensing something closing in he stares straight ahead as she comes into view, Siobhan in all her undead glory has passed the initiation period and is now a vampire. The turning complete, she has risen from the dead and the bond between master and apprentice is now unbreakable. They embrace fondly and after some proud praise from Krul, he prepares her for the introduction to her new gang. Entering Cathedral Tower with a new lease of existence – the last time she was here she was alive – Krul stands in the doorway of The Throne Room in front of The Vampires and The Witches and all present wonder what he is doing. Stepping to one side he allows Siobhan to enter. Clear to see she has been turned, some stand shocked, some snarl still considering her a rival gang member, others smile at the mocking and bragging rights it gives them over The Irish. Queen Rika sits fuming, the basking in the glory of monarchy is put on hold and knowing a turning of a mortal brings with it the vampire bond, Rika wonders where this leaves her. Focusing on Siobhan's mind she reads that the new vampire is nervous to the reaction of her new crew but at the same time excited to be able to live forever unless slain. This is all fair enough, Rika thinks, but shifting through her other thoughts like a flicking through a file, the witch queen comes to the emotion and Siobhan's newfound bond is gaining an affection for Krul, Rika's temper rises a notch and quickly changes to Krul's mind. Her fury goes into overdrive and yet she remains calm on the outside when all she sees is Enigma and leadership, Krul obsessed with gaining power, leading his people to victory and taking his place in history next to Niculi. His lost love is never far from his thoughts; Enigma was his one true love and even in death she is still defeating Rika for Krul's affection. The candles in the room blow out with a furious gust of wind only to instantly re-light by Tunder's click of her fingers. Krul glances over to Rika who glares back. Knowing he has more winning over to do, Krul tells Siobhan to mingle and get to know her new comrades before taking his place next to Rika on their thrones.

"Why did you bring us a new arrival?" Rika asks.

"To strengthen numbers," Krul replies, knowing the reason for the question but playing it down in his mind, suspecting Rika is already reading it anyway. "To kill our rivals but not add to our own numbers only destroys both us and our enemies, but to turn our rivals takes from them and empowers us," he tells her, feeling a confliction in his mind which he assumes is Rika attempting to alter his thoughts, but he remains strong and blocks it out.

"What relationship do you have with your new pet?" Rika asks in a jealous tone.

"Master and apprentice," Krul gives her the answer she wants to hear, to which Rika stares at him for a second and then smiles after his mind confirms the comment.

"Good," she responds gleefully. "Just make sure it doesn't become leader and lover," she adds, reaching across their thrones and taking his hand. Returning her mind to the glory of queenship, Krul looks across the room and sees Tunder watching them. The Dark Fairy holds her glare to a point it makes Krul uncomfortable. With a long way to go before true victory is declared, there will be more twists to the tale of war and conquest, and Queen Rika can read minds and bask in glory all she wants, but minds can be manipulated and there is still one prophecy she is conveniently forgetting.

Chapter 33

The standoff that has been ongoing for weeks now and with only the odd gangland killing, the gangs, in the main, are as they were. Krul, after returning to his people and retaking command with his protégé still under his wing – now full vampire there is no turning back for Siobhan. She is yet to meet Aiden and may never meet him again under the circumstances, but with The Irish leader knowing Siobhan is missing, as far as he is concerned the Irishman thinks his 3rd In Command is dead. The other vampires continued their reluctance to accept Siobhan, but that quickly changed to a welcome when they became used to the idea, and after all, she is not a member of The Irish anymore, she is a vampire. Victuis was surprised at first but found the news amusing – it adds to the insult of a rival and especially Aiden who almost exorcized Tunder. Aiden will be reeling from another vampire victory over his crew, first Cormac's death, now Siobhan's turning. Siobhan herself was standoffish with Victuis – he is the one who killed Cormac and Siobhan is still saddened by his passing only to be side by side with his killer; it did not sit well with her but now she is undead her allegiance has changed. Queen Rika has still been a bit off with Krul since his return, but the vampire's charm is winning her over – a smile here and an honourable comment there and the witch queen gives in to his flattery; added to the fact that Krul has levelled the playing field as The Werewolves were gaining too much power. The Vampires and The Witches are content with their haul; Cathedral Tower was once theirs and over the past few weeks it has returned to its rightful ruler, in their eyes at least.

However, tomorrow night the moon will be full and a return to bedlam is on the horizon. Cuthwulf and his crew have been deep in their defence of the land they have conquered and with the mortal gangs unable to take back their territories, and a vampire and witch decision to hold the tower and not conquer, they plan to let whoever wants the tower to come on to them and defend it to the death. This is where Zhen Yun is going to use The Werewolves to her advantage without them knowing it. Camped at the edge of the cathedral grounds, which over the past few weeks has been a refugee camp, Zhen has been spying on the cathedral and all around to watch for any weaknesses the forces of evil have. The Vampires need to leave the tower to feed and she and her crew have manged to pick a few off. The Witches are happy to remain; only a cat and a crow make brief appearances. When The Werewolves turn and attack, Zhen will use this as cover to enter the cathedral and hunt down those responsible for her loss. It has been a tough few weeks for Zhen, wanting to storm in and wreak havoc but that would be suicide – let Lycan rage bear the brunt of witchcraft and vampirism so Zhen can hunt down her target. Cuthwulf has defended well since Wulfric's death and Randall took it hard – they were like brothers and he felt guilty taking Wulfric's position as deputy, but in times like these it has to be done. They know more than anybody the full moon is coming and they have prepared well in advance for it, allowing The Messengers to return to Neutral Territory, which is not so neutral anymore as it is still under wolf control, but the few remaining Messengers have been allowed back with a werewolf guard. Just before the full moon these guards will be picked up by Cuthwulf and the gang and they will travel to the cathedral where the change will take place on cathedral grounds so there is no wasting time and the battle can commence. Cuthwulf knows the other gangs will not stop this because, one, they cannot, and two, they want as much firepower or any other power aimed at The Vampires and The Witches, so it is in their best interests to allow The Werewolves free passage to the tower.

Back at The Forests a small number of guarding gang members have been given orders to remain during the change and lock themselves in the secure chamber with The Cannibal prisoners to recruit some members. James Winston Wycombe has been living off the casualties of war and with plenty of those he has had an Aladdin's cave of choice, like a nomad from one turf to another he has found ways on and off each land and has had a survivor's mentality; but wanting to avenge his leader's murder he plans to see Cuthwulf soon. Unable to get to him in China Town, the irony is Cuthwulf will be easier to get to when he is at his most dangerous, as a wolf, because by then his troops will not be defending him and all wolves will be off doing what wolves do. Wycombe also has a fetish to fulfil, which will only add to his pleasure and to Cuthwulf's demise when he captures, rapes, kills and eats Jessica.

Father Gideon has been living in the halfway house between Cathedral Tower and the western territories – he had to remove the corpses of his gang members and give them a Christian burial. Their deaths were witch work judging by the way their bodies were left, the savagery sickened Gideon and it gave him motivation to not give up the fight and bring holy justice to the city once and for all. Aiden and Gwen, along with their depleted gangs, have been camped in an Irish/Pagan refugee camp northeast of the cathedral not far from BC Nation, Gwen assuming but not certain she is the new Pagan leader as she has given up hope of a return from Brigacos, and Bryson is missing too. Assuming The Vampires captured them during the battle, her hatred has grown for Victuis who she saw lead the attack and kill some of her people. After the story Aiden told her about Victuis killing Cormac, they have shared animosity for the vampire deputy and want him slain. They also, unknown to the rest of the gangs but it is assumed, are sitting back to see which gang will move first and at this rate it will be The Werewolves. The Irish and The Pagans have few numbers left after the defeat of the combined forces and few weapons, but they did acquire some extra guns and ammunition from the dead bodies all over the area they are camped.

A few weeks' standoff is about to end, and tomorrow night the worm moon will be upon 9 Gang City and carnage will once again rear its ugly head. Hatred and death will reign supreme just like it always has in this world, ever since God created man or Homo Sapiens evolved from Homo Erectus, or if ancient aliens terraformed Earth and made the human race – whatever the maker, the result is the same. This city has taken the extremes to the next level, the outside world continues with its life of sin, but 9 Gang City is a magnified version out in the open of what dwells in the darkness and the dwellers of the light are just as corrupt.

Chapter 34

C uthwulf has one final check of his troops and The Werewolves make their way west to Cathedral Tower. Picking up the few from Neutral Territory and a kiss for Jessica, the alpha wolf marches in to battle again. Dusk is upon 9 Gang City and the tension is gripping every gang member who knows the standoff is over and war will commence. Jessica bids a sad farewell to her love, knowing this could be the last time she sees him. Alice comforts her as Leo is preparing the guns for battle.

Krul is perched on the rooftop looking over the city to the east, waiting and watching the activity that brings either victory or defeat ever closer. His student Siobhan is on the other side, scoping the northeast where her old crew are creeping closer with The Pagans. Zhen Yun welcomes The Werewolves' approach knowing they will cause damage to the control The Vampires and The Witches have on the cathedral. Zhen has been counting the days until this moment. Also knowing that if things go well, she will be able to reclaim her land on top of slaughtering some witches, Zhen is pumped up for the fight that lies ahead and is itching to get into action. Aiden and Gwen have moved their depleted forces to the outskirts of the cathedral and Gwendoline is not holding any hope of Brigacos and Bryson being alive, she is now leader of her people, Arch Druidess Gwendoline. Father Gideon, the last of The Monks – Victuis successfully destroying the rest of his gang and 542 years of rivalry – the "heroic" CVS are represented by one man, can Gideon live up to his "The Great" title. Wycombe, unable to free his members from The Forests, is resigned to the fact they will be werewolf by the next full moon so makes his way to the cathedral for a showdown with Cuthwulf. A secret stash of weapons on Cannibal Farm has given him a gun armed with silver – either Cuthwulf dies or Wycombe. Tonight is the night.

Queen Rika sits on her throne and in her mind she is queen of 9 Gang but that is yet to be declared by war victory, so a guardian to the throne is more accurate to her position and officially Gideon is still leader. Every citizen of 9 Gang City knows it is only a matter of time before war resumes and Cuthwulf's army stops on the edge of the cathedral as darkness falls and the alpha wolf's eyes roll over black and an echoing snarl rings out. Zhen Yun watching the change for the first time through her scope is horrified by the sight of man turning to wolf, but to Krul it is just another creature he shares the darkness with. Cuthwulf's clothes shred as his body rips through, his teeth extend as his nose and mouth become a snout, hind legs crooked and a cross between paws and hands with razor sharp claws complete the change, and after a symbolic howl at the moon, war is here. Uncontrolled rage takes over and The Werewolves rush the cathedral, finding any way they can as gunshots ring out, Krul and Siobhan sniper from the rooftop. Cuthwulf smashes his way into Cathedral Tower as vampire gang members storm The Waiting Yard, Randall entering from the main entrance is flattened on to his back by a punch from Victuis, the two go head-to-head once Randall picks himself up with Victuis dodging a swiping claw and slamming Randall against the wall, which cracks and crumbles on impact and the wolf sprawls to the ground once more. Rising back up, Randall springs onto Victuis, sinking his teeth into his shoulder with the vampire returning the assault, biting Randall's throat. The two savage each other, causing damage that would kill a mortal with ease but these wounds will heal. The brutal embrace ends when Victuis prises the wolf's jaws open and floors him for a third time with a combination of punches before throwing Randall out of a window. He moves onto the next wolf.

Cuthwulf sends vampire after vampire sprawling, scattering, crashing in all directions, an untamed beast doing what an alpha wolf does best: dominate. Krul and Siobhan drop their sniper rifles and cock their Berettas in search of Lycan invaders through The Throne Room and down the infamous stairway where wolves are already creeping, Siobhan dropping one with a kill shot to the head. Following Jessica to the cathedral, Alice and Leo are doubtful it is a good decision, but they knew it was inevitable they would end up there. Aiden and Gwen remain camped but watching and listening to the horrors that unfold, biding their time until they enter the battlefield.

Supernatural powers go head-to-head, and The Vampires and The Werewolves are taking part in the most savage act of war this city has seen, which says a lot for the brutality of the battle, almost as if both sides know this is the final showdown, for now. Alice shouts at Jessica to stop, but her sister ignores the pleas and enters the cathedral. With no choice left Alice, Leo and their few remaining members follow into the danger zone, sticking close to each other. The Messengers huddle together in a defensive tactic with a stake and a gun each.

Zhen Yun prepares for combat now that The Werewolves have played their part, ordering her crew to scope the cathedral and sniper any foe that tries to stop her. She bids them farewell knowing this could be the last time she sees them. A speech of honour and respect with almost a tear in her eye, Zhen tells her surviving members she is doing this for Cheng and Yong, and after a bow from her entire gang Zhen Yun enters the witch's nest in search of her vengeance. On a witch hunt but still with stake and a gun, Zhen plunged her stake with expert aim through an attacking vampire's heart and removes his head with no time to waste on mere gang members; Zhen wants leaders. Seeing Alice torch a witch, Zhen smiles as the flames engulf the unfortunate victim, dodging fighting enemies and slaying the ones she can't, Zhen Yun has to quick draw when some werewolves close in; emptying her gun into them she watches their lifeless bodies return to men. Down the corridor Zhen enters what used to be the room used as a chapel by Father Gideon and his gang, now it is a dingy dwelling for the darker of rituals, an insult to faith The Monks hold dear. The atmosphere grips her and Zhen knows a witch lurks in the shadows but no sign – shooting a flame into the darkness nothing comes into view. Slowly searching the entire chapel making sure she circles around to not leave her back uncovered, the evil grows as she leaves no corner unsearched. Turning behind quickly, Zhen shoots of another burst of flame and sees a human-sized cat staring back at her. Princess Katalin ducks the fire and lashes out with her clawed hand, knocking the flamethrower out of Zhen's hands, who pulls her sword and swings at the witch. Katalin dodges with ease and takes another swipe, slicing Zhen's stomach, who winces but stands strong. Seeing cat's eyes staring back at her it is disconcerting seeing an animal so humanlike, but the discomfort is something Zhen needs to control if she is to come out victorious. Attempting to get to her flamethrower, but Katalin is keeping herself positioned between Zhen and the weapon, Zhen swipes her sword at the witch but quickly turns into a roundhouse kick, cracking Katalin on the jaw, sending the witch staggering backward. Zhen jumps into the air almost in slow motion bringing her sword down toward Katalin's head, but the cat's claws block the attack, sending chips of them flying into the air. A snap of the teeth just misses Zhen's throat but is close enough to shred her clothing, giving her a warning at no point can she lose focus, a witch will punish your mistakes worse than any mortal. Jumping into a multiple attack Zhen lands multiple blows to the furred face of her opponent and spins in the air with her sword aimed at the throat only to be thwarted again, and Katalin goes on the offensive with both hands clawing the China woman who has to back up, blocking both attacks, before the witch shapeshifts into a crow mid-air fluttering in Zhen's face trying to claw and peck her eyes. Katalin flies into the air to avoid a counterattack and immediately zooms back down for another assault, Zhen having to use all her defensive skills to keep those claws at bay and is able to land a punch, sending the witch sprawling across the floor only to rise back up as Katalin herself. Zhen feels her sword pull itself out of her hands toward Katalin and has to grip tight hold to keep her weapon her own; another pull from an invisible force, so strong this time Zhen herself is pulled forward with it toward the waiting witch, who stands with eyes transfixed on the weapon. A third attempt, but this time Zhen catches Katalin by surprise by stepping forward and throwing the sword into the force field using it as a counter weapon against the witch, sending the blade deep into Katalin's chest, exiting from her back and pinning her to wooden crucifix. Zhen retrieves her flamethrower and upon seeing the panic on Katalin's face the Chinese Empress knows she has the drop on her, pulling the trigger, covering the witch with flame. A shriek is heard from the fire as Katalin is engulfed. Keeping the fire coming Zhen sends her to hell. Katalin's head slumps to the floor and is reduced to ash on impact and Zhen stands to watch the bonfire, seeing the witch crumble in the flame, she is victorious.

Father Gideon hears the commotion coming from the cathedral and is the sound of evil he hears over everything else, the warrior of old has come home, his home in his eyes, still the leader of 9 Gang City, still with a holy duty for the greater good and a return to the soldier's way of life for Gideon The Great. Entering from the main entrance he is spotted by Aiden who is viewing the build through his binoculars and The Irish leader gathers his troops and marches into battle with Gwen in pursuit with her Pagan crew. Roars echo around the corridors of the cathedral, unholy in their origin in the false holy building that Gideon made as God-worshipping as he could. Blood splatter covers the walls and Gideon steps over what he assumes is the remains of a Messenger but he can't quite tell, it has been brutalised so much. A roar rings out from around the corner causing the monk to stop and cock his gun. The silver bullet takes its place in the chamber and the holy man squeezes the trigger when a werewolf bolts into view, the bullet hitting the beast square in the face, blowing part of the snout to bits and the wolf falling to die in a heap on the floor. Gideon steps over the man's corpse and continues his mission. Walking past a flaming witch chained to a stake – the conjurer is freshly burned as she is still flaking to ash – hearing a shuffle behind him, he stops, pinning himself to the wall for defence; knowing a werewolf wouldn't be so quiet he lowers his gun and holds out his crucifix. Darting around the corner ready to strike and with cross outstretched, Aiden jumps at the monk's sudden appearance, grateful for the back-up. Gideon nods his head in appreciation and leads the way, just as he did in the war and the feeling starts to give Gideon pleasure, the adrenaline, the buzz, the thrill of ridding the city of its darkest problems. Climbing the stairs and entering the High Council meeting room that The Vampires and The Witches call The Throne Room, that was one of Gideon's most enjoyable moments, turning Niculi and Ziana's throne room into the place where the democracy that conquered them holds its meetings. It felt like even in death they were still being conquered with every vote that was cast. He sees it has been returned to a royal room and the High Council table is gone and two gothic thrones decorate the head of the room. It seems Krul and Rika have assumed victory, but Gideon has fight still left in him, as a werewolf pounces onto Pagan gang members, savaging whatever body part it can sink its teeth into and is sent staggering into death when Gwendoline laces it with silver; Aiden setting a witch alight as Gideon stakes and decapitates a vampire. Bursting out on to the rooftop Father Gideon must decide quickly whether to help or allow the fight between Krul and Cuthwulf and Victuis and Randall – killing The Werewolves will only help the greater enemy, but slaying The Vampires will make Gideon a target for Cuthwulf and Randall. Turning to see an Irish gang member being hacked to death by an ambushing witch, he plunges his stake into it before being barged to the ground by Aiden who torches it with flame. Watching Cuthwulf floor Krul and pounce onto the vampire leader, who latches on to the alpha wolf's face with his fangs as Victuis slams Randall into a heap, Gideon sees his opportunity, hurdling gang members to get to the vampire deputy with crucifix outstretched.

"Demon of darkness, be gone from this world," Gideon bellows, and Victuis cringes to his knees, desperately trying but failing to shield himself from the power of the Messiah and the will of God. "The Devil awaits you in hell, go to your master and infect God's world no more," Gideon continues his exorcism.

Aiden rushes over with a stake, his mind full of vengeance and images of Cormac's corpse. Krul looks over in anguish at his friend's struggle, unable to help as now Cuthwulf and Randall are attacking him, vampire gang members are kept at bay by Irish and Pagan soldiers with Gwen leading from the front, witches can only try and fail in balls of flame as Victuis is defenceless to the assault. "By the power of God, die, you fiend of abomination," Gideon shouts as Aiden takes aim with his stake fully focused on Victuis' heart and about to slay. Tunder suddenly appears through teleportation to assist in the fight and her heart sinks when she sees Victuis inches from death. Leaning forward, she screams an unnatural scream, a high pitched ultra-sonic deafening noise that causes gang members to fall to their knees, clutching their ears in a failing defence against the sound. Tunder's new weapon in warfare, another notch on the belt of her magical power, sending shockwaves across the rooftop; walls begin to crumble and windows shatter, Gwendoline on the floor unable to move, her vision blurred as if her eyes are vibrating. Cuthwulf staggers back as a forcefield hits him and suddenly is thrown against the wall by the force, Randall is tossed so hard he hits the edge of the rooftop and falls to the ground below. Aiden drops the stake and holds his ears, already experienced in the effects of Tunder's magic, he is suffering again as the sound rings out across 9 Gang City. Alice, Jessica, Leo, Zhen Yun, who are not even on the rooftop, fall to the floor in agony of the weapon that is being released from Tunder's mouth in absolute fury. Queen Rika can't block out the sound as witches, vampires and werewolves are all laid out by its power. Zhen's army still camped and Wycombe who is on his approach to the cathedral are floored by her shockwaves. Krul is hurtled backwards and Siobhan in The Throne Room is sent back down the stairway by the forcefield, with Father Gideon being pushed back, crashing into the cathedral wall defenceless to the attack, dropping his cross and slumping to the floor. The Werewolves and bitten Cannibals back at The Forests are floored as the waves stretch the entire city. Only Victuis is left unharmed; standing as the scream still lays waste to any threat, Victuis walks over to Father Gideon, gripping his neck and lifting him against the wall. Tunder stops her assault. Victuis stares at the supposed great one, the leader, the tyrant, the man who thought he could save the world, as Gideon struggles under the supernatural strength choking him.

"He who thought he could slay me," Victuis says, the voice returning in which he spoke to Aiden, the recognisable tone, the familiar accent sends chills down Gideon's spine; his eyes widen with horror. Aiden, stuck in recovery from Tunder's assault, can only watch in disbelief when he realises who the voice belongs to.

"You are just the next victim of your kind who thought he was the saviour of mankind, you are a forsaken species that your own Holy book tells of God's disappointment, your Messiah's disciples drank his blood at The Last Supper and then the Son of God rose from the dead; vampirism is the supreme existence," Victuis tells Gideon, looking deep into his eyes so Gideon sees Victuis in his true form. Father Gideon struggles at the sight but his efforts end when Victuis sinks his fangs into the leader's neck, tasting the blood of the once heroic soldier now a victim of the force he tried to eradicate. The rest watch on as Gideon fades, drained of blood his fightback grows weak.

Dropping the monk to his knees, Victuis picks up a stake. "Now you are going to know how it feels," he tells Gideon and plunges the stake into his heart. Gideon gasps as he is penetrated and unable to fight back. Victuis, lifting a sword, swings with all his might, chopping off Gideon's head, sending it flinging into the air until it crashes to the ground and rolls across the rooftop.

Silence and shock grip the tower.

Tunder stands side by side with Victuis, the returned King and Queen of 9 Gang City back to claim their throne. Standing where they once used to watch over the city at all that was theirs, enemies come and go, fear and hatred grow, but life eternal and witchcraft sorcery have once again conquered mortality. Ziana's spell 20 years ago, a ritual for reincarnation, undetected by Gideon and unintelligible to the soldiers present, vowed a return for herself and her true love. All others are simply a chess piece in the king and queen's quest for glory and domination, and a return to darkness and terror for 9 Gang City awaits. There is a reason it is called supernatural, it holds a supremacy of nature, mortal nature is simply the unevolved version of super nature, so when people ask why God would allow such bad things to happen, it is because he has created a super nature to control the mortal nature and punish them for their sins, and in this world sins rule a human's own existence.

The mortal gangs scatter and flee, what is left of them will be hunted down later and either made to pay homage to supremacy or slaughtered for their defiance. Cuthwulf is sent crashing through the wall by a forcefield from Tunder, and The Vampires and The Witches bow on their knees to their returned masters. Victuis lifts a shocked Krul to his feet and embraces his friend and thanks him for his services to vampirism, his loyalty to the cause and hard work for the gang will be rewarded. Informing Krul of who killed Enigma, Krul's eyes roll over with anger and deception, his fury evident on his face, and he bolts off in search of revenge. Victuis and Tunder embrace as their mission is complete and look out over their land as a destiny is fulfilled.

Chapter 35

During the fleeing, Aiden hurtles down the stairs and catches movement out of the corner of his eye creeping like a vampire. Turning to defend himself he stands in shock and heartbreak at who is looking back at him. Siobhan gives her old leader a sorrowful look as if she has let him down and Aiden doesn't know how to react. His eyes fill and a tear rolls down his cheek, making Siobhan cry in response. Stepping toward her, indecisive in his action, she falls into his arms for a sad embrace but to also show him she still cares. Aiden has been like a father to her. Pulling her in close, he holds her sympathetically while stroking her hair for reassurance, not realising he is putting himself in danger – but Siobhan wouldn't bite Aiden, he means too much to her. They separate their hug and look at each other, no words, only tears and emotion; and after hearing The Vampires coming through The Throne Room, Aiden must retreat as Siobhan's new gang will not show him the mercy she has.

Aiden runs toward the exit with one stop and look back at his lost friend who returns the gesture as the tears fall. Aiden leaves the cathedral and flees into the distance. Alice and Jessica have been separated in the heat of battle, Leo helping his leader vanquish a witch, but their weapon has to change as they hear a werewolf approach. Randall, fresh from his fall at the hands of Tunder, hurtles toward them, sending Leo crashing into Alice and falling on top of her, pinning her to the floor. Randall pouncing onto Leo, who bravely fights off the wolf as best he can, Alice stretching for her gun that dropped as she fell, her fingers slide across the gun; she is agonisingly close. Leo's arm is savaged by Randall as his own blood squirts and splatters into his face. The wolf roars as he viciously slices Leo's stomach with his claws, the wounds deep and merciless as Alice reaches harder for the gun. Randall sinks his teeth into Leo's throat and the blood dribbles down onto Alice as Leo lets out a final breath and becomes motionless; Randall shaking him like an animal does to confirm it has killed its prey. Alice with one final stretch as Randall turns his attention to her, grabs the gun and lets rip the entire clip into a wolf whom she considered a good person in man form but as a wolf a brutal uncontrollable killer who has just murdered her friend. Randall staggers back as every bullet hits its target until the gun clicks. Everything falls silent. Randall's naked body a bullet-laced corpse, Leo blood-soaked and lifeless, and Alice still underneath covered in his blood. She leans into his ear and softly speaks his name, hoping for a response, but none comes; and Alice's emotions conquer her control, allowing the tears to flood for her fallen friend. Wrapping her arms around him for one last embrace, she weeps uncontrollably into him.

All alone and panicking, Jessica frantically looks for Alice and Leo. Inside the chapel, only a scorched cross and some ashes on the floor, along each corridor only bloodstains and body parts. No witches to stop her, but vampires chased some rivals out of the cathedral, and she can hear chanting and cheering from Cathedral Tower. It seems somebody thinks they have claimed victory and, seeing the mortal gangs run and the decimated werewolves, it looks to Jessica like 9 Gang City is returning to the dark days. With only a stake to defend herself with if a witch or wolf attacks, she will have to fight it hand-to-hand and that will not go well with a wolf. Getting the feeling someone or something is following her, she pretends to turn a corner but hides, listening for whatever is in pursuit. As it gets too close for comfort, she springs out with her stake ready to strike. Seeing Wycombe, she is surprised, assuming all this time The Cannibals had been wiped out and yet here he stands with a twisted look on his face as if at long last he has Jessica to himself. Taking one look at that twisted grin, Jessica lashes out at Wycombe, striking him in the face, instantly drawing blood, which only seems to spur the Cannibal on, grabbing hold of her. Jessica wriggles free and runs with her attacker giving chase, just as he likes it. As she flees, she looks for any kind of weapon to use but as she ducks for a gun he tackles her to the ground, landing to his pleasure on top of her. Years of lust and desire have come to this as Wycombe fondles a struggling Jessica who not for the will of trying is losing the fight – he is stronger than she thought and breathing heavily as he gropes. Screaming for help, Jessica quickly realises she would rather fight off a monster of darkness than a pervert of humanity, as Wycombe looks down at her aroused by her fear and discomfort. Grabbing hold of the gun he has in his waist, Jessica tries and fails to cock the weapon, Wycombe overpowering her to prevent Jessica from saving herself, but she manages to hold strong enough for the gun to fly out of their hands and slide across the corridor, just as a roar is heard coming towards them. A wolf's roar echoing toward them like a nightmare stalking in. Wycombe looks behind as he pins Jessica down and sees the shadow of a werewolf growing bigger on the wall, the candlelight adding to the atmosphere of horror. Cuthwulf spies his prey and hurtles toward them, latching on to Wycombe, claws and teeth locked on to make escape impossible. Jessica, crawling away as quick as she can to freedom, turns to watch Cuthwulf rip Wycombe to shreds, blood and body parts galore.

Flinging his remains into the air, Cuthwulf roars as he turns to
Jessica who realises she is not safe from her love and what he told
her is true, he is not the man she knows when he is Lycan. Jumping
to her feet and running for her life, he gives chase; hearing his growl
behind her she can almost feel his breath on the back of her neck he
is so close. Entering a room she slams the door as hard as she can,
hitting Cuthwulf. The door is smashed to bits as he enters the room,
swiping at her and falling to the floor off balance as he reaches,
giving her an advantage in her escape, bursting back out of the room
and down the corridor, hearing his pant still behind but further
away. Dreading the choice she has – die at the hands of the man she
loves or kill him – her options are fast running out until she clicks:
only silver can kill a werewolf, other weapons can harm and injure,
but the wounds will heal. Picking up a flamethrower, she spins on
her heels in a last-ditch attempt at survival and torches Cuthwulf
who, in a ball of fire, continues his attack, diving at her, a blaze of
rage. It doesn't stop him, in fact quite the opposite: flying even more
into a rage, Cuthwulf starts to thrash about, smashing into the walls
so hard it crumbles with the force. Jessica covers him again and runs
for her life. Cuthwulf runs after her; the beast sees only prey with
no ability to tell one person from another. Jessica with little hope
left turns the corner and sees Alice covered in blood, holding a gun
cocked and aimed. Jessica screams at her not to shoot, but Alice
is not listening, she has had her fill of werewolves and thinks it is
best to kill the approaching beast. Once more Jessica pleads with
her sister to show mercy on a monster that will never show mercy,
perhaps that is what separates human from animal. The smell of
burned fur pollutes the air as Alice gives in to her sister's pleading
and they both turn to run as Cuthwulf still slightly ablaze comes
into view. Slipping and falling to the ground, Jessica accidently drags
Alice down with her, fearing the worst until a pair of boots appear

at their eye level. Looking up to see Aiden standing brave with his gun cocked aiming at the wolf, Jessica springs to her feet.

"No," she screams, pointing the gun to the ceiling as Aiden fires; the bullets cause some of it to chip away and fall onto them.

"Jessica," Aiden bellows in fury. "For God's sake he is not the man you love, he is a monster," he adds as Cuthwulf closes in.

"He is the man I love just in a monster's form," Jessica correctly snaps back, knowing all they have to do is wait for sunrise and Cuthwulf will return to his man form. Aiden is having none of it and shoves her behind him with Alice in quick pursuit, dragging her sister away. Looking back as they flee, Jessica sees Cuthwulf smack the gun out of Aiden's hands and lunge in to bite but the Irish leader swerves the attack and dives for the firearm. Gripping the gun, Aiden aims at the alpha wolf as Jessica disappears around the corner and runs toward her freedom. Gunshots ring out and a roar is heard echoing around the cathedral. Jessica doesn't know if her man is dead or alive and is aching to return to see, but Alice refuses and clutches her sister to prevent her running back. If heartache ever felt so bad it is right now for Jessica, the man she loves could be lying dead as she runs for safety and the man who tried to save her may be ripped to shreds and have given his life for her and Alice, and yet they don't know and continue their escape. Another disturbed episode in 9 Gang City has a familiar haunting and horror to its unknown outcome, an unknown that tortures the mind and twists the soul, just another night in 9 Gang.

Chapter 36

Victuis and Tunder bask in the glory as they return to their thrones, 20 years of absence and neglect, 542 years of persecution and hatred, demonised and despised, their city returns to them. Victuis, knowing he could not have done it without Tunder and in return she cannot be without him, the couple supreme will reign once more.

"You only made it in here because I let you," Tunder says.

Victuis looks at her confused as Tunder smiles at him before turning to the corner of The Throne Room. Zhen Yun steps out of the shadow with her flamethrower and stake ready for slaying, the candle light flickering causing her face to come in and out of view.

"If people think mere witch hunters and vampire slayers are enough to take our throne then mortal arrogance really is in need of genocide," Tunder adds, as she stands to meet her challenge.

"Your sister is ash blowing in the breeze and soon you will follow her to the afterlife," Zhen tells Tunder.

The two stare at each other ready for their showdown.

"If that is so then I will tell Yong you miss him," Tunder goads, the last straw for Zhen as she fires flame at the witch to burn her just like she did to Katalin, but the result is much different. Tunder is a far more powerful witch; the flame disappears into Tunder's hands and is fired back at Zhen who has to dive out of the way, spinning in the air to avoid the fire. Zhen stares at her opponent, who glares back with menace in her eyes. Victuis sits like an emperor of old watching the gladiators. Tunder turns her gaze to the candles that light the room; clicking her fingers some of the candles extinguish and her hands become ablaze. Pyrokinesis is the power to control fire with the mind, a parapsychology that differs from Pyromancy which is divination through fire. Zhen Yun stands half defeated in mind knowing if a witch can control the fire that burns her at the stake, then that witch has surely become indestructible. A true display of power that cements Tunder's place at the top of 9 Gang City, a witch who has the power to return from the dead and control anything that can bring her death, Queen Tunder will live forever.

Shooting an inferno of flame at her challenger, Tunder almost toys with Zhen, The Throne Room lighting up as it burns only for the fire to die on the queen's command. Zhen drops her flamethrower and clutches her sword, Tunder returning the fire to the unlit candles which alight and cast their shadows on the wall. Zhen runs toward her target, leaping in the air, holding her descent and swiping her sword at the witch, who teleports behind her, kicking her to the floor. Zhen spins to her feet undeterred and wanting the witch's head. Swinging a kick to Tunder's head but quickly into a sweep, the witch falls onto her back. Zhen jumps sword-first to slay but stabs only the floor when Tunder teleports, saving herself. Zhen hits the floor in frustration but will not give up unleashing a heavy assault of punches and kicks, elegant but furious in their attack, Tunder blocking the blows and disappearing once again; but Zhen counters the teleportation and swings the sword behind her, slicing the face of the appearing witch who is caught by surprise as a trickle of her blood slithers down her face. Victuis stands tense at the wound. Zhen looks around at him, her hand never far from her stake attached to her waist. Tunder is furious, but remains focused; time to play with Zhen's mind. The witch transforms into Yong and stands before her. Zhen's face drops and emotion begins to conquer control, she must compose herself in the face of evil. The battle continues as Zhen and Yong exchange kicks and punches in an epic display of martial arts skills fit for any arena, but The Throne Room of 9 Gang City is the ultimate backdrop for such a battle. Majestic in its discipline and dedicated in its display, Zhen sends Yong flat onto his back only for him to rise instantly as Cheng and the Chinese leader schools his 3rd In Command in the combat arts. Zhen crumbles to the floor breathless, looking at the witch in the form of her leader, Cheng stands emotionless and an empty look in his eyes as if not a care in the world for her, another psychological attack on Zhen, the witch always looking for that weakness. Suddenly Cheng becomes Princess Katalin in transcat form, her claws swiping and clawing at Zhen who picks up her sword and blocks the attacks, chips of sword and claw fling into the air and drop to the ground as the two go full throttle at each other. Katalin becomes Cuthwulf and the beast rages, smashing the room to bits, snapping his jaws as Zhen dodges a bite only to be clawed across the stomach leaving three slice wounds. One final act of power and psychological torment for Zhen comes when she sees the wolf turn into herself and Zhen Yun faces Zhen Yun. Swords clatter and bodies hit the ground only to be brought back to their feet in a display of perseverance and self-preservation, neither wanting to give in, knowing one hesitation will cause death. The image Zhen unleashes a merciless attack on the real Zhen who dodges and weaves, but supernatural power takes the upper hand as human exhaustion sets in and the cracks of defeat begin to show. Zhen Yun's blocks become weaker and her attack become less and less, the image Zhen sees this and seizes her opportunity. Another barrage of sword attacks leaves Zhen breathless and injured and her defence drops; the image Zhen holds out her hand, a forcefield drags Zhen's sword into hers. Plunging Zhen's own weapon into her chest and teleporting behind her, reappearing as Tunder and sinking the second sword down the back of her neck and into her body, a soldier's death. Zhen Yun drops to her knees, the life leaves her eyes as her breath disappears from her lungs, falling face down she has died a warrior. Unknown to Zhen Yun and just as Ziana did with Celtic magic, Tunder has been studying the Chinese magic of Wu – a Wuyu was a witch in the Zhou Dynasty, a dynasty that Zhen held dear. Wugu is the ability to cast harmful spells and with many magical abilities from many different cultures in her power, The Dark Fairy can take her culture to the summit, the culture of witchcraft. Tunder reigns supreme as Victuis stands and applauds his queen's victory, another rival vanquished to strengthen the legacy of the King and Queen of 9 Gang City, King Victuis and Queen Tunder.

Chapter 37

Alice and Jessica step over corpses as they make their way to exit the cathedral. It has come to a point that the blood and gore have become just a part of life. Dead eyes staring at you and no matter how much you look away you have to look back and the eyes are still looking right into your soul, almost as if cursing you for still being alive and yet the sisters have become used to it. Bloodshed has become a routine and death is a part of life, but hopefully the end is near. No more killing and no more hatred is a pleasant fantasy, but they are what make this city what it is. Jessica prays Cuthwulf escaped the attack but hearing all of those gunshots it is doubtful and her tears cannot be held back. Alice hugs her, knowing what she must be feeling, the not-knowing can sometimes be the worst, but with the moon still glowing they cannot return to check. As they are about to exit the building, Queen Rika appears, blocking their way out. The sisters stop and hold each other for comfort.

"The war is over," Queen Rika states with a victorious smile. "The mortal gangs are fleeing like cowards and The Werewolves are decimated. Witchcraft and vampirism have returned to the throne," she says with a confidence she does not yet know is undeserved – she does not know of the revelation about Tunder and Victuis and still thinks she and Krul are the leaders.

"It looks like a return to the old days," Alice replies, not wanting to speak to the witch.

"Not old enough. There was a time your kind would be slaughtered for pleasure, perhaps I should show you?" Rika says, her grin growing across her face in a disturbed fantasy. "Ever the good girl, it's sickening, the holier than thou routine, the sinner reformed," Rika growls, becoming angrier as she thinks about Alice and her democratic ways.

"I am no sinner," Alice snaps back with a snarl.

"Your disillusion is even more irritating," Rika shouts, the air turning dark and tense. "Envy is a sin, you wanted Krul for yourself," she rants.

Alice and Jessica step back as Rika raises her hands to strike at them with a spell when suddenly Krul appears behind Queen Rika, sinking his teeth into her neck, gripping hard so she cannot escape. Rika gasps as she is drained and yet a slight smile drifts across her face as if she enjoys the contact from Krul, reaching round to hold him until he rips away from her, removing part of the neck, the blood splattering out and Rika falling to the floor. Alice and Jessica stand open mouthed at what he has done, Krul looking at them knowing they need an explanation.

"It was Rika who killed Enigma," he informs them.

Alice looks down at the body on the floor, the witch staring back without movement.

"She believed the prophecy about the vampire leader and the witch queen ruling again was about me and her ruling together, this meant Enigma was in the way," he continues with heartache thinking of Enigma and her suffering.

The sisters think about the prophecy, not knowing about who has returned; they almost believed that if it was true then Krul and Rika were who it was about and yet part of them knew there was something off about it. Rika was too presumptuous, an arrogance that she was chosen by witchcraft and not a witch that would earn her stripes and work her way up. Ziana had worked hard to get where she was, from gypsy girl to gypsy queen, from a witchcraft point of view she earned her way to the top. Rika assumed because of her position she just had to sit and wait for greatness, Rika believed she was the returned queen incarnate and Krul her king; she was wrong. Little did everybody know they were all just pieces of the game, one move after another they were played by Ziana's spell and time was left to catch up with her prophecy.

"Who is the prophecy about?" Alice asks, nervous of the answer but needing to know.

"Niculi and Ziana," Krul answers with a mixture of vampiric pride that his gang has conquered mortality but a disappointment that he is not the one. "But now they are known by different names."

Victuis and Tunder look out over the city, a loving embrace as the orange to the east shows its next sign of life, Tunder always had mixed feelings about this time of the morning because it meant Victuis had to leave her for a day, but at the same time it meant he was his most loving to make up for his absence. Victuis kisses her head as she smiles, thinking about the glory that not only have they achieved, again, but what is to come, the fear this will strike into mortal kind will be a whole lot more than the last. The mortal gangs and The Werewolves will try to fight back but it will be in vain, an unkillable force rules over them and if a false death should be cast upon the couple supreme, then time will deliver their throne back to them.

Chapter 38

After a couple of hours' sleep, Alice and Jessica packed their belongings, what little they have is enough to fit in one bag, took whatever car they could find and set off in search of a new life. No longer will they live in a place overrun with evil and tyranny, no more will they be servants to whatever dictator or elected leader orders them to do. A fresh start is on the horizon and Alice feels nervous about what awaits them in the outside world, being nervous after living in this city only goes to prove the human weakness of fearing the unknown. Jessica is caught in two minds whether they should leave or not – why does Alice think the outside world is any better? At least in 9 Gang City they have some sort of power and position and they have survived this long. She also has a longing to find out if Cuthwulf is alive or not, he never leaves her thoughts and it is love she feels without a doubt – she imagined their lives together, a gang union and a happily ever after, but lovestruck women often dabble in far-fetched fantasies. It would be a relationship of angst and heartbreak, in the back of her mind that small lack of trust for the animal in him would pollute her mind and break her heart, so it is with her sister she has her true loyalty. After speaking to Krul last night he told them he was returning to The Caves after cremating Rika at the stake, having a decision to make Krul's position in vampirism could take a huge upturn. Victuis has offered him the post of Pontiff in Romania, the returned king wants to join 9 Gang City with his homeland and Krul as its representative answerable only to Victuis himself. This is a high honour for Krul and if he accepts, his place in history is confirmed. Alice wishes him luck. Pulling up to The Caves' entrance to deliver a letter she has written for him, a final goodbye, she does not want to wait until sundown to tell him as beasts will roam the city freely now. The sisters stand and have a final look at the cathedral. If this was the only time they had seen it they would think it looks beautiful and peaceful, but they know the truth, a haunting demonic dwelling place that is an image of what it should represent. Alice touches her crucifix, a necklace around her neck with The Messiah nailed and dying; saying a prayer to herself for the city, the two ex-Messengers leave 9 Gang, leave the bloodshed and leave the horror.

Darkness cloaks the city, bringing unholy liberation to the forces that punishes mortality for their sins and Krul springs from his coffin with a glance to his side out of habit and sees nothing, but in his imagination, he sees Enigma smile at him. The door swings open as the first task of the day is complete, but this time it is not Victuis but Siobhan that greets him. A loving smile from his apprentice is returned with a nod of respect and leadership as the two share breakfast, a goblet of fresh blood from a corpse they found and drained. Krul smiles at the enthusiasm of his new student and knows she will be a great asset to The Vampires, a million miles away from the scared mortal she was just weeks ago; he is amazed at the progress she has made, still a way to go but she is doing better than he did at this stage of being a vampire. Krul has not told her yet of his job offer from Victuis, but he has decided he will accept the position, a place in history as the first Pontiff of The Vampires is too good to turn down. He has considered whether he wanted to leave 9 Gang – after all, this is his home now and where the action is, but with stories of unrest in Eastern Europe and reported indiscipline in the vampire ranks, Krul is the perfect fit for the job. He will give Siobhan the choice if she wants to come with him or stay in 9 Gang, she may want to stay close to Aiden. Krul understands she will always have an urge to visit her mortal loved ones, he remembers when he used to visit his mother outside the city, watching through her window just for comfort; he did not meet with her in person, he did not want her to see him in his new form, but just seeing her was sometimes enough. However, he hopes Siobhan will go with him on his new adventure. Taking the letter from the mailbox, Krul instantly recognises the handwriting. Alice has a very feminine and neat style, and standing on his rock for maybe the last time he reads the letter and as he does, he imagines Alice's voice in his head.

Dear Krul,

I am sorry I had to tell you this way but waiting for nightfall is too dangerous now, Jessica and I have decided to leave and start a new life elsewhere. It breaks our heart to leave but we know it is the right decision, we wish you all the best in whatever choice you make and we hope eternal life brings you eternal happiness. Once again we are sorry we have told you this way but know you will understand, Jessica sends her love,

Yours Always

Alice

X

Krul's hearts sinks a little but with his decision to leave for Romania it was inevitable they would not see each other much, perhaps never again, but that does not stop his emotion as he reads. Alice is right: Krul does understand and hopes they find a better life away from this hatred and death, and is happy they have made the right choice for the sake of their futures. Staring into the distance at Cathedral Tower, the next stage of vampirism has begun, the king and queen have taken back their thrones and witchcraft has evolved faster than humankind can keep up. The symbol of power reaches for the sky with only God above it and just like in Genesis, God has made a judgement.